Frances F⸻ld is a criminal lawyer, although she now only practises part-time. She lives in London, and in Deal, by the sea which, aside from her love of London, is her passion. Her previous novels (most recently *Undercurrents*) have garnered acclaim and awards, and have been widely translated.

THE NATURE
OF THE BEAST

FRANCES FYFIELD

ALFRED A. KNOPF CANADA

PUBLISHED BY ALFRED A. KNOPF CANADA

Copyright © 2002 Frances Fyfield

National Library of Canada Cataloguing
in Publication Data

Fyfield, Frances
The nature of the beast

ISBN 0-676-97493-7

I. Title.

PR6056.Y47N37 2002   823'.914   C2001-903523-3

First Edition

www.randomhouse.ca

Printed and bound in the United States of America

2 4 6 8 9 7 5 3 1

To Hilary Hale;
absolutely.

ACKNOWLEDGEMENTS

Novels are written in isolation, but inspired by human contact. (Email does not do the trick.) Thanks to Charles Cook, veterinary surgeon, for his help on the subject of dogs. Thanks also to Carolyne Osborn, creator of fantastic follies in miniature and whose book, *Small Scale Modelling* informs many of these pages. My knowledge of libel law was supplied by Robert O'Sullivan, an honest barrister-at-law and handsome with it. (For appointments, phone his clerk.) All mistakes and misinterpretations are my own, not all of them deliberate. Last but not least, my thanks to Brian Thorpe, for his ability to describe a building so well that the place enters the imagination and becomes entirely real.

FOREWORD

Letter to Helen West from Elisabeth Manser
August 8th

Dear Helen,

Here I am, sitting and chewing the varnish off my fingernails, when I should be writing a report, as you ordered. You've been very kind and supportive, but you always were bossy. *Write your version of this case in numbered paragraphs, beginning with your name and your role in the proceedings,* that's what you said. Only a real lawyer like you could make a request like that.

I can't do it. It isn't a *case,* it's an episode in a series of lives including my own and I want to be outside in the garden. I may well be a lawyer, too; this story is littered with lawyers, but I never really liked the law. Too dry and clever for me. *You* told me to write it down in a way to round it off and make sense of it, which is the sort of activity which suits you down to the ground, but not me. You think I know all the facts, and it's facts you want. Rubbish. Of course I don't know all the facts. Nobody ever does. To start with, I know bugger all about *love.*

Anyway, I can't write this report. Quite apart from the other problems about being truthful, I've no experience of rich people, which is one of the reasons which make this *reporting* so difficult. I've never known the sort of people who are so rich that they don't have to go to work, and have the houses and pastimes to go with all that. Which is why I didn't understand that Douglas and Amy Petty were different and therefore irritating to his nearest and dearest, for not being content with beautifying their house and showing off. If I was rich, I'd want to show off; what's the point, otherwise? Neither do I understand people who are dotty about dogs, and I only have the sketchy background I had for the case.

Numbered paragraphs, you said, as if that would make all the difference to my lack of discipline. The sun is shining and all I can hear is the sound of someone lecturing me. Your voice, or John's voice, so, I shall obey.

1) All right. My name is Elisabeth Manser. I am a non-senior barrister, although hardly junior in years, only in status. In the spring of this year, I was employed in the case of Petty v Associated Press, as the carrier of bags, researcher, gofer and dogsbody for John Box, QC, who is the man to hire in a libel case, on account of him having brains and a flair for tactics and a rather fine face. Juries love him, even when he sniffs. Douglas Petty was our client. He had been libelled and he wanted to fight his corner to preserve his reputation.

2) What reputation? Well, our client was once a glamorous bachelor with a notable career as a criminal barrister, before he disgraced himself ten times over. He has an amazing, melliflu-ous voice. Should have bottled it and sold it; there was nothing else to recommend him. He was a lesser celebrity of sorts, slightly famous for colourfully amateur charity stunts. He was bankrolled in his youth by an eccentric and rich, selfmade father, who spoiled him rotten and finally left him a house with a lot of money, hedged in with a lot of conditions. The condi-tions included the care of a stepmother and stepsister who had nursed him as a child through a freak attack of polio, which might explain a lot about his attitude to them. The other condi-tion of his inheritance was the carrying on of a dog sanctuary.

3) The dog sanctuary was started by his father in the stables of the house and it was/is weird. Weird, because it was more of a hospice for old, sick dogs ready to be put down. Douglas had this passionate belief that dogs should be allowed to live out their natural span unless they were in pain, and he was very outspoken about it. He married late, forty-fiveish, surprising everyone because he did not marry the dark, slim, slightly aristocratic kind of model he usually courted, but a proper size fourteen blonde nonentity with big knockers! A part-time beautician/aromatherapist, got picked up in a nightclub, got lucky and Douglas got a wife to bully.

4) The wedding hit the gossip pages on a dull day. Newspapers always liked Douglas. He was rich, charismatic, evil-tempered, with a wonderful house and a loud moral agenda. He was absolutely ideal for defamation. Such a silly, tinpot libel at a time when there was a dearth of other news, or no national paper would have run it. Who cared? Libel is a rich man's hobby.

5) Douglas and silly Amy Petty had been living in the house along with his stepmother and the dog sanctuary he was plan-ning to extend. Amy was helped and advised by her stepsister-in-law, Caterina, a frequent visitor . . .

Oh, sod it, I can't write this. I haven't, as John Box would say, the *objectivity*, or as you would say, the *concentration* to be other than lazy and careless. Besides, how can I write a report when I was part of the saga? I can't think in straight lines. I can only jot down a few separate scenes from what I saw and imagined and from what Rob, the trolley man, told me. I can only begin it with the first day, the first day when it began to *matter* to me, and then I can only let the whole thing follow a route of its own, like a train on defective rails, running on to somewhere. I think in scenes, because I played a part. An accidental part in the manner of an understudy who wandered into the role by mistake. That's all I can do for now, Helen. Set it rolling with the first scenes. I'll write the report another day.

Elisabeth Manser

Scene One

As the train sped through a slice of darkness and on into the sudden brightness of the spring day, she remembered being teased. *The trouble with you, Amy, is that when you say you see a light at the end of the tunnel, you mean a train coming in the opposite direction.* But she had never earned a reputation for pessimism. It was only the nervousness which was habitual.

No; she was a blithe spirit, rocking slightly in her seat in the svelte, half empty InterCity train, going from a small Kent town to London. The train gave the impression of condescension. It was too big for their suburban station and seemed to sigh to a halt there as if it was too much trouble to stop in such an insignificant place. It flowed towards cities like a snake on invisible wheels, utterly confident of its destination, and as she sat inside, near the back, she wished it would go on and on, so that she did not have to get off.

What if I told him? I'll ruin everything. I can't. I'll make everyone unhappy.

A lounge lizard of a train; a clumsy, elongated lizard, rather than a snake. Something on invisible rollers, slithering towards a city to hide under buildings instead of a rock. Amy was alarmed by her ever-increasing tendency to find some equivalent in the animal world in everything she saw. The process of making the comparisons had been confined to familiar human beings at first; thus Douglas was a Rottweiler with blunt ears, carrying the paper in a soft mouth, and Caterina was a kitten. The woman in the local shop was a horse, baring her teeth and flicking her tail, while the man on the checkout at the Cash and Carry was a pig. So obvious. The ticket collector on this train was a ferret with invisible teeth, his hair brushed into a spike of aggression; a ferret or a weasel, and the trolley man, Rob, was a mournful labrador. It worried her that the comparisons went beyond that and extended themselves to objects, so that here she was, sitting inside a lounge lizard on an upholstered seat which felt like a sheep. She lived in a house which was a big, sharp crystal. It had reached the point of absurdity. She was either living in a farmyard or a jungle, on the run from humankind. What would it be like in a courtroom? She would react as if she was in a zoo: she might laugh like a hyena and point.

There were a couple sitting diametrically opposite, arguing in the semi-silent way of circling cats who have not yet begun to fight, snarling quietly at one another.

The light at the end of the tunnel is only a train coming in the opposite direction. A shift of direction, the lizard turning east and the sun piercing through the gaps in buildings like a laser, straight into her eyes through the glass of her spectacles. She closed her eyes briefly, ready to bask in it, at home in this carriage, with her overstuffed handbag (which was like a puppy, fast asleep) nuzzled by her side and the man in the seat opposite shouting into his mobile phone. He resembled a small elephant speaking into its own trunk. 'Hallo Sylvie? Yah, yah, yah. I'm on the train. Just coming in now. Should be with you in fifteen . . .' Why on earth did anyone need to know that? Amy believed that mobile phone users simply spoke into them on trains to prove they had someone to listen. There was no Sylvie; she was an invention and he merely used the phone to stop himself sucking his thumb.

Amy bent her face to her magazine in case he should sense her observation, but he had caught her glance and smiled at her. *Smug elephant leers at grey squirrel.* He probably leered at someone every morning. Being leered at was supposed to be preferable to being ignored. She was wondering about that proposition and deciding she did not agree. She was wishing she was the sort of person strong enough to hit him.

Then the spectacles flew off her face. In that split second, she thought he had leaned forward and grabbed them away in some bizarre revenge for being viewed as an elephant. She saw the raw tentacles of a metal octopus whip against the windows in outrageous fury; she gripped hold of the puppy handbag and the whole world tilted sideways. A flying object hit the side of her head, hard. The elephant man bellowed with rage. *Will they miss me? No, they won't.*

Scene Two

Two men, one stocky and wolfish-looking, casually dressed; the other, thin and dressed in a suit. A woman in her thirties, too plump for fashion, also dressed in a suit. She was asking the questions.

'Is it true, Mr Petty, that your wife used to be a model?'

'What's that got to do with anything? I thought you wanted to talk about the dogs.'

'I only asked.'

'Well, unask. Irrelevant.'

'But if she used to be a model and a beautician, mightn't that influence her judgement? Her taste, I mean. You know, party girl and all that, and she was, wasn't she?'

He leaned forward, intimidating, his eyes shining with irritation, not so much infuriated as simply impatient.

'I repeat, what has this to do with anything?'

'Genes, Mr Petty . . . I think . . .'

'Jeans? She never modelled jeans, for God's sake. She modelled underwear for some catalogue, once, I think. Brassieres for Middle England. Before she gained weight or lost it, did something with it. She was never really a model. She was a beautician who did massage, ask her for God's sake. I'm far more interested in the fact that over fifty thousand unwanted dogs are put down every year. I don't know what she did before we were married. It's none of my business. I don't care. I never did.'

'Surely you must understand that your wife's previous occupations may affect her credibility?'

'Surely what? Oh for Chrissakes, you're as idiotically oversensitive as she is. You mean *surely* some dumb underwear model/ masseuse could not have become a perfectly satisfactory housewife in a house like this? Well she did. Without genetic modification. She's perfectly competent, although in one way, I take your point. Einstein she isn't, thank God. She doesn't need to be and she certainly wouldn't be with me if she was. Is that all?'

'Well, er, no. I was hoping to elicit some information about your life together. It is important for the jury to know, Mr Petty, just how dependent she is on you and how much she would lie for you, if necessary. I suppose she's busy at the moment, massaging someone. Doing a facial, if she still works.'

'No she doesn't. She's gone to London, Mzzz whatever your name is.'

'Elisabeth Manser, as you know. And don't lose your rag, Mr Petty. This is only a dress rehearsal for the sort of questions you might be asked in court, possibly by a woman like myself, only worse. Why do you always keep your wife in the dark, Mr Petty? Are you ashamed of her? Why has she never been available for comment?'

'Why? Because most people have the sense not to ask. She's never been a subject of interest. Besides, I couldn't keep her in the dark, she's frightened of it. And look here, you stupid cow, we might live in an age of equality, but marriage is still a very good way for a woman to get a bloody life. Have you ever thought of trying it?'

He was looming above her, voracious in his contempt.

'Sorry,' he said. 'What a bloody stupid, *irrelevant* thing to say.'

The interview ended. Elisabeth Manser sighed and left her seat.

Scene Three

Shake rattle and roll. He could see the Lloyds tower as he went through the carriages for the last time, collecting rubbish. Gave him a sense of achievement, as if he were the first person to see it. There were certain customers on this train for whom he had a soft spot. A serious soft spot, in her case, which meant a hole right in the middle of his solar plexus through which the wind blew in a gasp, as if he was hollow. Stupid really, for a hard man like himself, a thorn in the side of authority, temporarily slouching over this sodding trolley which had a life of its own. It was worse than a hyperactive baby in a pram or a wilful supermarket trolley; it lurched like a drunk, careered like a lunatic, danced like a teenager on Ecstasy and aimed for his shins like some renegade terrorist on a random mission to disable. It was crippling; it was vicious; it deserved to be shot. One of these days it would burp boiling water all over his blue, synthetic uniform and the shameful matching tie which he always ripped off before he went home. The water would make him melt, wane away, dissolve into a sludge of royal blue with yellow stripes, but not with the same immediacy as the way he wilted when she smiled at him in Compartment B.

The nicest compartment in this motley selection of carriages; nicer than first class, which was not worth the extra. It had regular passengers, including the man who looked like a rhino with a suit too small, the fashion girl who looked like a drowned rat, complained about the price of the tea every time, but drank it loudly, disgusting though it was. Then there was the morose doctor, the fidget who looked like a marmoset, the men with the laptops and the mobiles who never looked up, and then there was her. Pretty and slightly motherly and artificially blonde and just fucking gorgeous. *Woof!* Nice, really nice, as if she was waiting for him, ready to smile and listen and prepared to buy all his sandwiches if that helped. With a Marilyn Monroe type of sweet vacuousness, she always had the right change; none of this rendering a twenty-pound note for a single coffee. It was only two hours at most any of them spent on this train; what dumb prick could fail to arm himself with a quid or two in change if he wanted a drink? That was the way he judged people, unless they wore uniforms, in which case he hated them on sight. It was whether they had coins or whether they did not; those who washed their hair and those who did not. Nobody else based personal judgement on that.

There was the couple he had seen before, bickering quietly over the aisle from her. They radiated poison. When he thought about it, these idiots, repressed wage slaves, wives/assistants of wage slaves, metropolitan cannon fodder, were all a bunch of tossers and the air they breathed should have made him choke, but he just couldn't work out why, with those two exceptions today, they were so much nicer in here, near the back of the train, and why even the sodding trolley behaved better. It went smoothish among the stick-

ing-out legs and the briefcases. They were careless about belongings, stuff all over the place, but that was not a problem. Did he
like them? Too strong a sentiment. He just liked them better than
most, even if they did resent giving up their seats and clogged the
aisles when the train filled.

It was not that *she* was particularly talkative, and she was only on
the train once a week if that. Somebody's personal assistant, wife
or girlfriend, sent on errands. Yes, a wife – she had that family
look. Well dressed, but a few pale hairs clinging to her skirt. Ten
years older than him maybe, but still, *whooomph!* – the air blowing
a hole through his ribs as if he'd been hit with a big, soft ball.

She was smiling at him, clutching that big, soft bag she held
beneath her arm like a puppy, anxious to please and pleased to see
him, once a week, sometimes more, often as not, pretending to
read. She would always chat. Her husband might have been a
bully and she his pet. He could tell these things. He doesn't
deserve you, he would say to her one day. He's an upper-class git
with a house near Staplehurst who doesn't give a shit for you,
that's what he is and you're not from the same drawer, and if that
rhino in the opposite seat yells down his sodding mobile one more
time, I'll brain the bastard, OK?

You are *gorgeous*.

He turned to check the carriage. Saw that the man of the bickering couple had placed his hands round her neck and her hands
were grasping at his wrists in a peculiar kind of game.

Then the trolley wrenched at his arms and suddenly disappeared. Whisked out of sight. Then it came back like a flying
bomb, spitting fury and revenge and hot water. Knocked him
almost senseless and then veered away as everything tilted
sideways and he felt he was flying through a window. And at last,
he was in her arms, her hair in his mouth. Separated again,
dragged away, rolling, someone kicking his head and someone
else whipping him until he rolled back.

He shouldn't have touched her. Shouldn't have fantasised, not
with commuters in second class.

Should've controlled himself.

CHAPTER ONE

There was silence after Elisabeth Manser resumed her seat.

'I don't think that was a good idea,' John Box said quietly. 'Never a good idea to speak briskly in front of a jury. They want you to look at them straight in the eye, keep your temper and smile. I thought you were used to dealing with impertinent questions and insults from the press. I wasn't sure. I had to see how you might react. Just as well we had a rehearsal. Not good, I fear. You'll have to learn.'

'When I think of my father's humble origins,' Douglas said, 'it's a wonder these bloody journalists treat me with the contempt usually reserved for the landed gentry. I'm not a bloody politician. And I didn't expect cross-examination from a woman. Oh God, I *hate* women.'

'Not, if I may say so, a sentiment you should repeat, in the circumstances. And it's as well for you to appreciate the sort of questions and innuendos you will hear in the High Court. Possibly issuing from the delicate lips of a sweet young blonde, primed for the purpose of winding you up.'

Douglas looked at Elisabeth Manser, whose face he liked, but whose name he could never remember, to see if she was resenting his remarks, but she remained entirely expressionless. He rose from the straight-backed chair he had designated for himself, by mistake. It was the least comfortable in the room and he had sat in it for the rehearsal in deference to the guests, John Box, Queen's Counsel, and the woman, Elisabeth, laughingly referred to as his junior, as if either of them were other than sexless, ageless lawyers, seated in a rough semi-circle round the fireplace, with the empty chair at the outer edge. Even in the absence of Elisabeth, the chair looked angry. Douglas noticed that the seat was covered in fine hair, left by the cat, and he smiled with a brief satisfaction at the thought of what that might have done to the woman's black trousers. The chair occupied by Mr Box was far more commodious, wasted on such a skinny runt. A disgusting little prick, actually, far too tall, sitting so still, as if he was never tempted to move, fart, eat too much, laugh too loud, take his clothes off in a hurry and yell. From his own side of the room, Douglas wanted to shout himself, crossed his arms over his barrel of a chest and sighed loudly instead. A man in his position, with his own experience of the law, had to remember that the older man had other ways of kicking the shit out of people. Silence was one of his weapons.

'But I'm supposed to let you lead me,' Douglas said. 'Rely on your protection. I might have been a barrister once, but now, I'm the bloody client.'

'So you will know how lonely and vulnerable a *client* is as soon as he takes the witness stand. Nobody can protect him then. You, of all people, should know how brutal cross-examination can be. You know how a witness can be made to *writhe*. And the decision about who will do it is not mine to make. It will *not* be someone who wishes to accentuate a picture of domestic bliss in a beautiful family house. It will be someone who wishes to undermine you as cunningly as they may. And *you* must not let them do it, since I shall not be able to prevent it, except through constant interruptions which will make you look ever more foolish. Hence a rehearsal, to be continued.' He gazed down at his hands, linked on the papers in his fleshless lap. 'And as to all other decisions on the conduct of this case, you must continue to trust me. Absolutely. As you no doubt would once have insisted that your clients did you.'

'Is there any chance of some coffee?' the woman asked. Elisabeth whatever her surname was managed to be deferential and demanding at the same time. She was the diplomat who knew when to interrupt. 'I could get it . . .' Douglas sprang to his feet. 'Of course. Over there. In the thermos. Amy left it ready. Help yourself. I'm going for a walk.'

They were left in the room. Spring sunlight filtered through large windows; a draught swirled from the chimney and the trees in the garden swayed. In common accord, John Box and Elisabeth Manser moved without haste towards the tray containing coffee and biscuits, helped themselves and retreated to the same seats. In the distance, there was the sound of a door banging, a piercing whistle, a shouted command, another door. Looking through the windows, they could see Douglas, striding out of sight. He was the client who had convened a meeting at 8.30 in the morning and he was not a predictable person, but he was paying. John watched him, relieved by his absence since being in his presence was like sharing a room with a volcano unless his wife was there with him and by God, they would need her in court to vouch for his virtue.

'There is something fascinating,' John said, 'about a man who masquerades as a hero and is really a beast. To think of it.'

'I'd rather not think of it,' Elisabeth said. 'I'd rather he remained in the hinterland of minor, philanthropic celebrities, untouched. And I'd remind you, John, that that is exactly where he belongs as far as we're concerned. In a herd of semi-extinct wildebeest, revered for being handsome, if you like that sort of thing, contentious and fleet of foot. He's innocent, of course. All you have to know is that we have an innocent man, severely traduced by enemies.'

'Spell that for me.'

'What? Enemies? E – en—'

'No, traduced. If you ever use such a word in front of a jury, we've had it. Too much like Latin, too archaic. If you have to spell a word to a jury or explain what it means, you've lost the buggers. Speaking of which . . . oh shit . . .'

'Don't mention shit. Oh please, don't mention shit, please.'

They both dissolved into childish giggles. John sniggered into his handkerchief with a series of haw-haw-haw noises, like the muted braying of a donkey. He was a long and dapper man, wearing a faded but excellent suit, and it was his cadaverous face which lent him dignity. He haw-haw-hawed into a capacious piece of paper napkin which bore the legend of something or other. Pizza Express, Connex South; tissues he collected as he went around too absent-minded to equip himself with handkerchiefs. He had impressive, deep-set eyes, and his sense of humour, as Elisabeth resolutely refused to notice, was often reserved for the suffering of others. Tell him a cunning joke and he was puzzled; watch a man slip on a tiled floor and he was beside himself. His glee was always short-lived, but it made Elisabeth feel faintly guilty for her own laughter when they so rarely laughed at the same things. Affection, love, whatever she called it, was a random force, quite beyond rational judgement; chalk often adored cheese and besides, all the same, it was *bloody* funny.

Bloody, used in this context, was so far removed from anything to do with real blood, it did not impinge on the joke.

'Under our existing laws on privacy, such as they are,' John said, recovering himself and wiping half the smile off his face with the napkin, 'these photos are entirely admissible as evidence in any court of law. They were taken from outside a man's private property, from the safety of a tree' – here he began to snigger again – 'whilst looking into the garden. Oh dear. And in the others, the ones in the stable, they are stills from a security video which our plaintiff threw out with his rubbish. There is no property in abandoned goods. How can he have been so stupid? And why is it, my darling junior, that we give ourselves such licence to spy on one another?'

He was returning to an oft-repeated theme and it seemed artless to comment that without such licence to spy, he would not be in a position to earn his living and her own modest stipend would be severely diminished. He might still have owned houses and cars, but items of a different, smaller kind, and even if the licence to spy had not afforded him luxury, it would have made no difference to what he did, since he was addicted to it.

A parasite in the gut, his wife had remarked in her dry, committee voice and the memory of that smothered his laughter temporarily. John Box, QC, specialist in libel, would not have dared to ask his own wife to take the stand in his defence, which is what *this* client would be doing. He felt some sympathy for Mrs Amy Petty, which nevertheless dissolved in merriment again as he picked up the nearest photograph from the pile which scattered across the surface of the desk. The photos were slightly sticky to the touch and bearing the shameful traces of a thousand fingerprints. Everyone who had seen them had laughed.

The photo, enlarged to an obscene degree, had the blurry outlines of a badly executed video still. It was part of a series of markedly worse quality than the photos of dull-eyed dogs lying in straw or strolling with the listlessness of ill health. This photo showed a man, running across a lawn, pursuing a large, yellow dog. Both were of powerful build, oddly similar in the paleness of their colouring and halos of blond hair. In comparison to the man, the dog was a masterpiece of elegance, fluid in flight, tail held aloft like a flag of courage. The man was naked from the waist down. His torso was dressed in a garment resembling a striped pyjama top, held together over a barrel chest by a button or two, a substantially firm and large belly exposed. He had what appeared to be a stick in his hand – it could have been a whip – and his face was contorted, again in contrast to the calmer profile of the dog. Also exposed on the man was a prominent penis, caught on camera as a piece of body furniture held at about fifty degrees. There were heavy shoes on his otherwise bare feet. He looked monstrous. A view improved in the next frame in the sequence, when the angle of either the shot or the subjects had changed and he had caught the big dog, grasped it, fallen on it, the pale moons of his buttocks exposed and . . .

'Fucked it,' John said, sadly. 'Oh dear. And him with such a lovely wife, too.'

The coffee was fine and strong, the cream thick and the biscuits rich and crumbling on the tongue, a good replacement for break-fast for her while filling the ever yawning gap of John's appetite. She had a memory of another occasion, when the delectable Amy had provided them with lunch, on the basis of which Mr John Box, QC, had decided, with good reason, that she was exactly the woman to put straight her husband's injured reputation at the now imminent libel trial. Such a sweetheart, nicely warm and flustered; the perfect spouse to swear to the contentment and normality of her husband. Even if he did keep a menagerie.

'Of course he has no need to beat his animals,' John said. 'Or to attempt to fuck his dog. No need at all. Not with a wife like that.'

'Star witness,' Elisabeth agreed. 'Absolutely vital. Good woman. She'll stand by. Like good women do.'

They sipped, like decorous schoolmarms, not quite waiting for Douglas to come back, because that was not an event they could anticipate. Douglas was volatile. Neither counsel had ventured an opinion as to his sanity, even in private, but each treated him with the firm deference given to someone who was mentally unstable. Elisabeth touched John's hand, briefly, a gesture reserved for private moments, or occasionally the train, where no one noticed.

'I sometimes wish,' she said, 'that we had never volunteered for this case.'

'Nonsense. It's unique.'

In the distance they could hear the sound of dogs barking furiously and both shuddered imperceptibly. John gazed around the room, a familiar place through three similar meetings over the last month. It was an extraordinary house, not really designed as a house at all. It had been some rich man's foible in the last century, when the creator of it had used this valley as a setting to build a folly, consisting at first of a large, circular room, which was where they sat now. The room, with an ornately moulded ceiling and featuring a geometric frieze and large French doors looking out over a lawn, had been designed to ape the style of a gentleman's club, the Reform, perhaps. It had the look of a louche library, a place to be used for elaborate picnics at the far end of an estate. Then there were the additions which made it into a house, the large

rectangular extension which was added to the back two genera-
tions later to provide kitchen and scullery connected by a flagged
passageway, with stairs from there to bedrooms and bathrooms.
The result was odd to say the least. There was no real entrance,
apart from the French doors on the lawn or through the kitchen,
where the extra addition of a porch did little for the symmetry at
the rear. Seen from the front lawn and the willow tree, the line of
the gently domed roof of the round room was broken by the addition of a chimney. The whole of the exterior, front back and sides,
was painted bright, reflective white to make it seem more uniform
than it was. The original room was the only magnificence, used, so
history had it, as a palatial summer house for the ladies of the
family, but also, it was rumoured, as a sort of hellfire drinking club
for the men, for the conduct of debauchery away from the public
eye. Stables had been built for their horses. Subsequent to that, by
the time the place began to look from the air as if a bite had been
taken out of a circular structure and a huge box stuck on the back,
some family eccentric had been dumped here, again out of the
public eye, to keep a menagerie of animals collected from foreign
parts. The stables had then served a different purpose. Now both
those pieces of its history would make it suitable for a man like
Douglas Petty and his father before him. It was rather a man's
house. Women were irrelevant.

The room in which they sat was undoubtedly elegant in proportion and quite magnificent enough to attract journalistic
attention, although the decor left something to be desired. The circular contours created difficulties with furniture. The fireplace
was custom built. The moulded ceilings had been white once,
now an antique cream, with darker corners where the residue of
cigar smoke stuck, like in the ceilings of an old pub. The main feature was the stretch of curved, ceiling-height windows covering
most of the outfacing wall, with the huge French doors in the
centre. They brought into the room all the blinding light of a late
spring morning and the view of the gracious willow tree, vibrant
with fresh leaves. Saggy damson-coloured drapes were pushed to
the side of the windows, trailing to the floor and obviously never

disturbed. The faded cream of the walls and the semi-circle of armchairs, dwarfed by the size of the room itself, were in various states of repair.

'What a nice day,' Elisabeth remarked, letting the place charm her.

It would be exceedingly cold in winter, with or without the fire. The impression given was that the room was occupied by animals as much as by human beings. Visitors in dark clothing would leave covered in visible fur. The carpet was clean, but looked as if the struggle with animal presence had proved unequal. The large kitchen beyond, which Elisabeth had seen on a previous visit, was a better-kept place, where the war against the muck of the garden was waged if not won. All that effort, and the frilly cleanliness of the upstairs rooms, was probably down to the fragrant Mrs Amy Petty. What a treasure. She certainly needed domestic help in the face of a husband who entered and left like a gale-force wind, all the dogs in the stables and a mother-in-law. There was also a Petty sister, Elisabeth remembered, not yet seen, but still a point of reference as a frequent visitor. If John and she should ever live together, she thought idly, she would inherit far more hideous complications than that.

'We have to concentrate on the main points of the case,' John said, looking at his watch, suddenly busy. 'What was it about those articles and these pictures which offended him most? What harm does he want undone? Is it the ridicule he resents, the allegation of sexual perversion, or is it the accusation of cruelty?'

'Oh, the cruelty, I think. Don't you? I doubt he'd mind what anyone thought about his sexual habits, not with his reputation. Cruelty to a woman might be fine, but to a dog? Insupportable.'

They began to gather their papers, as if something had been achieved.

From the hallway beyond, they heard the click-click of a metal-tipped walking stick on the stone tiles. Moving slowly, pausing, hesitantly. Without further discussion they began to stuff papers, more particularly the photographs, into their bags with increased, silent efficiency. The footsteps turned away, and the sound of the stick tap-tapped towards the kitchen. They breathed out in mutual relief.

'I don't know why he persists,' Elisabeth hissed. 'He's lucky he isn't in prison. He should have been prosecuted.'

'I thought *you* might have influenced his reprieve,' John hissed back.

'Don't overestimate me. How could I influence anything? I only said I knew the lawyer who's been looking at the criminal side. Helen West. She's an old friend. We were at university together.'

'How terribly useful,' John murmured, 'to have a friend at the criminal end of the Civil Service.' He had an unshakeable belief in the power of contacts, unaware of how much she neglected her friends and how few the favours she had to bestow.

Elisabeth did not share his faith in friends. She looked at him blowing his nose and wondered why she adored him. It must be his profile and his eyes, deep blue in the light. Good looks, good brain, seductive.

A big room, full of desks, screens, people; the poorer end of the law.

'Mr Douglas Petty is a lucky man,' Redwood intoned. 'He evades the fury of the criminal statutes, or so you say. Briefly.' There was the minimum of paper in Helen West's file. Paper was discouraged for lack of space and all he considered was the first line of her written note on the merits of prosecution, or not.

It is impossible to estimate just how much buggery with animals takes place, the note read. *After all, the recipients of attention, unless they are talking parrots with a large vocabulary, are not really in a position to complain.* She was being flippant, as usual.

'Was that a nice change for you, Helen? You always complain of being bored.'

'I'm never bored. But it did make a change, yes.'

'Albeit another version of the same thing. Another contemptible male, doing the wrong thing with the favourite part of his anatomy.'

'A variation, yes. I meant it makes a change to deal with a crime which the Bible takes far more seriously than the law ever has,' she said crisply. '*If a man lies with a beast, he shall be put to death and you shall kill the beast.* It does seem unfair on the beast. Anyway, the issue is cruelty rather than bestiality, reputation above anything else. What else do you need to know? Douglas Petty was an infamous barrister with radical views of no known persuasion. Great success, but no sense of decorum. Got rich by inheritance from a colourful father, got sacked from the bar for the famous stunt of streaking through the High Court, remember? He's faintly famous for being famous. Whooped it up at all the right London parties, where he was rude to everyone, string of broken hearts. Would have been sued for breach of promise, let alone libel, if that had been possible. Remarked of one mistress, "She's a silly little tart, give me a straightforward bitch any day." Very quotable, always referring to bitches, viz, "There's nothing you can do with a bitch on heat; they don't care what happens to them." He was talking about vulnerable dogs at the time, to be fair. Married late, lives with sweet old mother and current wife. He keeps an inherited small sanctuary for dogs, on the basis, I quote, "Animals are so much nicer than people." Becomes more famous for this commonly held sentiment.' She coughed to attract his attention. 'Now, as you know, the law brackets bestiality with gross indecency . . .'

'Yes, I know all that. Get on with it.'

'Well, the newspaper in question say they received a set of photographs and a video, anonymously, which probably means they commissioned them. Having published them with a couple of inflammatory, hugely libellous articles, they then turned them over to the police with the righteous demand that Douglas be prosecuted for what they consider to be incontrovertible evidence of cruelty to his animals and buggery. Consistent cruelty, shots of animals with marks of beatings, etcetera. Well you know the way it is. Any evidence gathered by a newspaper is generally useless for a prosecution. They can't prove who took the video from which they distilled their incriminating pics; they can't prove the dates; they can't prove the tape hasn't been interfered with. The problem is that the pics definitely include him, doing strange things with dogs. Well, ambiguous things with dogs, while he was wearing his pyjamas.' She began to smile. 'Half his pyjamas.' She turned the page. 'He must have been keen, it was cold. You can pinpoint the time of year and his identity without much difficulty.'

'The bastard.'

'Probably, but the pictures aren't the surefire evidence the careless local newspaper thought it was. Might be enough to defend the libel action he's brought against the national paper which repeated the libel, but not enough by a long stretch for us to indict him. Civil lawyers are not like us; they don't deal with all this nonsense about the burden of proof beyond reasonable doubt. As for the pictures of animals – dogs, I mean – in distress, there are several of those, but no one knows when they were taken. He runs his dog sanctuary on strict lines. You deliver your sick or maltreated animal to the back door, absolutely no questions asked. Makes the RSPCA mad as hell. They've accused him of sympathising with animal beaters by guaranteeing their anonymity. Anyway, there's not one of these donors who's going to come forward and say "my dog wasn't like that when I gave it to him". So, pictures of injured beasts, which may have been abused by him or by their previous owners, don't say much.'

'Staff?'

She delved into the file, frowning, her glasses precariously balanced on her nose. 'No one at the time, temporary help, sometimes. A man he sacked just before, who won't say anything. Then, in the house, there's the mother, and his wife. Who seems a nice kind of floozie who will stand by her man and his income, and say he wouldn't harm a fly and anyway, was so busy in bed with her he didn't need dogs. Or the thrill of hitting dumb animals when he'd got her for the purpose, I don't doubt. No sign of any other abused creatures on the premises when they searched, but that was a whole month after the publication of the so-called evidence. I'm sorry, that's a lot to absorb, am I talking too much?' Her voice was louder, a hint in his direction to make him concentrate.

'You don't seem to like him much,' he said.

She looked surprised. 'No, but we don't prosecute people for being unreconstructed male chauvinist pigs. Or for being nasty and brutish.'

'Is that why the newspapers gun for him?'

She rose from her seat, placing a copy of her note in front of him. Her hair was untidy, the rest of her neat, clean and inscrutable. 'Don't be silly. It's simply because he's rich. A lawyer who once laid down the law, rich by inheritance and sometimes talks about morals. This is England, Redwood. Get real. He's everything we hate.'

She turned away, looked beyond the glass cubicle he occupied at the end of the open-plan floor, littered with desks, machinery and boxes. No one could think clearly in such a place. She was looking away to hide her impatience. At the far end of the room, a crowd of people was gathering, talking urgently.

'Is there anything which would influence your decision? Anything which would make you review it?' She turned to face him again, reluctantly.

'Yes.'

His face fell. 'Oh?'

She leant her elbows on his desk. He hated it when she got close like that. 'New evidence. A repetition. His wife turning on him. I'll be keeping an eye on this libel nonsense, if my friend Elisabeth Manser will deign to talk to me. What on earth's going on down there?'

The crowd at the other end had swelled and moved to the space by the windows which flanked the room. Prime position for the luckier ones was facing the light; second-rate citizens were lined against the back wall in darkness. Someone broke ranks and came towards them. 'Excuse me, has anyone seen Paul? Only we were worried about him.'

'Paul? Why?'

'Because he isn't here yet. He was on that train. Haven't you heard the news ?'

Elisabeth Manser and John Box waited, both wanting to catch the train, read newspapers, touch hands, and both hoping they might be out of the way before Mrs Petty, Senior hove into view. She did not have the same, slightly ditzy desire to please of her comely daughter-in-law, nor was she as easy on the eye. She had no potential as a witness in her son's cause because she rarely left the house, not even to go as far as the stables, was professionally infirm and would say nothing about him except to declare him a saint. For present purposes, she was a social obligation they could do without. The only mystery about the elder Mrs Petty was the way Douglas deferred to her.

Elisabeth stared through the windows, half lost in admiration of the view until with some relief she saw the client, striding back across the lawn in their direction. There was a dog at his heels. John wiped at the ginger cat hairs which stuck to his trousers below the knee. They had a stickiness which made them impossible to dislodge. The sound of Mrs Petty's walking stick came towards them down the corridor, unusually hurried. 'Douglas?' she was calling in her quavering voice. 'Douglas?' The back door slammed, forcefully. 'Douglas?' she called again as her head appeared around the door of the grand living room. Why did she repeat herself so? Elisabeth found the plaintiveness so irritating, it made her want to knock her over. As the dog might do at any minute, and then they would never get away.

In the event, son and mother coincided in the doorway. She clutched at his arm. 'Ah, *there* you are,' she said, breathlessly and unnecessarily. Her hair was the colour of pewter, beautifully styled. Her tweed ensemble matched her shoes.

'What is it, Mother?' The mildness of his tone when he spoke to her was always surprising. It was as if he risked punishment by speaking any other way, but then the threat of reprisal never seemed to stop him otherwise. Elisabeth suppressed a frisson of dislike. He was rude and crude and his wife had *bruises*, real *bruises* . . . She had seen them.

Mother paused, with dramatic effect. 'Amy did catch the 8.15 up to London, didn't she, darling?'

'I suppose so, unless she missed it.'

Her hold on the sleeve of his sweater increased into a clawlike grip. Her nails were manicured. Not a woman who attended to animals. 'I heard it on the radio. There's been the most awful, monumental crash. Headlong collision. Her train ran into the 125, or something, and she always goes to the front, doesn't she?'

Douglas detached her hand from his arm, walked the length of the room from the door to the French windows. Then he threw back his head and howled. The enraged, mournful, animal sound of it seemed to go on for ever.

Later, Elisabeth tried to tell herself it was the dog beside him which had made that inhuman noise.

CHAPTER TWO

The glance between Amy and the man with the trolley had been like an electric shock. Not for the mutual recognition of one another as allies, because they were already friends of a kind, but for what they had both seen, over the aisle, the man with his hands round the woman's neck, a piece of hatred in miniature. Then came the huge vibration. Whatever it was. Something which felt initially irritating and downright insulting, like being tripped up, or pushed and otherwise treated with outrageous rudeness. They sat, a little dazed, tangled with one another, breathless and winded for several minutes. The trolley man was in the seat next to her, without any apparent reason for him to be there, a puzzling state of affairs. All she could hear was heavy breathing.

They sat like dummies, awaiting orders. There were sighs of irritation, a few murmurs of disjointed talking, a chorus of *Oh, fuck this, what the hell*, nothing much. She had the irreverent thought as she saw that the luggage rack above the elephant man appeared to have emptied itself all over him, so that he was buried beneath two coats and a briefcase, that it served them right for carrying so much, messing with mobiles, laptops and being sulky when asked to move them. Elephant man's lack of protest was peculiar. He did not even try to move the coats which covered him. Amy tried to move her hand so that she could tidy him up, but her hands did not want to function, and the trolley man was pinning her against the window. There was a peculiar smell. They waited, dumbly, for announcements, obedient to authority, grumbling rather than waving fists and shouting.

Then there was a communal awareness, an increase in the level of unease, as they heard the sound of distant voices. Someone screaming from the next carriage, *Get outta here, it's getting hot, hot, hot,* and a vibration of movement. The sound of banging. An increase in the alien smell, people coughing. Without discussion beyond the repetition of the grumbling, they began to get up and form a disorderly queue for the nearest door. Amy was close to it, one of the last to move. The trolley man and the elephant man seemed afflicted with the same ability to delay.

The queue became rougher, more vocal. *C'mon, get out, for God's sake, get a move on.* Not panic, quite, but unpleasant. A woman began to cry. There was loud, insistent banging. The nearest door was behind her and would not open. She felt for the handbag and could not find it. The trolley man's pale face stirred against her shoulder as he braced himself against the arms of the seat and propped his chin on her shoulder. 'Did you see that?' he asked her, almost conversationally. 'Did you see that?'

'Yes.' The absence of the handbag distressed her. Others were pushing past while she looked for it. Vision was blurred. It seemed important to stand and follow, the urgency growing along with the heat. She noticed how others left their strewn belongings as they climbed over the wreckage of the trolley and pushed towards the door. Someone, somehow had opened it and smoke filtered into the carriage. There was pushing and shouting alongside her and she saw the man of the bickering couple with his woman slung over his shoulder, making room for their exit by pushing hard. Then the trolley man hauled her to her feet and they shuffled, almost the last, to the space between their carriage and the one in front. Facing the door, Amy wanted to go back. It was a steep drop to the track and she did not trust herself to jump. It was as if she was being told to jump from a plane without a parachute and the relative safety of the train seemed preferable, but she was pushed and she jumped.

Smoke, everywhere. People, looming up out of the smoke, standing disconsolately. By some common momentum, they began to move down the track in the direction of the station. The carriage in front lay on its side, windows smashed, figures in a fog emerging clumsily like a series of drunks trying to get over fences. Bloody faces, a number of bloody hands, weeping noises, moans, and in the distance, the wailing of sirens. They kept moving forwards, clutching at one another, some element of humanity making them offer support to the slowest, while all the time wanting to run.

The enormity of the damage occurred to her when she saw the figure of a man, almost surely dead, hanging out of a window, too high to reach, abandoned. 'Shouldn't we?' she said to the trolley man.

'No,' he said, roughly, 'he'll have to wait for the experts. We'd never get up there.'

'We must,' she said, pulling away. There was a yawing, creaking sound and the carriage shifted ominously. The crackle of fire. Someone pushed her on. She had lost the trolley man. There was nothing to do but go forward, get out of the way. There were more people now. Strange to see so many people carrying nothing; it looked unnatural. It was safer to look down than look up; she kept her eyes fixed to the track; she could watch her own feet and believe in her own progress. The pall of smoke was thicker, with great, gobby flecks of sticky black ash floating round like snow.

Her eyes caught the flash of something bright on the track, and she stopped. She was wondering how she and the trolley man had become detached; had he gone into the dangerous carriage or were there simply others who needed him more than she? A stray shaft of sunshine penetrating the smoke, quickly obscured, reflected the glint of something solid and gold. She could make out a gold ring on the track. Amy stopped and stared at it, bent towards it. Then noticed that the ring was attached to a hand, the hand protruding from the sleeve of a blouse, the arm outflung away from the body of a woman who lay quietly on the ground, the position of her head so distorted it appeared as if she was staring backwards. Eyes at the back of her head, open and fixed. Amy recognised the blouse of the bickering woman, with the man who had lifted her out of their carriage squatted beside her. 'Piss off,' he said to Amy, as if it were a natural thing to say and this a normal greeting. 'Just piss off.' Obediently, she stumbled on, beginning to cry. Kept on moving in the same direction.

Past another wrecked carriage, then another, the sound of sirens louder and the stench almost unbearable, a mixture of indefinable smells, none bearing close analysis, the combination worse than anything she had ever smelled with her nose so finely tuned to the nuances of perfumes and animal smells. The smell of singeing, vomit, blood, was overpowered by the acrid smell of diesel fuel. Then there was an order. Go back. The unruly column, obedient again, turned round and began to retrace their steps. From the carriages there came the eerie, disembodied ringing of mobile phones.

It was worse, now, even though they were being led. Men in yellow jackets, herding them without being able to shield their eyes. She tripped and fell over a greasy pile of clothing, which was warm and wet, but not recognisably human. The crying was uncontrollable. The plodding onwards seemed endless, more hazardous. Please don't stop, the order came down, keep moving, make space for the ambulance men. There were more obstacles to avoid, bodies, pieces of bodies, cases, polythene bags, cables, and the sound of dripping fluid. She forgot how many carriages. Perhaps they were going to put them back on the train again and take them all away.

Then she saw the woman again, that yellow blouse half-covering the outstretched arm, but by this time a man in an orange jacket was hurrying her on while he shielded the body, his legs astride the arm. She tried to tell him about the woman, but he said, *not now, you can't help*. She looked back at the hand, haunted by its helplessness and complete abandonment. Someone had taken the ring.

Behind the last carriage, the one in which she had travelled, they were herded across the track and told to walk down the other side. She could see a pylon, balanced across the train's roof, dripping with wires. This side of the train was fire-damaged; by the time they reached the next carriage along, the stench was appalling. The faces she saw were blackened, the clothes filthy and the presence of the orange and yellow jackets greater, moving among recumbent forms, shouting orders. Amy felt horribly self-conscious of the ability to walk and, because she was blessed with it, made herself walk as straight as she could without falling over. Among all the other sounds, there was again the intermittent bleating of mobile phones, a background chorus of pathetic pleas for attention, lessening as they scrambled down a bank, across a road and into a car park.

The presence of cars seemed odd, as if they had no place in this alternative world. A few shiny, clean cars, standing in rows, a reminder of another life. Dirty people leaned against them, leaving black marks and bloody handprints. People sat on the ground, stood, lay down. A sense of organisation grew imperceptibly. She found herself moving round, automatically, touching people, asking if they were all right, knowing she was less damaged, quicker to spot the sources of first aid and hear the voices giving instructions. The surface of the car park was sticky with blood. *You do what you can, what more can you do?* A distant memory of Douglas's voice, barking at her, and a woman whose shoulder she embraced, reminding her of a soft, sick rabbit she had rescued from the jaws of a dog, the blackened, ravaged faces of the people becoming those of poorly animals, a doe, a terrier, and that thin man over there, a giraffe. There was nothing she could do, nothing. She knew how to reassure a frightened animal; she had once possessed other skills, but all of her talents seemed facile and pathetic now. Even in hell, she was redundant.

She heard, with one ear, the discussions among the able-bodied about how many were dead. An idea had been forming, shocking in its clarity, born out of this familiar sensation of being useless, heavy, stupid. It was time to leave, was all. She had no contribution to make; she was as useless here as everywhere else; she should have gone. An idea which came full circle when a policeman approached with his pale face and trembling hands, trying to obey orders in the face of his own, profound shock. He asked for her name and address, and instead of the usual obedience, she murmured politely that she had given it already, to that woman over there, pointing to another uniform equipped with an identical clipboard. The boy looked relieved. His ability to write was impaired and he told her if she moved to the left of the place, that was where she could make phone calls and get help with getting home, as long as she was sure she didn't need a doctor. Amy thanked him; politeness was second nature. She remembered the mobile phone in her lost handbag and she was suddenly very cold, crossed her arms over her lightweight jacket and moved in the direction he had indicated. The word *home* had a hollow sound.

Home. She was not going home. There was no such thing.

That smell; that sickening smell. Burnt clothes, wet wool, the stench of carcase, blood, old food, urine. She tried to equate like with like in her sensory memory, but there had never been smells like this. Not even in the burying of a dog which had died and been mourned so long the digging of the grave was delayed to find the right place. A sweet, bad breath smell it had, for all the stiff, soft fur, a scent about it which made it easier to consign to the earth.

An hour and a half had passed, endless and timeless. She followed others down a side road, the ones who were particularised, finished with, ambulant, allowed to go, following one another like a line of hobbling lambs. They would have moved faster on all fours. The loop of road took them past more flak jackets. Human beings like sheepdogs, brindled yellow and white, urging them on with awkward gestures which wanted to be kind and turned out to be officious. Like lollipop men waving children over a zebra crossing. She felt like a refugee, not even wanting to be recognised. The lambs, walking away from slaughter, slower than they had approached it.

There was a conviction in her mind that none of this was in the present and all of them were extras on the set of a film made about war. Soldiers covered in fake blood, aiming for breakfast. The loop of side road took them back across another, unrecognisable service road over a set of hastily laid planks and into the station. A long walk. Then they were ushered across the station concourse. It looked so normal. Burger King, the Upper Crust, Cafe Select, all open and waiting for business, their operatives jabbering in diverse tongues, waiting, offering tea, anything, most of them crying. Kids. Apart from that, the concourse was eerie. White tiles, smutty with the smoky dirt of footsteps, destination and arrival boards, empty, silent as the ragged band shuffled past, eyes straight ahead, looking for whom they might meet on the other side of the exit. Some stopped and accepted drinks. Some were able to laugh.

She saw ahead of her the bickering man, the one who told her to piss off. She recognised the coat; she was used to noticing details. Beigey, dirt slicks down the back, no blood, walking with his hands clenched behind his back. As they reached the exit to the station, he paused and looked back, without undoing his hands.

She only smiled at him because she was puzzled; he should not have been there, but she could not remember why and because it was necessary to smile. *Excuse me*, she wanted to say, *but haven't you left something behind?* It was a good luck smile, as automatic as most of her smiles recently, a paper smile. They were faced by a phalanx of meeters and greeters who had come to collect. It was the meeting place for the survivors. If you wanted to go home, there was home to greet you in the form of a person waving a handwritten notice attached to a stick. *Paul! Sandy! Sis! Jack! Sally! Clara, Joe . . . Over here! Home.* The word made her sick.

The time on the station clock was midmorning; enough time to create this anxious crowd of lovers, friends and family, none for her. Eleven now, 8.15 when she set out. The smile which the man returned with a stare and a nod was a grimace of recognition, no more, and then they passed through the crowd like a pair of unrelated strangers, she hating him for a nameless reason, both of them ungreeted. The lonely ones, suddenly efficient, walking through traffic as if they belonged. Facing a road full of cars with no idea how to cross.

She was stopped at the entrance, asked if she wanted help. 'No thank you,' she said. 'I'm being met.' And she waved towards someone in the crowd, as if it was true.

Amy was dirty, conscious of the fact only as she became aware of the occasional glance in her direction, but she was in an area of dirty people. Around the station on this side of the river, grime was commonplace and no one cared to notice the quality of her grubby clothes. Sticky dirt, black, oily marks on quality fabrics. She had the idea that if she smiled some more, they would leave her alone. It worked. Hers was not a smile to attract; it was manic.

She was walking aimlessly and slowly and it took her some time to realise that she was, in her way, following a prescribed route. Away from the station and over the bridge. She felt lost without a handbag; it made her feel disembodied, panic-stricken. She stopped for a moment and patted her pockets. Her hands were filthy.

Amy Petty, petty Amy, *silly* thing. *Pretty Petty . . . the light at the end of the tunnel . . .*

There was the sound of her own footsteps, hard against the metal walkway of the bridge. The pall of smoke was now behind her and she did not look back. The sun on the water of the river was blinding. There was a dearth of people, abnormal silence. A breeze which made it seem as if the bridge was moving, instead of herself, staggering. The only imperative was to get to the other side. She did not like the south side of the bridge. It was ugly. There, now she knew where she was. Walking towards Blackfriars, a little steadier now, a plan emerging as if pre-formed.

Go to the flat. Not far now. She could see the dome of St Paul's. The traffic was jammed solid, tailed far back from the blocked roads around the stations. Cars, glimmering in the sunlight, and herself frightened that once she started to move across, the whole mass of them would move too. She crossed slowly, leaving the landmark of the river with regret. Down Blackfriars Road, towards

Clerkenwell, getting a few more sideways glances once she was beyond the area of dirty faces and mucky hands. She walked resolutely, relieved it was not yet lunchtime when these pavements would be dense with people, troubled by the sly thought that it might be better that way. No one was noticed in a crowd; crowds were secret places and this was not quite crowded enough. She reached the side street and the door to the block. The keypad was inside a box in the recess of the wall, the numbers as grubby as her hands. The numbers to press were embedded in memory.

It was the pied-à-terre of a handsome couple who lived in the country but occasionally needed the convenience of somewhere in town, and it was intended to be as quiet and anonymous as it was. Two flights up from the door, tucked in this back street. Douglas had owned it for years. A bachelor hole, once full of kitchen machinery, a stupendous supply of booze, rudimentary crockery and an overlarge bed. This was where he had first brought her, seven years before. Into a scrapheap of a place where discarded clothing from the last visit remained thrown into a corner of a kitchen where there was nothing to eat. Amy paused at the door. There had been no pretence and no blandishments. He had been a man who had missed his last train, went to a nightclub out of sheer boredom, and picked up a body for bed. She had danced with him because she was mesmerised by his voice. It was like dancing with a bear who neither listened to the music nor knew the steps. He had smelt of dog and his clothes were wrong and when he said, 'Let's go, shall we?' they got into a taxi and went the short distance to . . . here. 'Do you take drugs?' he had barked at her as the only attempt at conversation on the way. 'No.' 'Good.' They were both more than a little drunk, but in her case, not drunk enough for the clear purpose of the exercise. She was not really made for this cruising lark. She had stood at the door to this small apartment and seen the expensive squalor, litter and furniture jumbled together with no attempt to please or impress, touched with the aroma of neglect. She could smell garlic on his breath; she was impressed by him and afraid of him, but above all weary, suddenly sober and utterly depressed by the prospect of fucking someone who would never remember her name, for nothing more than the saving of a taxi fare home and being warm.

She stood unsteadily at the door and tried to remember what she had done. Waited for him to go to the lavatory and then left, closing the door behind her, while he was probably searching for a condom in the mess of his bathroom as a token gesture towards courtesy. No one had promised anyone the best of all honourable intentions. She had left this little flat out of an instinct for safety and a belated desire to preserve a shred of dignity. He had become, in a space of minutes, as repellent as she felt herself. A bloated shark with big, white teeth. A long time ago.

Her eyes felt as if the grit of the train along with burnt pieces of skin had formed into sand beneath the lids, scoring her eyeballs pink each time she blinked. She blinked now. This room, the living room, was awful after Caterina's makeover. Pastel shades, no mess. Green curtains and matching carpet still bearing the brushmarks of a hoover, no dust, no personality, like a hotel room maintained in a state of neutrality. Ready for human occupation and somehow resentful of it. Fitted wardrobes in the bedroom, his and hers. The sight of these pristine clean walls made her want to scrawl graffiti. The clock in the small vestibule where she stood with her view of the whole place announced that it was 11.45. The mirror on her left showed a woman with a grubby pleated skirt, shirt, jacket and no handbag, a wild gleam in the bloodshot eyes. A sluttish woman. Behind that image lurked the picture of how she had looked on the first occasion. Cheap black dress reaching an inch or two below the crotch and corseted to push up her bosom into twin melons, an excess of mascara making soot on her cheeks, a ladder in the tights. His estimation of her had been entirely right and probably still was. She had been lonely then, but not as lonely as now.

She needed a wash: shower, bubbles of soap, a scrubbing brush. She paused. The telephone was ringing and she suppressed the automatic move to answer it, took off her shoes, carefully, instead. Tiptoed over the small area of mown carpet as if the phone could hear her and washed her face and hands in the bathroom with all the nervous reluctance of a small boy who hated water. Dried her skin on a hank of toilet paper, sat on the lavatory gingerly and flushed all the traces away. Dabbed at the jacket ineffectually with more toilet paper, flushed that away, too. Began to hurry. The phone rang again, accusingly. They would be looking for her by now; it followed from that that someone would arrive. She could only take from here what no one would notice, and while she knew that Douglas was normally oblivious to the contents of the bathroom cabinet, she was not taking chances. She looked at the cosmetics with longing, her favourite things. From the Nescafé jar in the top kitchen cupboard she took the stash of banknotes, about five hundred pounds, she guessed without counting. Douglas never cared where cash went; there was always a reserve.

Back the way she had come, this time with her hair brushed and held back in an elastic band, the lunchtime crowds beginning to swell the view. Passing a restaurant window, she was acutely conscious of the dirtiness of the jacket. The dark print of the skirt absorbed more; dirt had become part of the design, but the jacket was different and her cleaning attempts had made it worse. On an impulse, she backtracked to the window, saw a small, smart, dark city watering hole, the sort of place she disliked. A place where a man brought a mistress and the sort of place she had been inside often enough, wearing the sort of clothes she was not wearing now. The window glass was smoked and the door stood open. She could hear a distant murmur of voices and smell beef and spices.

Inside the door was a full coat rack which Amy examined with two things in mind, the length of the garment and the sex of the owner. A man's coat would be no good, but she did want something which kept out the rain. There it was, olive green, lightweight, soft to the touch as she slipped it on. A little on the big side, covering her top to toe. She adjusted the collar and put her hands inside the pockets, making it her own. There was another kind of conspicuousness about the coat, though, as she walked along. The day had grown warm and the coats worn or carried to work had been abandoned now. She was overdressed and still cold. Again, never mind. She smiled to herself, briefly. After all, taking the *best* coat in the rack instead of her own was something she had always sneakingly wanted to do. One of those exciting, forbidden things, like pulling the communication cord in a train.

When she was back by the side of the river, she was glad of the coat because the wind whipped up off the water and the parapet of Blackfriars Bridge was inadequate shelter. The sun was bright again, the traffic still gridlocked, the air dense with fumes. She stopped and stood on tiptoe to look at the water, winded by memory.

This was where he had caught up with her on the night they had met. She, hiding down by the parapet and wishing she had a coat, and he, heralded by panting footsteps, coming into view in an ungainly jog, his face pink in the streetlight, seen in a moment of fear when she believed he would simply pick her up and hoist her over the wall and into the river; he was strong enough for that. When they had danced to that unmemorable music, her bosom had bobbed somewhere higher than his thick waist and the top of her head was level with his enormous shoulders. Squatting down beside her, breathless in his shirtsleeves, all he said was . . . nothing until he recovered his breath. Pulled a battered cigarette packet out of his top pocket and offered her one. 'Oh, for God's sake, you silly bitch. You'll catch your death. Have you got a light?' And at that point she realised she had left her handbag in his flat. He sat down beside her and began patting trouser pockets, extending large feet as he sat – feet, she noticed, which wore socks, but not shoes. 'And I,' he said, 'seem to have forgotten my sodding keys. We may have to stay here all night.'

Three attempts to light a match, and his face was illuminated as he cradled the light and bent towards her. A broad face, widely spaced eyes, huge forehead, like a high-bred, cruel hound. A limping pigeon had nestled next to her, hopped into her lap and then across to his. He did not shoo it away.

So much for fairy tales. Amy flung herself away from the parapet as if it were that which made her cold, and walked back. She could no longer look at the river. In the distance, she could see that the pall of smoke had died into a kind of smog on the further side of that other bridge. She felt sick with sadness and at the same time buoyant with a sensation of freedom as she walked on, the overlong coat gathering dust behind her heels.

'She doesn't answer her phone,' Douglas said flatly.

His stepmother stirred in her chair.

'She's always hated the mobile, Douglas, you know that.'

'She knows what it's for,' he said shortly. 'She doesn't have to love it to use it. She might have lost it. She's always losing it.'

'Yes, dear, she does. Did you try the flat again?'

'Yes of course.'

'The police liaison, whatever it's called, they said they'd call as soon as they've located her, didn't they?'

'Yes.'

'So all we have to do is wait.'

'I don't want to *wait*. Not wait and watch *that*.' The television murmured in front of them with a running commentary on the disaster. *It will take several hours to establish the extent of the casualties. The number to phone is . . .* 'And THAT!' he shouted, staring at the silent telephone. 'I should be *doing* something.'

'What can you do, darling? You wouldn't be allowed near, even if you could get there. The roads will be blocked and—'

'SHE CAN'T DO THIS TO ME!' Douglas shouted. 'She CAN'T, SHE CAN'T, SHE CAN'T!'

The dog ambled across the room and put a large head on his knee, gazing at him soulfully. He fondled her yellow ears. They resembled each other.

'Caterina will be here soon,' his stepmother said kindly. 'Just go out for a while, Douglas, dear. It might calm you.'

Rob, the trolley man, sat in the line outside the Accident and Emergency department. He had left the queue inside and come outside to sit on the steps in the sunshine, although he was not quite sure how he had arrived there. Maybe he had been led outside by the man who was questioning him, clipboard in hand and

Biro poised, both out of their depth and Rob weeping quietly and incessantly throughout, impeding the repetitions of his replies. Roughly how many people in that second to last carriage, Rob? Can you remember? No. Lots. Did they all get out? Yes, I was the last, I think. I don't know. Did any of them go through to the next carriage? I don't know.

His hands were grazed, his chest hurt more. Christ, it hurt, and the crying made it worse. I shouldn't have left her, he kept on saying. I shouldn't have let her go. I should have looked after somebody, at least.

Who? I mean why?

That woman. The blonde. None of your business.

But she might have wanted to die.

neglect had failed to kill them. What spark of humanity in a man made it impossible for him to kill his servant when he had already effectively destroyed it, Douglas had wondered. It takes far more guts to kill a thing than to neglect it, and no person would ever get close to these two now, except for Amy. In the third stable, left unlocked at night, two yellow retrievers called Sally and Josh, for no reason he could remember, slept reluctantly. They did not know about neglect; they had simply outgrown their elderly owner when the bitch was accidentally pregnant and the dog began to wander; they were all beauty and muscle and slaver, without a brain cell between them, and could be relied upon to bark and run for the house at the first sign of trouble, out of duty or cowardice.

The trouble with dogs, the vet explained, is that they confuse their loyalties. They are the only species of animal which can change tribal allegiance. Give a dog to a man and he will want to adopt that man as the leader of his pack, regardless of his weaknesses, inadequacies and lack of a tail. He will associate with man more closely than any other animal and forswear all kinship to his own kind. To the extent that if he is taken away from mother and siblings too early, he will not recognise them at all, will snarl at them with suspicion for ever after and cling to the human like baby to mother. On the other hand, if the dog should reach adulthood without human contact, he will revert to being a wolf. The two retrievers had reached the ideal compromise of pets. They were friendly with other dogs, but given the choice, preferred humans and raced towards them with fickle speed at the first opportunity.

Douglas knew he should refer to a dog as an 'it'; to do otherwise made him sound as if he was talking about people, but he could not refer to any of them as an 'it'. They were always 'he' or 'she'.

He bedded the two retrievers in the third stable with Dilly, an arthritic greyhound, who regarded them with vague contempt, as if she did not really enjoy the company. Dilly was peacefully ill, her tenure of life a daily uncertainty, but her complicated infirmities did not yet interfere with the desire to live, in particular to bask in the sun. She could die any time. Douglas patted her head with gruff tenderness. She had never wanted fuss, only recognition, did not stoop to crave affection and he admired her all the more for her dignified indifference even though this patient acceptance of disabilities was alien to him. He was dog-tired himself, a gnawing pain of anger settled in his throat.

The house was out of sight of the stables, on the corner of the drive which dipped at the gate and turned uphill to the back door. It would be better when the new quarters were built and attached to the house. The stables were not quite out of earshot on a still night, but a step too far for emergencies. Which was why at the back of the fourth, small stable there was a room of sorts, with a bunk bed for a human occupant. The mellow brick buildings, older by far than the house, were a relic of the grander times of horse, carriage and sweeping acres. Dogs loved the fields. Douglas attended to the dogs with fastidious, concentrated care. In his mind's eye, a map unfurled. Dogs, here; the car in front of the house, the road to the station car park, the hourly London train. A clear route of migration he never wanted to take. He coughed to clear his throat of what felt like a hairball of prickly fur.

Food, water, washing, bedding, guardianship and attention. There was another dog, a sick, undersized mongrel, residing back at the house and there was too much to do. There had always been too much to do. He concentrated on tasks, whispering, 'Sit down, you silly, go there, come here, eat this . . .' mindful of their diets, talking like a teacher in charge of a nursery, making his voice heard. He tidied up the fourth stable, the one with the bed, the map of the route to London still in his mind, not wanting to think about it. Amy had an attachment to the city which he no longer shared, some bit of her which was exclusively metropolitan, perhaps, but she would be back, walking through the door, anytime soon. No point waiting on her. She would be back.

He bent down to stuff the bedding into the industrial-sized washing machine which occupied the same room as a ton of dry feed. Felt a touch to his shoulder, hot breath on his neck. Flung out his arm to push away whatever had got too close. Felt the man gasp as if he had been hit, instead of merely slapped across a skinny thigh.

Douglas turned, winced as his knees creaked and stood. He

was getting too heavy; anger made him weightier. A wizened face, half obscured by a cap, yellow in the light, was scowling at him. It was the face of a pixie, looking older by far than his thirty-eight years. An ageless goblin. Douglas bunched his hands into fists. The man stepped back and sat on the bed; Douglas unclenched his fists.

'What the *fuck* do you think you're doing here, Jummy, you . . . *cunt?*'

Jimmy winced, as much at the mispronunciation of his name. Glasgow *Jummy*, a walking cliché, with his battered, ageless face, thick accent, wasted frame, roll-up cigarette hanging lifelessly from the side of his mouth until he grabbed it and stuffed it into his pocket. He was like a diminutive street fighter, pickled by alcohol and weather, far from home and beyond repentance. A randy little bastard.

'Aw, leave it out, Dougie, will ya? I scarcely touched you. Just saying hello. She hasnae come back, has she? I heard . . .'

Douglas sat down heavily on the bed beside him. The difference in their sizes became less significant. Upright, Douglas towered over him, looked as if he could have felled wee Jummy with a single punch. Sitting level with each other, it was more apparent that anyone who had a go at Jimmy would not go away unscathed. His agility was obvious; he sat still, but twitching; he would bite at the ankles or stab at the groin and go down fighting. He would scratch like a cat, Amy said.

'No,' Douglas said heavily. 'She hasn't come back.'

Jimmy scuffed his boots on the worn lino of the floor, nodded. 'I thought not. Heard about it. Thought to myself, Tuesday it is. Went to the car park at the station just now and there was her car, still. A few of them, poor buggers. In the hospital, is she?'

'No.'

'Ah, *shit.*'

Jimmy leant back against the wall behind the bed and blew out a sigh of disgust.

'Don't make yourself at home, you *cunt,*' Douglas snapped. 'You'll dirty the bedding.'

Jimmy was unmoved. 'So where is she, then?' he asked, hopefully, sitting up again and feeling for the roll-up in the pocket of his
trousers. He had a lot of pockets; pockets were his favourite thing.
Deep pockets in which things were lost, constantly.

'I don't know. We wait, and hope.'

'There's many dead. Burnt.'

'Thank you for telling me that, Jimmy. I really needed to know.
She may be one of them.'

They were silent for a full minute while Jimmy found the cigarette. Once it was established between his blackened fingers,
Douglas snatched it away and ground it beneath his heel. There
was no protest. Silence resumed, punctuated by shuffling from the
stable beyond and the sigh of a dog, dreaming.

'Well, I couldn't stand to think of it,' Jimmy said. 'I saw the car
and I came to see. If she'd been here, I'd have gone away. Then I
thought you might need some help.'

'Help? From *you*? You must be fucking joking. After all the
harm you did, I'd as soon have help from a rat.' It was calmly said
in that commanding voice of his.

Jimmy knew better. 'Help from anyone,' he suggested softly,
bending down, picking up the mess of tobacco with deft fingers,
putting it into another pocket. 'You'll need it, maybe.'

Bad enough with only two of them, latterly, attending to eight
canine cripples and the dogs up at the house. If Amy did not
come back, it was going to be impossible. Money bought food, not
help. There was so little money could actually buy, such as trust,
reliability. Money was an overrated commodity.

'You know I love them,' Jimmy whined. 'I'm just daft. Wee bit of
a problem, maybe.'

'A wee bit of a problem? You were supposed to be looking after
that poor sick bitch with her whelps, and what did you do? You
fuck that girl, both of you drunk as skunks. Set this bed on fire. Sal
nearly lost those pups. Help? From *you*? You daft sod.'

'I was good enough before, I can be good,' Jimmy said. 'You can
hit me if you like,' he added helpfully.

Douglas stood up and punched him on the jaw. The blow

wavered at the moment of impact, not full force, enough to make Jimmy's head rock back against the wall and tears start in the eyes. He blinked, shook his head slowly, eyes watering.

'You're a useless, two-faced, ugly bastard,' Douglas said. 'Come up to the house.'

Dusk was fallen, in the slow way of spring dusk within a month of the changing of the clocks. All bad things happened after dark. Countryside dark, not town dark, always more noticeable. A short walk if they had gone the straight route via the drive with the worn holes where the intermittent repairs with wheelbarrowfuls of gravel failed to stop the rot for more than six months. Rain found the weak spots, sluiced away the grit and left the hole deeper than before. Strangers like John Box and Elisabeth Manser would have stumbled, as indeed they had, oh dear, while habitual foot passengers moved unerringly. One minute was all between point A and point B. Not long enough for Jimmy. He did not want to reach the house and hear unwelcome news. Nor did he want to see wee Dougie's mam in the kitchen, wearing her rubber gloves and saying, 'Good evening, Jummy,' whilst she stirred some piece of poison in a pot which could have contained her painted nails for seasoning. Pure imagination, Jimmy, my lad. She just made him feel like shit, was all. Not her fault. Never said a cross word, never a real one either. He could see her now as they rounded the bend, a slender silhouette against the kitchen window. He knew who he wanted to see in there, out here, anywhere; the thought made him wince with grief and want to blub like a bairn. He put a hand to his cheek and felt it was already wet; his jaw hurt; he wanted a drink. Wanting a drink was constant; he was born lacking just the three double measures which made him feel right. Being sober and facing the elder Mrs Petty while his jaw throbbed and he wanted to cry was not a combination he could handle. His feet sidestepped the holes in the track and he could hear himself thinking, I'll go now; bad idea, this. Then, to his relief, Douglas detoured away to the side and led them down the path which skirted the house to the front where the living-room windows mirrored the lawn and the bench was rooted beneath the willow. He was not the only man here who did not want to go inside.

A curtain of dark was pulled on the day as they sat on the bench and Jimmy began his erratic search of his pockets for the remnants of tobacco and other bits he needed. Ten pockets in all, a great deal of fiddling. Douglas was halfway down his own cigarillo before Jummy took the first draw on his own. He could blow smoke circles into the still air, could Douglas, a trick Jimmy greatly admired. He was not blowing pretty patterns now though. He was fingering the mobile phone clipped to his belt and smoking as if the small cigar was a substitute for breath and his life depended on it. 'You're a shit, Jummy,' he murmured. 'An absolute shit.'

'And so what are you, faceache? Some fucking saint or what? You're a *cunt.*'

'*Bastard.*'

'You're the bastard. Makes two of us. *Cunt.* Aah'm just a drunk. You're just a turd with money, you. You're just bollocks, you. You wouldn't give me a chance. Not you.'

They smoked furiously. Jimmy's jaw ached less; Douglas's huge left hand fingered the phone as if willing it to speak.

'Not *yew,*' Jimmy continued. 'Not great big yew, Muster Big Guy, yer fucker. I fuck up, fuck yew, you say. But she's a good woman, her. She'd have give me the chance.' He dragged the last gasp from the charred Rizla paper and started again about the exploration of his pockets. The task exhausted him and he began to cry. 'I canna bear it. She's never *dead*, Mr Petty. Is she?'

'Possibly.'

'You fucking great *shithole*. She never is?'

'I don't know.'

They went to the back door. Of common accord and long habit, both took off their boots and threw them into the porch with all the other boots. Douglas shed his coat: Jimmy never had a coat except for three days a year. A coat impeded him; he wore instead several layers of thin, decrepit sweaters, which, in the days when he had worked at the stables, had gone into the washing machine along with the dogs' bedding from time to time and smelt roughly

the same. The kitchen was empty, with the look of recent abandonment, as if Mrs Petty, Senior had become exhausted by the
peeling of potatoes which lay, half done, on the draining board.

'I expect she's gone to call in the cavalry,' Jimmy said.

Douglas nodded; their eyes met in a moment of understanding
as they sat heavily at the kitchen table. A cat peeled itself out of a
box by the Rayburn, stretched and moved to sit on Jimmy's lap, as
if he belonged and had not been missing for two months. Douglas
could not understand the attraction of Jummy's body either to
cats or to females. Must be the smell of him; the succession of
sweaters with holes.

'She'll be calling up your sister, maybe.'

'Already has.'

Jimmy remembered not to let out a sigh of relief to be inside this
kitchen again. Too soon for that. He liked the daft, white dolls'
house which perched next to the sink; he liked the uneven red tiles
on the floor, the constant warmth of the Rayburn, the battery of
equipment he did not understand, the heavy wooden chairs, the
clutter of paperwork which always had to be moved off the table
and the sense of being in an engine room. There was always a litter
of yellow Post-its, containing Amy's lists. They were her particular hallmark, stuck to the fridge, the table, everywhere. It was the
only room in the house which counted and he rarely went any further. The sight of a pot of drooping tulips on the window ledge
above the sink renewed the threat of tears. Amy always had to
have flowers in here and she always kept them long after they
were dead.

'Och, Dougie,' he wept. 'What are we going to do?'

'Oh for God's sake, stop grizzling, man. Helps nothing. And
yes, I could do with you back. I fucking wouldn't if I had a choice.
I must be mad. That poor bitch might have died.'

'But she didn't die, Douglas, did she? Amy got her right. And
you know damn fine it wasn't me talking to newspapers . . .
could've been Dell, digging the dirt on you.'

'Have you got rid of that scrubber?'

'Oh yes. Far away, gone.'

A bottle of whisky appeared out of the kitchen-table drawer. Douglas slopped two generous measures into small tumblers. Jimmy refrained from grabbing the glass with both hands. The gesture of the whisky meant, OK, start work tomorrow. He nodded, the closest he could get to saying thank you. Thanks and apologies were not on his agenda. Then he caught sight of an apron hanging over a chair and his eyes filled again.

'And when my sister comes, you stay well clear of her. No closer than a bloody mile, you hear? You can be as rude to her as you always were to Amy.'

'Oh, for sure,' Jimmy said. He always had been rude to Amy; his affection for her a well-kept secret. 'I canna believe it, Douglas. She'll walk in that door any minute. She's just having you on.'

'That's not what Amy does, Jummy. Not in this house.'

'No, I suppose not. What about her family, Douglas? Someone you should tell?'

'No,' Douglas said. 'Apart from us, absolutely none.'

'Was she an orphan, then, or what? No brothers or sisters?'

'No,' Douglas repeated. 'She came without family.'

They fell silent and listened for the sound of Mrs Petty's cane. A man did not say fuck or cunt in her company.

It echoed in her mind, the sound of the stick. When the evening closed in, Amy was glad of the coat because the fickle heat died with the sun and it was only spring yet, not summer at all; she began to panic. The choices which existed in the middle of the day no longer seemed viable. Euphoria had died and something else had replaced it. The component parts of shock and guilt, hunger as well, although the thought of food was sickening. She sat in two cafes and one burger bar, faced with coffee, microwaved apple pie or cheese roll, unable to eat the food, only drink the coffee and find herself shaking. Now she tried tea instead, in another burger bar where she was the only one nursing a single Styrofoam cup rather than eating out of cardboard containers the mess of food which looked worse than what she spooned out of tins for the cat. Life has spoiled me, she thought. I have learned to cook and resent crowds: taught myself to live in a way I once found alien and impossibly difficult and now I can't adapt. I have got used to an entirely different set of sounds. I need not have bothered coming back once a week to keep myself acclimatised; the therapy did not work. I am homesick. But this is my new home.

Trafalgar Square was home to no one. A magnet for tourists and pigeons, a gathering place for strangers. Before midnight, the police would clear the benches and in the early hours of the morning, someone would tidy up the litter and it would all start again. The evenings longer now; time shorter. She could find a hotel, but she did not want a hotel, because the money would be gone in two days and she did not have a cash card to put in a hole in the wall, even if she could have used it. She was dead. She had seen the *Evening Standard* posters – TRAIN CRASH! FORTY DEAD! – and here she was, sitting here, one of them. Her thoughts were less of the dead than the disabled. She thought, briefly, of the trolley man and wondered how he was. It was better not to think. Thinking, like food, made her nauseous.

How silly to imagine that there ever had been any doubt about where to go. Amy clambered off her stool, searched for her hand-bag and felt foolish for forgetting she did not have one. There was not enough to do with her hands without it, except stuff them in the pockets of the coat and pretend she did not want to keep stuff-ing them in her mouth to bite the nails. Short, square nails, neatly trimmed, not like her mother-in-law's nails, painted a different colour every week. A vanity of hers. Sitting on the bus, she found herself looking at hands, concentrating on the fingers which curled round a newspaper or a book lying dormant in a lap.

It began to rain. The bus edged round the square and then broke free of the clog of the traffic, escaping up the broad road to Westminster. Ran free from Pimlico into the hinterland of the metropolis where tourists did not go. Going south. She could almost imagine she was going home. The place where you put your heart, and left it there. Not the housing estate where she had grown up, surrounded by rigorous hygiene, where curtains were pulled at the first sign of dark. A goldfish bowl, where the fish inside swam around in relative safety provided no one could see.

The bus journey was endless; stop, start, welcoming on board a different population. More hands, laced together on the bench seat opposite, guarding a bag, a stomach, an umbrella, or propped on the side to rest the head, or poised to dive inside a bag of crisps. Thumbs crept into mouths as darkness fell, a little nibble of a forefinger as someone remembered the thing they had forgotten on the way home. The territory ran out of useful shops but never out of buildings. Smaller streets, mock town centres with lights coming on now. The bus emptied. She sat on the bench seat almost alone, linking her own hands and trying to look relaxed.

Get off here. The roar of traffic from the ring road, an urban motorway which sounded like hell. Down this road to the shop on the corner. The Paki newsagents, as he referred to them, where she looked in the window, shielding her eyes the better to concentrate, and examined the advertisements. ROOM TO LET, a tired postcard among all the others explaining the existence of an e-mail expert, a plumber without qualifications, a three-piece suite and several tarts. No point going in here and asking about the room. He would tell her what he had told her before. No one ever takes it, darling. He only puts the card in there to make sure he gets fifteen visitors a week, which he does, regular. Likes company, turns them all down. The card was still there, folded innocuously inside its plastic folder on the display with all the others, innocent among the sly invitations to sex, but quite at home. She passed by. The centre of London was far away. The fifty-year-old semi-detached streets were too ugly to suffer the lure of a fashion makeover. They had never been tempted to gentrification. Amy turned off the main thoroughfare into a narrow road where the cars were crowded on to the pavements, bumper to bumper, shiny wet with the drizzle. Some looked as if they belonged to no one and had landed where they were by mistake. Three men crowded round the bonnet of another, staring at the engine and arguing about it. The litter was damp and flattened into doorways. She passed a house which reverberated with the *boom, boom, boom* of stereo sound. The next house bore the gallant signs of effort, with fresh painted window frames and net curtains behind the double glazing, while the next looked dark and empty, the windows thick with dust and a cracked glass panel in the front door.

From the outside of the houses, it was impossible to gauge how many people lived within. Successive property booms had passed this area by and moved north to places served by more than the erratic bus service and the far distant station. Bayview Road, it was laughingly called, summoning some vision of the sea instead of the contrasting sound of the railway line running behind the back gardens. A local wag had altered the sign on the wall, changing the Y to a T and the B to R. Ratview.

The house she had reached was not the worst in the row since it did not have an air of neglect and the cars immediately outside possessed all of their wheels. Their bulk blocked most of the light to the ground-floor windows but it did not seem as if the occupants would mind. The curtains dragged untidily across the front window, with their dun-coloured lining facing the world, looked as if they were never drawn back; the bunching of material on the window ledge had the look of undisturbed permanence. Amy stood on the step and rang the bell. A car cruised slowly down the street, filling the valley with the echo of more loud music. She turned to watch it. When she turned back, the door was already open with a figure retreating down the hall in a mute invitation to her to follow. She went inside.

'I suppose you've come about the room,' his voice floated back in neutral tones. 'Come in, do. Close the door.'

She did as she was told, noticing the smooth, almost noiseless click of the latch, and followed his right turn into the room with the curtains. Heavy curtains, which allowed no chink of light either out or in. The room was so bright, it hurt her eyes. There was a distinct set of chemical smells – paint, glue, white spirit – clean smells which she liked. They were sharp scents which cleared her nostrils of the other smells which had lingered since the train – blood, diesel fumes, burning.

He was a bright little bird of a man, about sixty-five and nimble, standing with his hands in the pockets of an old cardigan which stretched to his knees with the wool of it bobbled and flecked with different colours of paint and dried clay. He was pale with apple pink cheeks, big eyebrows which moved when he smiled and no more than a dusting of white hair on his head. She was taller than he, but not tall enough to see his skull. He was so clean-shaven that his chin shone and the smile on his wide mouth creased his whole face into a look of delighted curiosity. He usually minded his manners.

Almost always. His manners, she noticed, were all about being careful and precise in everything he did and wanting to preserve his environment. She was not the person, or even the category of person, he was expecting and it seemed to confuse him. She did not know if his turning away, back to the task in hand, was deliberate or just something he did to hide indifference or disappointment. Or maybe the task was more important. He had picked up the thing he was mending and held it together with his two thumbs and first fingers. It was a tiny chair, made from balsawood, high-backed and almost as tall as a matchstick, the seat as broad as his thumbnail. He was pressing one of the tiny legs into the seat from which it had become detached. It required a certain kind of glue.

'Broke,' he explained. 'Some person sat on it too long. Too heavy. Bit like you.'

Amy tried to smile. He concentrated on the chair, staring at it as if willing it to stick. She looked round the room. The drawn curtains hid treasure. There were shelves on three sides with tables in front, crowding the room. On each of the tables was a dolls' house. The frontage of the one he faced opened like a door, revealing the rooms and stairs and inmates otherwise visible only by peering through the windows. Each house had a theme; she knew that already. One was a gentleman's club, with a library upstairs, where tiny old men in waistcoats sat in armchairs with newspapers, while in the main room below more of them sat around a fireplace. One younger gentleman stood with his back to the fire, raising the tails of his frock coat to warm his behind on the coals created by shredded red and gold foil paper in the grate. A butler hovered with a tray.

The dolls' house with the opened front, from which the broken chair came, was different altogether. This was a brothel with pretensions to Victorian grandeur, with flock wallpaper on the walls, genteel and delicate furniture painted gold and gaudy furnishings of net and plush velvet. Painted ladies lay in deshabille on three chaise longues in the living room, attended by a demure maid in black and white. Upstairs, another miniature woman lay in a hip bath with her clothes, including a corset, strewn over a painted screen. It was the brothel on a Sunday, with no customers in sight. The ladies were bored by their own elegance. She did not look closely; he did not encourage it, but she still admired. Amy was too big for the limited space left in the room. The tiny figures she could see through the windows made her feel even more enormous. She stumbled against the edge of the table with the open dolls' house, making it rock. The young man with the raised coat-tails fell over. She reached inside and righted him carefully.

'I've almost got enough for my big exhibition. And my book. Isn't that nice?' he said, checking to see that the miniature had been returned to the right place.

'Hallo, Daddy,' she said. 'I can see you're busy. But I've got to stay a while.'

'How long?'

'I don't know,' she said. They did not embrace; they never did. She thought of the vast space of the circular living room at home and the willow tree outside and began to cry.

'You told me I could come here. I can't go back and I could look after you.'

'My darling child,' he said, without moving towards her. 'You're so defenceless. I wonder how different you would have been if you had the slightest capacity for retaliation. Where did you get that coat?'

'I found it.'

'And I found you. This is your home now.'

CHAPTER FOUR

Elisabeth Manser always wanted to go home. Or outside, where spring was having a debate with summer about which of them was winning. Inside here, it made precious little difference. She and John Box sat on the stone benches which lined the vast hall of the High Courts, five steps up from the tiled floor, facing the dun-coloured stone of the archways opposite. The archways led to curved stone stairs, disappearing to the floor above. High above them, the leaded windows of the east wall let in a colourless light, offsetting the dramatic stained glass of the windows at the far end. The building had the dimensions of a cathedral. The tiles of the floor, set in huge mosaic patterns of warm colours, made it less like a cloister and more like a vast railway station, built as a temple to the steam train, with the height of the roof more suitable to absorbing the sound of machinery than echoing the music of worship. The presence of gigantic stone in the huge pillars, balustrades, vaunted ceiling, archways, steps and multiple decorative motifs made it feel as enclosed as if they all sat, stood and moved in an underground cave. Voices echoed; a shout became a whisper; ordinary conversation became a mumble, the place too large for eavesdropping and perfect for secrets. The whole, huge space lent itself to privacy and defied hysteria.

There were no rules against cigarettes. Cylindrical ashtrays stood here and there against the walls, tiny against the scale of the rest and as unnoticeable as smoke. The size and the stone reduced the human element, their bad habits, bad breath, peculiar costumes and everyday clothes, to complete insignificance. A millionaire would have less presence than a gargoyle.

'So much easier to think about one's client when one hasn't seen him for a week,' John said, ready to return to his theme. 'Easier to sympathise from a distance. The law's an ass, you know. We have no real right to privacy and yet we persist with our strong concern to protect the rights of reputation. Shutting the stable door after the horse has bolted.'

'Yes,' Elisabeth agreed. 'No offence to focus your telephoto lens on a bedroom window and record how little a woman wears in bed, but publish and be damned. Rather like giving your scavenging journalist access to all the tasty scraps and then telling him he cannot digest them into words.'

'Poetic, my dear, but scarcely accurate. Who cares about privacy, anyway? Provided your life is as dull and ordinary as most lives are, you attract no interest. You're entirely safe, and you can beat your wife or your dog with complete impunity. You need no law to assist you. If you have courted the limelight, well, a different matter. I do so dislike the kind of client who beckons attention for her cleavage, but is furious when she is snapped being sick at the party. Which is a difference with our Douglas Petty. He doesn't seek attention, never did, but somehow, he incurred it and it remains consistent. There's many a public relations expert who would like to know the secret.'

'But it is tantamount to dislike,' she said. 'The one we love to hate. No public relations company would want to emulate it.'

John blew his nose on a large red paper napkin, rescued from somewhere, speaking simultaneously. 'The grieving widower. Poor woman. What an awful way to die. I hope she wasn't frightened.'

An odd hope, she thought. It was the lunch hour and therefore a time of relative calm. How Dickensian they must look in this setting. The High Court enclave was almost obscenely opulent in its decor and at the same time severely uncomfortable. The stone seat, inset into the wall, had the gradual effect of stiffening the spine. Both of them leant forward, resisting the chill of prolonged contact with the unyielding wall. Neither of them had chosen it as the ideal place for conversation. They had been passing through, using the front entrance in the Strand and aiming to exit through the back as a short cut into Carey Street. There was nothing awkward in this sudden sitting down. She fancied they resembled two garden gnomes, turning to stone, as if the daily apparel of wig, gown and suit had stunted their development, petrified them into something quasi-permanent and definitely old. Elisabeth suspected that John might like the place *because* it was uncomfortable as well as vast and anonymous in its vastness. Or he might like the opportunity to sit here and watch the women pass, walking quickly and peculiarly framed against the tiles. He had a way of observing women in particular, the brief, frank examination of someone looking for something to admire, like a hurried visitor to an art gallery who was curious but had no intention of buying. It was so objective, she found it impossible to resent.

There were two ways of walking in the High Courts, the brisk walk of someone who knew where they were going, or the pretended brisk walk of the majority who did not. The staircases on the left led to an impenetrable warren of impregnable doors, the maze of nightmares.

'But highly convenient, in one sense,' John remarked. 'By Amy Petty's death, Douglas gains sympathy, surely? Even if she isn't there to add to his credibility, she's a force *in absentia*. An absent piece of virtue who cannot be cross-examined.'

'And no risk she'd break down in public and say he was a bully. No risk that the defence could find some murkiness in her background to make her look . . . dishonest. A person prone to lies. A gold digger.'

'Oh, come now, we could have objected to that. Entirely inadmissible. And what could they have found? There's nothing.'

'Which is odd, don't you think? I'm not suggesting they could have raised whatever they found at trial, only used it, threatened to publish it, to get him to back off. You can always find something.'

Elisabeth felt nervous. It was always present, beneath the surface, when she was with him. He was so analytical he intimidated her as he always had and that had nothing to do with love.

'No, I disagree. She might have been a scrubber, how I hate that word. An opportunist, maybe, but she wasn't important enough for notoriety. The cloak of ordinariness is a good enough armour. Even if she did indeed model underwear and work as a mortician.'

'*Beautician*,' she corrected, standing up briskly. 'But Douglas won't stop on her account, will he? Wouldn't that be nice?'

'How can you say that? I do hope not,' John said fervently. 'My practice is half what it was a few years ago. I mean, look at the lists.' He waved in the general direction of the freestanding noticeboard near the entrance. 'One hundred and fifty judges in here, and not one of their eminences trying a libel case at the moment. We've priced ourselves out of the market. Scarcely anyone takes the risk of libelling anyone any more. But that stupid local paper did and the national compounded it. Then they enter a defence; they don't even get themselves off the hook by making an offer of amends. So rare, alas, to have opponents as ill-advised and careless as this. I *need* this case. There are other reasons too, of course. *We* need this case. I shall advise him that widowed or not, his reputation is still sacred and any settlement they suggest is inadequate. I want a *fight*.'

His voice cut into silence. An excellent speaking voice, like Douglas Petty's, but without the latter's peculiar resonance. Elisabeth thought of the courtrooms upstairs, where the relentlessness of stone gave way to equally relentless wood panelling and the creaking oak of the floors. She thought of the crackling tension of the mornings and the sleepiness of the airless afternoons in those rooms, and wondered if he needed anything of the kind. Without Mrs Petty to decorate the occasion, the scenery would be monumentally dull. And there was something behind this case which made it more disconcerting than its originality. A slipstream of malice, rare in its irrationality and indifference to money. Surely there was nothing else worth an argument but money; in real life, yes, but in litigation, no. Why care about reputation if you were rich enough to survive the loss of it?

Elisabeth shivered. They walked across the tiles towards the rear entrance, John blowing his nose again. The sound was infinitesimal; even the loudest of farts would not attract attention.

'This was where Douglas did his naked run,' she began.

'Where did she come from?'

'Who?'

'*Her.*'

A girl tripped down the steps in front of them, illuminated from behind by the light streaming through the stained glass. It turned her into a silhouette with a cloud of hair, her neat black suit invisible, a figure with legs, a thing of beauty. Once she was out of the light and they turned to regard her, they could see what she was, of indeterminate age, high heels, good legs, plain face.

'Do you know,' John said, 'everyone has moments of beauty? If only they knew and if only it were enough.'

She smiled. Their footsteps up the steps were louder here than on the tiles. They could turn left or right at this point, take one of the side exits, quicker, if either of them had wanted to hurry. He became indecisive at moments like these.

She thought of Douglas Petty, running naked through here for a bet, his big body spotlit by the windows.

'Just as well Petty was the wrong kind of advocate. Only ever did crime. If he worked in here, they'd have to call the Tipstaff and get him arrested.'

'He *was* arrested, just outside the doors, remember?'

'Ah yes, of course. An amazing disgrace. He did a streak from the back to the front, didn't he? Then got disbarred. What an absolute ass.'

Elisabeth hesitated. 'John, this libel . . . I know who printed it, but who started it? We don't know, do we?'

'The rival animal sanctuary? One of the many people he's offended? An old lover? Who cares? It doesn't matter who started it. Money in the bank, this one.'

They took the exit to the left with the windows above. Kissed by the doors, briefly but not furtively, and went separate ways.

Elisabeth went via Chancery Lane, past Ede and Ravenscroft with its display of formal clothes. The dummies on which the costumes sat reminded her of overgrown dolls, like the models displayed inside the High Courts. The High Court models were encased in glass, at the foot of the first set of stone steps which led to the left, just behind the entrance. They stood in their gloomy passageway, displaying the traditional finery of the Judges of Europe, as if to reassure the litigants who passed that the apparel of the judiciary upstairs was no more elaborate than anywhere else. The items in the Ede and Ravenscroft window were also uniforms; suits of stiff wool gaberdine and evening dresses like armour. Elisabeth disliked costume. She disliked the wearing of her wig, even though she believed in it. It made her into an advocate, defined her role in judicial proceedings, encouraged the person she was beneath the gown to behave accordingly and it was the very antidote to vanity. Not that vanity was one of her sins; she could not concentrate long enough for grooming and there was nothing to be vain about. There was instead a yawning gap of insecurity, indecisiveness and the constant belief that her world was as tenuous as her career, and that she herself was nothing but a fraud.

She did not want to go back to chambers, she wanted to go home and start again tomorrow. There was plenty of work to do at home. Better to go home in the early afternoon when the trains were less crowded and the detours to the line less irritating. It shamed her slightly that she was able to shrug off the horror of that train crash, still prominent in the daily headlines, and catch her train on the parallel route without a second thought except for impatience about having to go to an alternative station and the whole business taking longer. She should have been more hesitant and less practical, she thought; she should be boycotting all trains, in deference to the memory of Amy Petty, whom she had liked. But people died and life continued, that was that, and since she had neither the money nor the inclination for a flat in central London, she was a commuter and a second-class citizen, in a way. Second-class barrister also, hanging on the coat-tails of a lover. Who did she think she was? A fish out of water who should have gasped for mercy long since. A woman without grooming who needed a wig to cover her hair, working a career for which she did not feel remotely competent, although John always said otherwise and sometimes she believed him, and if she was as serenely confident and ambitious as she appeared, she would not be living where she lived, and she would not be in the fourth year of her affair with a married man, whom she loved to desperation without even being able to approve of him. It was an odd way to live on the brink like this, feeling constantly not up to it, whatever it was, waiting for it all to crash. With the knowledge that, if it did, the pieces of her wreckage would be remarkably small.

She was halfway to the regular station before she remembered it was still closed, due to open again next week once they had removed the remnants of the crashed trains to allow life to continue as if it the accident had never happened – beyond the recriminations which would reverberate for a year or three and the civil actions which would provide lucrative work for three dozen lawyers. Now that would be the perfect symbiosis, acting for a victim of negligence, behaving like an indignant humanitarian whilst earning high fees at the same time. There was nothing like well-rewarded altruism, but she would not have been up to that, either. She got quality work because of John's blatant favouritism. It was a subject of comment, Elisabeth's practice being better than she deserved. Occasional sex in return for patronage. Sometimes she believed it was true. Usually she knew it was not. She loved him and she was afraid of him. Even more afraid of admitting defeat.

Detouring into the Tube for the creaky Northern Line service to London Bridge, she had a sudden fellow feeling for Amy Petty, based on nothing but her own sense of inadequacy. That was what Amy had been like, all the time giving the impression of trembling on the brink in a way not obvious to John, only to herself. Call it feminine intuition, a phrase she loathed even though she did not doubt the existence of such a thing. It was a mistake to have meetings in the house of a client; you learned too much from a house and a client should remain a stranger. You should not be sent off into the kitchen to make tea with the client's wife, to watch her fuss and apologise about the dirt on the floor. Elisabeth did not despise those who made a career of housewifery; she envied them. It was a daunting task in its own way and a noble calling. Amy had taken her to see the dogs. That was where she was competent, but she did not think she was, any more than Elisabeth considered herself a natural lawyer or a star anything, for that matter. She was a thirty-five-year-old, unkept and sometimes unkempt mistress with a very small house and garden far outside the walls of a big exciting city which she had never quite grasped or enjoyed.

The roof over the platforms of London Bridge station was probably a little taller than the roof of the High Courts, she decided, but there wasn't much in it. She was thinking of the size of the Petty household in comparison to her own, which she kept with indifferent care, apart from the garden. She was thinking that if she had been Amy Petty she would not have been up to her job, either, not if it entailed keeping a man like Douglas Petty happy and getting beaten up by him, to say nothing of his mother, and she was wondering at the same time exactly when the moment was that Amy and she had fallen into liking with one another, however briefly. As she sat in the train, fishing in her bag for the packet of mints she usually carried, all dusty at the bottom, she suddenly remembered Amy remarking in the kitchen, 'He's nice, your man. Do you know, he looks just like a *whippet?*' And then, before Elisabeth could interrupt and state in her best icy tones that John was not her *man*, she was simply his assistant, Amy put her hand over her mouth and murmured a flurried apology. 'Oh, I'm so sorry, what an awful thing to say, but I like whippets. They're fragile-looking, you see, but ever so tough. Sorry.' Busying herself with tea things like a nervous waitress, so that Elisabeth had laughed out loud and not bothered with any denial. The woman had a sixth sense about her relationship with John, but like feminine intuition, it would be easily ignored. 'So what do I look like then?' she had asked to prove that she did not really mind anything the mere wife of a client might say. The question had startled

Amy and given her pause for thought, but so short a pause, she had obviously thought about it already. 'You? Overgrown cocker spaniel mixed with terrier, nice colouring.' 'And yourself?' Elisabeth had asked, still smiling and oddly flattered, eyeing the Post-its on the mantelpiece, covered with neat handwriting. Amy had shaken her head and lifted the tray, her long sleeves falling back from her wrists. 'Battersea Dogs' Home special issue,' was all she said. 'Although Douglas says I'm more like an Afghan. They haven't got much brain.'

When the sleeves fell back from Amy's arms, Elisabeth noticed the bruises. Old, pink and yellow bruises. Nothing was said about them. Remembering that, Elisabeth shed a tear for Amy Petty and chewed on a dusty mint. Three meetings in that house and on each occasion, it had presented itself in various states. It had not been a quiet house, or one where a single room was left undisturbed for long, despite the number of rooms. All that livestock. On that second occasion, they had all thanked her for the coffee except that bastard husband of hers. He hit her; how else did she get bruises? *Mongrel with good taste. Grizzled grey bulldog, several owners.* Elisabeth fumed.

The journey to her outpost was forty-five minutes, but this train went two hours further than that, right as far as the coast. Sometimes a man, woman or hermaphrodite, Elisabeth never noticed which, pushed a trolley through so fast there was scarcely a chance to stop the damn thing and ask for a tea bag in boiled water. She preferred to get on her train clasping good coffee purchased at the station, fussy about that, trying to forget her hunger which was more of a thirst and remember the fact that a brief, dry kiss in parting from a man who looked like a *whippet* was, nevertheless, worth having.

But the words of the article which had defamed Douglas Petty echoed in her head. *Why does this one-time defender of law and order take in his waifs and strays? Is it so that he can sentence them to this?* And alongside that the picture of the defrocked Douglas with the raised stick, chasing the dog across the lawn, with the caption *Dougie frolics with doggies, but why in the dark?* And *why,* if it were not true, would anyone seek to reveal Douglas Petty as a man not only cruel but perverted? All right, there was a rival animal sanctuary run by some woman, but where was the *money*? Who could possibly stand to gain? And, most importantly, why, if he was such a monstrous, reactionary bully, did a woman like Amy stay with him? Money, the root of all loyalty. Not a bad motive either; there were certainly worse. A bargain was a bargain. The kiss lingered, as if her cheek had been pinched.

Douglas kissed his stepsister in the perfunctory way of a brother with greater things on his mind. He put his hands on her shoulders and placed the kiss in the general direction of her left ear, followed up by a gentle slap between her shoulderblades, as if his giant hand was looking for a place to land without encountering anything sharp. Caterina had an angular shape, with the kind of spiky hair which looked permanently arranged above a long, slender neck and the sort of physique designed for elegance. She was made for flowing drapery and large chunks of interesting, metal jewellery. As she was now, recently out of bed, she looked more like an overgrown waif who could fold herself piece by piece into a chair. The loose jumper, tight jeans and bare feet suited her forty-year-old face, which was youthful with skin stretched tight over high cheekbones and enormous brown eyes. She took hold of his hand before he moved away, pressed it lightly to the side of her almost beautiful face, and then released it. She watched his progress to the other side of the table with a look of concerned devotion, as if he might slip before he reached his chair. He reached for the packet of cornflakes.

'You were up late last night,' she said in her high, singsong voice which surprised people. An almost childish contrast to the voice of her stepbrother, which was deep and carrying, even when he swore beneath his breath.

'I usually am.' He was not encouraging conversation. Caterina sighed, unfolded herself from the easy chair and came to sit opposite him. Douglas poured milk on the cereal and munched solidly without any sign of enjoyment. Bacon, eggs and all the accompaniments were not available under the regime Caterina imposed out of preference for the muesli and yoghurt type of sustenance. Cornflakes and toast were a compromise arrived at without discussion after a week. She did not think Amy would have achieved this, but did not say so. She knew when to limit her remarks.

'Locking yourself away,' she teased. 'Not good. Oh my poor Douglas, I do feel for you.'

'I know you do,' he said between mouthfuls, 'only I wish you wouldn't say it.'

There was a silence. She shrugged to suggest she was not really hurt and smiled. Caterina had a wide mouth and her smile had a devastating charm. He smiled back. They were, in their way, a handsome pair of step-siblings. When he was a barrister and she a twenty-year-old student, he had been proud to be seen with her and announce the relationship to jealous male friends. Did he have friends in those days? Yes, he remembered them; harddrinking bachelors, quite unsuitable for his status in life even then and all disappeared now. They either took up the domestic mantle or abandoned him when he was disbarred. It was only Douglas who had been able to sustain bachelor behaviour into the age when it was less than dignified. Right up until the time he met Amy and made his late marriage at forty-five. A man with money does as he pleases.

'Yes, yes, dear,' she said. 'I know you don't like *emoting*. But do remember that it is allowed in others . . .'

'Cat, don't think I'm ungrateful for all you're doing. I am grateful, very. You've been a terrific buffer zone these last few days. I may as well have been guarded by a Rottweiler. It's allowed me to . . . well, come to terms in my own way. Get on with things.'

Get on with *dogs*, he might have said. Walking the dogs, feeding the dogs, comforting the dogs in their loss and leaving her to deal with Mother and the police and all the rest which she had done with great efficiency. Years of intermittent work in public relations had developed that singsong, listening voice with overtones of authority. She was a good listener. Officials of all kinds respected her voice.

'The police are still puzzled, you know,' she said carefully. 'As well as embarrassed, for lack of a better word, in their failure to find a body. There's a nice officer deputed to talk to me who seems to take it personally. He also takes it personally that he's not allowed to talk to *you*, so perhaps you'd better, next time. It's just that . . . well, there was only one fatality from her carriage, which was near the back, a woman who fell and broke her neck getting out of the train. Tragic. They know which carriage Amy was in because they recovered her handbag—'

'The puppy,' he murmured.

'The what?'

'Nothing, go on.'

'And they think she either walked through to the front of the train, before it crashed, forgetting her handbag. Or she was in the loo and went in the wrong direction once the crash happened. It's so easy to get disorientated on a train, I've often done it, now, where *was* my seat, especially if I'm thinking of what I'm going to do next. She might have gone forward by mistake. Into the carriage which burned.'

'Amy would forget her own arm,' he said shortly. 'Did anyone see her?'

'They haven't quite got round to all of them yet. Besides, he reckons people will remember the crash and nothing else. They asked me to ask you, what was she wearing?'

Douglas was listening intently, drumming his fingers on the table. Then he was silent for a full minute as the clock ticked on the wall, the cat sighed in the basket by the Rayburn and she grew impatient.

'Ask Mother,' he said finally.

'Mother was still in bed when Amy left.' There was another long pause.

'I don't remember what she was wearing. I never do.'

She rose from the table, gracefully, removed his cereal bowl and took it to the sink. He stared at the toast rack, thoughtfully. There was such a contrast in their movements, Amy's and hers. Where Amy was noisy and frequently clumsy – she could make a row, even laying a table – Caterina was silent and deft. She could eat without a sound.

'I'm sorry I can't help with the dogs,' she said quietly. 'I wish I wasn't allergic to them at close quarters. Someone else keeps ringing. A woman from a sanctuary, you've mentioned her before . . . is she the one you said can't decide whether she's totally New Age or a born-again virgin? Oh and that lawyer, Box, whatever his name is, wants you to call. When you can. I told him you probably didn't need him any more. Nonsense to go on with that silly case in the circumstances, isn't it?'

'I don't know about that. I'll speak to him.' There was a warning note in his voice she was careful to heed. He was not about to abdicate all decisions.

'Are you sure you can't remember what she was wearing?'

'No. I told you, I never notice.'

Caterina smiled. 'Never *did* notice,' she corrected automatically.

He had an overpowering desire for the company of dogs. When she looked up from the loading of the dishwasher, he had gone.

Practising the deep breathing learned in yoga class, designed for concentration and useful for the creation of a soothing persona, Caterina left the domestic chores for which she was exquisitely well trained, and went in search of her mother. She was as yet not entirely sure where she might find her, since Mama had the habit of varying her routine, especially in the mornings. At least, it may have been a habit; or it may have been the result of such a dreadfully *upsetting* week, if not an upsetting year. Caterina was a frequent enough visitor in this house to know the regimes, but she was not entirely familiar with how the morning bit worked. At the moment Mother was inclined to wander. Not, thank heaven, in the physical sense, but simply in conversation when her son was around, perhaps because she did not know quite what to say, or so Caterina had advised him. She isn't really being indifferent, she had explained to her darling brother, but you do have to realise, my love, that at that age, they've been to a lot of funerals already and take bereavement rather more for granted. A slight exaggeration, she had to concede, since Isabel Petty had not attended a burial service in many years. Appearances did more than justice to her years. Her porcelain skin belied it; she had the figure of one of those frail, stooped angels in the graveyard, built on wire and able to withstand the foulest storms.

The rain outside was dwindling, the grey day beginning to show promise. Mother might have stayed in her room with her tea tray or she might have come downstairs to sit in the same chair of the living room, to look towards the garden where she would not walk until it was warmer and even then with small footsteps, for fear the heels of her shoes would catch in the dampness of the lawn.

And there she was. Like a Tibetan spaniel, Amy had once said in the days when she and Caterina had been friendly. She's like one of them because the head is small in relation to the body and the muzzle is fairly short and blunt without being flattened or wrinkled, and Caterina had been amused by the comparison until she began to wonder what breed of dog she herself might be taken to resemble; a Saluki, she hoped (lithe and graceful with the head of an aristocrat), but there was a faint feeling of unease that Amy might make a different comparison altogether and think of her as a cat, or worse. This pretence of mourning was really a bit of a strain.

Isabel Petty had a way of sitting which made her seem so still she was almost invisible. An unfamiliar person might walk in and out of the room without noticing her presence, as if she was a permanent fixture in the chair she always occupied in here. If she were not acknowledged, she remained silent. Perhaps the fact that so much of her life had been spent married to an autocratic man and, after that, alongside a son of similar disposition made her wary of initiating conversation. Perhaps it was laziness or disinterest.

'Would you like some coffee, sweetheart?'

'Oh, is it that time already?' Her head peered out from behind the newspaper which she always managed to read without rustling, a feat Douglas had remarked upon as impossible. Midmorning coffee was not appropriate until she had devoured every item of the national and international news and begun on the crossword.

Her mood would be ebullient if she had finished it by lunchtime. She lowered the newspaper soundlessly and smiled sweetly at her daughter.

'Oh dear,' she went on. 'How time flies when one tries to distract oneself. I should be doing something useful, shouldn't I?'

Mother's usefulness was limited by her appearance. Her hair was piled on to her head and pinned into a neat French roll, in a labour-intensive style of the 1950s. She wore a skirt which was heather-coloured, a cashmere sweater in cream and her stockings and shoes matched the skirt. They were colours in which her daughter would not be seen dead, but they suited her mother's style. The clothes were unsuitable for work; they were the clothes of someone who had once dreamed of owning such clothes when she was taking down shorthand in another era. She had worn different clothes in her working days, which had captured the attention of her boss, who had announced his intention of making her a lady instead of a deserted mother. A challenge to which she had agreed, although the transition was more in his mind. She had always been a lady who insisted upon ladylike behaviour in her presence. She had been a fine cook; she had always wanted a son and adored his son. They all three adored his son. Isabel Petty never raised her voice.

'Oh, no, don't worry about anything,' Caterina said. 'All under control. Well, more or less.'

Nothing could be further from the truth, but both took comfort in the idea. The priorities were to keep Douglas as content and stable as possible, offer him the succour of a pleasant environment and emotional support should he require it. He showed few signs of needing it, and he was, as always, conspicuously polite to them both, something they seemed to copy in their own conversation, always aware of not letting the side down. It was far too soon to remind Douglas of how much the food had improved.

'If we had a memorial service of some kind for Amy, I wonder who would come?' Isabel Petty asked, more to herself than her daughter.

'I don't know, Mummy.'

'Well, we shall have to think of something. In due course. He won't be up to it. He was in his study, last night, writing away. Well, I mean, I don't know if he was writing or not, one is never allowed in there, but he stayed there ever so late. I do wish I could sleep. Makes me feel so sluggish. Yes, coffee would be lovely. In here, shall we? The sun'll be out in a minute.'

The room had grown cleaner and freer of dog hair over the last few days. For lack of anything better to do, Caterina had had a go at the windows, inside and out, taking a morning over it, with a stepladder sinking into the flowerbed as she cleaned away rain marks from the outside and the grease of cigar smoke from within. Clean windows made everything cleaner, encouraged dust to fling itself into the hoover and the colour of the rugs to emerge. Caterina itched to do something with the curtains and knew that within a few more days the temptation would be overpowering. Douglas would hardly notice and once this death was confirmed, she could make a start on Amy's clothes. Somebody had to do it.

There was a series of photographs in now clean but usually tarnished silver frames on the oak table by Isabel's chair. Three in colour of Douglas and Amy's wedding, where the sheer volume of Amy's dress seemed to obscure everything else like a barrage balloon in the sky, and three more, older by far, black and whites. Douglas's father, dead these many years, but laughing uproariously every time he tried to avoid posing for the camera. Petty Senior, wearing his son's judicial wig and looking a fool, always having the last word. A man with a firm belief in primogeniture as well as responsibility for the fairer sex, so that he left to his wife a small stipend, to his daughter a gift of cash and to his son, a fortune and a collection of convalescent dogs, along with the instructions that he should look after the women until hell froze over, or be damned for eternity. Damien Petty had made the last of his fortunes in lawn mowers, never used one once, took his attitudes from prehistory and his language from Dickens. Except among friends, when he told them that the sun shone out of his son's arse.

'So she's dead, then, Douglas.'

'Yes, Jimmy, I know. Do you always have to state the obvious?'

'Where will we bury her?'

'There's no more room for burials, Jimmy. You know we stopped that a while since. Call the vet and get her taken to the crematorium.'

Together they lifted Dilly the arthritic greyhound, wrapped in her blanket, took her out of the stables and laid her on the paving stones.

'Let her keep the blanket and rest in the sun for a bit,' Douglas suggested. 'I don't like leaving her in the dark.' He uncovered the black and white head, closed her eyes and tucked the blanket round her neck. 'If that poor bitch had ever known kindness before now, she could have lived another three years,' he said. 'Let her get a bit of sun. She loved to sit out here.'

Jimmy nodded, suspicious of sentiment. The blanket looked incongruous in the neatness of the yard. Jimmy doubted the vet would treat the corpse with so much respect, probably would not even come himself. People were staying away from Douglas at the moment, probably because he was able to mention words like 'crematorium' and 'burial' without flinching. He seemed savagely indifferent to the death of a wife, although moved by the demise of gentle Dilly and her shorter span of days.

They went into Dilly's stable and began the task of clearing it out. A scrubbing from top to bottom, clean bedding. From inside the thick walls, where warmth lingered as if trapped from season to season, they heard the sound of a van pulling to a halt. Jimmy looked out of the door, hesitated and groaned; Douglas went on working, deliberately deaf to sound, the way he was in the last week when anyone called his name or the telephone rang. The engine stopped and footsteps moved towards them. Then there was a scream of outrage.

'*Bastard!*'

'She's asking for you, Douglas,' Jimmy said calmly. 'Take your pitchfork, I would.'

It was a reminder of an old discussion; would it be better to bed the animals with old-fashioned straw so that they could behave like

ancient farmhands, wielding pitchforks to clear it and burn it
cleanly, or was this too much trouble for words? Straw pricked and
rubbed and harboured insect life, could scratch an arm raw, whatever its cleansing qualities. So it was wool and cotton and
washing-machine-durable blankets, better than they had in most
houses, Jimmy said. Should have sewed ribbons on them. Douglas
took his sunglasses from the breast pocket of his shirt and put
them on, winking at Jimmy, which was a sight Jimmy had longed
to see, before picking his cap off the floor of the stable and pulling
it low over his forehead. The headgear and the dark shades
effected a strange and sinister transformation, completed by the
small cigar he lit quickly and carefully, changing him into a vision
of a louche racehorse trainer at the races, a city bandit disguised by
nothing but his baggy jeans, a bit of a wide-boy, with muscle. Pity
he was clean-shaven, Jimmy thought. A beard would have made
him look like an assassin.

'*Bastard! Bastard! Bastard!*' the voice outside shrieked, then lowered to a keening wail. 'Ahhh, you poor thing, ahhhhhh. *Bastards!*'

'You've gained a plural,' Jimmy suggested. 'Better get out there,
before there's more of yous.'

Douglas patted his chest and strode to the door, one hand in his
pocket, the other controlling the cigar. The sun shone on to the
paved yard of the courtyard, fickle as all hell, as if it had been there
all the time. Half in and half out of the sunlit corner where they
had laid Dilly to rest, the shrieker stood, her hand poised in benediction over the black and white head with its collar of yellow
blanket. It was a large, fat hand, with rings on the fingers, and the
body behind it dressed in a long, open-weave coat the colour and
texture of hessian with various dun-coloured layers beneath trailing over boots, the whole of her trembling with rage like a motor
engine at traffic lights. Douglas was looking at the crown of her
bent head, long hair, white at the roots, variegating between dull
brown and chestnut before it touched the ground as she bent over
the bulk of her own body. '*Bastard!*' she yelled again. Her hand did
not quite touch Dilly's muzzle.

'You do repeat yourself,' Douglas said, standing close, so that when she unbent she was at risk of collision. 'Can I help you?'

She turned her head, flicking at his face with a flurry of hair and lethal earrings which dangled to her shoulders, then took a step back. She smelled of lemons, hay and the unwashed creases of a sagging body overlain with sharper perfume worn specially. There was brief, unspoken recognition of the fact that each found the other acutely distasteful.

'I've come for the dogs,' she said. Her voice was deep, vibrant with indignation. 'I've got the van, so let's make it easy. They can't stay here, can they? They'll all die and get slung in a corner, like this one. Let me look at her. I want to make sure she wasn't beaten to death.'

Douglas blew a thin stream of cigar smoke straight down into her eyes. 'Hallo, Delilah. Nice day for it. Been shaving with a blowtorch again, have you?'

She took a step backwards and almost tripped over the recumbent form of Dilly. Douglas grabbed her arm with unnecessary force to keep her upright. On her bosom, a large ceramic badge reading 'DELL THE ANIMAL SANCTUARY THAT CARES' clanked against a silver chain necklace. The same words were emblazoned in red on the van, parked askew at the entrance to the stable yard.

'Don't touch me, you beast!' she yelled, shrugging him off.

'Don't fall over the poor animal then,' Douglas said calmly. 'Didn't nurse her to have her crushed post mortem by a heavy-weight.'

'You *pig!*'

'Oh stop being such a lout, Dell. What do you want?'

She could not stare him down through his reflective glasses. All she could see was a distorted reflection of herself. She put her large red hands on her ample hips. 'I told you, I've come to take away the dogs. You aren't fit to look after them. They might have had a chance before, and now they haven't any at all. Dying like flies, obviously. Probably starving without a woman to feed them. *Bastard.*'

'Come on, Delilah. You've always wanted these dogs, because

you haven't got enough animals in that place of yours to justify the money you wheedle out of the public. Not much of an empire for you, is it? Perhaps that's why you want mine. People'll start asking about why you need two Volvos. Even if you have got God on your side.'

'Oh, isn't that just typical, Mr Petty? Contempt for poor people as well as poor animals. All you wanted was power and what do you do when you've got it? Kill the poor buggers. How can I let these poor things stay here with you? My conscience would kill me. You, you can't even grieve for a wife, can you? What was she to you? Just another *bitch*—'

'Watch it, Delilah.'

'*Me* watch it? What have I got to watch? Just give me the damn dogs. And may God have mercy on your wife, she must be glad to be dead.'

Douglas caught hold of the sleeves of her long coat and yanked it down over her shoulders, pinning her arms to her side. There was the sound of ripping material; she whimpered in protest as he turned her round, fingers pressing into the lardiness of her shoulders. She whimpered louder as he spun her round to face the door of the stable and walked her towards it.

'Rape!' she screamed.

'Yeah, serial rape,' Douglas said.

She felt his grip tighten and then she screamed in earnest, just as he let her go. Framed in the stable doorway there was a pair of protruding buttocks, skinny, white and moving, Jimmy bent over with his trousers round his ankles, bare bottom exposed, waggling his hips. Mooning.

'Let me go!'

'Nobody's stopping you,' Douglas said. 'Just go.'

She adjusted the coat and looked at him, ready to spit. Then she smiled. Too late he saw the girl on the other side of the van, with the camera, catching it all. The dead dog in the corner, with her head in the sun, himself with the shades over his eyes and his hands on the woman, and wee Jummy's rump, wagging a tune.

Delilah posed, displaying her torn coat to the camera. Tottered towards the van like a martyr running from a lion and collapsed into the passenger seat. The van sped away.

'Aw, *shite*,' Jimmy muttered, fastening his trousers and fumbling for a cigarette. 'That's fucking done it. Am I sacked again, Douglas?'

Douglas threw his sunglasses on to the stones and ground them underfoot, then smiled for the first time in a week.

'Keep that up, you'll get fucking promoted,' he said.

The cleaning woman let herself into the Pettys' London flat by fortnightly arrangement. It was one of her favourite jobs because all she had to do was make a mark on the place to show she had been there, like dragging the hoover across the carpet, rearranging the odd item, dusting the dust and leaving the odd, tasteful fingerprint to show she had tried. Sometimes, if someone had been in residence, there might be a humble note on a Post-it, pointing out a particular task, *Can you have a go at the stain in the sink, thanks, and take out the rubbish?*

She always knew when someone had been, even without the note. The velvet pile of the carpet reacted to the lightest footprint and a bathroom used was a giveaway. So she cleaned more than usual, buffing the enamel on the cream bathroom suite to a state of shine, although it was hardly marked, and looking into the cupboard above the basin. Such a lovely range of unaffordable lotions and creams. Seen *that* one advertised, and *that* was a favourite of her daughter. With a fingerful brushed over her face, she could see why.

In the living room, there was an answerphone on a table with a light blinking to show messages waiting. It was a bit old-fashioned, she thought; a silly expense when a mobile would do, but she had never seen the light winking before so she pressed PLAY. A disembodied voice crept into the room.

'*Amy Petty, answer, why don't you? I hope you're there. Don't worry, I shan't come looking. Not yet.*' Click, whirr.

'*Amy, you know I'll wait.*' Click.

'*Amy, there's no point in freedom without comfort. You must need money. For God's sake speak to me.*' Click.

'*Message for Mrs PITTY . . . we have your drycleaning ready for six weeks, OK?*' A voice in the background interrupting, saying, shushh, not that one. '*Oh, sorry, Mrs Pitty. Didn't know you was dead.*' Click.

'*Amy? Amy? Don't go away. I'll find you. Stay where you are.*' Click.

She was rather shaken by these brief recitations and could not work out if the voices other than the drycleaner's were the same person's. The machine was older than any she recognised, without instructions to save/delete/repeat. She unplugged it from the wall and dusted it thoroughly. Drifted back into the bathroom, took out all the almost full jars and put them in her bag. Dead was dead.

CHAPTER FIVE

Amy Petty missed her fine face creams. She had taken, in the last few days, to smoothing her empty hands over her dry face compulsively, as if her empty hands could feed her skin. It stopped her feeling so woozy. *He'll find me. I know he will find me. Someone will find me . . . Stop it.* The sun would be shining on the white house; the kitchen at home would be catching the light from the side window. There would be a breeze in the trees, mud on the floor, not this dust. She could see the willow tree, bursting into leaf . . . Amy stirred from her daydream. She was not going to take any more of the calming pills he gave her. It was kind of him, but she felt better without them.

'It's not so clean in here, Dad, does is have to be like this?'

'Are you saying it's dirty?'

'I didn't say it was dirty, just that is wasn't exactly clean.'

'It isn't a laboratory, Amy. And I don't want you clearing it up. That's what you do at home, but you don't do it here. Prison used to drive me mad like that. Cleanliness next to godliness, all that rubbish.'

She put the tasteless yellow spread which was not butter on to her toast and ate, slowly. At *home* there would be butter. How childish to long for butter, but to all intents and purposes she was a child for the moment. She had been a child for over a fortnight.

'I thought you quite liked it in prison.'

'I never said I *liked* it,' he said crossly. 'You are stupid. Years of hell, apart from the workshop. Arts and crafts to clean our dirty little minds.' He wagged a finger at her. 'It gave me a hobby and a sort of living, so I should be grateful. Everything comes in by post and goes out by post. I love the post, live for it, did that in prison, too, although I never got a letter from you. Pass the jam, will you?'

She touched the pot, detaching her fingers from the stickiness. 'But you didn't learn about dolls' houses in prison. You always made them.'

'Yes, I suppose,' he said absently. 'Only not all the time.'

He always sat a distance away from her, not always in the same place at the kitchen table, but as far away as space allowed. The table where they ate acted as a staging post between the outside world and the rest of the house. For each meal, the items that had gathered in the meantime were moved to one side to allow room. If she sat at the narrow end, he would move the pile of magazines, pipecleaners, paperclips and small postal packets so that it lay between them. She passed the jam jar over the heap, lifting herself out of her chair to do so. Today, he looked like a chicken, or more like a small cockerel, with his white hair stuck up in a comb. He was in a talkative mood.

'So what would you have been doing if you had been at *home*, then?' he asked.

'Oh, probably cleaning,' she said with a smile.

'There you are then,' he said comfortably, and then as an afterthought, 'You look so much better than you did.'

She knew this was not true, but appreciated the kind intention. Her hair had been turned from blonde to dull brown with a rudimentary dye he had provided and her own efforts with scissors had reduced its unruly volume to a passable bob, not quite the same length on both sides of her face. Her skin had grown paler and her cheeks were pink from the constant heat of the kitchen, a look he seemed to prefer to the weathered flush which had not survived the first ten days. She had a touch of pallor, like his own. A newspaper rustled, folded by his plate; she wished she could open the window, but if she did, she would not like what she could hear; no trees, no mewing of the cat. She shook her head to clear the fumes of sleep. She had slept so much.

He was an inveterate reader of newspapers, which collected on the front doorstep early in the morning along with a selection of magazines and catalogues. The delivery of the wrong newspapers was a source of loud complaint, although he conceded that his was a difficult order, what with a different paper every day, a rabid tabloid one day, *The Times* the day after, the *Guardian* the day after that and this local Kent paper every week, the one he flourished towards her now. She did not think he could ever be the sort of old man who could fall down in his house and be ignored for days. The papers on the doorstep would tell the tale of a man with eclectic tastes, seriously indisposed. She looked at him with desperate fondness. *This* was home.

'Looks like your stupid spouse is in trouble again. I only take this thing because I can get it by post, sent for it after I saw your wedding picture. Long time ago, eh? "Beauty and the Beast", or was it "Pretty Woman marries Playboy"? Some page four headline like that, and a picture of you with that great big frock. I always wonder who chose that dress for you.'

'His stepsister helped me.'

'Ah, she would have been the one standing by the side and looking like a model. You call it *help*; I'd call it sabotage. Dear, dear Amy Fisher, if it weren't for newspapers, I'd never have known where you'd gone. Once I had some idea of where you were going to live, I started getting this paper, still do. It's such a *bad* paper. Anyway, your widowed husband has lost his rag again.'

It shocked her. *Husband; widowed.*

'Let me see it, Dad, please.'

He held it playfully, between finger and thumb, as if it was contaminated. 'Only if you promise not to get upset. I don't like to see you upset. You were screaming in your sleep.'

'I promise.'

'You've a good pair of hands,' he said, washing his own under the tap and bouncing out of the room, whistling.

She had been making an effort to be like him, but she did not share his addiction to newspapers – in fact, had come to regard them as the very bane of existence. They were the intruders into homesteads, the harbingers of doom; they destroyed harmony and stopped more conversations than they ever began. They were something she read with caution, except the magazine sections with the features on lives which she could enjoy reading about while doubting they were true, and the cookery and household and cosmetics sections which she devoured with interest while others argued the toss about politics. Amy could never allow herself to get angry about things she could not change and did not think she could change anything much, except, perhaps, her clothes, her face creams, or the colour of the walls, and even the latter had proved difficult. What a silly person she was. She looked around the room. How soon this way of life had become normal in its simplicity. Her father ate bland food in small quantities, variations on a grilled chop with vegetables, and he insisted on cooking it. That was the evening meal; daytime food was toast, beans, cereal and fruit, which hung around the kitchen always slightly past its best. Food was not important and that was a relief. Nor was the shabby decor. Her father could have decorated his small house from top to bottom; he was fit enough and artistic enough, but he never bothered. This room, like all the rest, teetered on the brink of unsavoury ugliness, but saved itself from complete condemnation by his cursory efforts to keep dirt at bay. The only thing she found particularly hard to tolerate, even in her befuddled state, was a fridge littered with inedible leftovers. She could demand their removal or throw them away herself; but she was a guest, a child, and it was not his fault that he was so frugal, it was a necessary part of his existence, she told herself, just as the careless over-provisioning of her own home had been part of hers. And she supposed that her adapting to this other existence had been made easier by the fact that she had always known how little you needed to survive, never quite at ease with affluence, but she had also come to realise that she had arrived here on a tidal wave of shock, a state which made her more docile than normal. The passive state was receding now she had got used to the sound of the trains running through her head every hour of the day. It wasn't home, though.

Home. She made an hourly effort not to think of it, but thought of it now, trying to push back the wave of misery that threatened to drown her. There was an image of the willow tree in the garden on the day she had seen it first, the sound of a barking dog, and early-morning blackbirds which would be at their rowdiest now. The back door open to the draught of spring, the fields in the distance and the solace of endless space. All she had ever wanted, she had known that as soon as she saw it. That house was quite imperfect enough for her; it could never make up its mind what it was supposed to be: the two of them were alike in that way and fell for each other easily. Come to think of it, that home had something in common with this mean little house in terms of what it was like to live in it, insofar as she was still the visitor, never the mistress, and the sphere of her influence was small. Amy Petty Nobody. *Stop it.* She reached for the newspaper.

There was a feel to it she did not like: it felt as if it would disintegrate into the soggy pulp it was made from at any minute; the harm it could do out of all proportion to the rough flimsiness of its texture. Nothing on the first page, plenty on the second. A violent photograph. Douglas Petty, cigar in mouth, partially disguised as he pulled the coat off an older woman whose face to camera was twisted in a scream, with two other photos continuing the narrative, one of them of a swaddled dog, lying neatly, another of a bare bottom. *GRIEVING WIDOWER GREETS GUEST! I was terrified, said Delilah Hall, owner of Dell Animal Sanctuary; I only went to offer help. Petty can't bring himself to say a single thing about his wife's tragic death – is he human? So I worried about his dogs . . .* A close-up of the bruises on her arms. *And what did I find? Brutality.*

Amy smiled. She smiled a lot. That stupid Dell was really silly. What did a few bruises matter? Then she picked up the magnifying glass her father used for small print and focused on the swaddled dog. She drew the glass further away to improve the image of the head, touched it with the tip of her little finger and began to cry. Rollie Fisher, the bantamweight father who did not resemble her, came back into the room, stopped whistling and spoke quietly, pointing at the paper.

'Look, you knew what he's like. A pig of a man. That's why you took the chance to leave, because of him.'

'Is it?' she said. 'Did I ever say that? You know I don't talk about it.' And then, under her breath, so that he could scarcely hear, her finger still stroking the head in the photograph, 'Poor Dilly.'

'Poor who?'

'Nothing.'

Rollie Smith sat down unwillingly at the other end of the table, trying to hide the slight impatience of a busy man who kept to a routine and found it difficult to interrupt his daily regime. She felt she had no right to monopolise him and disturb the order of things, even though he loved her. Love, the anchor of the soul, as necessary as food. A man's habits were difficult to break. He wanted to be in his workroom and was making a big effort to readjust the day in order to help her. Father and daughter quality-time. She brushed away the tears.

'You've done the right thing, my darling, even if not in the right way. The right thing was to get away from him, by whatever means. Do you know, I shall always feel responsible for you marrying him. If I had been a proper father to you, instead of an absent father, an *imprisoned* father, you might have found a different kind of partner altogether. You were looking for the father figure because you hadn't got one. That's my theory, anyway.'

'You mean people marry the person who makes up a gap in their lives?' she said, with difficulty.

'Possibly.'

'Well, if that's what I did, it's hardly your fault, Dad.'

'No,' he said furiously. 'It isn't my fault. It isn't my fault that I ended up in prison because of your mother's lies and the gross incompetence of the law. It isn't my fault that I was denied any access to you, but I still feel responsible for not being there. You might have done entirely different things with your life if I had been. Still, at least I'm here now, eh?' He straightened the items on the table into a neat pile of paper and got up, slightly embarrassed by his outburst and not knowing what to say next.

She was quite prepared to agree that her mother told lies. It was the feature about her which she could remember best, Mother's penchant for fantasy which amounted to lies, her pretence that Amy's father, her first husband, had not only *died* but gone to heaven, a fiction so often repeated that it ought to have become suspicious, although for an eleven-year-old girl subsumed in her own misery, it was not. The abrupt moving of house, school, the new man, produced with miraculous speed as if by a conjuring trick, were more than enough to fill the waking hours and provide the stuff of nightmares, while Amy's mother elaborated on the nature of Daddy's heaven. She described it fulsomely as a large house, surrounded by fields, with a stream at the bottom of the garden. It took Amy a long time to realise that the fiction of Daddy's heavenly house was simply a scaled-up version of the dolls' house he had left for her, with dogs by the fire in the kitchen and, out of the back windows, a vision of green trees and lawn painted on to the inside of the window panes. The back of the house was covered in painted ivy. Amy kept it in her room and took it with her when she left that home.

He touched her lightly on the shoulder and withdrew his hand quickly. She would have liked to have held on to it for a while, but somehow knew she should not.

'Poor girl,' he said. 'Look. Go out and walk, or shop or something. No one's going to haul you off the street or anything like that, you know. I do hate to mention it, but you are dead, to all intents and purposes and nobody seems to think otherwise. I've scoured the papers. They've been full of train-crash horror and all that, but I'm afraid the first mention I've seen of you was an oblique reference to that non-grieving husband. No one's going to point the finger at you.'

. . . Dead. It is now presumed that the fireball which followed the impact was caused by up to 2,000 gallons of fuel spilled from the trains.

One coach of the high-speed train and the middle carriage of the turbo were burnt-out shells.

'Poor Dilly,' Amy said absently.

He was standing with his hands on the back of her chair, jiggling it and giving the impression he was about to pull it out from under her if she did not move of her own volition. 'I think the sun's shining. And you've always got your mac in case it rains.'

There was the terrifying feeling, once she was out on the street, that the door behind her would remain permanently closed and either she would have to scream and shout to be let back inside or she would be forced to wander for ever and a day, descending from pavement to gutter, from room to cardboard box. Think what you've got used to already, she marvelled at herself; you've already worn the same clothes for days, even though you wash your underwear and shirt every day and put them on creased and crumpled the next. What would it be like if she could not even do that? And the money – dear God, she had left most of the money indoors too; she could not last longer than a day, but then she remembered that this was not the first time she had been out, and he had let her inside as soon as she returned. Why would he not? On the third day, he had treated her like a brisk surgeon, desperate to get the patient up and walking, pushing her out of the door and telling her to go to the shop. This was the third time and the first when it had not been raining. The sun was a revelation, so bright it winded her, making her pause on the doorstep of the house with the drawn curtains where light, however grey, was slow to penetrate. He had muslin tacked over his windows to let in diffused light upstairs and the first time she had seen it, three years before, the sight of it had unnerved her. It was unnatural for someone to turn their own presence into a shadow in case anyone should observe the detail from the street, although over the last week she had been grateful for that flimsy barrier between the outside world and herself. She hated curtains, but she could understand his paranoia now. It came from the fear that at any moment, someone would look in and say, *there he is, get him,* making him vulnerable in the privacy of home, without any chance of running away, and she knew what he meant, felt it herself. It was not a new sensation; it seemed to her to be something familiar, revived from a long time ago. Perhaps the net curtains of childhood, rigidly installed in the new house after Daddy had died and gone to his heaven, had something to do with it. Hiding was second nature.

And it was an inconsistent fear, because it did not stop her father from leaving his council-owned terraced property to walk down the street like anyone else, shop at the newsagent and the more distant Spar shop which was the source of most of their bland food, with the only difference in his demeanour being the fact that once he had left the house, he ceased to whistle. Nor did the covered windows make him reluctant to ask indoors the visitors who came in pursuit of the room to rent, only to be told after a brief chat and a cup of tea that it was already let. If they seemed the right kind of person, he might show them the dolls' houses. Daddy was not afraid of encounters, only those he could not control. It was as if he wanted to inspect the human race, in his own time and on his own terms. Only when she reached the end of the road did she realise how hungry she was for the presence of human life and what a benediction there was in the fingers of sunlight which touched her pale face, kindly.

There were not many human beings. There were only cars. First the variegated, crowded-on-to-pavement cars which lined both sides of the street and sat sulking in the sunlight. Cars which were as much the subject of argument as noise, for ending up outside the wrong door, taking up personal space, blocking light from windows, looking ungainly. Cars and vans which colonised the road and squashed people into their houses, as if it was the cars that owned the place. Like cockroaches, she thought irrelevantly; dead cockroaches, waiting for an order to march. She could get into one of those cars and drive away. The thought of being inside some moving object was disturbing; she would not be able to control it.

At the end of the road, she turned left and walked again. The road itself had been quiet and now the noise was thunderous. Two

lanes of vehicles rumbling by in each direction, slowing to a halt at
the traffic lights fifty yards away. There was a metal barrier in the
middle, separating one column from another, in case they should
quarrel. To cross the road and find the multi-purpose shop was a
long walk across the junction at the lights. Standing in the island in
the middle, waiting for the green man, she felt peculiarly exposed
and faint among a sea of cars. Here, the motor was king and the
pedestrian an awkward freak, easily flattened. *Moving cockroaches
eat beetles*. The feeling of exposure was the white light of
anonymity; she could not have been less significant in this landscape of metal. The green man appeared and she crossed. The red
light was the invitation to death. Wait for the light to turn and the
engines to rev, then jump.

But she had never wanted to be *squashed*, not even when she
had been so loaded with secrets and divided loyalties that the
burden had been intolerable. She had only wanted that impossible
dream, a life of quiet industry with dogs all around and that version of heaven which was attributed to her father and might also
have been a lie. *Daddy gave me a dog.*

There were no trees; sunlight bounced off metal, with nothing
to feed. What would she be doing by the time this spring heat
turned into real heat and the road burned under her feet and her
own death was history? She could not think of that. She tightened
her sweaty grip on the polythene bag which held two ten-pound
notes. She needed new, cooler clothes and could not think of that
either. Her feet ached; she did not want to be out, and she did not
want to be in. The bullying cars made her furious with their arro-
gant dominance. The air was poison.

Further away from the main road, there was still a dearth of
people on foot. A block of flats on the right provided shade; there
was scrubland and a few stunted bushes between that and a sister
block, a mere twenty floors high and modest in comparison to
others which loomed behind them. She made a note of the shrubs.
At least her father did not live in one of those flats. He had his own
garden, tiny and neglected and blighted by the railway line, but his
own.

It was on the corner of the road facing the minimarket and the garage alongside that the idea came to her of what she would do with the time, now she was *better.* Dig his garden, listen to the trains, make something out of nothing and wait for a plan. A poorly row of bedding plants standing outside the garage shop made her think of that. They were the bravest things she had seen all week, pansies and pelargoniums, waiting for someone buying petrol and fags on his way out of here to remember the window box waiting at home. She could not remember if she had come out with any specific errand; she had simply come out, but now there was only one thing to buy in this wilderness. Even at these inflated prices, twenty pounds would buy a lot of plants. She could come back for the compost. It could take the whole morning. Amy forgot her promise to help her father in his front-room workshop because she was overjoyed with her own distraction and, at the back of her mind, she knew that he was not telling the truth when he said she had a good pair of hands. Not for his kind of work, she didn't – her hands were like flattened hams, big, spatulate, with blunt finger ends. When she spread them wide, they could cover a back, and she had the well-developed shoulders of a masseuse.

That was the part of her beautician training she had liked most, even though she had embarked on it straight after school purely because it was a course her mother had advocated since it meant you could probably ensure having work for the rest of your life, which was a consideration for a big, raw-boned girl with a sweet smile and not much upstairs. *Should have been a gardener; should have been a kennel maid, even then.*

She could feel her fingers twitching as she approached the garage, eyes fixed on the wilting plants which were in worse condition than they appeared from the distance of the other side of the road, making her anxious to get them away. How silly to feel like that, especially as Dad's garden was hardly a better haven at the moment, but this kind of anxiety was almost a pleasure. She had not felt as purposeful since leaving home. *Home.*

There were a few brown leaves around the edges of the pansies and the petals of the purple flowers looked faded and dry, but there were also buds and emerging shoots. She passed from these to the verbena, which looked spindly and unpromising, with the little flowers still a distant promise, sly things, which could quadruple in size and poke their way almost through brickwork. There were smaller bags of compost with handles, so that she could heft two at a time going home, and surely there was some soil under the debris of Daddy's garden. There were parts of his dream he had neglected, but then Mother was a liar to suggest he had ever craved garden and trees, unless they were painted on the inside windows of a dolls' house. Daddy never looked at his garden.

She was feeling and touching the plants with her big hands when she became aware of the noise of argument from inside the garage. There was no immediate cause for a row like this at a quiet time of morning with one customer busy at the pumps, no other noise but the not-so-distant roar of traffic and the hum of the pump as the salesman stood by his Ford, waiting impatiently as he held the nozzle inside the tank of his car and watched the price tick away on the dial. The surface of the forecourt around the pumps was slick with grease and water, as if someone had been out with a hose to wash away petrol spills. There was a removal van parked alongside the wall, next to the air pump, looking as if it had been left for another day. By the third of seven pumps, a deserted minibus was parked with an air of resignation.

The petrol meter stopped and the salesman with the Ford remained where he was, with the curved nozzle stuck into his car, dreaming for a minute as the sun crept under the canopy and warmed his forehead, thinking of the next destination and also of the same argumentative noises from inside the kiosk which was big enough to be a shop, where everyone went to pay in these bright daylight hours. At night, money and cards were received through a grill thick enough to stop a bullet and all the frivolous things – plants, barbecue bricks, flowers – hid inside.

There was always a story at the back of an argument. Amy went into the shop, followed by the customer who had relinquished the hose and finally remembered that he had fed his starving car at pump six, both of them curious about what was going on. There was a tenor to the raised voices which made them safe rather than threatening. It was not a fight, only a row.

'Listen, what'm I supposed to do?'

'Dunno, man, get the fucking thing outta my place. I dunno what to do. Get it outta here. Was you knocked it down.'

'I never, it was there, and I never run it down. Just come out sideways and biffed the wheel and now look at him, poor sod, not dead or nothing, looks like it might be, but it ain't my fault and the sod's on your premises. I'm not waiting for no police.'

'Get it outta here.'

'What, like it was me brought it in, it was fucking here, I tell ya, just fucking appeared, it did, what'm I supposed to fucking do—'

'Drive slowly, mate, is all, steaming in here, like you own it, I dunno.'

'Half dead, anyway. Sling it out the back.'

'Nah, leave it alone.

'Scarcely touched it, honest, it just bounced off the wheel when I turned in here, never saw it. I didn't go *over* it, honest, never felt it . . . and there it was howling, it *came* in here, I never brought it . . . Tried to bite me, so it can't be dead.'

'Well it can't stay here, can it? Doesn't look like it's going anywhere now.'

'Call the police, I say.'

'Is it a he or a she?'

'Fucking thing damn near bit me . . .'

Against the back wall of the shop, furthest from the door, was a fridge containing cold supplies of milk and soft drinks, freshly stocked. The customer from pump six stood in front of it, uncertainly. ''Scuse me,' he said. 'I wanted a Coke.' Then he looked at her and blenched. She quite understood; she did look odd. From his feet came a low growling sound and he stepped back hurriedly, giving Amy a view. A large mottled dog, part greyhound, maybe even three-quarters, lay against the fridge door. It was a vaguely brown colour with grey round the muzzle, a white star on the chest and a white stripe up the middle of a long nose; the coat was smooth and it had a thin leather collar. Somebody's old dog or an old dog which was once somebody's. It looked exhausted but the growl was intimidating. One back leg lay flat against the ground; the other, held slightly off the ground and unnaturally angled, quivered.

'Do you remember that story last year?' the man at the checkout said. 'About that greyhound which ran out straight off the track at the end of a race at Walthamstow stadium and just kept on running? Perhaps this is it and it never stopped.'

There was the muffled laughter of confusion. They were not really angry; they did not know what to do. Indecision made them callous. 'What about my Coke?' pump number six asked plaintively. He was in a hurry, wanted out of here.

Amy did not notice. She squatted down near the dog, drawn to it like a magnet to metal. She may have pushed him aside to get so close, she didn't know. The fridge hummed and the lorry driver, the one with the loudest voice, shouted at her.

'Don't you go near him, he's nearly had my hand off! Dangerous, *don't*.'

'He's a *she*,' Amy said.

'It's dying.'

The animal looked at her through a single wary eye, not moving its head from the shiny floor. Not so old, she thought, feeling for the collar and turning it gently, but no spring chicken either. The sex, from the splayed back legs, was obvious enough. No head wound, no obvious wound at all, simply that wavering back leg and the dull eye of pain and fear. There was no tag on the collar, but marks on the neck where the leather had worn at the fur, one notch too tight for comfort, the beginnings of a sore. She found the buckle and loosened the collar, making soothing noises; she stroked it behind the ear and the eye closed for a second. The group in the shop fell silent. Amy took her hand down the bitch's back, feeling the spine, touching the quivering leg; there was a growl and an intake of breath from the audience. 'Shhhh,' she murmured. The dog shushed. Then she got one arm between the dog and the fridge door, hauled her up and stood bent over her, holding her beneath the chest with her own arms forming a sling.

The dog turned her long nose, Dilly to the life, with that long white stripe, but not Dilly at all, another dog, because Dilly was dead and this one was not due to die, not yet. She was only hurt. Amy removed her arms and kept a light hold on the collar. The dog stood uncertainly, but unaided, on three legs, the last still shaking, dipping to the floor, touching and curling back. Amy took a couple of steps backwards; the dog limped towards her.

'Does it want water ?' someone asked.

'Give it a Coke.'

The man from pump number six sidled behind the dog and got his Coke can from inside the fridge, letting the door clunk into the renewed silence. He paid with a credit card, accepted sullenly apart from the click and whirr of the machine. He left quickly. The rest watched, to see what else Amy would do with the dog.

'If it walks out like that,' the lorry driver said, 'on three bloody legs, it'll only get killed.'

'No, it won't,' Amy said, stroking the ears again. 'I'll take it home.'

There was a sigh of relief, without any alternative suggestions, except when the cashier said, 'What if someone comes for it?' doubtfully, not wanting to be caught in the wrong or accused of theft.

'I'll be back tomorrow,' Amy said.

'You haven't got a lead.'

'She doesn't need a lead.'

'Shall I take you in the bus?' She could see the minibus driver, wishing he had not said that.

'Please.'

She sat in the seat behind him in the minibus, holding the dog which trembled and did not like cars. It took longer to go round an elaborate one-way system than it had to walk, and by the time they got to the top of Amy's father's street, the driver was regretting his generosity even more, because she could not tell him the way by road. No sense of direction.

'Got a way with animals, have you?'

'Yes,' Amy said. 'I suppose I have.'

Which is more than I have with human beings. Just a thought as she lifted the animal out of the vehicle, listening to his comment about how strong she was and wasn't it heavy, then she waved goodbye, and thought as she stood with a reassuring hand on the dog's collar how this might make her father very angry indeed. The bitch licked her hand and quivered from head to thin, dilapidated tail. Amy did not care who might be angry. This animal was going to get well. And she hadn't been an idiot, either. Two trays of plants and a sack of compost came too.

Rollie Fisher stood at his bedroom window with the lit cigarette he would never smoke in the workroom downstairs. Too much inflammable stuff down there. Should not smoke at all. Would never drink again; drink had almost done for him, once. Here, he let the smoke float against the muslin pinned against the window frame, thought of the exhibition, and looked hungrily into the street, disappointed to find it so empty. It was the wrong time of day again; he tended to forget time or only acknowledge his favourite time of the afternoon, when he waited and watched, winter and summer. There were few enough children in this street and such as there were meandered down the road at about four o'clock, shrieking abuse at one another. There were three little Asian girls, who managed to be tidy and subdued even at the end of the school day, and he waited for them, often in vain. They were busy children, not always allowed to walk home alone, and when they did, and he saw them, he smiled. Now Amy was here, he might get her to ask them in.

He stubbed out the cigarette, hating the habit and loathing the smell, looked at his own, spatulate fingers, the shape of which his daughter had inherited, and concentrated on the planning of the next project. He took a pill from the cornucopia of medicines in his bedside drawer. Doctors were generous with old men who said they could not sleep. His exhibition, when it happened, must contain rare and unusual ideas, a *new* version of the dolls' house. He was a model-maker, an artist or inventor, not someone who simply played with the thing and sold traditional, gimcrack furniture through magazines. Model houses did not have to be cottages, Victorian dwellings, cosy shops, places with lace curtains. They could be fairy-tale palaces, visions of heaven or hell, whatever he wanted them to be, creations upon which the imagination could fasten in order to stop itself going mad. This morning he had fashioned on a pipecleaner base a particularly bent figure, and this afternoon, he would add to the gentleman's club, or maybe the brothel, some image of a judge, with a full wig and his trousers down . . . One day, he would create a Garden of Eden out of modelling clay. All the same, he wanted to make something conventional next. A sweet shop with a red roof, looking as edible as a cake.

What was that, coming down the road in his direction? Oh God, his big clumsy daughter, followed by a *dog*. The longer she stayed, the better, but he hated dogs.

Elisabeth Manser stood in her kitchen and looked out at the garden she had made. She was five minutes from the station and she was going to miss the train, dammit, but it was too nice to leave and she was furious, also gripped by an unreasonable anxiety that the bedding plants – verbena, lobelia, names like gracious women – which she had planted out the weekend before, might die before she got home late in the evening. A parallel anxiety about how they might drown after being so liberally doused with water at dawn, and how they might be affected by her own anxiety. She leant against the phone on the wall, angry that it was affixed and she could not pick it up and throw it.

Good news, good news, John had said. Douglas Petty's going to go on with his case. He's so bloody angry with the latest report, he's absolutely determined. Determined about what? she had asked, and hoped she had not yelled, spoken the quiet way he preferred. Determined to not let them get away with it, John said, pleased. Mr Petty says the original libel affected his marriage and made his wife unhappy. He wants his revenge for that. He has to do it to protect *her* reputation.

What? Did this vainglorious brute have the nerve to say that he was going to continue with a futile libel suit against a couple of newspapers in order to honour his *wife*? Had he actually explained to John that the latest newspaper report, albeit only local, made him even more anxious to exonerate himself from the original allegations of cruelty and bestiality, because these reflected on his *wife*? Because, he said, if he were to look as if he was ignoring it, it would also look as if his wife had been turning a blind eye to all this stuff, and that, in turn, made *her* look as if she condoned it, deliberately failed to notice if animals were being abused, or something like that. That might have been what Douglas Petty had said, or it might have been John Box paraphrasing it to make it sound even more hypocritical, i.e. first the client had wanted to protect his own reputation and now he wanted to protect the reputation of a dead spouse. Really.

He probably wanted something to do, Elisabeth thought. Something to fill the gaps left by a death and the fury which follows death in the same way that it follows defection. Douglas Petty had always been a restless man, but it took that restlessness to the limit for him to continue waving his stick in the direction of a national newspaper, in memory of his wife. She looked at the paperwork on her kitchen table. There was a study in her house, equipped with e-mail, fax, paper, books, but she still ended up in the kitchen with a view of the garden, because it was the nicest place and there was always food at hand. A place where she could survey her cooking pans. If John ever left his wife and lived with her, he would surely be fatter than he was. The paperwork on the table was what he called her homework; her vital task of researching all things known about the client. He was, after all, almost the only sodding client. She had to get her head round it. Her head was feeling over-large with her newly washed hair; should have used a conditioner. She had dirty hands, too long in the garden, not enough reading.

She should act like the intellectual she was not, *think*. The newspaper could plead justification for what they had printed if what they had implied was *true*, i.e. Douglas Petty was cruel to animals, guilty of unnatural practices with a certain golden retriever, guilty of hypocrisy and cruelty to dumb beasts, *at the time* the photo-graphs were taken. If they could not prove current guilt, then they had a second chance of defending themselves if they could show that he had done something similar in the past. Something which meant that he had a tendency to the current actions, could easily have done them, was that way inclined, so that what they were saying about him in the present was far more likely to be true than not. What he did after the damn libel did not count unless it was literally a duplication. Beating up a rival dog lover was not a duplication. Elisabeth found a bar of chocolate hidden at the back of the fridge and eased her left hand round the tight waistband of her skirt while she ate it, guiltily, with her right.

Was there something she had missed? The homework was the dredging of press cuttings far and wide, the exploration of any mention of Petty, damn his eyes and his silly name, to see if there *was* anything in the past to support the likelihood of the present innuendos being true. She had also explored the reasons for his relative celebrity. After all, the man had done nothing but raise the roof with certain boorish pursuits. The charitable bit had always been there, in the form of some venture like running the London Marathon in sky pink Lycra while smoking cigarettes, all in aid of lung cancer. That was in his thirties and an odd thing to do for a man with a figure like a squat chimney stack, but nothing special. She eased the waistband again, pondered briefly the subject of vanity and comfort food, ate the rest of the chocolate because it was there. There were other sightings, less philanthropic, such as dunking the head of a parish priest into his own font when he had refused baptism to the child of a heathen friend, drunkenness, broken relationships with bimbettes quite inappropriate for his career as a barrister and only possible because of money; drunk-enness, knocking the helmet off a policeman; kidnapping a police horse and then a police dog. Fame was not based on achievement, she had to conclude; it was based on flimsy incidents where a person stood out from a crowd either by accident or design. Then there were too many women of B-list anorexic celebrity status, criticism from his peers, a picture emerging of a party animal who was frequently crass and never apologetic, and only accused of hypocrisy because by day he donned a suit, conducted his hangover to court and looked the solid embodiment of the Establishment, as keen on law and order as he was to break it. The real fame, though, was the streak through the High Courts.

Elisabeth sat and sighed at this point, turning over pages and wishing John had read her copied pages with greater interest. The public had taken Douglas Petty to heart for that *streak*. Probably a late-night bet, that he would shed the pinstripe in Carey Street by the railings there and run, stark bollock naked from the back entrance of the High Courts of Justice, down the stairs and all the way across the vaulted hall with the mosaic floor, dodge the guards and run through the swing doors at the front where he would get a taxi in the Strand. That was the bet which he almost won; he was the only man led away with a copper's helmet held over his gonads, captured by the cameras on the far side waiting for the appearance of a film star and her cheating husband. The tank of his body was wrestled to the ground; he was disbarred for disrespectful conduct and stayed a wee bit celebrated ever since.

There was nothing in this which allowed the defendant in the case to plead *justification*. Douglas Petty was simply a silly willy.

'Who beat his wife,' she said out loud. 'And probably a bore in bed, too. Had a better chance with a dog.'

If she had her own way, she would never leave home.

CHAPTER SIX

There were a number of irritating things that went with the commuter existence, some of which Elisabeth secretly liked. She lived a quick walk from the station, without any of the complications of trying to start a car and manoeuvre it into the car park, which was worse, to her mind, than walking in the rain. She could watch other commuters jockeying for space with their shiny vehicles and pity them for it when she travelled early, or admire the serried rows of useless cars when she walked across the space midmorning to wait on a virtually empty platform, feeling superior in the knowledge that her day was not nine to five. The major irritant was the train timetable, varying in predictability in a way that bemused staff as much as anyone, but again, she liked that. This little station, smaller than its car park, was on a loop where mainline trains detoured at peak times to provide services ancillary to the small train she awaited now. Despite fine blue livery, the three-carriage trains were prone to delay and the signals on the branch line seemed to have a mind of their own, although things worked, most of the time, on good days. There was a delay of ten minutes which might stretch to more and it would make her late for the meeting with John and another client, but never mind. All a good commuter could do was put herself into the hands of fate on bad days, and be grateful that they were not on the line from London to the coast carrying the trains which had crashed over two weeks before. This may have been a shorter, less significant line, but all the cars in the car park belonged to people who were alive.

She sat beneath the canopy which covered the platform for half its length, content to wait. Train time was thinking time. The second shower of rain drummed on the roof and the sparrows protested loudly, an interesting noise and all the better for thinking. She never craved perfect silence; it filled the head with buzzing.

She looked up at the rowdy sparrows; two other waiting passengers stared at the weeds on the track. That was what Douglas Petty was, a rowdy man who stormed about making a noise. The sort of young man first made infamous by the death of his father and always up for a dare. A man who raised money for charity in the manner of a famous disc jockey, gaining notoriety for being willing to make a fool of himself. There was nothing in those newspaper reports of old that allowed the defamers to plead *justification*, except, well, the underlying *violence* of the man. The way he had lashed out when arrested after the streak, taking three of them to hold him down; the way he had kicked a car in another incident; the way he clenched his hands when he spoke; the sudden shouting, springing up, ready to attack; the aggressive energy of him. The bruises on his wife which she had seen; the plain talking which was almost violent; the dismissal of an enemy with the words 'He's a cunt' and a chopping movement of the arm which made it clear he would knock that person's head off if that person was in the room. The way, when the tribunal of his peers had met to decide that he was not a fit person to practise law at the English Bar, he had roared at them about being silly old farts and been forcibly dragged from the room. Uncomfortable at close quarters.

The rain stopped and the racket of the birds grew more subdued as they flew from their nests on foraging expeditions. Rich pickings in the spring. They were busy, busy, busy.

But there was nothing cruel about the man, surely. They would be able to plead justification for allegations of hot temper and even ungovernable rage, but there was nothing he had ever been reported to have done which smacked of the coldness of cruelty. But cruelty, she thought, watching the other, quiet passengers, does not have to be cold any more than it has to be systematic, and it might not even involve any enjoyment in the inflicting of pain. It was just as cruel to beat an animal or a person because they got in your way or would not do what you want as it was to beat them in cold blood. The effect was just the same. Bruises, wounds, shock, and, worst of all, the fear of fear. Amy Petty had been sorely afraid.

The train arrived, grumpily. Three-quarters of an hour for a short distance as the crow flew, but probably longer today as the train limped down another branch line to take in an extra station the last one might have forgotten. Elisabeth got out the Kent newspaper from the day before and gazed at the photo of Douglas Petty in violent confrontation with Delilah Hall from the animal sanctuary. Smiled at it and then grimaced, realising she should not smile, even in private, when faced with a depiction of a valued client behaving in an ugly way and looking like a bandit. But the persistent fact that she could not ignore was the fact that in looking at this picture, she herself found Delilah Hall to be a more frightening specimen than her assailant. Now there was prejudice for you: one woman disliking another on sight of her photograph, and purely on the analysis of her coat and her dreadful hair and the obsessive look of her. Elisabeth did not believe that anyone, male or female, could be genuinely engaged in any practical purpose if they wore sodding great earrings like that. Delilah Hall looked as if she had dressed up for the occasion. What lies there were in pictures, but all the same, the fear of the woman might not have been feigned. Petty was undoubtedly violent. Rich, spoiled, violent. He would even put his feet up on the seat in a train.

She was tempted to put her feet up on the seat opposite. Bad manners, but irresistible in a totally empty carriage midmorning with no one to say 'don't'. So she did and caught sight of the shoes she wore to do the garden, nasty canvas lace-ups, once white, now stained brown. *Shit.* They were a problem she had not contemplated; maybe there would be time to buy replacements at the other end; they looked ridiculous, like some awful reverse fashion statement, and they were dirty. Elisabeth curled her feet beneath the seat and decided not to think about them, yet. There was time for that. Concentrate on Douglas Petty, so that she might have something useful to contribute when next he was discussed, perhaps this afternoon, after the other client.

John did not care about this recent little scandal, he said; it was merely local newspaper stuff. Mr Petty did not mind accusations like that; it was only the inference of cruelty to his rescued dogs that made him want to play the Russian roulette of the law. And now he wanted to gamble on behalf of a dead wife, who might have been frightened of him too. *Crap.*

Elisabeth was pondering that uncomfortable thought in the luxury of her empty carriage, enjoying the view of the same bank of primroses for some minutes before she realised that the train had actually stopped. Damn. The coffee drunk in her kitchen was a long time ago; she was thirsty and restless, wanted something to do with her hands; wanted to throw her disgraceful shoes out of the window, and now she would be really late. She looked down at her fingers and saw soil beneath her nails. She was not her best. John would be annoyed.

Then there was a rattling crash and her blood ran cold. No, surely, nothing to cause alarm, but no one with whom to share the sudden fear. Trains did not crash every day of the week; they crashed every few years and it was not her turn. The door connecting this carriage to the next was flung open and the trolley came through, battering against the wall and then back again, rattling its contents. She breathed out slowly and then shrank back against the window. The man and the trolley were not getting on well; it was heavily overloaded and not entirely within his control because he was shaking so hard she could imagine his teeth were rattling in between the strangled words that came out of his mouth. His face was the colour of chalk, like someone about to be sick.

'Fucking bastard, fucking thing, bugger, bugger, bugger . . . *shit.*' He kicked the trolley and then noticed her. 'Sorry,' he muttered. 'Did you want something?'

'Tea, please.'

He held the plastic cup beneath the water spout level with his chest, but his hand shook so much the water slopped over the edge and on to his wrist and he yelped loudly. Then he tried again and managed to fill it half full, although the coordination of holding the cup and pressing the button for the hot water seemed to take every ounce of strength and even then, some of the water went on the floor. Perspiration exploded on his forehead; he staggered wildly.

'Stop it!' she yelled. 'Stop it! Stop it and sit down.'

He did as he was told, feeling for the armrest of the seat as if he could not quite see it, and flopped into the seat opposite hers, his colour alarming. She looked at him for a second, then stood up beside the trolley, found the packets of sugar, emptied two into the half-full cup, teased the teabag which floated unattractively and put the cup down on the shelf beside him. 'Careful, it's hot. Where's the milk?' He pointed. Elisabeth found three cartons the size of tiny egg cups, tore off the tops and poured them in the yellow-looking tea. Disgusting. The teabag floated like a corpse. After a minute, he grabbed the drink in both hands and sipped it unsteadily. Colour returned to his face in the form of two spots of red in his cheeks.

'Sorry,' he gabbled. 'I'm really sorry. I shouldn't have come back to work, stupid really. They said are you all right, you can stay off for weeks, but I said no. Stupid.'

The same clump of primroses stared back through the window.

'S'funny,' he said. 'I'm fine when the bugger's moving, but when it stops and I don't know why it stops, I come over all strange. For two pins, I'd jump out, I fucking would, really, but it's best to keep going.'

She was as confused by his verbal diarrhoea as she had been by her own instinctive reaction to sit him down and give him tea from his own trolley. She did not usually act with such spontaneity, always felt she would be the last to pull a communication cord while she thought about whether it was the right thing to do. The hectic colour of his cheeks, spreading now to the tip of his nose, told her she had done something right and she took a sideways look at the trolley to see if she could improve upon it by offering something more medicinal than tea, such as brandy. Perhaps not; she leaned forward across him to open the top part of the window, heaving on it to pull it down, one of those stiff windows in this old train. They were nearly all old trains, the sort she liked, and she wondered if she would be behaving like this if there had been anyone else to witness. He went on talking, but the trembling was less. He could manage the cup with one hand. There was an empty hole in one ear, she noticed, as if he had forgotten an ear-ring he had worn for years. As she watched, his spare hand went to fondle his ear lobe, as if thinking the same thing. He was talking more to himself than to her, wrapped in a sick and shaky world of his own.

'Lost it in the crash, don't know how. Only I wanted to go to work. No point sitting at home, not where I live, does my head in, that does. Put me on a different route, though. I was all right yesterday when there was someone else and plenty of people, even though I did throw up, once. It's not when it's pissing along all right, it's when the bugger stops. And you can still see the tower from this line. I wish they'd get moving.'

'Maybe you should go up front and tell them,' she suggested, light dawning on her confusion.

'Oh yeah, yeah. A lot of difference that'd make. There's probably a mouse on the line.' He cackled at his own wit.

'Leaves,' Elisabeth said. 'Snow.'

'Blossom, fucking blossom, that's it . . .'

'Good weather. Newspaper on the track, rogue rabbits . . .'

'Wrong kind of rain, more like.' He paused and gulped the tea. She did not envy him the taste.

'Shall I get you some more?'

'No, thanks but no thanks.' He smiled unsteadily; a nerve jumped beneath his eye. '*She* offered, you know, one day when I was poorly. Said she'd go down the train for me. We had a laugh. Well, not poorly, not like yesterday. I had a fucking great hangover that day, to be honest. Did my head in.'

'Whoa,' Elisabeth laughed. 'You've lost me there. Am I right in thinking you were on one of those trains that crashed?' She sounded pompous to her own ears, but he nodded vigorously, gazing at her, dying to talk away the symptoms of panic. She had the impression that once the train started again, he would move and she did not want that. Her laughter was artificial, but he did not seem to notice. He had the vulnerable figure of a lanky lad and a face far older; he fingered the vacant ear with more irritation than fondness. 'But I don't know who you mean,' she said, 'when you talk about "*she*".'

The train creaked and he listened to the sound, startled, then gazed out at the primroses. She found herself checking the bank to gauge how difficult it would be to jump out, waiting, oddly, for the train to tilt and almost bracing herself to counteract, sitting up straight as if she really was a sensible person. He grinned, waved the almost empty cup, put it down and continued rubbing his ear. She felt like a teacher, itching to tell him to stop. Stopping was not an option for him; the empty carriage and the creaking stillness of the train had the same effect as a confessional. *Cross-examination consists of never seeming to ask the questions*, and she sat here now, as if she was indifferent to the answers.

'Funny you should mention that,' the trolley man said as if they had been talking for hours, 'only when I come through that door, I thought you were her. You'd got your handbag on your lap, see? She always used to carry hers as if it needed looking after. And she sat at this end of the carriage, usually, when she could, I mean. And she always had tea, never coffee. Staplehurst, she got on. Waved to me when she got off. I sometimes got on at Ashford. I used to say, are you going to have a nice day then, and she'd wrinkle her nose, like that' – he wrinkled his own, which was now scarlet – 'and say, not really, how about you? And I'd say, I'd say . . . I'd say . . . something. She'd say something like, that ticket collector we've got today, he looks just like a ferret. He did, you know, he really did.' He laughed.

'And was she in the crash, too?' There was the sudden, intrusive image of Amy Petty, sitting as she sat now, hugging her handbag.

Elisabeth tried to dismiss it as nonsense and felt light-headed with strange excitement. The trolley man scarcely listened.

'She always dressed nice,' he continued, 'but always a bit wrinkled, if you see what I mean, looks as if she'd had a cat on her lap, and yes, now you mention it, she was in the crash. I helped her off and she helped me, and they want me to look at videos to see if she walked back through the station, 'cos she shouldn't have died, she really shouldn't, not in our carriage, only I dunno where she went. I keep telling myself that she just walked off somewhere. Running away. Not getting in that carriage that went up in smoke. I don't believe it.'

'Couldn't she have just walked away?'

Her voice seemed to penetrate, at last. He leant forward, earnestly, elbows on thin knees, head supported by fists, foot tapping the floor. They were scuffed shoes, brown once, with his navy trousers creased at the knee, the rubber soles of the shoes making a small noise.

'Well, that's what I thought, but it wasn't that easy to do, I mean, I wanted to walk away, but I couldn't, I just followed the band all over the fucking place. You did as you was told. So I reckoned if she walked, she wanted to walk, really wanted to. And I was trying to work out if I saw her on the videos, this afternoon, what should I say?'

Again, the excitement which made her impertinent. 'Why don't you start at the beginning?' Elisabeth said. 'You'll have to remember what she was wearing. Did she always wear the same things?'

He saw nothing odd in the questions; he was too far gone for that. There was a crackled announcement mentioning signals. The trolley man shook his head.

'That's the trouble, see? They stop at every bloody signal now, black, white, green, you name it, get out, check it, phone for advice. Ah yes, a patterned skirt that day, wool stuff, bit warm, I would have said. Lovely skin, nice hair, bouncy, bit like yours really.'

So that was what Amy and she had in common: the big hair of slightly blousy blondes. The image of Amy Petty with her slightly tanned skin and floppy blonde curls grew into sharper focus.

'And her name?'

'Never knew that. She knew mine, though.' He pointed to the name tag on his lapel. 'Rob. Probably remembered it too, knowing her. Yes she did. She said thank you, Rob, when we got out the train.'

'She got out of the train after the crash?'

'Yeah, course she did. We all got out. It wasn't a train like this, though. These ones you can open the doors. Then I lost her. She might just have got back in.'

'Why?'

'To help. You can't explain what it was like, you just can't. It was terrible . . .' He began to shake until the sunlight invading the carriage in kind contrast to the rain calmed him. She had no idea how long they had been stationary: she was mesmerised by his voice and his pale hands round the cup.

'And now *they* want you to look at video footage to see if you could see her, is that right?'

'Yeah, that's right. Not just her, though, there's a few they just can't explain. But if she did walk off and got as far as the station, and Christ, I bloody hope she did, she had a reason to do that, didn't she? I'm not going to say, yeah, that's her, there she is, if I do see her. Get them looking for her, why should I? She must have a reason . . .'

'When do you have to look at the videos?'

''Safternoon. Ah, shit, here we go.'

The train sighed, moved uneasily; the primroses disappeared, replaced by the backs of houses, a station platform for Grove Park. Rob stood up, tested his legs by pressing his hands against his knees and stamping his feet in turn, looked at his watch, embarrassed.

'I think it's cruel to make you do that,' Elisabeth said loudly over the creak of the train. 'Making you do that. Brings it all back.'

He shrugged, beginning to tremble again. 'What makes you think it goes away? Look at the state of me.' He held out his hands, shaking wrists, bloodless fingers.

'Who's going to go with you?'

He shrugged again, surprised at the question. 'No one. Who'd fucking go with me? My mother?'

It was the day for silliness and recklessness. She looked at her watch, realising the meeting was almost missed and she had not even apologised; she could see her disliked mobile phone sitting on the kitchen counter from which she was always forgetting to retrieve it, but the trolley man, Rob, was somehow uncannily likeable, shambling, vulnerable, brave and none of that stiff upper lip; she felt maternally defensive of him and so curious she was watching herself turn into the kind of officious busybody she would otherwise despise.

'I'll go with you, if you like,' she suggested casually, picking up the newspaper and documents which had leaked out of her case on to the seat, stuffing them back. 'I'm a lawyer. Do this kind of thing all the time.' She handed him a card.

'I'd never have known,' he scoffed, recovering now and taking in the grey suit and the almost uniform neatness of her, marred by a crumpled collar, the mud in her fingernails and the hideous shoes. 'And I can't afford it.'

'Sure you can, when it's free.'

His face, now pink, split into a wide smile. It was such a smile, like a light switched on inside his skull, to illuminate an expression of sheer good nature that she could immediately see why Amy Petty might be pleased to see him. It would be easy to let him brighten the day, plain stranger though he was, and she felt slightly, hysterically mad.

'OK, you're on. Four o'clock, platform six. It's in an office. I'll take you.' He paused, both of them regretting the making of a commitment, yet still wanting to make it. 'You won't make me *do* anything, will you?'

She tried to sound careless and authoritative. 'The whole idea is that you aren't forced to do anything. I'll be there.'

He pushed the trolley against the door. 'I don't see why you should,' he said. 'And you probably won't.'

The Lloyds tower was visible on the right and the scenery was brick. There were hoardings either side of the track, hiding everything to the left. The station was open for business again for the first time today, trains sloping in and out, slowly, queueing for a platform. The clock above the ticket booths had stopped. Hurrying across the concourse in the direction of the Underground, Elisabeth felt nothing but foolish and who did she think she was? *You probably won't be there.* No, she probably would not. She was out of her mind, buzzing with excitement.

She walked up from the Embankment, crossed Fleet Street and deliberately wasted more time by cutting through the High Courts. The shoes were entirely forgotten until she paused at the back entrance, trying to conjure the image of Douglas Petty stripping himself of his pinstriped suit and brogues, then shedding his underwear, leaving not a stitch before he began to run, and wondered who had taken the photos then of his pile of discarded garments and who was supposed to collect him, afflicted with a nagging memory of a refinement to the whole act which might have been her imagination. Afflicted, too, with the memory of that barrel chest, the swinging prick. Did he wear nothing but a wig? She must look it up again, later, and think clearly now. Forget about the trolley man, put him away.

She no longer cared enough about the meeting to hurry; John did not need her for this conference. It was only another case, a defamed businessman who thought he was better known than he was, attending to be told in gentle terms that the pursuit of a libel action against a magazine was likely to be as counter-productive as it was costly and although the suggestion of an adulterous affair on some minor gossip page was probably untrue, the allusion to it had been phrased in such a way that it was merely a suggestion that this married man was at it again; hardly a dent in his unimportant reputation to infer he was indulging in a lifetime hobby and no effect whatever on his company's credit ratings. No case. He was angry because he had almost lost a wife.

Useful things, wives, Elisabeth thought as she sidled into the room with an apologetic nod, finding the corner desk which hid her feet, met John's steely glance and noted the pristine state of his shirt and tie, so fresh they could have come straight out of the packet. They had been better off on their own, he and the client, who was similarly dressed, perhaps by a similar spouse, the two of them talking man to man, with John telling the other how much better it was not to open the can of worms which was his life. John hated to give negative advice. The client paid for it, but not nearly as much as he would pay for a trial. His room overlooked the square of Lincoln's Inn Fields, where the new leaves on the trees glistened after the rain and the blossom had been blown into a carpet on the ground. Now that was luxury.

The client was in the stage halfway between blustering anger and acceptance. She could feel the displeasure of Mr Box, QC, settle around her like a pall and she resisted the urge to ease her grubby shoes off her feet in case her toes revealed themselves as even worse.

Amy Petty may be alive, she wanted to shout, but then the coldness of his expression lowered the temperature and dulled the need to say anything. There was no middle way with an affair like this. The balm of his approval, like the praise of a father on an insecure child, was everything she had lived for at first and still craved. Almost as much as the touch of his hands on her skin which was never often enough to be familiar; still had an almost alien strangeness after all this time. But the pleasure she took in making that thin face crease into laughter bore no comparison to the agony of misery he could cause in her without even trying. She made it easy for him to wound her by being so vulnerable to criticism before it was even spoken, began to react to the edge in his voice and the expression in his eyes even before she had any right to guess that she was the cause. Only with him, not with anyone else. The weariness in his tone might have nothing to do with her lateness: it might be the result of a bad night and an irritating interview, but it felt already as if it was for her. How odd that she could survive the most scathing remarks of a judge and the choice insults of an opponent without turning a hair, and still quail at the prospect of a brief and probably kindly admonition from him. She wanted him to reach into a pocket for a piece of red paper napkin to blow his nose and make him human, but he was rising from his seat, smoothing back the thick grey hair, extending his hand to the client, who took it, reluctantly. Elisabeth shook hands too, enough for a brief introduction and this polite and meaningless farewell. There was not only dirt in her fingernails, but a streaked stain of spilt tea on the back of her hand. She showed the man out, down the stairs and into the square, her only contribution to his case, apart from the backroom research which informed his chances. No reason for him to know about that. She paused for a chat with the clerks before going back upstairs, determined to ignore the shoes as the client had. The conversation with the trolley man and the urge to tell John about it became more distant by the minute.

John stood by the window, looking at the blossom driven down from the trees by the rain, tapping his fingers against the pane.

'Where were you?'

'The train was ridiculously late and then it stopped . . .' She stopped too.

'I'm sorry I interrupted you at your housework this morning. But it seemed important at the time. And I did have the illusion that if I spoke to you at nine, you might manage to catch a train at eleven for a prearranged meeting at twelve. A little challenge for you. Silly me.'

The reference to *housework* stung. Why did she devote time to home and garden if not to be proud of it whenever he saw it? To watch him sink into a chair, say this is nice, or where did you get that?

'Signal trouble,' she said. 'They're being extra careful. Blossom on the line.'

He did not laugh. 'Only an idiot uses the excuse that every two-bit criminal uses when he's late for court. Trots it out without thinking, how come everyone else manages public transport without getting mugged by it? *I needed* you.'

She stood in front of his desk, looking down at two enormous feet. 'No you didn't. It doesn't take two people to give advice. It was you he consulted, not me.'

'Just as well then, isn't it? Always better to go to someone who's capable of catching a train, I find.' He blew his nose, discreetly, a regular handkerchief this time, all of him laundered and fresh today, as if he had been put through the cleaners. 'And of course I needed you or I wouldn't have asked you to inconvenience yourself. You have such great placatory powers, you women. He's such an irritating man, I almost hit him.'

'Well I'm very sorry I wasn't there to *almost* stop you. I could have made the tea.'

'Coffee,' he corrected gravely, without irony. 'He wanted coffee. And we both needed a woman in the room.'

Like a male doctor with a female patient. She was realising too late that she was wrong-footed, and that she had been uneasy about acting as semi-silent witness to two men of the world, talking about the best way to limit public awareness of the consistent infidelity of one of them. She had not wanted to watch him acting as an embodiment of virtue, discussing adultery as if it were any old subject, like cricket or football, just another fact of life, only important if it was discovered. Did not want to hear her own lover debating the best way to minimise the hurt which might be felt by a wife, or the prospect of expensive revenge. It made her uncomfortably guilty; it had influenced her dawdling this morning easily as much as thoughts of Douglas Petty and it made her silent now. She did not want to rock the boat; she would drown. She pushed her fingers through her hair, to hide the silence.

'Don't do that,' he said mildly.

She blushed, stopped doing that and remained silent, although her hands itched to do something, such as fiddle with her necklace, smooth down the collar, check her tights for runs, remove the shoes. Amy Petty with her similar hair also blushed easily, turning her smooth skin an unbecoming shade of brick: Amy Petty and she, they were both in awe of their men. The trolley man turned pink in patches, beginning with his nose. She had never monitored the progress of her own blushing and she was not going to mention either of them, not now.

'Don't do what?'

'Make yourself look ridiculous. Any more than you have. You

look like you've walked through a hedge.' And then he smiled, but it was already too late. She felt like a dog whipped soundly for a trifling offence when a mild cuff round the ear would have done. She thought of the trolley man's empty ear lobe and shook her head. John was folding up the Skoyle papers and tying them neatly with tape. Downstairs, the computer ruled; upstairs, there were still old-fashioned habits. She had lost her tongue. He unbent from this minor task and talked to her with face averted.

'Maria's going to be away tomorrow night, I said I'd stay up here, but I could come and stay with you. Could I?'

'Yes,' she said. 'Yes of course.' She was glad she had planted the plants and pruned the apple tree in that tiny space and she always said yes, even though he did not need her. He came to her side and smoothed her hair, briefly, always cautious about touching her in the public arena of his room; so often, like now, anxious to shoo her out before the clerks downstairs began to comment as if they did not already. He was as particular about her as he might have been in his own home. The smoothing of her hair felt as if he had put a torch to it and still she said yes. Even though he was going to drive from his large place to her small one and park his car a hundred yards away, she still said yes.

In his diary, yes. An appointment.

She was on ground level, kicking the blossom beneath the trees and trying to pretend the movement of her feet was accidental rather than whatever it was. Sad, the release of a woman of thirty-three, who, with the onset of summer, slept with a man once a fortnight, did not have enough work and spent Saturday evenings tending her garden and an awful lot of time on trains, without even having the sense to want it otherwise.

She followed the throng on the narrow pavements of Fleet Street. She cut down Fetter Lane and went into the church. She went to her own chambers and talked about the lack of work. She took forever to buy a pair of shoes and find the right rubbish bin for the ceremonial disposal of her own. She bought socks in the Sock Shop, a cheap silk T-shirt against her better judgement and a sandwich which she took down to the river where she could lean on the parapet and consider the Blackfriars Bridge without the faintest idea of who the black friars were, as well as looking at the railway bridge which ran from this side to the bunkers of the South Bank. All to pass time. Then she hitched the strap of her soft leather briefcase over her shoulder and walked back to the station, far too soon, passed more of the time with a good cappuccino, the 20p lavatory and a newspaper which she tried to pretend engrossed her with vital information as she lingered in the vicinity of platform six, pretending not to wait. She felt dirty; her hair looked like a burning bush of artificial blonde curls; one day she would train it to be smooth. Useless to eye the clock; the clock was closed.

''Allo.'

'Hello there. Where do we have to go?'

There was no more conversation than that, no indication that Rob was pleased to see her as he turned on his heel and led the way across the concourse to the side entrance and then down the street and into a room. So normal the room it was almost discomforting, with the look of occupants who spent their lives inside it. Smoke-free, businesslike, three men with desks and a TV screen. She had expected a cinema. So had Rob. He began to giggle and held on to her.

'Who's this?'

Elisabeth did not let him answer. 'His legal representative, OK?'

She was used to obstruction after introductions of a similar kind, but here it was sweetness and light, no names, no pack drill. Might take an hour, OK? You want tea? Coffee, she corrected and then changed her mind and accepted tea, because of her bladder.

It did not take an hour. Rob, the trolley man, who did not know her from Eve but had a nice face anyway, clutched at her arm in their plastic chairs. She patted him consolingly, as if they were friends of long standing.

They were watching a black and white tape of the walking wounded as they paraded across the concourse and out to the front. Some upright and brisk, some impatient, some dazed. Tell us where you want to stop, Rob was told. Some of the people on the video did stop. They looked at the clock, as if for redemption, they wavered and turned, they tried to deviate out of line and go to the exit they normally used and they were shepherded back, all to go out through the same arch, into the same light, to be captured on video. It seemed a final insult to their dignity to herd them all in one direction purely to be recorded on tape in states of shock. It was cruel.

Singed hair, dirty faces, weeping eyes, people without belongings. What would she feel if the only person on the other side had been a John Box lookalike telling her to straighten up her act and smooth her hair? Would she have fallen at his feet, grateful for recognition? At the end of ten minutes she forgot what she might have done or felt and was weeping. They looked like a tribe of lost souls, landing on an alien planet.

See anyone? the voice said, someone nudging the trolley man. Like I said, we freeze the frame, make a picture whenever you want. Elisabeth could feel the dampness of his palm, placed flatly over her knuckles on the arm of the chair.

Then, from the left, came a tall strider in no doubt about where he wanted to go, but appearing to notice something on his coat at the elbow which bothered him and made him shrug his shoulders and rotate his arms as if warming up in desultory fashion for exercise, and then going back to holding one arm in another and looking at the damn elbow, like someone consulting a watch in the wrong place. Stretching his arms over his head, next, then putting his hands in the pockets of his raincoat.

'I remember him,' Rob murmured into her ear.

'What?'

'Nothing. Fuck, nothing. Bastard.' He shivered violently and then said, louder, to the listening audience, 'That man, the guy flailing his arms, he was in my carriage.' The tape was taken back, then forward, frozen, resumed when Rob nodded. So that they could see, a few uneven paces behind the tall man, Amy Petty, with plentiful yellow hair, walking slow and determined with her arms crossed across her chest, turning to look at the clock until she got near the exit where she wavered, uncertainly. She was not significant among these others, but Elisabeth knew her immediately. So did the trolley man. He gripped her arm and let the tape run on for a whole minute. He waited another three with every sign of indifferent calm, and then he was violently sick. His undigested hamburger and coffee formed a pool by her shoes, but he did not say anything, except to apologise.

Someone mopped up and they resumed, less heartless than efficient. Watched to the end as the last stragglers straggled through.

Occasionally, he asked for the tape to be stopped again, but he did not say anything.

Neither did she.

In the circumstances, it seemed hypocritical to accept thanks for their cooperation, but Rob did it gracefully although with ill-concealed anxiety to be out of there. Smiles all round and she followed meekly, as if he had been John and she the carrier of his bag. He loped back round the corner while Elisabeth struggled to keep up with him, until they stood at the side entrance to the concourse. There he stopped.

'I could buy you a drink at the bar,' he said, jubilation trembling in his voice. 'To fucking celebrate.'

'Celebrate?'

'She's *alive*,' he hissed. 'She's fucking *alive*.'

'Yes,' she said. 'Yes, yes, yes, a drink, but not *here*.'

It was not the rush-hour crowds which inhibited her – their frantic zigzagging towards platforms with their burdens of luggage, shopping, business bags, coffee, tea, chocolate eaten on the run, while others waited, open-mouthed, staring at the departure boards as if they were the clue to life – but the presence of Douglas Petty, solid as rock in the midst of them, refusing to be budged with his size and presence forcing even the most hurried to detour and avoid contact. He was scanning the crowd, glancing at the faces as they swept around him. He looked like a father waiting for a child, covering all the angles, unsure of the direction from which his child might come. He managed to be both lonely and threatening. The child, when it got there, would be in for a bollocking. He was carrying a small purple bag, a feminine article which looked as if it might contain a gift.

'We're going somewhere else,' she said, snatching Rob by the arm. 'I've just seen someone I don't want to meet.'

The crowds thinned out to busy trickles of people. Douglas moved to Cafe Select further away from the trains and stood with a double expresso. A pigeon paddled round his feet. They were rats on wings, intrusive vermin, but he did not shoo it away and dropped crumbs of his cake for it to gobble. He did not want the cake and he was fond of pigeons.

He ticked off the list he had made on a Post-it stuck on the back of his diary. Lists were necessary; they focused the mind. The ticking-off of tasks gave him a sense of achievement.

Tuesday 4th May
Go to ghastly flat, check it out
Cash and Carry
Phone vet, query bill
Letters
Train 2.33
Home

Not an impressive list of achievements, nor even an impressive list of duties. He had done the most important. Douglas turned for the journey home. He hated trains.

CHAPTER SEVEN

Douglas sat in the station car park at Staleybridge, waited for the next train to come in, and counted the days. Fifteen since the crash and the cars of the four dead who had departed from here long since collected, along with the tributes of flowers he had seen from a distance but never approached. It was prematurely dark when he set off through the small centre, round the one-way system and away from the town. The distance was less than two miles but he had already entered a different zone and the city he had left might have been on a separate planet. His eyes ached from the artificial light of the carriage. The small town slumbered, bereft of amusements after eight in the evening apart from two pubs, a restaurant and the window-shopping of the single, select street.

The headlights of the old hatchback strafed the banks of the narrow country road which deviated from the main highway towards his house, picking out primroses, bluebells and blossom. In contrast with the quiet self-containment of the town, the woods which flanked his route teemed with nightlife which he could sense without ever seeing the secret rituals. He disliked the hazards of an early morning drive in summer, when rabbits and birds came out to bask on the relative warmth of the tarmacadam and lost all instinct for survival, so that however slowly he crawled through the lanes to avoid them, there was always some bloody corpse in evidence, flattened by a vehicle in the headlong rush to the station. The commuters were like the Gadarene swine driven by a curse. He did not suffer from a similar impatience at that time of day, but then did not have to go to work, and that privilege alone should be enough to make him tolerant.

It did not have that effect, although he knew his situation was enviable and he had taken great joy in his freedoms. Douglas considered that not going to work should be the height of any sane person's ambition. Why else scrimp and save and get and spend, if it were not for the privilege of being able to stop and consider the lily? There was never any difficulty in filling the days, which seemed, in winter, to be unmercifully short, although the prospect of the endless light of summer was not the delight which other years had promised. He shifted in his seat, changed gear to slow down on the bend with the overhanging hawthorn bush where last week he had seen a fox flitting across the road like a cunning shadow. He could have sworn it had winked at him.

He turned left into the small valley which contained the house, sheltered from the Downs beyond, less than half a mile to go without any of the usual lifting of spirit. Fifteen days, he repeated, only fifteen. He accelerated angrily for the final, straight stretch. Then his headlights caught the golden dog, trotting towards him in the middle of the road, nose to ground, tail aloft like a flag, raising its head at the last minute, so that its eyes caught the reflection of the headlights and shone back, blindingly, like a pair of brilliant torches aimed at his windscreen. Douglas slammed on the brakes; the dog stopped, transfixed, and the car screeched to a halt with a couple of yards to spare and he sprang out, swearing. The dog moved as he approached only to wag its tail and then let it droop in anticipation of disapproval. Douglas felt for the distinctive collar, a thin leather band in red with name, address and phone number on a plastic disc hanging from the buckle. Then he held the dog by the collar, felt briefly for a warm, wet nose and led him to the back of the car.

'Josh,' he scolded. 'If you were a girl, you'd be a whore. So who's a randy hound, eh? You.'

The dog clambered obediently into the back and settled down with a big soft head placed on the back seat, regarding him mournfully through the driving mirror. 'I don't know,' he told it. 'You're all over the place looking for a bitch in heat and you don't even charge them. Shame on you.'

He drove on into the hollow by the stables and parked by the entrance, leaving the lights on full beam to catch the colour of the mellow brick, and the dog began to whine. Jimmy was outside, hurrying towards them, the worry etched on his face turning to relief.

'Oh Christ, you got him. I'd my back turned for a minute, I'm sorry, I shouldn't have . . .' His breath through the open window was minty fresh. 'Sorry,' he repeated, the words difficult to say, stepping back as Douglas swung himself out and stretched.

'Never bother, Jimmy. Can't be helped. This dog could get out of Alcatraz if he had the right scent. I don't give a damn if he mounts every bitch in the county, but he's got no road sense. He can die on the job, but not under a car. I'll take him up to the house. Everything all right?'

'Fine.'

'No intruders with poison arrows?'

'Nope.'

'Get off to the pub then, I would. Listen out for gossip. We can't keep guarding the place like a fortress. None of them's on the critical list.'

'I can come back here and sleep.'

'Could you? Even assuming the enemy's not gunning for us this evening. It'll be easier when I build the new place.'

'Are you still going to do that?'

'Of course. I'll leave the car here. 'Night.'

His footsteps crunched away into the dark with the golden dog sulking at his heels. Jimmy shook his head. Leaving the car as an indicator that someone was with the dogs every single minute of the day and night would not fool anyone with an ounce of intelligence, or even the cub reporter from the local press who had been there again today, but Douglas was right. If the alarms they had installed meant that neither of them could ever be absent, there was little enough point in installing them at all. They had to pretend that life was normal. Jimmy looked at the house, where lights twinkled welcomingly, shook his head. Someone was trying to ruin this man and he was not sure who. It was too much to ask of a man to guard his women as well as his dogs.

'There,' Caterina said to her mother in the living room. 'What do you think?'

Mother sat in her regular chair and peered at the windows. The heavy curtains, which were usually thrust to one side and rarely pulled, so that they spent most of their lives bunched against the wall on either side of the curved window with dust gathered in the folds, had been taken down and shaken out, the dead flies of last year removed and the fabric rearranged so that it draped the window from the centre, looped into grand theatrical folds at the side with huge tassels hooking the weight to the wall. Almost a day's strenuous, back-breaking work; Caterina was proud of it.

'Makes the window look like a stage,' Mother said indifferently.

'Exactly.'

'Douglas would prefer not to have curtains at all.'

'Exactly.'

Mother smiled. 'I didn't know you had the strength, dearest, they must weigh a ton. It does make the room look grand. A place fit for a party. What a waste this house has been. I may as well have moved out to the kennels and let the dogs live here. I can't wait to move.'

Caterina touched the tassel at one side, straightening it up, stood back again to admire. 'He'll sell, in time. You just have to be patient. If no one brings any more dogs and he loses his reason for being, he'll sell. If he persists with that libel action and loses, he'll sell. That's what you had in mind, isn't it?'

'Or he'll stay and see reason. Give up gracefully and take to a life with a bit of style. Not a house annexed to an animal hospital. Ridiculous.'

'You didn't mind so much before dear Amy arrived.'

Mother let her sewing fall into her lap. 'No, but at least one had a chance,' she said petulantly. '*We* had a chance to rid him of his obsessions and make something more of himself. This place could be so beautiful. It *will* be beautiful. So inconvenient of Amy to die like this. Gives her a status she hardly deserved.' The venom in her voice was all the more resonant because she spoke so quietly. Caterina wondered if her mother was really insane and smothered the thought; look at her, a piece of perfection, mending her own lace blouse with her uncannily good eyesight. Caterina looked at the white hands which took up the needlework again so gently and had a moment of realisation about how other people might see them if they knew how rotten they were to their elegant back-bones with sheer envy and yet she could not feel any shame about it. They loved Douglas; they had always loved Douglas. They were entitled to be as they were; they were only what they were made to be. Everyone was entitled to fight for the birthright which had been given and then taken away and anyone would scheme to save something precious that was being spoiled. They were the only ones who knew what was good for him.

'I'm sorry all the same that Amy had to go quite like this,' Mother went on calmly, redeeming herself slightly with this expression of regret. 'What an awful way to die.' She paused trag-ically and then smiled with an awful serenity. 'But at least it saves alimony. Do they still call it that? She'd have been gone within the year, probably; she was working up to it.'

'You were very nice to her, Mummy.'

'We *both* were,' Isobel corrected.

Even in private, they talked in a careful code as if they could be overheard. The effect of the restyled curtains on the room was undoubtedly dramatic, especially after dark. They blocked out the uncomfortable expanse of the sky and reminded Caterina of a plush restaurant in a country-house hotel, designed for opulent candlelit dining, but perhaps a little sombre at breakfast. The other thing it reminded her of, less comfortably, was the stagey curtains at a crematorium, behind which the coffin slid quietly to oblivion. Still, they emphasised the curve of the room and gave it the grandeur it deserved.

'Whoever chose damson curtains had a lot to answer for,' she remarked.

'Nobody chose them, they were *there*,' Mother said. 'Nobody but me thought there was any point getting new ones after Daddy died. Douglas said they would do, he always says that.'

'Did you hear the car?'

'No, did you?'

Caterina hated the silence, willed herself to hear vehicles and voices, anything but the hooting of an owl, the dawn- and evening chorus, or the barking of dogs, which was worst of all. She disliked being in a house surrounded by this blackness where the kitchen door was not locked at night. The kitchen door stuck; it was another irritating thing waiting to be fixed and that was the sound she heard in the distance now. She sank into the chair nearest that of her mother and took up the newspaper. 'We'll really have to plan this memorial service, you know. People will think it so odd if we don't,' she said demurely.

'What people?' Mother asked, hearing the same sounds. 'She didn't have any friends. She only talked to the dogs.'

The kitchen smelt of savoury casserole, probably ready for him to eat. The cat had been mewling outside, running down the path to meet him and weaving in and out of his legs as he opened the door, so impatient to be on the inside and close to food that it forgot it might defeat its own purpose by barring his progress. He kicked the door open wide and let it through first; the mewling increased in proportion to the smell. The cat was a lazy scavenger, addicted to anything cooked for human consumption rather than the blander alternative that came out of a tin. Douglas lifted the casserole out of the oven and spooned some of it into a bowl, which he left on the counter to cool for the cat while it continued rubbing his ankles in an orgy of cupboard love. Exactly the kind of company he needed, selfish but undemanding provided he understood what was expected of him, quite unlike the women in the room beyond, whom he did not understand at all. The cat should have been fed sooner than this. He spooned a little more into the bowl, indifferent to the rich smell of a bourgignon flavoured with herbs, onions, wine. Bloody filth. Waiting for the cat's dinner to cool, he wandered over to the dolls' house, which stood by the sink, taking up space that would have been useful to a dedicated and practical cook, something Amy had never managed to be. The dolls' house attracted dust and grease and required meticulous cleaning from time to time, one of those activities for the proverbial wet afternoon when there was absolutely nothing to do but attend to details and there were not many afternoons like that. Douglas looked at it curiously, the one thing Amy had brought into this house apart from a selection of clothing, lotions, potions and creams and a few pairs of shoes she treated with reverence. She had acquired nothing else but this strangely accurate facsimile of the house in which she had come to live. See? She had told him, see? This is our house, I mean your house, and in a way she was right. There was a living room, with the garden painted on to the windows and damson-coloured curtains, where the master sat in a chair with two dogs at his feet. In the kitchen, a woman worked at an antiquated black range, with another dog in a basket and a cat sleeping alongside. Upstairs, there were two frilly bedrooms, with another dog adorning a counterpane.

Douglas picked out the figure of the master, noticed the poor state of his rather decayed clothing, admired the frayed tweed of the jacket and wondered how it might be repaired. He had never been curious about the manufacture of the doll and it only made him think of weary afternoons at primary school where they had made things out of Plasticine instead of playing and where the idea had been *not* to pulp the different coloured strips of malleable stuff into one multicoloured ball to stick in the ear of some other boy. The project had been to make something nice, mould figures or at least a cat composed of two round shapes, one for the head and one for the body, not forgetting ears and tail. All he could do was disrupt the class.

The figure in his hand remained as it was when removed, sitting in the same position as it occupied in its wing chair, with both arms at right angles and one leg crossed over the other. Inside the chair, the doll looked impressively life-like, but in the palm of Douglas's large hand, it seemed curiously deformed, like a dead lizard. If he held his finger and thumb apart so that they were parallel, that was the height of the figure if the figure had been able to stand. He got out his glasses to examine it more closely. The leg would move within limits and the clothes were constructed like real clothes, made to be placed on a standing figure during an appointment with his tailor and squashed now into permanent creases from having sat down all these years. A clumsy seam at the back of the trousers had split, revealing a substructure of tape. Looking at the feet below the trousers showed him that they consisted of small lumps of clay, painted grey for socks and black for shoes and the calves were made from twisted wire. The ingenuity of it suddenly delighted him, but then the modelled head, which he had handled roughly, fell off into his palm, revealing a pipecleaner neck. He easily put the head back on to the stem of the body and sighed with relief, but the head was at the wrong angle, with a tiny porcelain face looking upwards, making the body seem distraught. He adjusted it as much as he could and put it back inside the house, where it sat less easily in the chair. 'Arseholes!' he yelled.

The cat was up on the counter, sniffing the too hot stew and Josh was whining to go out in pursuit of lust. Should have had that dog seen to, but he hated to emasculate a dog. He sat at the table, tempted to put his head in his hands and feel his temples in case his brain was bursting, but instead he bellowed at the cat, 'Get down, you stupid twat!' and the cat obeyed. Something was often achieved by shouting; it invariably made him feel calmer. He put the cat dish in the fridge to cool for a minute while he washed his hands and put the casserole back in the oven. Then he put the cat's portion on the floor and watched her eat with delicate greed.

Caterina sidled into the room. 'Hallo, didn't hear you!' The first untruth of the evening. 'Are you hungry?'

'Sorry, no.' He stood shielding the cat on the floor so that his sister would not see what it ate. Josh resumed his irritating whining. 'You go out on a lead, or not at all,' Douglas said, turning to his sister as the cat finished. 'I caught him out on the road. Off hunting.'

'As you men do,' she said.

Douglas felt in his pocket for the small cigars, spoke quietly. 'Cat, tell me something. Why did I ever marry anyone as silly as Amy?'

'What a strange question! I can't answer it. She had fine qualities and you were running out of options,' she said carefully.

'Where did she get the dolls' house?'

'I've no idea. Awful thing.' She paused, not quite sure what to do in here to occupy her hands. Everything was clean, every dish washed or out of sight. He hated it like that, felt he should walk about on tiptoe in socked feet for fear of making marks.

'. . . But there was something, Douglas . . . I don't know how to say this, but she was hiding something. I mean, it isn't only men who go out hunting, is it? Those regular trips to London when she never seemed quite able to explain what she'd done or where she'd been . . . do you think there might have been . . . ? Did it occur to you?'

'How discreet you are, Caterina. And yes, it did occur to me that there might be a lover lurking somewhere since I'm not oblivious of the fact that she is fifteen years younger than me, but it only occurred to me after Mother raised the possibility. Then I considered it and dismissed it.'

'Why?'

'Because I would have known. I didn't ask her what she did or why she wanted to go because she didn't want to elaborate and that was entirely up to her. Not much of a life for her here.'

'Douglas, she had everything she could possibly want. Adored the dogs, too, absolutely mad about them.'

'She worked hard. She was entitled to stop.'

'About once a week for three years,' Caterina said flatly. 'Enough to keep a lover happy, especially if he was also married.'

'Oh, shut up, please. For all I know, she might have been going to see a doctor, in the time-honoured fashion of Edwardian ladies who find themselves unable to conceive. She might have gone up once a week to spend the whole day on the Ferris wheel. She might have gone to get away from dogs, or me. I don't *care* where she went. As long as she came back.'

'I think that's called knowing what side your bread is buttered,' Caterina said.

'I'm amazed at you. What are you trying to do?'

'I'm trying to make you accept human frailty, including your own. That bloody newspaper was right. It isn't natural to behave as you do. If you could accept her as a human being, you might be able to mourn. Come and have a drink at least.'

He lit the cigar, suddenly weary in the way he was if he spent a day with only a small ration of physical exercise. It was as if he had to expend the energy in order to acquire more. The smell of the tobacco leaf was reassuring, mollified him, and he allowed Caterina to lead the way down the flagged passageway to the front room where he went to her chair and kissed his mother lightly on the cheek and waited for the full-bodied smile of welcome which always pleased him. She tugged his hair and tutted at the cigar he was waving in front of him. 'Shouldn't do that, dear,' she said sweetly, without really meaning it, the words only another form of greeting. It was only a mother who could speak to a son with a rebuke and make it sound like a welcome. He sat in the opposite chair, crossed his legs and waited for Caterina to bring him the whisky. The master of the house, like the doll in the dolls' house, lord of all he surveyed. Then he looked up and saw the damson curtains, ruched into ornamental swags, hiding the moon.

'What the fuck . . . ?'

He ignored the glass which Caterina presented to him and strode to the French doors almost concealed in the middle, battled with the cloth to find the handle and flung the window wide.

The alarm sounded from the stables, like a sore-throated siren. The dog that had followed him into the room galloped for freedom. Douglas followed.

He ran over the lawn, which was spongy beneath his feet, brushed his way through the willow tree with the drooping branches snatching at his face, cursing the wrong kind of shoes and the lack of a torch. His feet hit the track to the stables and pounded on, stumbled once, gathered speed. A minute, no more than that, but still too far. He splashed through a puddle and went on, the breath rasping in his chest, punishing him for the cigar which he threw in front of himself as he ran and watched the small spot of light land on the ground. The alarm grew louder, accompanied by a cacophony of barking, the dogs' voices joined in a chorus ranging from basso profundo to shrill yelping. The gate to the stable courtyard was open. The barking ceased unevenly as if his presence was sensed, except for the small dog which went on after all the others and then stopped abruptly. He checked each stable, talking to them; nothing wrong, went into the stable with the bed and the control switches to reset the alarm. The nightlights lit the yard with a serene glow and as he went to close the gate, he saw the new dog, heard its breathing before he saw it. He switched on the spotlights.

The head of the thing was half out of the sack used to transport it. He could hear the weak, scrabbling sound of claws scraping at the canvas of an old post office bag, mercifully loose at the neck. It looked as if the whole parcel had been flung over the wall; he hoped whoever it was had at least opened the gate and carried it inside. The dog stared at him with frightened, bloodshot eyes and bared teeth. There was a fresh wound by the ear: someone had struck it to keep it quiet. Probably safer to keep it in the sack.

It was not the first time that a new charge had arrived this way. Douglas sighed and wished he had not sent Jimmy to the pub. He gently picked up the animal, sack and all, found it lighter than he expected and wondered why he was surprised. Animals arriving here rarely had much flesh on their bones and he hoped no bones were broken. He began the slower trudge back to the house. That clean kitchen was the best place for this and if he were going to be called out at night, the vet preferred to be close to the whisky.

He could see the tyre tracks in the mud by the gate and paused to look down with the dog still light in his arms. The night was deliciously clear with the moon showing up the stucco of the house and making it glow white beneath the scudding clouds. The scent of the courtyard herbs after the rain lingered in his nostrils while the dog smelled rancid and sick. Breeze rustled the friendly trees and despite the anger, he felt completely at home. It's a lovely place, he told the dog; you'll like it here; the forecast for tomorrow is healing sunlight; what do you like to eat? The animal was beyond protest, shocked almost to death, and he was afraid it might indeed die without Amy to weave her magic. Amy, come home. The bluebells have begun and the May blossom will be out. You can walk this dog on the Downs.

Elisabeth had the wide-awakeness of the not entirely sober and her face as seen by herself in the train window during the journey home was one she would rather not share, with a puffiness round the eyes and the jaw made slack by the unkind reflection in the black glass which distorted her into something freakish. It made the crumpled collar grey, smeared her mouth into bulbous lips and her hair as if it was a clutch of nesting snakes turned over by a spade. Her throat felt like cactus. There was no such thing as a nice place to drink in the vicinity of a rush-hour station; there were only bars full of screaming spenders, shedding the day like a second skin. Thin girls and thick men, separating themselves from both work and home, challenging each other to drink the fastest. Or there were the clandestine meetings, not always hurried assignations in the quieter corners with a furtive holding of hands, women who looked like she might have looked when she met John sometimes, not hiding, but not shining either with the sparkling shimmer of the skinny unattached, waiting only for summer to bare the flesh from ankle to thigh, hip to bosom and announce they were there to be caught. She wished she had ever been like them, but instead, she was the one in the corner, wrecking an evening for the prospect of half an hour with a man before he caught his train.

And such lies they all told each other in the bars, about who they were and what they did; she could hear them, low-decibel lies, loud lies, lies by evasion. In a different sense, she had also lied, or at least been economical with the truth, to use a phrase overworked in the law, and Rob the trolley man deserved the truth, even though, in defence of her present feeling of shabbiness, she told herself it would be almost impossible to explain, especially when he thought he had found an entirely spontaneous friend. And so he had, but the other agenda she carried, like a weighted knapsack by now, was not easy to explain to someone like Rob with his instinctive dislike of persons in suits, whatever their sex; he might not have spoken to her at all if she had not looked like the pretender to status which she was. He had a chip on his shoulder a mile high, which did not prevent his fierce affection once any individual had struck him to heart; he was an odd mix of cynical and naïve, a hater of authority, and if she had once announced that she had a vested interest in the identity of his missing pal, well, she did not know what he would do. Divorce her after a day on the basis of their incompatibility. Elisabeth found herself giggling, whoops; not good, try again; she had drunk one overpriced, gassy lager too many. No, several too many.

She almost missed her stop and then strode out of the station with the fixed determination of someone pretending they could walk as soon as the anaesthetic had worn off. Sped through the route to her dull terrace, reflecting upon the idiocy of time. The journey this morning had felt like the equivalent of a whole day and the travelling home seemed like five minutes. There was no such thing as time, only a perception of it. God had rained water on her new plants; she could forget about them for the time being. The wine in the wine rack was a more tempting prospect than food. Blotto was an excellent idea.

She turned into her street and as soon as she was near the front step, the security light came on with a comforting glow. There was no sound of TVs or loud music; the neighbours were all far too discreet until barbecue time in high summer, supposing it ever showed, when oily vapours would waft across her clematis along with the sound of parties to which she would not be asked. Elisabeth did not really want to know her neighbours any more than she wanted to examine the psychology of the trolley man, and it was only her lack of curiosity in that regard that made her feel guilty. His loneliness was like a clarion call to her own; she should respect it, but she did not want to do that. She wanted to find Amy Petty, all by herself, and that was all she wanted to do.

Key in lock, light goes out once inside. Mobile phone in same place, proper phone in bracket on wall, with a light to signal messages, good. Wine in fridge, home forever in need of cleaning, cat had peed in sheer disgust, bad. She dumped her bags and kicked off her new shoes. Found pad of paper and pen and started to make notes:

How find Amy P? Look, you pillock. All you do, looking. You aren't a lawyer at all, you're a backroom person who knows about finding press cuttings, et al. You know where you go for birth certificates. Is the Fisher I had down as her maiden name her real name? Might be.

If you were on the run, where would you go? Mum and Dad. She hasn't got any. Who says? Hubby says! Everybody's got one or other, even me, only I wouldn't go there at the point of gun, cos they think I'm a success. Why shouldn't she have them? The sort not fit to introduce? Everybody's got someone, somewhere . . .

A pause for a gulp of wine and an effort to make the hand with the pen more businesslike. It was a nice pen, some special make of fountain pen John had got for her, perhaps to lend some dignity to her shambolic signature and cryptic notes. Real ink looks nicer on the page. Cold-blooded bastard, ink in his veins. Her giggling shook the crockery; she became more businesslike.

Obvious, innit? Birth certificate and work back. Not as if you had anything better to do. Look up fishy Fishers. Any mention in press? No need police computer (if only), try bad debtors and stuff.

Oh shit. She staggered out into the garden and managed to aim the vomit on to the paving where she could hose it down. Jesus, the garden cost more than any room in the house and she was a lousy drinker, not an expensive drunk since a little on a big stomach seemed to go a long, long way. She came back inside, remembered the answerphone message.

Darling Elisabeth, I'm a crabby old devil and I'm sorry if I was rude, however late you were. The trouble is that I am incredibly lonely without you. Everything goes wrong without you, my talisman. Hope you understand and know you do. I love you.

She put down the phone, suddenly sober. How could she be afraid of John and also love him?

Amy Petty did not notice the state of other people's houses. She was the one who went inside and wondered why anyone ever apologised about their mess. When she looked at a room, she saw the shape of it and registered it on a scale of one to ten for comfort. When she looked at a garden, she looked for space and colour, the more vivid, the better. No taste, Caterina said.

The back garden of her father's house looked, by the light of the moon, as if all colour had been leeched from it. There were a few valiant shrubs around the edges of a cracked concrete yard which sprouted tough dandelions. A buddleia hung precariously from the back wall, the only thing she would want to preserve; she had seen these often on the brick escarpments flanking railway lines; they seemed to like the height and flowered in the face of misfortune. She longed for the sound of the owl that lived in the garden at home and she would have sold her soul for the murmur of wind in the trees. Instead, she heard a train go by in the cutting and, when it had passed, the background hum of cars.

She had cleared up all the cardboard boxes he had thrown out here, torn them apart, pressed them down, bagged them, then set about turning the old coal bunker into something else. It was a square, concrete box, open at the front, designed to keep fuel dry, and it was now a kennel with a clean interior which still smelled of coal. Amy was very tired.

Her anticipation of her father's anger when she came home accompanied by a crippled dog was entirely accurate, but she had underestimated the scale of his displeasure. She may not have known him very well, but the reaction surprised her all the same. Stupid of her to forget that not everyone shared her defensive devotion to dogs. After the outburst, he had retreated to his workroom and stayed there apart from a few forays out for tea and sandwiches. TAKE IT AWAY! he had shouted. But where would

I take it, she had asked. The police? The RSPCA, who would keep it a little while and then destroy it, humanely of course, but still before its time? They destroy thousands of dogs every year, Daddy; dogs have no rights as soon as they are abandoned. Only for a few days, Dad, please, until I can make it better. He was so angry, it crossed her mind to wonder if it was safe to leave the dog in residence while she went back to the shop for supplies, in case it reacted to his resentment, but she knew he would not harm it and there was no alternative. She was right about his decency, of course. Somewhere in the late afternoon when she was clearing the yard, he had placed some food in an old pan on the floor for the dog, which chose to ignore the leftover chopped-up sausages and portion of rice from the fridge and slept instead. Water was its only requirement; gallons of water, which cost nothing. It settled into the kennel she had made, bedded down on the old eiderdown from her bed, with the extra padding of a moth-eaten blanket she had found. Daddy had nothing new.

Amy looked at the space she had created with extreme satisfaction. A good day's work, even if her father was still refusing to speak a word and was unlikely to come out of the dolls' house room, even to say good night. She knelt by the kennel, fondled the dog's head and heard the thump of a tail. If the dog lived out here or in her room, it need never bother him at all and once he saw it sleek and well, he would be proud of their acquaintance.

Amy fetched the pan of food which the dog had ignored, intending to place it by the kennel. There would be better food tomorrow when the beast was hungry. Then, as she carried it from the kitchen into the relative darkness of the yard, something in the pan caught the light. She shook the container and looked again.

Beneath the rice, there were shards of glass.

CHAPTER EIGHT

Amy Petty nee Fisher looked hard at the pan with the glass shards only clumsily concealed beneath the pallid boiled rice and wondered from where he might have laid hands on them. It was against her father's nature to break things; she was the clumsy one, he had remarked the day before when she dropped a tumbler and he had hastened to sweep it up, spiriting away the remains into his workroom. There was a use for everything in there.

She closed her eyes and tried first to imagine the possibility of mistake and then to think of why he had taken it away and for what use. As she prodded the shards, she could feel the sensation of glass in her own mouth, imagine her teeth crunching on that alien texture, thought how long it would take her to attempt to spit it out. Such a sensitive thing, the mouth, the way it tested food for sweet and sour, dry and moist, welcome, unwelcome, and all inside a split second of instinct, but hunger deadened instinct and a dog chewed less, especially a starving dog. A dog would eat what a cat would disdain, but the dog out there in the back yard had been too traumatised for this unappetising mess. She wrapped the lethal food in newspaper and made a dish of bread soaked in milk, which it sniffed first, then ate when she made to take the dish away, sighed, as if the effort was great and it did the world a favour by being so obliging. It was not the kind of cunning dog that courted love by showing gratitude in a semblance of human manners; it pretended to ignore her. Amy sat by the kennel and watched as it settled again, one eye open, watching. A train ran by in the escarpment beyond the yard and the damp ground vibrated gently. She had an overpowering need to say something; a sense of profound shock made her want to speak in order to make sure she could control her own voice without screaming.

'You're OK here,' she told the dog, 'because I should have been a vet, or perhaps not because I've never met a vet who wasn't impatient. My father, would you believe' – she nodded her head in the direction of indoors – 'bought me a dog, once; stole me a dog for all I know, but it was still mine, and because it was mine I read every book going about dogs so that I could take care of it. It was *mine*, but when my father *died*, as they say, and we moved, the dog disappeared. I've been replacing it ever since, I reckon. How's that for psychology?' She adjusted her too heavy, severely dirty skirt over her knees and leant against the barbecue. 'My mother didn't tell me to kiss it goodbye, someone just got rid of it and told me it had gone to heaven with him. How old are you, buster? Sixteen going on seventy? What was it like to be young? A lot of fun, I bet. Do you want any more?'

The animal closed its single, watchful eye and let her stroke its head.

'As for that man in there,' she whispered to it, 'I am his only child and he was a teacher in a primary school. He taught them reading and writing and how to play with Play-Doh. He didn't go to heaven; he went to prison for seducing the girls. Long stretch. I never knew that until much, much later. Framed, he says, at a time when people were hysterical about such things. Is that true? I never stopped loving him. He gave me a dolls' house and a dog after all, what more can a girl want? I still love him. That's the way it goes.'

The light came on behind her, far up against the back wall, in the bathroom. That had been his vantage point to watch what she had done in the afternoon. The dog whimpered.

'Shhh,' she said. 'Shhh. Let him listen.'

Speaking out loud in this even tone of voice so as not to alarm the dog had an oddly calming effect on herself. She was so silent in this house, lived here like an inconvenient lodger on sufferance.

'He found out where I was after I married Douglas,' Amy continued. 'And sent me an article he had written about dolls' houses so that I would know it was really him. Don't tell anyone, he said, so I didn't. I'm excellent at keeping secrets, like my mother. I came and saw him, I was sorry for him and I've always wanted him to love me. That's part of the reason why I ran away. All those lawyers and newspapers would have found out, wouldn't they? They find everything out and what would his life be like then? I've read about people like him being lynched, almost. Driven away, and this is all he's got, his dolls' houses, his miniatures, and me. And then, I wouldn't have been much of a witness for Douglas, would I? Amy, the pervert's daughter. What would Douglas think about not being told?'

She could feel her voice rising and did not care. 'But that was only part of it, not even the biggest part. The worst thing is . . . what do you think? Not being loved? No, you can get used to that, *you* should know; I *was* used to that already. It's being undermined, being hated in a way that isn't even personal . . . And not being able to say . . .'

'Not being able to say what?'

Amy did not jump, she had half-expected to attract his attention and lure him down. Nobody spoke out loud without wanting an audience. Rollie Fisher stood at the kitchen door in a pool of light, looking sad, dishevelled and tired. She glanced at him over her shoulder, folded her arms and looked up at the sky. Never quite dark here, not like home, where the dark was like a soft blanket she could pull over her head without suffocating.

'Not being able to say to your husband that the two people he loves best in the world are his greatest enemies. And knowing that if you suggested such a thing, he would think you were mad.'

She turned on him and laughed without humour. 'I never thought that talking to a dog was a way to get people to listen,' she said. 'Perhaps I should have tried it before. Why did you try and

kill this poor dog, you stinking, *sadistic, inadequate BASTARD?'*
She clamped her hand over her mouth, frightened by the words
and wanting to swallow them back. They tasted like glass.

He shuffled. 'I didn't . . . I didn't think it would actually *eat* it. I
thought they knew better. I just wanted you to know how angry I
was.' He slumped against the door frame, trembling with the effort
of standing so still. There were tears in his eyes. 'I'm so sorry. So
sorry. I don't know what possessed me. It was in the pan, I just put
the stuff on top by *mistake*. I'm sorry.'

'That's what my mother said when she told me you hadn't died.
Or gone to heaven,' she added. 'She had to wait until *she* was
dying and no one knew where you were. I've heard quite a few
sorrys. I can't distinguish between the real ones and the other
kind. *Sorry.'*

He rallied, stood straighter. 'Your mother was having an affair
and she wanted OUT,' he hissed at her. '*She* spread the rumours
and put the police on me. I was *innocent*. All for her freedom, not
mine. It was a *mistake*, do you hear me? I'm SORRY.'

He began to cough, guttural spasms wracking his chest and
turning his face purple. The phlegmy cough went on and on until
she moved towards him and patted him on the back but he
retreated from her, waving his hand as if to say, don't, it'll go in a
minute, and hacked loudly until it ended, leaving him stooped
and painfully old. An old man who fumbled and made mistakes.

'Go to bed, Father,' she said. 'I'll lock up, just let me. Go to bed
and I'll bring you some milk.'

He nodded and tottered through the kitchen, out of sight, footsteps receding on the worn carpet of the stairs as she followed him
inside. She could hear the sound of running water and the flush of
the toilet. The sound of nextdoor's music penetrated into the room
and for once she was grateful for the irritation and listened until
the end of a half-heard song. After a while, she went upstairs,
knocked and entered his room, placed the milk and a saucer full of
the plain biscuits he liked on the rickety table by his bed, not quite
caring if he was really asleep. Streetlight seeped through the tightly
closed window with the view up the road and made his skin look

yellow. It was a small room, everything in it looking as if it had always been old, just as he did. She knew that he sat on this old counterpane on his carefully made bed for an hour in the afternoon, unaware that she registered his habits and movements. She was trying to work out how they resembled one another and found nothing at all, although in other lights, they had the same eyes, the same large hands. Then she went downstairs and double-locked the front door. His workroom was still brilliantly lit; distress or whatever it was had made him forgetful of switching off the light and of his reluctance for her to enter his lair unless he was there, too. Inside, there were fourteen dolls' houses, a workbench, several one-room tableaux, innumerable catalogues and magazines, car-spray paints, acrylic paints, poster paints and the smell of glue and turpentine which distinguished the place. There was an old typewriter in the clean corner where he recorded what he did for the book he was writing, *Modelling in ¹⁄₁₂ scale,* and where he conducted an acrimonious correspondence with other model-makers and enthusiasts. *Dear Madam, Your letter to* Miniature Model Making Monthly *on the use of cold porcelain was entirely misleading . . . Dear Sir, The house you described in your article as an original model supplied by Hamleys in 1929 is clearly NOT. The windows do not match with . . .*

She turned to the pages of his notes. *Building miniatures from scratch is the greatest challenge. Almost everything is useful. (My wife has a system of filing spare bits and pieces in the large yoghurt pots we get for the grandchildren, which are useful themselves! All numbered, of course.) Preliminary models can be made from all kinds of packaging. The boards at the back of school notebooks are particularly useful. The lack of wooden punnets for fruit is a shame, these days, but chocolate boxes, egg trays, canes for plants and tinfoil wrappings are invaluable, and takeaway meals often have useful containers. Christmas decorations can be used to resemble table decorations or the trimming on a fancy garment (a piece of tinsel can be a boa, for instance), tinfoil can be used for mirrors and special effects. A piece of broken glass, say from a mirror, or any object with a flat surface, can be used to make a miniature lake. Cardboard absorbs moisture from*

the atmosphere, though, so it will warp in time unless you coat it with
varnish . . .

All written in the same enthusiastic style of the letters pages of
the magazines devoted to the making of tiny dolls and their abodes
which Amy had read during the nervous distraction of her first
week inside this house. There had been a mixture of motives for
her reading in those first days, initially to distract herself during
the waking hours when she had been listless with nightmares and
second, with the thought that if she learned, she would be able to
help her father in his endless endeavour to create the miniature
masterpiece. She had read the magazines in the kitchen, secretly
puzzled by the obsession of those who devoted lives to the making
of *toys* with the same passion an architect might bring to the building of a cathedral, and she had listened to him talking about the
writing of a book, but nothing here could explain why ever would
he want shards of glass from a cheap, broken tumbler, and why, in
the writing of this chapter, did he claim a wife and suggest a style
of living which belonged not to himself, but to someone else?
Writing as if his house were full of the detritus of a normal family
life. There were no takeaways, chocolate boxes or celebrations of
Christmas here.

There was only a dump of a house, in which he made his alternative worlds, out of romance or competition. Preparing for an
exhibition which would stun the world and make it accept him.
She had no idea why he should lie and wanted to dismiss the dis-
quieting thought that he lied with automatic flair, all the time.
Then she considered his life; of course he was bound to lie. No
one was going to read a letter or a book about wholesome pastimes
if the author of it confessed he was a convicted paedophile who
had refined his hobby into an art form whilst serving at Her
Majesty's pleasure. They would draw the simple parallel between
dolls' houses and children. Poor man; it was necessary for him to
lie. But the inventive, quarrelsome adults who read the magazines,
bought the kits and swopped notes like trainspotters through the
columns of the several publications did not create these tableaux
for the touch of sticky fingers and the witnessing of childish

delight; they did it for their own amusement, in the same way that it used to be grandfathers who spent afternoons with the Hornby train set rather than the grandsons. They probably did it to escape from a daily life that lacked the necessary romance. Or they had a hidden agenda.

She still could not see why he had wanted to preserve the broken tumbler, or why, even in private, he should elaborate upon the lies surrounding his existence. When he had said *sorry* for the accident with the glass in the bowl, he had been entirely sincere. A deliberate act of frightful sabotage had already been translated in his mind into a *mistake*, and that was what he would believe tomorrow, by which time there would be no other suggestion. It was a rapid conversion of fiction into unshakeable truth and he probably did it all the time. As natural as breathing, the same type of liar as her mother-in-law. But surely such instinctive. rapidly formed lies did not surround the central facts of his life. Amy found that idea impossible to contemplate. You could tell a lie, but you could not live one. She could not even tell a fib; they stuck in her throat like a piece of gristle and refused to budge until she choked, making silence preferable.

Her skin was sticky and dry. She longed irrelevantly and frivolously for a scented bath, a delicious face scrub and a thick creamy moisturiser of the kind her face could drink in through the pores and leave her feeling pampered and relaxed. The pleasures in life were the small ones; the evening bath at home a reward for the achievement of the day. There was no alcohol in this house; otherwise she might have attached it to her arm via a drip and anaesthetised herself. She would remedy that tomorrow. Buy some wine as a luxury for herself and her father, look after him, remind herself that they loved one another, because that, of course, was the essential truth. He loved her and needed her, which was why she was encouraged to be here. He was a man treated abominably by life; he had been falsely accused; his life, like hers, had been wrecked by the presence of other liars far worse and that was the real truth, and if she repeated it often enough, it would become truer.

Amy went back to the kitchen and out to the back yard to check on the sleeping dog. It had been grossly unreasonable of her to bring it home; she must have forgotten for a moment where she was. Not at home with Douglas, where the collection of an injured stray was a matter only for congratulation and debate, but here, where she was needed.

He doesn't love you, you silly little clot. The words, whispered out of the darkness, remembered from another time, struck a chill to her bones. *He doesn't even admire you; you aren't the sort of person he could ever admire. And that's what you wanted, Amy, isn't it? To be admired, not ignored.* Poisonous words from somewhere else, intolerable echoes from another place, carrying in their wake an inconsistent homesickness. Words that had been said beneath the gentle shade of the willow tree, which she could see in her mind's eye now, and still the longing for home was so strong that she could imagine herself scrambling down the bank to the railway line and running east, just to get closer. She would go; she could go; she could brave it when the dog was better; she could walk it, like a hobo. She could stand in this pathetic space she had created, keeping company with a dog that did not really like her and weep the night away.

Instead, she went back inside and began to clean the kitchen. If she looked up at the ceiling, she could see cobwebs gummed into corners and drifting down the walls. If they had been live cobwebs, she might not have been able to remove them and kill the busy spiders, but they were abandoned homes, ruined by grease and overburdened by dust. She would take down whatever she could reach with an old stick duster and a chair; she would clean each surface to within an inch of its life and she would scrub the wooden table so that she could see it was wood, all to forget the sound of the trees at home and the existence of liars. And she would buy her own newspapers tomorrow, instead of reading the pages he fed to her. That was what she would do.

The cutlery drawer had the musty smell of the hurriedly washed; it was cheap stuff and she would polish it to a shine, but she had days and days to do that. After she had found somewhere to walk the dog and practise talking out loud. It clarified the mind.

★

'It was your sister's suggestion,' John Box said gently to Douglas, two days later, 'that I might represent you in the first place, and she further suggested that I might extend that to covering your wider interests and not just the interests of your libel case against the whistleblower. Excuse the nickname. I never mention real newspapers in conversation because it makes me so angry. Call it a kind of discretion, if you like. Childish. You could have someone far cheaper than I to shield you in your dealings with the police *et al*, not quite the strength of this side of the profession, but your sister suggested you might appreciate someone already familiar. Is she right?'

'She's always right. Just get on with it.'

John blew his nose. Elisabeth noticed the blue handkerchief that had rested by the side of the bed, distracted by the fact that he had just said something which seemed important although she had missed it. How sweet and needy he had been the night before. The handkerchief disappeared into his pocket before she could guess at its origin. She thought she knew them all.

'I only wanted to mention,' John went on with equal gentleness, 'that a QC is rather expensive as an alternative to a postbox. You might be better off relying on your solicitor.'

'The man's a greedy little shit,' Douglas said with no acrimony in his splendid, musical voice. 'And silly as arseholes.'

The man in question did not seem to notice his dismissal. Nothing could have added to his discomfort and he did not know where to put his legs. Caterina laughed a sisterly laugh and patted her brother's knee with one hand, then leant across the distance of two feet to touch the elbow of the fourth person at the meeting, the solicitor who was readjusting his skinny body into a new twist, so that she had to reach further as he slouched to the opposite side and almost overbalanced. There was nothing else he could do that could gain him the attention he was obviously seeking to avoid, but he could not stop twitching in his desire to be out of here. Insults went over his head, but the small flies and the sudden heat got right up his nose.

Douglas nodded in the direction of Elisabeth, who managed the discomfort of her deck chair by sitting back and remaining still in case any movement of her shapely but heavy frame should drive the wooden legs further into the damp ground.

'Well, that's frightfully considerate of you, old man,' he drawled. 'And you're quite right to mention it, but since Caterina *is* always right, you may as well be the liaison officer. Unless, of course, you want to pass it over to your deputy here.' He pointed rudely and obviously to Elisabeth. 'I mean, she must be cheaper. Even if she is half-asleep."

'Only half,' she murmured, straightening up as much as possible. 'I was just admiring the tree. It's so beautiful.'

They were sitting in the circle formed by the weeping willow, all of them on assorted oddments of chairs which had the appearance of being recently hauled out of cellar or attic for the first airing of summer. The deck chair in which she sat had a canvas speckled with mould and she sat in it regardless. What all of those present envied about her was her ability to relax like a cat and forget where she was. A dog sat at her feet, adopting her. Caterina was the only one who looked in command of her own posture, but she had the benefit of sitting on the wooden bench which always stood beneath the tree, next to her brother, whose suggestion it was they should convene in the open air. Most unbusinesslike, reminding Elisabeth of school lessons al fresco, where nothing was learned. She had never been able to work out of doors. Caterina had disapproved of the suggestion, but Douglas had insisted. The chairs were there already and the decision was a *fait accompli*. Caterina's quickly suppressed annoyance had given Elisabeth unexpected pleasure. It was the first time she had met the woman and her immediate reaction was dislike. It might have been the height of her, the slim perfection of her perfectly creased linen trousers and the artful top with the cap sleeves that did it, but Elisabeth doubted that since she always admired the well-dressed. Nor was it the fact that John and she appeared to be acquaintances at least of long standing; she kissed him on the cheek, for God's sake, and what was Douglas Petty doing letting her choose his legal counsel? Caterina had his air of command with none of his redeeming features, although

Elisabeth was surprised to find herself thinking that he had any of these. Strange, how you had to see someone as dislikable as he was in the company of someone worse in order to see anything remotely admirable in them. Such as the accuracy of his rudeness. That solicitor twisted on his stool really was a greedy little shit. Adequate to formulate planning permissions for the new kennels, useless for anything else. Elisabeth knew what he charged, for which he did very little. But the day was hot; a blissful, insect-buzzing heat rare for early in the year and it felt like they were being given a treat.

The willow tree, fed with rain and now blessed by the sun, was at its best. Elisabeth would have lived here for the willow tree alone. The tree had grown tall but crooked, so that its graceful branches, weighted with pale green leaves of amazing delicacy, drooped in an uneven circle away from the slender, speckled trunk. The longest branches swept the ground; it gave the perfect degree of incomplete shade, so that the sunlight twinkled through the leaves, dappling the ground and all their faces. And it created the perfect degree of background noise, a mild and musical rustling sound, like the swish of long evening gowns. A very feminine tree, beneath which Douglas sat, looking like a satyr, making him far preferable to his sister, who looked like a *snake*. She must stop this. Elisabeth felt that the identity of Amy Petty had taken up residence in her brain, although John looked less like a whippet today. The white façade of the house glimmered through the leaves, glowing in the full sun of the afternoon.

'I tell you what,' Douglas said. 'John can deal with the libel side of things. Elisabeth deals with my wife's affairs. She didn't make a will and she didn't have anything to leave; should be easy.'

He spoke with such brutal casualness that Elisabeth forgot the redeeming features. 'I don't know anything about probate,' she said. 'That really is a job for a solicitor.'

'Well, hoity-toity,' Douglas said, 'I'm sure you can learn. I didn't think you people ever turned work away. No job too small and all that. Not like when I was at the Bar. Work oozing out of every pore, however bad you were. You shut the door on them and they crawled through the window trying to get at you. I reckon I had the best of it. It can't be much fun now.'

She leant forward to retrieve the teacup she had placed on the ground for lack of anywhere else to rest it, took a sip and placed it back down. Looking up, she saw Caterina nod imperceptibly in John's direction. Quite the old friends. She could not think why the recent knowledge that it was Caterina who had chosen him to represent her brother should be so infuriating. Not that the choice was bad; John was the best, after all, but Douglas should have chosen for himself. Ah well, that was the way of it, she thought ruefully. We all want our men to take advice from women, have the sense to abdicate control and be led by us, and yet despise them when they do.

'It isn't so much the probate aspect of things,' Caterina said in her singsong voice. 'It's finding out when her death can be declared official, that sort of thing. Difficult,' she added, with a reverential lowering of the voice, 'without a body. I don't know what you do. It's a question of research. We have no *closure*, you see. Poor Douglas can't make appropriate decisions until we get that.'

'Including appropriate decisions about continuing with the case?' John prompted gently.

'There's no decision to be made about that,' Douglas said sharply. 'We have to go on with it. I told you why. If I let a sodding newspaper make me out to be an animal who beats and buggers other animals and I don't fight it, then how does that reflect on my wife? She'll simply be remembered as someone who conspired to make me into that animal. Encouraged me, stood humbly by and let me do my worst. Amy would kill anyone who was cruel to a dog. I can't have anyone think that of her.'

Elisabeth noticed his use of the present tense, wondered if it was accidental.

'Douglas,' Caterina said with a deadly gentility he did not seem to notice. 'What does it matter?'

'It matters to me.'

The branches of the willow tree stirred in a sudden breeze,

covering the silence. Elisabeth reached for the teacup again, even though all it contained by now was a brackish brew the colour of rust which had left circles on the inside of the china to mark her sips. It tasted like real Ceylon tea, the kind she liked least, and it scarcely quenched her thirst, but it was not to be ignored. Douglas had made the tea and it was Douglas who dragged them out here beyond the cool of the living room. You sneaky bastard, she thought with a venomous admiration; you have organised all this to get us at a disadvantage and you've done this before. It worked on all of them, John included, except herself, because she was hugging a secret and she loved the sun and the tree, which put everything else into the realms of nonbeing, or almost did. The sun made her an indolent dreamer; it was the most sensual of comforts; whatever vexed her mind or if she had been told that hell would freeze over the next day, she could always sit in it at the faintest excuse and treat herself as a piece of bread ready for toasting. The sun turned her into an idiot; a deck chair was heaven and even though this was not the day for the smart-heeled shoes she longed to kick off her feet, or the tights, or the long-sleeved blouse she wanted to rip off, and even though she was a worried and guilty woman, it still felt great. She struggled to sit upright and overturned the teacup with her foot.

'I'll do whatever you want me to do, Mr Petty. I don't know the answer to your questions at this moment in time' (God she hated herself for talking like that, so pompous) 'but I'm only junior counsel to Mr Box and I can only act under his aegis. Otherwise, I'm unemployable.' (Christ, that came out wrong, she wanted to take off her shoe and throw it at the branches.) 'I mean, I'm only his assistant and I can only take orders from him, not from you.' Even worse; she sounded like Miss Whiplash with an addiction to bondage, looked towards John for approval and saw him nod, even though his face was blurred with sun and she could not be sure what the gesture meant – go on; don't go on, or shut up. She went on. 'Certainly I could find out anything you want to know. Research is my strong point.'

Yeah, all you needed was an accidental meeting with a trolley man and the habit of silence which came from sheer uncertainty. And twenty-four hours' research into the mystery of a living woman who was supposed to be dead, resulting in not a lot, yet, apart from thinking about her all the time and not being able to say so. There was nobody she trusted with this virgin knowledge; no one, and anyway, Amy Petty might have weaved her way out of that damn station to do nothing other than become a suicide statistic in a rented room, or another body in the river, the sort that drifted from bank to bank until unrecognisable. The sun dived behind a cloud and she was shivering, smiling brightly and shivering. 'Do you mind if I get some water and would anyone else like some?' she asked. They all shook their heads no. 'While you discuss this with Mr Box? Don't worry, I know my way.'

Getting out of the deck chair was easy, moving aside the branches of the willow tree with a semblance of dignity was harder on the spongy ground with the heeled shoes. She walked as fast as she could to the French windows of the crazy room, fought with the curtains which blocked the light from outside and swore. There was the older Mrs Petty, sitting like a monument to patience by the side of the fire as if waiting for it to be lit, while peering over her half-moon spectacles at a newspaper, her sewing in her lap, the very soul of calm. She looked just like a potted plant. A favourite aspidistra which has stood in the hall for a long time, or maybe a peace lily no longer in flower but demanding attention, and she bestowed on Elisabeth a smile of distracted sweetness. Elisabeth hurried down the flagstone corridor, into the kitchen, aiming for the sink and the tap. *Does my head in*, the trolley man said when he had phoned the night before. Well, yes, she said, I suppose it does, and now she knew what it meant, but all she wanted was water.

A man sat at the table, slurping a mug of tea. He had begun to stand up at the sound of her footsteps and then when he saw who it was, sat down again, nodded. 'Afternoon.'

'Hello. Do you know where they keep glasses?'

He grinned. 'Do you mean the *good* glasses or the everyday glasses?'

'The chipped ones, I'm only the hired help.'

'Use a mug then, there's a couple in the sink.'

She rinsed one out, filled it with cold water and drank it down.

'Tea's the best thing for thirst, I find,' Jimmy remarked.

'Depends on the tea.'

'Can't stand that poncy Earl Grey stuff,' he said conversationally. 'Real mouse-piss. Are you one of those fucking lawyers poncing about on the lawn and wasting his money?'

''Fraid so. Who are you?'

'Jimmy, hired help, like yourself. Only with the dogs, though. Which makes me useful at least, which is probably more than you are.'

She refilled the mug and drank again, slower, and put the mug down with a bang. 'Why is *everyone* in this household so fucking rude?' she asked. 'Is it in the water or do you take lessons?'

'No, it just comes natural.'

Elisabeth laughed, refreshed by the water and the rudeness which was oddly liberating. He laughed too, his face creased like an old leather shoe.

'I've heard about you,' she said. 'You're the one who got sacked before Mr Petty got into trouble with the newspapers, so you were a fat lot of good to him. And I've seen a photograph of your bum, the other week. I rather enjoyed that, I must say, but I don't think you're entitled to call me useless when you don't even know what I do.'

He inclined his head. 'Point taken,' he said.

She sat down beside him, carrying the empty mug. 'Any more of that tea?'

He poured from the pot into the mug and slopped milk on top, accepting her company. His hands were dirty and he smelled of dog and nicotine. The cat which was curled in his lap stretched and jumped off, resenting the intrusion.

'Will they be long out there?' Jimmy asked. 'Only I'd like a word with the master.'

'You're having me on. You don't really call him the master?'

He grinned again. 'Sometimes. It was a joke I had with Mrs Petty. We both used to call him the master when he was out of sorts.'

'Were they happy?' she asked recklessly.

He showed no signs of resenting the question. 'Sure, to begin with. Everyone is, aren't they, to begin with. Completely fucking mad about each other. Loved the same things. No, I mean they really were, before . . . Oh, fuck it. Only don't ask me to talk about her, it makes me cry.'

'Well, alleluia,' Elisabeth said. 'At least there's someone willing to cry for her. *The master* seems remarkably dry-eyed.'

'Well, he would be, wouldn't he? He doesn't believe she's dead.'

'What!'

'He doesn't believe . . . He *can't* believe. He'd go to pieces, else. Uh-oh, that's enough.'

A loud greeting echoed down the corridor and Jimmy got to his feet hurriedly. 'That's Caterina. I'm off. You want to watch out for that one, she's worse than she looks. Eats fried balls for breakfast.'

He was out of the back door before Caterina appeared, flowing into the kitchen like silk. 'Ah, there you are,' she said, as if it was not entirely obvious. 'Wondered where you'd got to. They've changed their minds. They all want water.' She moved deftly, found a tray, crystal tumblers from a cupboard and a tall jug which she filled with mineral water from the fridge. Elisabeth looked round the kitchen. It was far more streamlined than she remembered from the time she had come in here with Amy and admired the homeliness. Furniture had been moved; there was less clutter on surfaces and the dolls' house which had got in the way was relegated to a corner. The kitchen had never been tidy, but now it was aggressively clean.

'Here, let me carry that.' She took the tray from Caterina.

'Thanks. Watch out for the flagstones. They're a bit uneven.'

Caterina said this as she swept out of the kitchen, leading the way. Elisabeth followed, cross with herself for volunteering to help and feeling rebuked, admiring the other woman's carriage and the way she walked as if she had been taught to dance. The passage-way between the rooms was comparatively dark for the distance between the door and the hall where the stairway began and the light poured down, reminding her of the heat outside. The tray was heavy and she trod carefully, remembering the warning about the unevenness. She turned into the living room, feeling the thick carpet beneath her feet. The new arrangement of the curtains framed the room and darkened it; she was looking up as she stepped through the open French doors, tripped on the step and let go of the tray. Two of the glasses flew through the air and bounced on the lawn; the rest crashed on the steps as she rolled on to the grass, still holding one handle of the tray.

Caterina stood over her, hands on hips, looking down at her with exasperation rather than downright anger, amazed at her clumsiness. Then she thrust out a hand which Elisabeth took reluctantly to haul herself back to her feet. Caterina was strong, for all her slenderness; her arm was sinewy and her palm cool and dry; Elisabeth relinquished it, looked at the damage. Broken glass littered the steps.

'I'm so sorry . . .'

The other woman folded her arms and stared at her. 'Do you know, you're just like Amy. Sort of thing she'd do. Excuse me while I find a brush. We can't have the precious dogs getting this in their paws.'

Elisabeth rubbed at the grass stains on her knees, wondered if it was true and she was just like Amy. She was certainly no longer herself.

She stumbled back to the shelter of the willow tree, mortified.

'I thought I heard the sound of breaking glass,' John said.

'Yes, I'm sorry.' Elisabeth turned to face Douglas, who still sat on the bench. 'I just dropped a tray . . .'

He was not listening. He was looking at the object he held in his hands, an item which had just been presented to him by the solicitor. A clear polythene bag with a plastic seal, containing what seemed to be a handbag. Tan-coloured, like one she had at home.

A bag, anyway, but scarcely gift-wrapped. A bag belonging to a dead person and sent home, in lieu of herself, to be buried. It looked like a laboratory specimen sealed in an airtight plastic cover in case it might contaminate, not to be touched in case of germs. A last souvenir, a confirmation of finality. The greedy shit of a solicitor had got his revenge, delivering to Douglas what had been officially delivered to him. Douglas was the colour of chalk; his bare arms rigid by his sides and his hands hovering above the ugly package. Then, in the manner of someone horrified by a snake which had landed in his lap, he picked up the thing and hurled it at Elisabeth. The aim was accurate and the bundle bounced against her chest, soft and heavy, winding her. She fell back into the deck chair and held it to her chest. The feel of the polythene was peculiarly unattractive.

'You can begin with that,' he said, wiping his hands down his trousers. 'Just get it out of here.'

Elisabeth cradled the handbag as if it were alive. A sleeping puppy.

From the distance there came the sound of Caterina moving across the lawn, humming to herself, carrying the fresh supply of water.

CHAPTER NINE

This time they went back together on the train, although to different destinations. They were driven to the station by Jimmy in a beaten-up hatchback with suspicious stains of long standing on the upholstery and so old that everything about it creaked ominously. Another attempt to discommode them, Elisabeth thought as she sat in the front with Jimmy who stared ahead and flung the car around bends as if both he and it hated the road. John and the solicitor sat in the back and clutched at the handles, talking to one another. She pulled the seatbelt across herself, clipped it, then used the time to push the exhibit bag into her own empty briefcase. The case was the wrong shape, but the bag could not be carried around naked and the arranging of it made a chorus of polythene creaking sounds. Jimmy had the windows shut; he wanted them to be hotter and stickier than they were, eyed her sideways and went faster. The ten minutes seemed longer. She looked across and down, marvelled at the skinniness of his thighs, like a jockey's, nothing but muscle and bone held together with threads of thin fuse wire beneath the frayed cotton of his trousers as he changed gear with the same aggression as a man whipping a horse to win. There was something about that tan-coloured bag he wanted to devour: once it was out of sight and they reached the outskirts of the town, he went slower. In the back, they continued talking, tight-lipped.

At the station, Jimmy leapt out and opened the back doors officiously, saluting like a chauffeur without a hat, a parody of insolence. Out of sight of the others as they parted in the car park, Elisabeth slapped him on the shoulder, her hand meeting a sharp ridge of bone.

'Thanks,' she said pointedly. 'That was fun.'

'Fuck off,' he muttered under his breath. 'Fuck *off.*'

The heat persisted. John and herself waited on the platform for the train which would take them to Tonbridge where he would leave and she would change for the branch line.

'The train's not for fifteen minutes, time for a drink?'

'Where?'

'Nowhere.'

'It's not long. Home soon.'

'Yes.'

The late afternoon was airless and listless, infecting them both. Meeting with the Pettys had left them shaken. It was not as useful as it might have been for her to live fairly close to John as the crow flew. They were on a different part of the commuter belt, scarcely connected. She had seen photographs of his house, the sort of house that ate money; a mock-Tudor thing with acres of space for a privately educated family to leave, one of these years. She was not a convenient lover. The relationship might have flourished better if she had lived in the City in a flat accessible during working hours.

They waited together but separate on the functional station, built to withstand wind, prettied up with tubs of geraniums still in bud to add a touch of class.

'I wonder if that dreadful man knows more about the libelling of Douglas Petty than Douglas thinks he does,' John said, referring to Jimmy. 'And why on earth does Douglas employ someone like that?'

Elisabeth pretended to consider. Her mind was on other things,

relieved all the same to find his mood so equable after an uncomfortable and largely wasted afternoon that had not featured
deference from anyone, even herself.

'Considering what it must be like to work for him, I don't suppose he has a lot of choice. I rather like Jimmy.'

'Anyone with money has a choice,' John said with a trace of
resigned envy, speaking as one who never had enough. 'Still,' he
added, 'Caterina might manage to get rid of him.'

Elisabeth cleared her throat of dust and looked downline, shielding her eyes from the sun and suddenly back in the here and now.
'Where did you meet her?' she asked casually. 'You never told me
you knew her so well.'

'I don't, really. Met her years ago. She worked for a magazine I
defended, successfully, as it happens.'

'What does she do now?'

'Corporate publishing. You know, in-house magazines for
banks, that sort of thing. She's a very able woman, *when* she
works.'

For someone who did not know her well, he seemed remarkably
well-informed and Elisabeth felt the brief thud of jealousy, over-
come by curiosity. 'So, she's a bossy bitch with contacts in
newspapers,' she said. 'Well, well, well. What I don't understand is
why Douglas is letting her rule his roost.'

He did not rush to Caterina's defence and there was a small
comfort in that. He looked at her, interested in her opinion, choos-
ing his words carefully in his endearing way. 'Guilt, I expect. He
has it all, she has nothing. The terms of his father's will insisted
upon unfairness. They're beholden to him and he is beholden to
them. Papa didn't believe women could make their own decisions.
I believe our Douglas was ordered to revere the womenfolk, at
least *these* women. Not others, obviously. Rather like Mafia fathers
and sons – Mama and sisters are sacred, but you can shoot the
others if they get out of line.'

'It would have put the cat among the pigeons if Amy had produced babies, wouldn't it?'

'I don't know,' he said, bored with it. 'But she didn't in five years, poor soul. She had dogs instead. Perhaps she and Douglas didn't copulate, who knows?' He paused to squint at the sky, spoke sadly. 'The greatest secret of all time is the true state of anyone's marriage. No one on the outside can ever really know. Even those close to it don't know. For God's sake, even the parties to it often don't know.'

'He hit her,' Elisabeth said.

'You've suggested that before,' he said, a touch impatiently. 'And I think you're wrong. You don't know much about men, do you?'

The platform alongside them was suddenly filled with raucous children turned out of school to go one stop down the line, home to tea. Three boys tussled with one another and threatened to fall over the edge while two more shouted encouragement and a posse of girls watched, scornfully. John watched the girls and she watched his profile, admiring and resenting his ability to reduce her to silence.

'My children will be off our hands in a year or so,' John said. 'Not like those. Then I'll be free. To be with you, if you still want me.'

It startled her, this intimate pronouncement, coinciding with the slight vibration which signalled the imminence of the train. It made her uncomfortable; it was out of context when they should have been talking of anything else. Did he mind the fact that Douglas had instructed her in the matter of his wife's death, for instance? It was as if he knew that she was being pulled away from him and had to say something to reclaim her attention. She smiled at him and touched his hand, to let him know he had succeeded.

'You don't mind this division of tasks, do you?' she said as they sat in the corner of the carriage furthest away from the marauding children, who settled down to the serious chewing and swopping of sweeties produced from pockets, all pretension to adulthood forgotten.

'No, why should I? I know no more about the finalisation of death than you do, and I don't want to know. The solicitor should do it, but never mind. All our roles are up for grabs these days. How odd of Douglas to throw that handbag at you like that.' He did not, she noticed, criticise the client either then or now for outrageous rudeness to his junior. It was up to her to tolerate that kind of behaviour and meet it with equanimity, just as he did.

'I don't think he could bear to touch it,' she said. 'Was that on account of hate or love, do you think?'

John shrugged. 'Who knows? Fury, that her death was confirmed by the return of her property? Angry that it meant no one was looking for her any more? I don't pretend to understand him. There was never any real doubt about her death. She somehow got into the wrong carriage where thirteen people were incinerated into ashes. Even if he had precious little feeling for her, the bag was a pretty callous reminder. They could hardly send it back in pretty paper.'

The train gathered speed.

'They're a pretty callous pair, those siblings,' she said.

'Nobody's that callous. Not even Caterina Petty.'

'How do you know?'

He shrugged, irritated and cagey. 'As I said, I don't. She's put me in the way of work, that's all. But I do know enough to find her quite impossible to like, however handsome she is.' He sighed and stretched his long legs, crossing one over the other, elegantly. He was one of the old school who hitched up the knees of his trousers before he sat; she found it endearing. It showed prudence and consideration; she could see him being taught to do it as a child at the same time he was taught to hang his shirt over a chair.

'She is rather beautiful, isn't she?'

'If I were a woman,' John said, 'a *beautiful* woman, I think I would be perfectly content. Utterly satisfied that the very presence of me was enough to give such pleasure. I would feel it entitled me to everything. Why isn't it enough simply to be admired? Why do you all want so much?'

He was not demanding an answer. The train stopped and all the children piled off, screaming. Elisabeth was not listening to him any more; she could see a corner of polythene sticking out of her briefcase and she itched to tear it apart and there was another part of her which was furious with him for not sharing that avid curiosity. Why should he? The woman was dead; she was no longer beautiful and he had ceased to be interested and she herself had an unreasonable fear that Rob might be working on this line today; glanced around, hoping not. When they got down from the train, she felt guilty to feel so relieved to be saying goodbye.

It added to the other guilt, which ranged from anything to everything, apart from her clumsiness in breaking the Petty crystal, which was, in retrospect, faintly enjoyable. She could hear the sound of it now, a shocking little echo; a tale on which to dine out, if she had friends with whom to dine on a regular. basis, but John and their affair had isolated her without her noticing, and that fact intruded now into a conscience already riddled with regret. She never saw Helen West any more; she never saw anyone. Friends drifted and she had let them drift once she could no longer explain who it was she saw or why she invented excuses; she could not trust herself to trust gossip. *Careless talk costs lives*, an old adage which applied to her and marooned her even more than all those evenings of waiting for the phone, afraid to miss the chance of speaking to him.

She could not open the ugly exhibit bag with its heartless appearance and vicious seal while waiting in the public eye of a busier station than the one from which they had embarked. They were reaching rush-hour time; she could not tear at the seal with her teeth, so she had to think of something else. Such as what was John doing, mentioning a future so specifically, was he saying, wait for me, please, or what? She would not have continued with this, however besotted, if he had been one of those whingeing men who claimed their wives did not understand them, all that crap. Or a man who blamed his spouse, or criticised her to excuse his own infidelity. John never did that; he adored his two children and agonised, in his cool way, about the conduct of his life. He would not like ridicule and contempt. Please do not betray me, he had said; I offer you nothing but myself from time to time and that is all I offer, there is nothing else to be had. And now he was, altering the dimensions of the goal posts and introducing a hope she had never entertained, although it had always been there. *I'll be with you if you want me to.* Elisabeth shivered. She had never tried to take him away; she did not want the responsibility of another woman hating her.

Her train came in, packed. She guarded the briefcase as if it contained a gold ingot and it felt heavy enough for that, weightier by the minute, and she handled it with the guilty care she might have given to smuggled goods as she stood in the aisle, keeping balance with one hand on the pummel of a seat and the right side of her body dragged down by the case which she could not bring herself to put down on the floor because of the absurd fear she would forget it. See her own stop with such relief that she would push her way out of the carriage with her own handbag, leaving the case behind, as if she would. There was no space for dipping into the newspaper which was also in the case; no real inclination, either.

Another twenty minutes of crowding without the relative silence of rustling newspapers. She marvelled at the way the phones came out and passengers chatted, issuing instructions towards home, planning meals, finishing business or pretending to be busy in a series of pointless conversations which made her sigh for being so lacking in a certain something, something that made her leave her mobile in the kitchen because it was just another thing to carry and forget and she hated, hated, hated the dreadful challenge of saying anything important in public. The case grew heavier. Nobody noticed.

The train made her angry, as it often did when she was granted uncomfortable, claustrophobic thinking time. She pushed her way out as rudely as she dared; her own, small house beckoned like a beacon. It was still warm on the way back from the station to her door, where the security light came on regardless of the daylight. One month before the longest day in the year, and the light and heat seemed endless. The cat yowled. She fed it, opened the kitchen door on to the area at the back she referred to as the

garden. A small back yard, ready to burst into bloom, made possible by a ridiculous mortage, kept on a promise. She loved it.

The answerphone blinked; so did the insulting mobile. Elisabeth
got the polythene sack out of the briefcase and tried to tear it
open, but it was strong and unyielding. She could not find the scissors. Nothing for it but the serrated carving knife, the sharpest in
the block, but approaching the parcel with a lethal weapon in her
hand seemed hideous; she felt as if she was about to murder it,
standing there with the blade poised like Lady Macbeth. It was so
stupidly dramatic, so she sat instead, pulled the bag towards her
and made a small, tentative hole with the tip of the knife, tore it
larger, and took out the tan-coloured handbag as gingerly as if it
was alive.

It felt alive. Slightly warm to the touch, with a circular base and
a drawstring top, pulled tightly closed and the leather strap handle
dark with dirt. It smelled of cinders and good soft leather, worn
softer by constant use, comfortable slung over a shoulder. It had
an expandable shape, into which anything could be stuffed, not
the kind of bag Elisabeth favoured, because it was the sort in
which a woman would spend half her life, scratting around inside
its depth, looking for things, but a good bag for the purpose. A
person could carry a life around in a bag like this.

The contents were disorganised, jumbled together in a mess
which made Elisabeth decide to upend the thing on the table and
look at it all in total rather than item by item, although it seemed a
horribly impertinent thing to do and she was not sure if it was
more intrusive because of her belief that Amy was alive. A bag like
this was sacrosanct, an area of privacy rarely shared; if she were to
put her hand inside another woman's handbag without permission, it would be a form of assault if not theft. She was always
faintly ashamed of her own and would never want it examined,
because the endless mess of it revealed all her deficiencies, so she
made a mental apology to Amy Petty and told herself that this particular bag had already been neutralised by the touch of others.
Someone must have gone through it.

Some nameless police official, who would replace all the

contents and fix the exhibit seal. Exhibit A, a life, returned to next of kin. Why the fuss? The contents were only typical and smelled sweet. A waterproof makeup bag, full of cosmetics. Foundation, mascara, lipstick, eyeshadow, brushes, excellent quality. A small tub of exquisite moisturiser, Floris perfume which had leaked, hence the smell. Amy Petty liked her cosmetics and probably never travelled without them. There was another cloth bag, with a sachet of shampoo, toothbrush and paste, a miniature tub of cleansing lotion, all of which surprised Elisabeth. Did Amy know she was going away for longer than a day, or was this a precaution she always took? A diary, stained by perfume, a brush, comb, endless paper tissues, house keys and a bulging purse which was the same colour as the bag.

A hundred pounds in cash, a lot in these days of payment by card, but there was nothing odd in liking cash, useful stuff. A full array of credit cards and numerous bits of paper. Amy was the type of person who only cleared the many compartments of her purse once a year when it became so full it split the seams. Receipts by the dozen, for groceries, household stuffs; she favoured Tesco, Waitrose, Brown's Pet Supplies, and a local high-street chemist which kindly itemised what she purchased. Clarins creams. And then spread through these was a clutch of small receipts for a newsagent's with a blurred print address in SE23. Small expenditures of four or five pounds featured in these. Elisabeth tried to guess what. Cigarettes? Amy did not smoke, as far as she knew. A box of chocolates to take to a friend?

At the back of the purse there were appointment cards. Dentist in Wimpole Street; that would explain some of the London visits, but not every week and none recently. Facials at a local beauty shop, next one due last week. A massage therapist for aromatherapy. Amy took care of her face and teeth. She did not buy books and spent nothing on clothes, if this collection of receipts was a true indicator of habit, but she did like a bit of pampering and Elisabeth was faintly disappointed in her. She laid the appointment cards in a neat row and turned them over, absentmindedly, as if she was playing patience. On the back of the dentist's appointment card was a tiny, printed sticker. *Rollie Fisher, Miniaturist and model-maker, 12 Ratview Road SE23.* Not *Ratview,* on closer inspection; *Bayview.* Someone had playfully written over the B and the Y. It was a very small sticker, like the kind used on apples.

Slowly, Elisabeth flexed her fingers, counted to ten and left the table. SE23. Same as the newsagent's with the remaining numbers of the postcode blurred on the receipt. What the hell was she doing in SE23? SE23 had absolutely nothing to do with the rest of her life. Had anyone else looked at these? And if they had, what would they be looking for? They would simply be establishing that this purse belonged to this woman, nothing else. But there was far more. Elisabeth poured a large glass of wine and pulled the other papers out of her briefcase. All she had got so far on the search for Amy Petty. Her birth certificate, easy to get once you knew her date of birth, which she had known since first taking instructions from Douglas. John always insisted on taking full particulars from clients. *Amy Fisher, born 1965. Father Roland Fisher, schoolteacher. Mother Ursula, nee Jones.* Deceased in '93, that much she also knew.

In the initial stages of a libel case, John wanted to know the identity of anyone who might be affected by the libel. When a man comes to be held in contempt, the ripples spread wide; it affects his family, his cousins, his relatives by marriage and the extent of the effect could be reflected in the amount of compensation. Was there anyone else apart from yourselves who was distressed by this publication, he had asked. Caterina and my mother, of course, Douglas had barked. Amy's lot are conveniently dead and she was an only child, that's right, isn't it? Amy sitting quiet and nodding agreement.

The phone rang, horribly shrill in her quiet kitchen. For a moment she was confused; the silence of the place and her own concentration made any sound alien, and at first she did not know which phone, picked up the mobile and put it down, touched the other one. Let it go on to answering service; no, it was too insistent, but she had an awful dread of answering it, as if everything she was piecing together would disappear in the sheer effort of conversation. As if Amy would dissolve into mist as soon as she was talked about, something she had felt for days. Amy the illusion, dispelled by word of mouth.

She whispered into the phone, waiting to hear her, with the ridiculous impression that the voice would be Amy's, admitting her existence and wanting to speak. Amy had once possessed her card and her number. Both she and Douglas had. They were credentials presented on first meeting, like badges of identity, something given to prove you were real, like the identification badge shown at the door by the man who came to read the electricity meter. *Amy does not have your card any longer, you fool; she is not thinking of you just because you are thinking of her and rifling her handbag.*

'Hallo? Elisabeth Manser here.'

'Oh it is, is it? What took you so long?' There was a choking sound at the end, and she could imagine him reining himself back from saying *you silly bitch*, his deep voice instantly recognisable.

'Good evening, Mr Petty,' she said, louder and more formal.

'What's *good* about it? S'fucking raining, or didn't you notice? An' I'm a bloody fool. Fucking hell—' There was the sound of a stumbling crash. 'S'cuse me, lost the fucking glass. Again!' Then he laughed, a full-throated sound which reverberated around her kitchen and was oddly comforting. She had never heard him laugh, always imagined, if she had thought about it all, that it would be abrasive. She sat up straighter, looked at the wine bottle on the table full of papers. Only half-gone; she was better than he, obviously.

'Bit pissed,' he was saying unnecessarily. 'Jus' a *bit*.'

'Good for you,' she said, reaching for the glass. 'I'm still working on it. What do you want?'

He terrified her; he beat his wife; this was what was meant by Dutch courage. No, that came from gin. Courage, in her case, came from impatience and irritation and the fact he was not in the same room.

'D'you know,' he slurred, 'Jummy says you're OK? Okey-cokey.

Never noticed myself Always wearing daft shoes, you. Daft shoes and big hips. We like that. *Biiig* women, *yesss*!'

'What do you want?'

'Wha' do I *want*? Oh for Chrissakes . . .' His voice tailed away into laborious breathing, interrupted by the slurp of a drink and the sound of swallowing, then a long silence. 'I wan', I wan' . . . You gotta send me back that bag . . . That fucking bag, why did I threw it at ya? I dunno. I was stooopid. I wannit. Bring it back. Now.'

'Now?' she said, politely incredulous, consulting her watch. There were sounds of laboured breathing and another swallow of drink.

'Now.' She could see that big head, nodding. 'Now would be fine.'

'You gave it to me. You gave me *a fucking* job to do and I'm doing it. You threw it at me.'

More laborious breathing. 'Yeah. I did.'

She waited, like she waited in asking questions, distancing herself and letting the silence do the work.

'Hated that bag,' he said. 'Never did like that colour with her. All those country *browns*. Only woman I ever knew suited blue. Lace and pretty things. Like you and the Queen Mother.' He sighed. 'Wen' to the flat, I thought . . . *she* went to the flat and took away her face creams, she *took* them, yes she did, she was *there* . . . I can't force her, just got to wait . . .' Then he seemed to rally into the silence which she did not fill and compose himself. 'Bring it back,' he muttered. 'Bring the fucker back. Shouldn've los' it. Is all I got. I need it. I *want* it.'

'Why? So you can eat it? Throw it to the dog?' She could almost smell the breath.

'You bring it back. Shouldn' have given it you.'

She remained silent, listening to his breathing.

'You come back here, Big Lizzie. Need you, too. Come and break a few more things, will you? Never could stand those fucking glasses. Too heavy for drinking. Come back . . . I'm the master of the house, or at least, I've got him with me.'

She let him take another drink. Whisky was the drink he would suit. Her hand held the receiver tightly.

'The dog died, darling,' he said wearily. 'The new one. Someone had tried to cut its fucking throat. Think tha' might have been Dell, don't know though. Come back.'

The phone went dead, leaving what was to her mind the saddest sound in history. That buzzing sound of abandonment, being cut off, ignored, finished.

She would have to give back the bag, but not yet. He had the tone in his voice of someone who had been crying. Not only a pig, but a drunk, sentimental pig. Elisabeth had the temptation to cry herself, but went to find the *A–Z*.

SE23. A life in a handbag; fragments thereof.

Jimmy turned on the new mattress in the stable, felt the scratches on his arms from where the destructive Alsatian crossbreed had kicked with his legs as he held it for the vet. He liked that dog, it was his favourite. He liked the ones that bit and tore up blankets and destroyed everything they could reach, because the poor bastards had been pushed from pillar to post, shifted from house to house and never fed – snarled and snapped and swore as if to hide the broken heart and ravenous hunger. When no one looked, he sat with them and told them stories and fed them stuff. Never for as long as Amy had done. She would croon and feed for weeks until they stopped tearing the bedding to shreds; she groomed them into trust as if her life depended upon it. Never talked as much as when she was talking to dogs.

He was drowsy when he heard the footsteps, and heard too, through his heart rather than his head, the shuffling of the three dogs occupying the room next to his own. Maybe Douglas coming back, but he was gone, two hours since. Jimmy swung his feet off the bed, glad of his boots and his status as fully clothed, and began to whistle. There was a variety of sounds which wakened the dogs. They were impervious to fucking and whistling – cocked an ear at that and went back to sleep. *Natural* sounds made no impact. Not the sound of the grey owl, or the squeak of prey, or the quiet footsteps of a familiar. They were wise fools, dogs were. He listened with their ears. Not Douglas, but another member of the pack.

Caterina was carrying a flashlight, because she was not attuned to the ruts in the track like her brother was to the extent that he could walk it three sheets to the wind and sideways. She was careful and delicate, and a familiar scent because she came here often enough and far too often for Jimmy's taste. All big eyes and no hips, noiseless until she sneezed, quietly, but somehow ostentatiously, as if to prove she was there and did not like it because of this allergy of hers which prevented her from close contact with dogs. Nor did he like that quiet sneeze and her soft footfall over the stable yard. He turned on the radio by the bed. That never disturbed the dogs, either; they knew what it was, a soothing sound of mumbled voices or music.

He was standing and ostensibly busy with the door wide open for escape by the time she was over the yard. He was trying not to look shifty as he straightened the bed on which he had been lying, feeling in his pockets for a smoke and knowing she did not like that. Her perfume came before her, like a noxious cloud to which he was not immune, because he loved all the smells of women.

'Hi there, is there a problem, or what?' he said cheerily, as if she was welcome, biting his teeth on his own reaction. *Skinny bitch, boneache, spaghetti legs, too clever by half.*

She smiled and he noticed she had donned her lipstick as well as her flashlight for this simple trip down the drive so well on the right side of midnight you could hardly call it late for a townie like her. Good God, rumour had it they ate at ten at night, while he would have called himself hollow three hours before that. She was shaking her head. A well-groomed bob of black hair swung across her cheeks, obedient to her every move, and her brown eyes were like pools of shitty muck. She always turned her head when she smiled, as she did now, presenting the better profile, and in this thick, electric light, which sent deep shadows over her features, he could see not the slightest resemblance to her thickset, blue-eyed brother. Stepbrother, he corrected. Not the same kind of blood.

'I came to see if you were all right,' she said softly, as if she was some sodding spy on a foreign mission and taught to speak in code. 'I'm afraid Douglas is a touch *hors de combat*, if you see what I mean. Might have left you in a pickle. I wasn't sure if you were here.'

'Of course I am.' *Horse de whatsit* was not his vernacular; why didn't she just say *drunk*, he would have got the picture anyway. *She's a bit like a fish, all smooth and shiny with muscles all round her middle.* Muscles on her eyelids, too, fluttering in an attempt to express concern, or maybe a reaction to the light as she eyed the bed where they had slept, Amy, Douglas and he, on separate occasions.

She nodded. 'Are you sure?'

'Of course, *ma'am*. I do this all the time.'

'I know,' she said. 'How cosy you make it. I only wondered . . .' she hesitated prettily, 'if Douglas had been all right to you. Such a mood, you see. He does tend to *lash* out when he's like this.'

'Has he hit me, do you mean? Not recently.'

She had no conception of irony. 'There's really no need for you to stay here at night, you know, not when it's so much warmer; it really isn't fair of him to insist. I think you ought to stop.'

'He doesnae insist. And it's not every night, only when . . .'

'Don't do it, then.'

'Could I not see you home?' Jimmy said evenly. 'So kind of you to come out. All this way.'

The smile did not falter. She smelled sharp and clean. 'I was also wondering if you might help me with the garden tomorrow. If you've time, that is. It's all getting out of control.' She spread her hands in a gesture of helplessness. They did not look too dirty to him. Jimmy had watched her out there; all she had done so far was spread poison to kill the slugs which had eaten their way through a clump of hostas and left silvery trails over the French window steps.

'If I've time. I'm no gardener, mind.'

'That would be awfully kind of you. Oh excuse me!' She sneezed again, loudly, and found a handkerchief with her left hand, while the right still held the flashlight, pointing to the ground in a pool of light and illuminating her feet. Neat black shoes, suitable for a funeral.

'Bless you,' he said automatically, and was rewarded with the full smile.

'Good night.'

Her footsteps receded towards the house, with the flashlight dancing before them. Jimmy stood in the yard and lit a cigarette. So that was the way of it, then. She was not going to fight with him; she was going to befriend him. Save him from her big, powerful brother. Make civilised creatures of them both. In the way Amy never tried.

And she had not come here to enquire after his health. That was out of the question.

Aw, Douglas, man. Wake up, will you?

It was the night-time reminded Amy most, even when the traffic on the main road waned and there were moments of comparative but never complete silence and the area was a depressing reminder of all that it was not. Today she had remembered the date, felt the stealthy encroachment of summer and noticed how, even at this hour of the evening, the light was slow to fade. The long hours of daylight were nothing but a waste. It was the second evening that she had walked in the darkness with the dog loosely attached by a piece of rope looped round her hand and attached to a bandana of softer cloth round the animal's neck. It would look bizarre by day-light, but anything went by night. She followed the familiar route to the garage where she went every day and the man in the shop was a kind of friend. Faced with a barrage of cars, the dog quiv-ered. No one had claimed her; no one would. She limped painlessly and was improving, without enjoying the exercise that was the ostensible purpose of the nocturnal stroll. Like Amy, the dog belonged somewhere else, but it was important to get them both out of the house and remind them they had working limbs. When she was out, she talked to the dog. There was a different man locked into his box in the garage at night, so she did not wave as she passed and walked further up the road, thinking she was rather like the dog, a creature in search of interesting smells. Jasmine, syringa, wet grass, finding instead the cloying scent of cars and the elusive smell of food. A bus rumbled by; it was only because she had left the money behind that she did not race to the bus stop further up the road and raise her hand to arrest it. Get on, pay, go to the station on the route she knew, get the train, go *HOME*. Amy turned back, and although the big road was empty, she did not trust herself to cross, and waited in the eerie emptiness for the little green man to give her permission.

She still felt naked without the bag and mourned it, but without the bag there was nothing to steal or stalk, and besides, she did not care. She was so subsumed with longing to be walking down the path from the back door of the white house to the stables, where she could smell the herbs she had planted and hear the real sounds of the night, that someone walking behind at the same erratically slow speed was not a problem. There was nothing to be afraid of any more; there was no fear worse than the thought that she might never see that place again. When she turned into the car-strewn road where her father lived and felt for the keys on a string round her neck, she was afraid of nothing but that, kept her eyes ahead, her hand on the rope. As she stood by her father's door, the footsteps went on by.

She closed the door behind her, quietly. Equally quietly, she settled the dog and went to bed. The homesickness was always better in the morning, when there was so much more to do. She would not swallow the pills he left for her. By this time, she had learned to close off part of her conscious mind, but not to sleep without dreaming.

Chapter Ten

In the morning there were fewer silvery trails on the broken concrete of the yard in the early sunlight. They had seemed almost pretty yesterday until Amy saw how the snails had eaten away at the verbena plants from the garage, still in their plastic pots for lack of anything else, their promise diminished by the ravages of the night. Silvery trails on the foliage too, hopeful shoots snapped before their prime. Slugs or snails, she could never tell which; greedy monsters and the only creatures in the natural kingdom of snakes and rodents, insects and other pests that she despised with a thoroughness bordering on hatred. They had no moral code, these molluscs; they consumed the freshest of greenery regardless of its innocence; they thrived in the damp and the dark of walls, operated by stealth and would even eat one another. They had blind faces and bloated slimy bodies beneath those smooth shells and they thrived on destruction.

Any desire to be organic or vaguely environmentally friendly went in the face of this kind of enemy. She had decided she would kill them with the bright turquoise slug pellets also available in the increasingly useful emporium of the garage, but once she had got this lethal material home and looked at the warnings on the label, the plan changed. By now, the daft dog ate anything it could find, regardless of shape, size, colour and smell; nothing could be left in the vicinity of its appetite. Salt killed snails too; they could be induced to drown in a dish of beer and she could protect the base of the pots with impassable material, like tree bark, sawdust, broken eggshells, none of which things were easily to hand. Or there was the simpler expedient of waiting in ambush, picking them up, putting them in a bag and walking somewhere to throw them away, but she had balked at that and scattered salt, with partial success. Salt was also cheap; in the first two weeks here, she had spent nothing; in the last, one hundred and fifty pounds. Even dog litter and redundant slug pellets were expensive. There was another kind of problem in the offing. She tried not to worry herself about that and made herself count the compensations of her current existence on a bright morning after a restless sleep which refreshed her only enough to convert the homesickness into a sub-acute pain. It remained a chronic condition; she carried it round like an illness, but there were consolations and at least she and her father were on speaking terms. He had demanded an inventory of yesterday's shopping expedition, expressed interest in the yard, accepted the improvements and seemed to mellow with the sunshine although he retreated back to his curtained room as much as ever and hurried in from the daylight as if it might damage his skin. Rollie Fisher had recovered from the sulk, although not from the racking cough; he had regarded the clean kitchen without comment but at least without disdain, and approved the new neatness of the garden with particular reference to the pathetic showing of flowers. Nice, he said, very nice, in the manner of someone patting her on the head and giving her permission to proceed. Neither the dog nor the broken glass were mentioned. This morning, he had gone shopping. He was still in charge of food.

'Do you know,' Amy told the dog, 'that he and I might have had one of the easiest conversations we have ever had? I don't mean just recently, but ever. He might feel easier with me around when I'm doing something rather than nothing. Everybody likes me better when I'm busy, even you. I'm best tolerated when *they* think I'm not listening. Stupid and over-industrious, Caterina said that about me, but I like working, it's as simple as that, and there's only one person in the world who does not think me stupid. There is no such thing as *too much work*. Do you know, in my wild days, I almost became a tart? That wouldn't have been very good, I'd never have managed the money. Are you comfortable, dear? We'll go for a walk later, not in the dark.' She examined the inside of the kennel. 'You'd do me a great favour if you would stop ripping the bedding, although I know why you do. And I'm sorry I can't feed you as much as you want, but, my dear, I do know best.'

The dog was not sociable; it was wary, ravenously hungry and destructive, but its eyes were bright, its leg was mending and even after a few days of proprietary food, the coat was thicker. This one was a neurotic animal, requiring food and stability more than affection; the old blanket was torn to shreds and fouled. It would consent to be stroked over and around the left ear, but not the right because of something painful there. Amy wished she was a vet with a dispensary, rather than a self-taught, instinctive nurse. The dog liked conversation, provided she never turned her back as she talked. It did not care what she said.

'As far as my father is concerned,' Amy was saying, 'don't expect *love*. Tolerance does just as well, I promise you, we can live with that.' She was busy removing the torn bedding; the kennel needed insulation from the cold of the floor. 'Easier for you than for me,' she added. 'He isn't your father and I would really be a fool if I hadn't already noticed that he finds me entirely repellent, in the physical sense, I mean. I think he always did. Are you all right?'

The dog closed one eye. It was half in, half out of the kennel, torso stretched languidly to feel the sun, the one ear cocked to hear threat. Then it scuttled back into the bunker, curled into the furthest corner. Amy turned to the sight of a head poking over the bowed wall at the furthest end of the yard. A train rumbled by in the cutting, chilling her slightly with its sound. The head was the head of a girl, eight years old or thereabouts, with a perfectly spherical face of brown skin, lit by enormous dark eyes and crowned by black curls, offset with a single gold stud in one ear. Amy recognised the face; she had seen it from the window among a posse of girls en route to school, early in the morning. It was one of the faces her father waited to see, coming back down the road in the afternoon.

'Hallo,' Amy said.

The head grew into a head with shoulders as the child heaved herself further over the wall and leant on it with her elbows. She was wearing a yellow sweater.

'You've got a dog,' the child announced.

'Yes, so we have. Why aren't you going to school?'

'I've got spots.'

'That's a shame.'

'*You* look funny,' the child said, releasing an arm and adjusting her precarious balance to point.

Amy looked at her skirt, fashioned from the endless supply of old curtains of garish colours her father kept, and felt the collar of her shirt, which even after washing still smelt of him. 'I suppose I do. Do I?'

'Yes.'

There was a conversational impasse. Amy scattered more salt.

'Are you his girlfriend?' the child hissed, suddenly confidential.

'Whose girlfriend? Do you mean my father?'

'Oh.' There was palpable relief, and then a rush of whispered words. 'Your *dad*. He's got lots of *dolls*, hasn't he, with *houses* for them . . . has he?'

'Who told you that?' Amy asked, coming nearer as the child became self-important, bursting with superior knowledge.

'Our lodger told us. He went to your house first. And your daddy said there was no spare room any more, but he showed our student the dollies' houses. Our student plays football. My mummy says your daddy makes the dolls' houses to get little girls to come in.'

'No, he doesn't,' Amy interrupted. 'It's his hobby. He likes to make things.'

'Can I come and see? Can I, can I, can I? It'd be all right if you were there . . .' the child stopped, conscious of Amy's silence. It was not a feigned silence; she simply did not know what to say.

As if on cue, the dog emerged from the kennel, issued a single indignant bark and went back. Immediately there was a babble of instruction from the other side of the wall, and the head disappeared unceremoniously. Then there was the sound of scolding and the back door of the house next door banging shut. Amy was shaken. Daddy's secret life was not as secret as he assumed it was, but surely he *must* know that, even if no one came any more to view the room he never let. *I was keeping it for you,* he had told her; *I never meant to let it.* The presence of a woman in the house did not go unnoticed, even in a street as sublimely antisocial as this. Still shaken, she went inside to look for alternative bedding for the dog. Rollie Fisher never, ever threw anything away. There must have been an extremely acquisitive phase in the early stages of his occupation resulting in the stockpiles kept inside the ugly wardrode in her room, the contents of which had the look of a charity shop. His subsequent collecting was as eclectic as his newspapers and it was futile to attempt to determine what he had in mind. He often explained to her, with evident pride, how it was that almost anything could be recycled into a dolls' house. Small pieces of curtain material for wallpaper; tissue paper for frilly frocks; the material from an old shirt, of which there were many and one of which she wore, for miniature sheets on miniature beds or the apron on a parlourmaid. The copious old curtains looked as if they had been donated from someone who had realised they did not deserve a place in anyone's home. Amy had turned one of these into the skirt she was wearing which did not fit particularly well and added so much to the oddity of her appearance that even the child remarked on it. Orange flowers down to the knees; blue and white striped shirt on top; no wonder the man in the garage embraced her as a simple eccentric; no one could look as discordant as this and have any capacity for harm.

Your daddy makes dolls' houses to get little girls to come in. It'd be all right to come in if you were there . . .

Was that why he had welcomed her? As an alibi? With a frivolous irrelevance which embarrassed her, Amy longed for a large sample of Clarins *multi-régénérante* night cream, a long bath in herbal foam and the touch of lace. She sat on her small bed in the drab imprisonment of her room at the back which was scarcely improved by the removal of the muslin from the window, wishing that the sun would not shine, a selfish wish, she knew, since it shone on everyone else and was welcome. It made the dog better, her father more amenable and the house brighter, but against all expectation it also increased the intensity of the homesickness to such an extent that she moved in a daze and could not think beyond the next task. Take now, for instance; what was it she had come into this room to find? Her handbag; she was always looking for the nonexistent handbag; that was a constant preoccupation; there was always something she wanted from her bag; it was part of herself. She was looking for something dispensable to use as bedding for the dog, because it would be a while before the creature learned not to tear everything to pieces. She was looking for displacement activity, so that she did not have to think of the child. She *must* think of the child and how to protect them all.

Instead she sat on the bed and dreamed. Took herself back home to the shade of the willow tree, saw herself on the bench beneath, looking towards the dazzling white façade of the house, surveying the garden through the veil of leaves, and wondering again what to do about the snails which would have eaten the hostas by now if no one was guarding them. She had been a clumsy, wait-and-see gardener, even with the help of books on *How to Create a Wilderness*, but there would still be harebells and campanulas, bluebells in the shade, speedwell in the grass, all the blues. Hardy annuals in the flowerbeds around the steps which led to and from the room she loved best, the minimum of lawn and the maximum of meadow; dreams of a pond where the half acre of land sloped downhill and became marshy in the dip. Five glorious summers in which she had never noticed the weather and made her best attempts to be *busy*, to justify this miraculous existence she had been given and ignore the rest . . . until it was too late.

Sitting here in the airless room, she knew with the slow-burning certainty which had increased by the hour that she would have to go back before she could resolve anything here. Go back, once.

Once, just the once, before the money ran out. Once, before she could reconcile herself to *this*. There were crucial things she had to do before the money ran out. She counted on her fingers, like the child in the next garden probably did, reminding herself of what she had come to find.

Newspaper; Rollie Fisher had newspaper stacked, piled and stuffed all over the place. There were newspapers twisted for use as draught excluders in the bathroom; newspapers bundled and kept for various purposes; there was newsprint wrapped with string in untidy piles. The base of the wardrobe, which leaned to one side, was welded to the floor by the solid weight of newspapers. Maybe he kept it against nuclear fallout – people did that once, in the days when they built underground bunkers against the end of the world. She tried to understand, even as she sat where she was and thought of the newest newspapers which had arrived that morning. They did not have the musty smell of these. The dog would like them better. Some days, Daddy scarcely read the things. She stared at the open wardrobe with the wobbly hinges. There was just enough space for a few folded clothes before the heap would touch the unused hanging rail at the top. He would never have meant to let the room. The room was a decoy. You would have to be desperate to take this room. He did not need rent, he lived on benefits and financed his hobby by making dolls for dolls' houses. He made shuffling runs somewhere with dolls in bubble wrap, little corpses in polythene . . . might have got the postman to collect them from the newsagent's. *My mummy says he makes dollies' houses to get little girls in . . . I can come in if you live here too, can't I?*

Sometimes the homesick sensation was akin to a heart attack, because it felt as if it must be fatal, this time. Better to move, but in the darkness of the stairwell it was worse. She steadied herself, clutching at the rail, and then went back. *Go home, go home, go home. No, CAN'T.* Not yet, not now. It was worse than his coughing. *Ughome, ughome, ughhooome,* echoing at night.

Downstairs, the front door banged: she could hear him whistling on his way through to the kitchen while she remained as she was, sitting on the stairs, fighting for breath. Then she went down, loathing the texture of the synthetic carpet beneath her feet. How could he live in this near squalor and create, by contrast, the exquisite interiors of the dolls' houses? Why this passion for ugliness?

The new newspapers were spread over the kitchen table. Amy had forgotten her plan to get to them first before he selected what she should read and spirited away the rest. There now, she was being ridiculous to read anything into this. Here was a white-haired old man, reading his daily intake of news and getting ready to rant about the state of the world he otherwise ignored. He looked like a sheep today, baa-ing at her by way of midmorning greeting as he looked up from the page. Amy put the kettle on, comforting herself with ritual.

'Look at this,' he said quietly, flattening out page two of *The Times*. There was a montage of photographs, each of them pass-port-sized, some clearer than others, and each with a brief description of the person portrayed. *The Final Roll Call of the Train-Crash Dead . . . None of these people should have died.* Amy sat next to her father; he moved further away and left her to examine the page. She scanned the photographs, looking for herself and finding her own face in a blurry image of a head dressed in a wedding veil, thought briefly of who might have supplied the photograph, and then scanned the rest. Thirty-three; so many it made her angry, the murderous wastage of it all. What had any of them done to deserve this? She found herself looking for a familiar face, looking at the men first and thinking of the trolley man, hoping against hope that she would not see him there. But why should she? They had all got out of the carriage, even the smug elephant man with his phone; it was not their carriage that had burned.

The dead were mostly men. Amy looked at the photos of the other women, and as she looked, stopped. There, at the beginning of the third row, was a particularly clear photo which struck a chord. The woman who had sat opposite, with the hands of the man round her neck in the split second before the crash. The woman who had been carried off and left by the track with her arm outflung and the ring on her finger which someone had removed.

A memory suppressed and now outrageously, brutally clear.

'Why did she die?' Amy said out loud, incredulous and furious. 'They were having a fight; he'd lost his temper, lost it completely, didn't care who saw . . . but we saw. She didn't *die*. He *killed* her. Either he strangled her or he threw her on the track and broke her neck. Then he walked away. Like . . . I did.' She could feel nothing but a sense of excoriating shame. 'Me and Rob, we *saw* him. He wanted her *dead*. He *used* that crash to do it! *She should not be DEAD.*' Amy realised she was shouting.

Rollie was listening closely and seemed to understand. 'Shouldn't be dead?' he asked. 'Neither should you. What do you propose to do about it?'

'*Tell* someone.'

He began to laugh. A giggle which turned into a guffaw, became longer and louder before interrupting itself to cough. He laughed and he laughed and he laughed.

It was then that she began to realise that whatever he had felt towards her, it was not love.

She had played herself into everyone's hands. If he had *loved* her, he would never have taken her in. He would have sent her home. He thought of her in the same way she thought of snails. With loathing, hatred, contempt. Amy went into the back yard and stood trembling next to the dog. Go *home. No, not yet.* Go OUT.

It was perfectly simple. Go to Bayview Road and ring the bell. Or knock on the door. Elisabeth squinted at the *A–Z* mapbook of London and tried to visualise what the area was like. Densely built, criss-crossed by trunk roads, foreign territory to her, like most of the hinterland which spread from the centre. Rather a box in the suburban loop touching the ever smaller green belt than a house in the other kind of suburbia that had nothing. There was a vast superstore labelled at the northern end of SE23, as if it were an ancient landmark and a sportsground. The map would not tell her if there were trees. There was a railway line marked in black, but the local station was two squares away on the map. Buses and cars, then. Buses had always been a mystery to Elisabeth; she recognised no form of transport other than the train, the Underground and her own two feet, all of which got her around the small compass of the places where she needed to be. South of the Thames was the foreign territory she glimpsed from the train. What a snob she was to dismiss what she simply did not know. There were probably a million contented people in SE23, loving every minute and fantastically fit from walking everywhere, bargain properties and leafy cul-de-sacs she had never seen. Elisabeth got out the bus map, admitting that she was secretly afraid of the whole adventure and disliked the idea of the bus most of all.

But there it was; it had to be done and here was a bright sunny day to be doing it in before she had to consider the returning of the handbag. She would have to do what the client said and he was quite right, he should never have thrown it at her. It was all they had to bury or cremate; she could see it, ceremoniously consigned to flames in a bonfire in that glorious garden of theirs in front of that glorious room, with the Petty family watching the smoke. Perhaps she should take the handbag with her to Bayview Road, but she might lose it and it was not hers to lose and besides, a woman with two handbags would look lopsided. Elisabeth realised she was postponing an expedition she did not wish to undertake. Half the day was already gone and she had only got as far as Charing Cross.

A glance at her bank statement, the most unwelcome thing to arrive with the morning post, was not an incentive to spend time on non-fee-earning pursuits. Whatever the fate of Douglas Petty's libel case, it was not going to earn anything for anybody in the short term. Whereas prompt legal advice about how to deal with this death would pay something, for sure, a consideration which made her wince. Earning money by research into a death which she knew had not occurred was really biting the bullet of hypocrisy. So even if she had imagined there was a choice about finding this damn bus and going to godforsaken SE23, there really was no choice at all. Already she had delayed. The bank balance made the easier option of taxi travel a bad idea and there were other reasons for that, too.

Amy Petty had left the station with *nothing*, sweet fuck all, *nothing*. Elisabeth wanted to do the same. Her unused credit cards were in her wallet. Unless her knickers were stuffed with cash and she had planned the whole bloody crash, she would have left that place as a pauper. She must have had somewhere to go, or nowhere. Perhaps there was a man, a knight errant, with prospects. If she closed her eyes and made a wish for Amy, she would invent for her a lover of gentle habit and no complications who was content with an afternoon a week, while saying come live with me and be my love and I shall hide you. Someone who could transport her to a garden in the South of France and let her live without bruises. Fat chance. It would be nice if such a person existed but Elisabeth did not believe it. If Amy had gone anywhere, she had gone by bus with the coins left in her pockets, unless they let her ride free.

The one-man-operated double decker which she took from Trafalgar Square presented a granite-faced driver behind a Perspex screen and a phalanx of machinery. No one got inside this damn bus without money. Flat fares, so she paid the maximum, went upstairs and consulted her map. She felt surreptitious and found maps more difficult than words.

Wise of Amy to choose this time of year to disappear. The central city bloomed and the Thames, traversed briefly by the bus, glimmered like a gold-embossed invitation to extravagant pleasures. Then the bus turned east, away from the riches of it all, and Elisabeth was lost. She had the sad realisation that she would have felt braver and more confident in far more ramshackle transport in some hot, Third World destination, where her relatively pale skin would have made her a stranger to be helped, while here she was the only one who did not know where she was. Somewhere along the convoluted route she began to follow it, and all the same, forty minutes later, found herself reluctant to get off.

It was her constant bad conscience rather than the view that made her doze for some of the journey. She was a sleepy animal, easily lulled, constantly lured into closing her eyes when the sun beamed even through the prism of glass. She woke, knowing it was minutes rather than hours, consulted the map, recognised the name of a street. Thundered down the bus stairs and was out of the doors half a mile too soon. Walked. Practitioners of the law always protested that they knew how the other half lived. It was not true. She knew nothing about crime except for theft; she knew about bad blood and reputation, but she did not know what it was like to live here. The bald instructions of the *A–Z* were accurate. No trees, only roads, which meant when you followed the map, which suggested you could cross the big road *here* in order to find the small street *there*, the map told a downright lie about the relative size of everything. She faced a thunderous highway with a garage on her left; three crossings later, she found the turning to Bayview Road and turned away, because she did not quite know what to do now. The alterations on the street sign, *Ratview*, made a great deal of sense; she would have laughed at it if she had any sense of humour left. Once that went, she was in deep, murky shit, left with nothing but the realisation that she should have eaten something more than dead cereal before she set out. Food was the fuel for bravery. Anything was possible on a good stomach.

Amy, she remembered, walked easily in her hour-glass shape, propelled with a certain elegance via powerful hips, big bum, small waist tapered into narrow torso below a generous bosom which bounced. Not a million miles from herself, apart from that uncannily gorgeous face which haunted her now and was, as she realised in her seconds of hesitation, the reason for her being here at all. It was not only man who was seduced by female beauty: Amy had the face which mesmerised. A face lit with artless kindness and a complete absence of malice. Elisabeth passed the window of the newsagent, where her own reflection was marred by the advertisements in the window. You're not so bad yourself, girl, get on with it.

The newsagent's was an island which attracted single swimmers from the anonymous streets and squat tower blocks that surrounded it. They sneaked into this minicentre for humanity in

pursuit of fags, milk, newspapers, sweets and computer magazines together with a selection of videos. It gave the impression of
the sort of place where the kind of magazines and videos not supplied by Disney might be available from the recesses of the
counter, behind which an old man sat in a pall of boredom, looking as if a robbery might be just about sufficient light
entertainment to keep him awake. Not that it was the kind of area
where such violent criminal activity seemed imminent unless
someone commandeered a truck for the purpose. It felt unthreat-
ening to Elisabeth, merely sinister for the lack of people moving
around on two legs instead of inside vehicles. In the middle of the
morning, a display of Jellytots, mini Smarties and lollies on sticks
was the only sign that children existed.

Senselessly, she looked at the display and selected two packets
of fruit pastilles for the bottom of her handbag, plus a packet of
cigarettes for emergencies. She paid and he handed her change
from the ten-pound note, with a receipt, remembering what the
law said about receipts. They should always be given, or at least
available on demand; the receipt must enable the purchaser to
identify the seller, which meant in practice that a receipt in a shop
like this was usually neither given nor required and would be as
anonymous as a bus ticket unless the seller had developed the
punctilious habits of *Oza's, Hurst Lane, SE23*. Lane? This was at
the junction of a virtual motorway, guarded by railings to stop the
deaf, dumb and blind from straying into the road. She nodded
thanks and went outside.

The private detective of fiction would have purloined a photograph of Amy Fisher and said, *Have you seen this woman?* Yeah.
And the man behind the counter with his heavy glasses would
have said, *No.* Elisabeth was no detective and she had not
rehearsed; she was a refugee from logic on alien territory and she
walked down Bayview Road for the second time without any idea
of what to say but knowing that she felt such a fool to herself that
she would have to knock on the door even if she was hoping that
no one would answer and she could go home.

★

In the event, there was a perfectly ordinary bell and insufficient delay before it was answered for her to phrase an innocuous question or fix a smile. The door opened quietly to reveal a sweet old man who stood there with his white hair standing up in a coxcomb and an apron over his clothes, looking as if he had been interrupted.

'Mr Fisher?' Her voice sounded to her own ears like a ghastly stage whisper which the whole street could have heard.

'Who says so?' he replied playfully.

'Oh . . . er . . .' It was on the tip of her tongue to say something daft, like *I've come about the room,* so that he would know immediately that she was an impostor and he would slam the door in her face and she could run away, but then inspiration struck in the form of her memory of that tatty little sticker, fixed to the back of a card, and she stumbled on. Such a small sticker, for a small object.

'I'm *so* sorry to bother you, but are you *the* Mr Fisher, the miniaturist?'

Something about the question appealed to him; he stood straighter, as if he had been saluted. 'I could be.'

'Oh good, wasn't at all sure, you see, but my name is Elisabeth Jonathan and the thing is my daughter's crazy for all that kind of thing . . .' (Oh Jesus, *what* kind of thing?) '. . . and she's ill and . . .'

'Do come in.' She followed him into the hallway and immediately saw what looked like an old curtain slung over the newel post of the facing stairs, catching her eye only because of the garish combination of black and orange and the fact that it was the only thing to notice apart from a pile of newspapers and colourless Artex paper on the walls, staying in her mind as the door closed and the hallway was plunged into darkness. Her eyes adjusted to the gloom soon enough for her to follow him left into the front room. It was stiflingly warm from the heat created by the spotlights which lit the series of miniature buildings ranged against the closed curtains and on the workbench at the rear. Somehow the view from the door was orchestrated to make the houses leap straight at the eye and after the brightness of the day outside it was like entering a theatre. She gasped.

'Your daughter, you said?'

'Yes, Maria, collects *little* things. Dying for a dolls' house,' Elisabeth gabbled.

'I *have* been known to make dolls' houses to order,' he was saying, 'but really I prefer to buy the shells and concentrate on the interiors. Furniture and figures are *really* me. More a miniaturist than an architect, how clever of you to know. How old is your daughter and how did you get my address?'

'Oh *gosh*,' Elisabeth gushed, all trepidation gone and invention flying high. 'She would *love* this. She's ten and she's had meningitis. I don't know *how* she got the address. I think it was stuck on the bottom of something, I don't *know*. Oh, this is *wonderful*.'

The last part was not feigned. Conscious though she was of the necessity to give this suddenly created child a name and, possibly, a personality, Elisabeth was genuine in her jaw-gaping surprise and her pleasure pleased him too, inspiring him to a level of almost boyish confidence. She had the feeling that both would burst into spontaneous laughter, any minute now. New best friends.

'This is what I'm working on at the moment,' he said, gesturing towards the workbench. 'Not a proper house, as such, more like a tableau. It's my haunted house, papier-mâché, moulded rather than built. Gives a nice texture, don't you think?' It was a wonky, off-centre model, more like a tall cottage lilting to the left. 'I shall paint it a nice sludgy colour with lots of ivy up the side walls. Rats in the basement and rather traditional ghosts.' He giggled. 'But when I have my exhibition, *this* will be the centrepiece.' Without actually touching her, he seemed to drag her across the room to the house with the Victorian façade which stood in the centre of the other seven ranged across the front of the curtains. Deftly he lifted a hinge to the right of the façade and opened the front to reveal the complicated interior on three floors. 'My brothel,' he said, giggling again. '*That'll* show them. All *they* ever make is silly shops and cottages. Mind you, I'm also making a shop.'

'They?'

'Miniature-makers. They get together at fairs, purely to squabble. They don't like the avant-garde. I'm above all that.'

'Oh.'

It was not the house he showed her now which had drawn her first, but the cabinet house to the left of it, with a stunning façade, reminiscent of something her father had once taken her to see. A closed house which would open to dreams and many rooms of splendour. That was what drew her eyes, but obediently she looked at the one he wanted her to admire. It was a beautiful, witty construction, reaching from the waist height of the table where it stood to her shoulder, so that she scarcely had to stoop to see a lady in her bath upstairs, a gentleman lounging downstairs, two whores, wearing corsets and little else, busy about their ironing in the kitchen, one with a cigarette hanging out of the corner of her mouth. She laughed with delight, looked closer, stopped laughing and then began again with a falsity she hoped he would not detect. All these little inch-high tarts were prepubescent girls. Not a bosom in sight. Except for the fat lady in the bath with her grotesquely painted face and she was the ugliest of them all.

'Fantastic,' Elisabeth said. 'My husband would *love* it, but my daughter prefers animals. You see, I wanted to get her a *stable*, no I didn't, I wanted to get her anything she could add to, something where she could go on collecting pieces to fill it. Do you *have* any daughters, Mr Fisher? They're a pain in the neck. *Oooh*, look at this!' She deliberately moved away to stand and gaze at the cabinet house. 'That's what I'd like her to have. And I promise she'd take care of it. Do you have any children, Mr Fisher?'

He was standing alongside her, carefully shutting the door of the brothel, only as much on his guard as he might have been with a big woman who looked as if she might be better at riding a horse than fingering delicate objects.

'The best thing you could do is bring your daughter along and let her see,' he suggested mildly. 'I expect she's very pretty, looking at you.'

'Not *yet*,' Elisabeth said, beginning to enjoy her own creation and imagining herself at ten. 'She's plump and she's shy and she has to wear specs. Do you have children, Mr Fisher? I'm so sorry, I asked you that before.'

She noticed then, before he stepped back from her, how those blue eyes were almost translucent, at the same time that she realised he was propelling her out of the room and striding ahead to open the door.

'Children, Mrs Jonathan, at *my* age? Grandsons, *yes*, courtesy of my son, and I must say, I'm glad they don't visit very often. It is absolutely *vital*, I find, for an artist to live alone.'

'Granddaughters would appreciate this more than sons, I suppose.'

'I wouldn't know, Mrs Jonathan. I used to teach little girls and most of them preferred games. There's no telling what they like.'

He had suddenly had enough of her. There was not going to be the offer of a cup of tea and a prolonged chat, which was disappointing in one way and a relief in another. She was blundering; she would not be able to keep this up; sweat trickled down the back of her neck and she wanted out, badly.

'I see what you mean. If I asked you to make something for her, I'd get it wrong, wouldn't I? I usually do.' She laughed heartily and slapped her thigh. If she did not look as stupid as she felt then Roland Fisher was blind. 'Perhaps I could get her to write to you?'

'Yes, of course. Get her some of the magazines and books. Bring her to see.'

He was not actually pushing her, but the movement forwards was inexorable. She was being ushered out into the gloomy hall, past the curtains and the newspapers, looking forward to the opening of the door, standing back to let him go first. *Click*, and a chink of daylight. Then, as the door opened, she felt something warm pressing against her calves, a large, hairy presence inserting itself between them, pushing towards the light. Elisabeth screamed. The door slammed shut. '*SHIT, DAMN, you BAS-TARD!*' His voice thick with fury. She heard the sound of a kick, then a yelp, felt the dog twist against her legs and try first to fling itself against the door, then turn back, twisting to avoid the kicks. Not her kicks; she was frozen to the spot and all movement ceased. Then the panting of breath and the dog scuttling away.

Suddenly she was alone in the gloom. In the near distance, from the dolls' house room, she could hear a crash and a scream of rage and the only thing she wanted to do was run. Instead she stumbled back in the same direction, following the sound. The warmth of the room hit her, brought tears to her eyes.

The dog was trying to get away. It had leapt up at the workbench and knocked down the papier-mâché house which lay on the floor with the animal crouching behind it, trying to seek refuge beneath the bench, unable to get in there because of the piles of newspaper. Roland Fisher was advancing, hammer in hand, the dog whimpering, the man growling.

'*No!*' Elisabeth yelled at full volume. '*No!*'

He stood in the middle of the spotlit room, with the claw hammer in his raised right hand. The hand remained as it was for a full second, then faltered. His shoulders slumped and he turned to face her. The dog had frightened her first; now it was the venom of the man. The dog became still, waiting to be beaten to pulp.

'Oh my word,' Elisabeth trilled. 'What a nuisance. Oh *do* put that thing down. You might damage something valuable.' She moved past him, picked up the haunted house and set it back on the bench. 'No harm done. You *naughty* dog.' The hairy thing slid by her and out of the room. She smiled brightly and adjusted her handbag. '*Awful* things, dogs, aren't they. Why on earth do you keep it?'

'I don't, it's my—' He checked himself and was abruptly fully in control. '—friend's.'

The hammer was replaced quietly on the workbench. This time, he saw her out without incident. Elisabeth gulped at the air like a fish coming to the surface, remembered to wave gaily at the door closing behind her in case he waited to see if she would, and set off up the street at a canter. Her steps were unsteady; as soon as she was three doors down, she stopped, looking for somewhere to sit. There was nowhere, so she moved on slowly. Nothing in her mind was able to compute. She was trying to remember the location of the bus stop. Turn right, one hundred yards down on the other side of the road. For once, the roar of the traffic was comforting. She began to walk quickly towards the crossing. Not a soul walked ahead or behind.

Then, in front of her, waiting to cross, she saw the woman. Elisabeth was moving quickly towards her at first simply because it was another human being and she wanted to be near one, any one. She was watching a white woman with heavy carrier bags dangling each side, no handbag, dark hair. The lights changed; the woman walked over the road to the island in the middle across two lines of grunting, fuming traffic.

The most significant thing about her was the awful colours of her skirt.

Elisabeth began to run.

The dog ran faster.

CHAPTER ELEVEN

She was almost at the traffic lights when the dog overtook her; the sight of it skittering past and up to the traffic lights made Elisabeth stop suddenly. She could see the figure of the woman in the patterned skirt over the top of the railings which bordered the road, standing in the middle. Then the realisation that that *bastard* had let out the dog to follow her and run into the road; sent it to chase her, bite her, but the thing was suicidal; she made a grab for it, too late.

The figure in the skirt was waiting for the next green light, while the northbound traffic in the section of road Elisabeth faced grunted into ominous life and began to shudder. She made a futile wave at it, as if to say, *stop, stop*, the gesture only resulting in her stumbling forward towards the railing, and as the cars began to move, the dog darted into the road without hesitation, prancing ahead as though it was deaf and blind. She could not look. There was the howl of a horn as an articulated truck reapplied the air brakes and the cab juddered to a halt with a squeal and a delayed *thump* as the car behind collided with the rear. The cab was halfway across the lights, the towed container slewed sideways across two lanes. Elisabeth could see neither the traffic lights themselves nor the central reservation, heard the crunch of car metal, no deathly squeal of pain. A motorcycle manoeuvred around the locked vehicles with callous speed and roared away on the offside. The truck remained in place; she began to cross in front of it, nervously, putting up a hand to ward off danger, just as the lights changed to green again and the driver of the lorry opened the door of the cab to wave his fist. He seemed a long way off the ground, shouting at her *bloody, fucking* dog, but the man from the car behind was running the length of the lorry, yelling even louder. Elisabeth jogged for the small island which separated the carriageways, feeling marginally safer as soon as she reached it, shielded by the bulk of the traffic.

The woman in the skirt was bending over while two heavy tins rolled away from the bag she had dropped in order to clutch the dog by the scruff of the neck. The traffic travelling west stopped, the first two drivers staring left at the stationary lorry with curiosity. There but for the grace of God go I.

The silly bitch was embracing the dog and the sight of it made Elisabeth want to puke. One glimpse of her face as Amy turned briefly with a vacant smile and Elisabeth knew who she was. She poked the stooped figure in the shoulder, waited the split second for her to turn again and then made rapid, shooing motions to the far side of the road. *Go, go.* Amy nodded; the three of them scuttled across like guilty children. It was not mutual recognition: Amy was responding only to the urgency of getting away from trouble and the instinct to run. The one shopping bag she still held bit into her wrist while her right hand gripped the fur on the back of the dog's neck, making her run at a crouch with her back bent, irritatingly determined all the same, never letting go of either. The deafening traffic alongside them began to move again in a succession of high-sided vehicles which blocked them from view of the lights and argument. In this fashion they moved about fifty yards, Amy leading, Elisabeth following, Amy scolding the dog and Elisabeth wanting to hit it. They turned left, into a side road flanked by empty ground on one side, a block of flats straight ahead with parked cars in front. A patch of green appeared at the side with a single, stubby tree entirely out of scale with the surroundings, the first tree Elisabeth had seen. Once closer, she could also see that the patch of grass was more earth than green and the tree not large enough to offer shade, but Amy seemed to regard it as a destination. She let go of the dog, growling an order. Then she tipped out the contents of the polythene bag, twisted it and tied it round the dog's neck in a makeshift collar, unselfconsciously absorbed in the task as if nothing else was important. Only when she was finished tying a knot did she look at Elisabeth directly for the first time. Closely, but not with any great interest.

What colour were those eyes of hers? Blue? Elisabeth could not remember. They seemed to have changed, or maybe it was the pallor of her skin, or the ghastly hair, brown with a hint of pale yellow roots, the opposite of the norm.

'Amy . . .' Elisabeth said weakly.

Amy shook her head, vigorously, nodded. Shrugged in resignation and wrapped her arms protectively over her chest. 'Shall we sit down, Elisabeth?' she said. 'My legs have gone wobbly. And I'm not even sure what we're running from. It gets to be a habit.'

They sat on the uninviting grass, Elisabeth out of breath with an unaccountable desire to scream. Amy adjusted her skirt, to save it from the dust in a superfluous gesture for such a hideous garment. She was not out of breath. Her pale calves, protruding from the skirt, had the firm muscles of regular exercise.

'Thank you for helping with the dog,' she said formally. 'Not everyone would have done that. It may be extremely ungrateful, but I'm not. I think it has a death wish.'

That makes two of you. Elisabeth was silent. She wanted to ask, *what the hell do you think you're doing*, but she could not find the words. 'Oh *fuck*,' was what she said. 'What a mess.'

Amy nodded agreement. She was recovered and her sang-froid was exasperating, especially since she did not seem to feel an immediate need to say anything more. The silence was filled by the panting of the dog in tune with Elisabeth's laboured breathing; she moved away from where it sat obediently, apparently pleased with itself. It was a disgusting dog and it was this sour observation which finally provoked her to speak.

'I think you're supposed to be wondering what the hell I'm

doing finding you in the middle of the road in this godforsaken area when you're supposed to be fucking dead,' Elisabeth said furiously. 'And nearly getting myself killed in the process. How can you just *sit* there?'

Amy plucked at a blade of grass, held it up to the light and examined it. She seemed so relatively relaxed that Elisabeth's exasperation grew, but instead of slapping that delicately large hand, she was arrested by the sight of chewed and grubby fingernails which filled her with a sudden empathy and pity. They were peculiarly similar to her own.

'You said I was like a cocker spaniel,' Elisabeth said. 'Perhaps that's why you remember me.'

Amy nodded again and Elisabeth wondered which of them was the least insane. Amy seemed to read her mind. She smiled an incongruous smile which was nevertheless as Elisabeth remembered it, enchanting.

'Yes, you are. The unusual-coloured variety. You may think I'm entirely mad.' She chewed at the grass root. 'And you may be right. Forgive me, but I've quite lost sight of how other people might see me. It doesn't seem relevant and I haven't really had time to think of it. And, for some reason I really can't explain, I was sort of expecting you. You, or someone.' She hesitated. 'Not at the edge of the road, you understand, but somewhere. Perhaps I was just expecting a face to appear in a window. So I'm very glad to see you, really. I scarcely knew you, but I rather liked you when I was alive. A trustworthy person, I thought, like a spaniel. I suppose you've been to see my father. I should have thought about him pushing the dog out. Quickest way to kill it, after all. Anyway, I'm glad to see you because I've got to tell someone about the man on the train.'

The tree offered a fraction of shade after all, but the heat Elisabeth felt was not on account of the sun. Perspiration oozed from her hair down the back of her neck. She pushed damp curls back off her forehead. The ground was hard. She thought of the willow tree in the garden of the Petty house and what a pitiful imitation this one was. The calm authority of Amy's tone made her stammer.

'I've got your handbag,' she began. 'There was a sticker . . .'

Amy clapped her hands; the dog leapt to its feet. 'You've got my handbag! How wonderful. You've no idea how much I've missed it.'

Again, Elisabeth wanted to scream. She began to scramble to her feet and found it surprisingly difficult. From a position on her knees with her knuckles supporting her weight, she spoke firmly. The face of the dog was level with hers and its breath was sour.

'Listen, Amy, I'm going to go and find a taxi out of here, go home and tell the police and your bloody husband where you are. You've caused mayhem. How selfish can you get? How *dare* you just disappear and leave everyone mourning you . . .' She was choking with anger, furious to find herself shouting in clichés.

Amy frowned, waved her hand dismissively. 'Don't be silly. Nobody will have shown the slightest sign of mourning me. At least I don't think so. *Please* sit down,' she said humbly.

Elisabeth sat. There was such palpable truth in the statement about not being mourned that it quite took her breath away. It was not the pathos of the sentiment and her own inability to contradict it, but the cool sadness with which it was made.

'I'll try to be helpful, shall I?' Amy said. 'Oh God, I'm hungry.' She hunted amongst the shopping strewn on the ground, found nothing. Elisabeth dug into her own handbag and found the pastilles she had bought in the shop, broke the tube and handed Amy the half.

'Thank you.' The dog, which had been sitting indifferently between them, sniffed. 'Not for you,' Amy said. 'Your teeth are bad enough as it is. Where was I?'

'The beginning.'

'The beginning? Oh no, I can't do that. The beginning's all too long ago. Excuse me, it's difficult to talk to a human being. I'm better talking to dogs. I should have said how nice to see you. My manners have gone completely, you see. It's amazing how quickly it happens.'

Elisabeth tried to breathe regularly. *Remember this woman was legendary in her own household for being* thick. *And she was beaten.*

There may be precious little difference between being terminally stupid,
abused and downright bonkers. Whatever it was, it was infectious.

'Yes I do see, Amy. Are you all right? I mean, not ill?'

'Of course I'm not all right. I'm dead. And you're quite entitled
to consider me mad, but please don't join all the others in thinking
me stupid. My logic might be warped from time to time, but it
does exist, even if I'm more inclined to act in response to instinct.
Don't you? I can't imagine it was purely logical deduction from
the contents of my handbag that brought you to this wasteland.
Wouldn't be my first choice. Instinct must have played a part.'

Elisabeth was dumbfounded. She kept her eyes down and
sucked on a fruit pastille, felt Amy's hand touch her arm.

'It was kind of you, Elisabeth, as well as silly, to make this expedition, for whatever reason you've done it. I'm grateful. And I'm
sorry to burden you with this, but unless I know that you *aren't*
going to go straight back to Douglas, I shall go and lie down in the
middle of that road, is that clear? I don't see why you should care
if I do, but please understand I'm perfectly capable of doing it.'

Elisabeth nodded.

'Besides, you owe me something. No, that's wrong, you owe me
nothing. Perhaps Mr Box does. Douglas should never have been
encouraged to start off that libel action. That was the catalyst. I
might have been able to stick it out if it wasn't for that. But I had
a secret, you see, and I really thought the libel action would smoke
it out. My father.' She plucked at the grass. 'He taught art and
crafts to schoolgirls. He was convicted of trying to have sex with
them. He served twelve years in prison, disappeared and remained
disappeared long after I found out. Then he got in touch with me
after I married Douglas. He was ill, he said. Wanted to meet me in
secret. So I did. So secretive, you wouldn't believe. Worse than
meeting a married lover.'

Elisabeth found herself blushing.

'I couldn't risk anyone finding out about him. You know what
people do to paedophiles. Stoning, for starters, newspaper exposure, house burnt down. I believed my father when he said he was
innocent. I believed him because he built me a dolls' house and

gave me a dog and because my mother was such a liar. I believed him because I never stopped loving him. You don't, you know. I believed him when he said the libel action would smoke him out and set the hounds of hell on him. I believed that it would be all my fault. The only thing I didn't believe was when he said he was only in prison because of Douglas. He only says that in his sleep. Then he wakes up coughing.'

The fruit pastille was in the soggy state where it stuck against teeth. Elisabeth was all aches, pains and information-overload. 'You've lost me.'

'Douglas has something to do with this,' Amy said, looking at her as if she expected her to know and this was a piece of obvious, universal knowledge. 'But I don't know what. I don't know what to believe any longer. We'd grown fond of one another, Dad and I. He's very persuasive and I'm very weak. He said he would be my secret refuge for ever. He said the only unconditional love you ever get is from your father. He said I would need a refuge one day, and I did.'

There was a long, bewildered silence. Elisabeth peeled back the foil on the half-packet of pastilles and ate the last two. Her stomach rumbled and bile rose in her throat. She could only recall the man with his dolls' houses and the venom in his eyes and believe him capable of anything; she was reeling from indigestible facts and now the sweat had dried, chills crept between her shoulderblades and made her want to scratch. Staring ahead, she could see the route they had come and hear the murmur of traffic. Somewhere over there was a sportsground and a school, according to that lying, monosyllabic map which never mentioned the lack of trees and the real dimensions of the lethal roads.

'I want you to find something out for me, and I want you to do something for me,' Amy was saying. Her authority and the rapidity of her speech were nothing short of miraculous. 'Get today's *Times* for a start. Third left in the second row of photos of people killed in my train crash is a woman. Can't remember her name because I never knew it. She was in my carriage. She didn't die by accident. She had a man with her who was so furious with her he was ready to throttle her in public. Tell somebody. That man killed her. There was no reason for her to die. And he took her ring. Nobody should get away with that. I can live with a lot of things, but I can't live with that.'

Elisabeth got to her feet, head dizzy. She clutched at the branches of the tree which was more of a shrub, felt the brittleness of twigs.

'That's the most important thing,' Amy continued, dry and businesslike. 'And then, if you don't mind, I would like you to find out what it was my father was supposed to have done. I've always believed most of what he says and I can't any more. I can pay you, but not much. And you don't have to keep quiet about me for ever and ever. Just until I know. Give me a phone number. He hasn't got a phone.'

'Here's a card. Got my number and address. Phone the mobile. Where are you going to put it? Oh for God's sake, this is crazy.' The image of the fortunate, docile Stepford wife with so little to say and no will of her own had receded into a red mist and left nothing but dithering confusion. She watched her take the card and stuff it into her bra without thanks. 'And *why*,' Elisabeth spluttered with a return of the fury which rose to hide her own feeling of being the stupid one and the one entirely out of control, 'do you imagine I'll do any of this? Why the hell should I?'

'I don't know why. Because you've got this far. Because I might well die if you don't.'

'Of what this time?' Elisabeth snapped. 'Insomnia? A dog with bad breath? A broken heart?'

Amy smiled her enchanting smile. 'Oh, that happened some time ago. It's lasted well, all things considered. You can have bad teeth and still manage to eat. There's not much of my heart left and I'm so sorry. I've no right to expect anything at all. You'd better go home and do exactly what you think best. I'd like it if you'd give me a couple of days' grace, though.'

They were both on their feet. Amy looked at the strewn shopping, perplexed by it until she found among it a roll of pedal bin liners, put everything in one, including the rest of the roll. They began to walk, slowly, Amy holding the dog by the polythene loop she had made.

'What I don't understand,' Elisabeth said, adopting Amy's dry tone, 'is why all this stuff with your father made you take this overdramatic turn. Awkward, yes, but surely not the end of the world. You could have told Douglas.' She had a momentary, vivid memory, not only of that willow tree, but of the bruises on Amy's arms in the coldness of spring. Perhaps telling Douglas was not an option.

'I should have told Douglas,' Amy said. 'Right at the beginning when my father first wrote, I should have told him and trusted him. But I didn't. I listened to my father instead; I was overjoyed to see him. I was biding my time, but secrets get to be habits, don't they? They become elaborate and impossible to explain.'

Again, Elisabeth blushed.

'But it wasn't because of my father that I walked away from the crash. That wouldn't have been nearly enough. There was far more to it than that. I'm sorry,' Amy repeated. 'Because I explain things to dogs, I forget I haven't explained them to human beings.'

'I thought you ran away,' Elisabeth said, speaking louder as the infernal traffic noise increased, 'because he beat you up.'

Amy stopped so suddenly they collided with the dog sandwiched between them. How Elisabeth loathed that dog, even though she was glad it was alive. Amy's face was pink; tears welled in her eyes and spilled down her cheeks. 'But that's *ridiculous*,' she said. 'Beat *me*? I didn't go *because* of Douglas. I went *for* Douglas. I went because they were too strong for me. I went because I thought he really would be better off without me. Can't you see that?'

They were proceeding down the main road now, with the traffic roaring, *yeeow, yeeow*, alongside. No wonder nobody ever came out. Elisabeth had an unshakeable conviction that if she did not do exactly as she was told, then Amy would do exactly as she said, go and lie down in the middle of it, until she was like a squashed hedgehog on a country road.

They reached a bus shelter where the flimsy walls, made only for protection from rain, failed to baffle the vibrating noise.

'What else?' Elisabeth yelled.

'Give me two days,' Amy yelled back. 'I'll phone you.'

'What?'

'Two days . . . PROMISE?'

'OK, I PROMISE.'

'This is your BUS. You will be all right, won't you?'

That was the last Elisabeth remembered. A look of genuine concern from a woman with nothing to lose. Concern for *her*. The bus emerged out of a distant line and drew into the layby created for it and nothing else, with a desultory efficiency. The doors slammed open, *whump*, and then as soon as she was on the first step, propelled there by a shove, the doors *whumped* shut behind her and the whole edifice was moving before she fumbled for the fare. Handbag, purse inside handbag, coins inside purse, dammit, coins were useless, fingers were useless. A tin of dog food had found its way in there; she hated dogs. Swaying on her feet, she found the purse and some pound coins. The machine spat a receipt; Elisabeth was propelled to the back as the bus gathered speed, sat with her handbag on her knees. It weighed a ton and seemed to grow before her eyes.

Get home. Phone . . . *who*? Who would believe this? Who could be trusted with this? No one.

Amy slammed into the house and went straight through to put on the kettle, looking for him, hoping she would not find him, trying to stop the furious tears. *How DARE she?* She took the polythene-bag collar off the dog and pointed it at the garden. Mid-afternoon; he would be keeping station upstairs, waiting for the children to come home, so he could watch. The door to his workroom was shut; the house was quiet, the door out the back open. By the dog's kennel she could see the dog's bowl, half full of food she had not left. The dog strained towards it. She went out into the yard, looked at it, brought it back inside and threw it in the bin. She fed the animal from one of the remaining tins. Went upstairs past his silent door, into her room.

The money she had left in the wardrobe was gone. The other

half under the mattress was still there. It was only a matter of time before he found it. She took a hundred pounds, picked up the rope for the dog, went downstairs and made herself eat. Bread, butter and mousetrap cheese in large quantities, unpalatable, workmanlike food to line the stomach and give her ballast. At the table she wrote a note for her father.

I am taking the dog to a safe home and may be back late . . .

There was more to say than that, surely. It might be better if they communicated in writing. Questions, such as why do you hate me? Is it me you hate, or is it Douglas? Was it me you wanted to destroy, or is it him? She waited at the table for the afternoon to wane, drumming her fingers and crying fat, useless tears. Heard him cough his way down the stairs, as if deliberately alerting her to his presence before he went into the dolls' house room and shut the door. She *could* be calm; she had proved it. She had to plan the journey.

The bus took forty-five minutes, depending on its timetable and the traffic. The trains went from Charing Cross on the hour. The journey was an hour. The walk home across the fields would be half an hour. She wanted to arrive so long after darkness that everyone would be asleep.

Going home now, she told the dog. Running short of time. She won't tell anyone tonight, I'm sure of that. Amy fetched the coat from where it hung neatly on the back of her bedroom door, slipped it on and there was another person. The olive green coat lent her a respectability which would not bear the close inspection it was not going to get. Accompanied by a dog on a rope lead, she could pass as a country eccentric of the kind who had no time for makeup or vanity, even to do credit to her dog. She had seen far worse.

Quick, quick, the bus . . .

The mirror image of herself reflected in the doors of the bus told a different story, but not so different that it worried her. An accurate depiction of a poor, drab woman, prematurely aged from thirty-five to fifty, with badly scuffed shoes and an inconsistently good coat only slightly too warm for the time of year, sitting in a half-empty bus at the time of day when all the mysterious occupants of the hinterland were travelling back from the centre rather than towards it. She stroked the fabric of the coat, which was soft, with satisfyingly deep pockets for the house keys, the wodge of toilet roll, and the small proportion of the money which was not tucked into her bra with Elisabeth's card. A person travelled lighter without a handbag, armed with nothing but a bottle of water and a plastic dish in the standard-issue polythene carrier, without which life was untenable. Who needed a handbag?

The excitement grew; she let herself dream. The house would be empty; she would be able to range freely, touch everything. No one would see her or guess her presence; it would be easy to explore, take pictures of it with an imaginary camera in order to make a volume of memory she could keep. Each night away from it, she climbed the stairs and tried to remember what lay behind each door; she lived in the garden, looked into the round room and lingered beneath the tree. She knew every inch of that house better than anyone else. Whoever was there, she would be able to hide from them; there were so many nooks and crannies for a ghost, and that was what she was. A light, lithe spectre, able to slip in and out of windows, the invisible woman. She might even be able to purloin her favourite pair of shoes from their room; she might raid the bathroom for the night cream, collect fresh underwear . . . Dream on. The dead were allowed to dream. *Home*. See home, just *once*, please, please, be as you are and let me in just this final once.

Let me see Douglas, once. Hear his voice.

The dream diminished at Trafalgar Square. Crossing through the sheer density of the crowds seemed impossible, although the details of their appearance were reassuring and made her realise she was the soul of nondescript in comparison. In the window of McDonald's she could see dreadlocks and pierced noses, black battledress and torn leather, ancient denim and shimmering pink, crowded together as if marshalling for a riot. They had nothing to do with her; she had never been one of them; she had never drunk her coffee alongside creatures such as these, even before she died. It was only the dog made her feel substantial, straining at the rope leash in pursuit of another dog crouched in a shop doorway with an owner already clad in a sleeping bag, ready for the night. Amy dropped a five-pound note in the begging bowl, more for the dog than the man, and dragged her own beast across the road into the station. Sanity returned. It was past rush hour, shops closed, concourse still busy. A crowd gathered beneath the board which showed the destinations of the trains, waiting for information and ready to canter in the direction ordered, a small queue for tickets. She stood in line with the dog, listening to the snippets of conversation, watching the others, finding herself looking out for a familiar face and not sure if she was relieved to find none, realising with a sickening dread how difficult this was.

It was the sound of the trains, not the disembodied, anonymous engines she had been hearing every day, but real trains, close. The sound of her own voice, which requested the return ticket in a perfectly normal tone and said thank you when it appeared on her side of the glass, was as alien as her own ability to pick it up and move away from the queue towards the right platform, walking steadily with the sulking dog. The homesickness still burned like acid indigestion; there was no choice about this journey, none at all; it was absolutely inevitable, only there was something she had failed to anticipate. The train.

The train was enormous. It sat there at the platform, making its rumbling, whirring, ready-to-depart noises. She stopped at an open door, one hand in her pocket, crushing the ticket, fingers mobile, the rest of her paralysed. It was a monster and she was supposed to get inside its belly; once she was inside it, it was going to *crash*. She could feel the vibration of jarring impact, feel the weight of her handbag pressing into her chest, smell the burning and the stink of diesel. See the elephant man with his phone, covered with stuff from the rack, hear the screams and taste the blood in her mouth from where she had bitten her lip so hard it had bled down the back of her throat. *Oh Christ*, she could not get on this train.

But the dog knew. Shivering on the bus, hating every mile, trying to make itself smaller and smaller beneath the seat, and here, it strained at the rope leash, panting to board and whining with joy. Eyes wide open, refusing to focus, Amy let it lead her, almost pull her up the steep step into the second-last carriage and into the seat nearest the door where she sat, trembling uncontrollably. The dog settled under the table at her feet, as if it travelled by train every day and knew all the rules about how dogs should make themselves inconspicuous. She could feel the warm body of it against her legs and kid herself that it was offering protection. Jolt; movement. They were close to the lavatory, convenient for vomiting. She was in there, heaving up the bread and cheese as soon as the train began to move. The face in this mirror was full of terror; she was frightened at the sight of it.

The dusk outside was a blessing; she made herself look out of the window and fix her eyes on the lights as the train rumbled over the bridge. When the beast gathered speed, and the lights became a blur, she closed her eyes. With eyes shut, she could feel safer, even with her hands clutched into white fists on the arms of the seat, waiting for the crash. Then she opened them again, because if she could not see, she could hear more and the sound of the train was painfully loud. Deliberately, she made herself stare at the other passengers she could see if she leaned sideways and looked down the aisle. *Got to get you home, dog, too, quick, before you get murdered.*

The man in the next seat opposite looked like a monkey, with a small wizened face. The woman next to him looked a marmoset. The ticket collector coming down the aisle was the ferret. Once this was established, she would breathe. She pressed her eyes open. The home station was small enough to miss in the dark; she must not miss it. The watch told her there was time to worry about that and she did not believe it. She looked again at the passengers as they emptied out. A twitching grasshopper, a girl with legs like a newborn colt, a fat woman with widely spaced brown eyes over an enormous bridge of nose, a good-natured cow. It was not insulting to be called a cow. Cows were nice. Breathe in, breathe out, slowly. The weakness would have made her slow to get off, but the dog was having no argument. Out from under the seat, discreetly at first then dragging her by the rope lead. Then over the bridge to the exit with a few others, not that late. The darkness had the fresh look of novelty. She could remember the other kind of relief she used to recognise when she had got as far as this on the route back from London. Relief, first, and the dread coming second as an aftertaste as she looked for her car. She could never remember where she had put her car, because the configuration and number of cars always changed between the time she parked and the hours later when she collected. She looked for it now, surprised not to find it. Puzzled to see the dead remnants of flowers in a pile by the exit in a normally tidy place. A couple of doors slammed as the late-working commuters hurried away.

Her car would be long gone. Someone efficient like Caterina would have collected it. Caterina would be at the house and Amy did not like that. Somehow, it took some of the urgency out of the mission. So far, all means of transport to get her this far had seemed excruciatingly slow; now she had lost the impatience.

She wandered down the High Street unselfconsciously. She knew how people failed to recognise someone they did not expect to see and she was aware of looking markedly different from her normal appearance. The dog itself was a disguise; there had never been the need to bring a dog into town. Nor had her hair ever been this colour, or her face this thin or her body clad in nondescript green. Amy preferred whites, blues, creams; it was Caterina who suggested the beige linens and brown silks which suited her own sallowness.

All the same, if she skulked in shadows someone might notice her in this place which reeked of neighbourhood watch and good citizenship; if she moved like a person living in one of the neat town houses that ran off the High Road, out with a dog for an evening stroll before the rain, no one would turn a hair. The dog was as well-behaved as if it had come from one of those houses and never been anywhere off the leash. Neither of them behaved like runaways. She did not linger by the windows of the smart pub, even though no one ever looked out of these mullioned windows; people only looked in. That was where she had seen Caterina having a drink with Dell from the Animal Sanctuary and the other man. She got to the end of the street and set off down the road out of town, keeping to the pavement until that ran out and the street-lights stopped. Then she walked along the verge. Two miles was not far to a person used to long walks. A couple of cars passed. She walked on without turning, facing the oncoming traffic. The air smelt of rain.

'Rain would not be suitable,' she told the dog. 'Rain would make us wet and miserable and heavy. I hope it doesn't rain.' That would be the only thing she would care about; the prospect of rain and its effect on her shoes. Her mood fluctuated between weariness and exhilaration; nothing mattered apart from seeing home. Not going home; seeing it, just *seeing* it. The willow tree would shelter her from the rain; the rain would muffle sound. Rain was not such a bad idea. Amy hummed as she walked along, looking ahead, swinging the lead and enjoying the sound of the dog's paws on the tarmac as it trotted beside her. They were both proud of the mended leg.

At the next bend, where the may blossom was covering the road when last she had seen it, she turned into the fields. The fields were riddled with footpaths and dark or light she knew them all, had walked too many dogs to ignore any of the routes. Including dogs that were best walked at night, because they were so ugly and scarred they would frighten the other walkers. And Dilly; poor Dilly, who preferred to walk at night. The smell was intoxicating, peaty, acrid, sweet, dispelling the memory of other smells. There was nothing to fear in this kind of night and she had never been afraid of it. It was hers to command. She entered a copse of trees and shivered with sheer pleasure at the sound of the branches, like the sound of waves on a seashore. Perhaps that would be the only way to dispel all memory of this place; live somewhere else with equally soothing sounds, like the sea. The screech of a bird of prey cut across the whispering of the trees. It did not alarm her. Something always had to die in order for something else to live. Death was so often for the greater good of the living, including her own.

I couldn't save you, Douglas, not without making you hate me. I couldn't expose you to the wreckage of all you hold dear . . . those others were there long before me. Stop thinking of him. Put him entirely out of mind. 'Listen,' she said to the dog. 'Listen, isn't it lovely? When we get home, you have to be very, very quiet. No barking.'

Walking up the valley, she could see the outline of the stables and veered to the right, keeping her distance. If Jimmy was there, his ears were sharp. She knew how the alarm system worked and she knew how to evade it, just as she knew how not to set the dogs barking, if she was careful. Supposing she had lost the knack? That was for later. Amy cut across the dip at the back of the garden and slipped between the branches of the willow tree. There was the house, glowing white. There were scudding clouds racing across the moon which glowed like a huge oil lamp swathed in muslin, the forgiving light of it changing the aspect and shape of the building and never revealing it as less than beautiful.

It's only a house. Not it isn't. It's my house and a special house. Mine . . . why did you drive me out?

She sat on the grass, next to the obedient dog. Sometimes dogs needed a big shock to make them obedient; they needed that bit of fear. *Like a woman.* Who said that? Douglas, are you there? Amy whispered to the dog, 'Let me tell you about this house. *He* liked it because it was never finished. Because it's half a house with one magnificent room. See that? The way the front there comes out in one great big, sexy curve of windows that no one else sees? There should be a drive sweeping up to this, but there isn't. They built a dome, but it isn't a dome any more. It's half a dome. A folly, they call it, with all sorts of bits added on.' She fondled the underneath of the dog's chin where the hair was grey, the only other place it liked to be touched. Jimmy would sort out the ear infection, one day soon. 'It has *historical importance*,' she whispered. 'Like any hellfire club, dowager house, yeah, yeah, yeah. Some lord kept his llamas here, and his *snakes*, would you believe? It was always a menagerie surrounding that room. See the lights at the back? Someone upstairs. A new addition, *darling*, circa 1950. *Ruined* it.'

In the hushed mimic of her mother-in-law's voice, Amy realised that something was terribly wrong. Light was supposed to come out of the big, curved window, shine on to the steps and reveal what was within, but the steps down to the garden were dark. She had never once closed those curtains in the whole of her tenure, never wanted to do anything other than rip them down or, failing that, finally regard their presence with indifference as long as they slumped to one side and did not interfere. That room was supposed to be lit with sunlight or moonlight, so that you could see the fox slink across the garden, the grey owl as it cruised away, the mole as it made a hole, the willow tree as it grew and bent, as if vexed by concern, under the weight of snow. You should be able to see all your friends at once and hear their noises, scuttling, preying, fighting, growing, dying, creaking, barking. The windows of the grand room looked back at her like big, dead eyes, reflecting nothing but the oil-lamp moon and her own, uncomprehending stare.

'Shhhh, *siiit.*'

This to the dog, who sensed the acuteness of her distress. Then there was a light. The French doors opened and two people stepped out, one smaller and stockier, the other, taller than he, supporting him by the elbow and shrieking '*Whoopsadaisy*' in a high voice as he stumbled. The fraction of light framed them nicely. They were backlit like sculptures in a museum as they kissed.

CHAPTER TWELVE

Her first reaction on seeing the black wall of curtains hiding the room was one of outrage. It was as if someone had put a filthy old blanket over the whole house and shrouded it. The whole point of this odd house was the light released through those vast windows, streaming in from the outside during the day and returning the compliment by filtering out from the room and over the steps more gently at night, so that the house and the land were all part of a whole, reflecting each other. To blacken the windows at night was to make the house small and mean and the people inside it shameful prisoners. To close those curtains was to despise it.

The reflection of the hazy moon in the dark windows mattered more than the sight of her husband and Caterina letting themselves out of the French windows like a pair of conspirators, only to embrace, like lovers. *Like lovers*; the phrase had resonance. Was it possible to be *like* lovers without actually *being* lovers? There were newspaper reports which suggested it was perfectly feasible and frequently desirable. It was sometimes politic to act like a lover. They looked so good together, these two, like ideally paired celebrities posed for the camera. Seen from the distance of a hundred feet, backlit by that mean little fraction of light escaping from behind, it was not so much a kiss as a hug in which his body was awkwardly stooped and each rested a chin on the other's shoulder in a brief contact from which he pulled away, quickly. She knew every nuance of his movements; an embrace from Douglas was an all-enveloping, wholehearted, arms and legs, rib-crushing exercise with nothing perfunctory about it. When he stood away from his stepsister, he staggered slightly, as if he was drunk or exhausted. Yes, he was a little drunk; there was a certain way he muddled his feet when he was like that, and all the same, Amy was breathless with hurt. It did not make any difference if he was influenced by whisky and resisting the affection he was being offered; the fact remained, he had still entered the circle of Caterina's graceful arms and stayed there, however briefly. She seemed to be scolding him now; she pointed him back into the room as she might have directed a disobedient pet. Amy was too far away to hear the words; only watched as he went back inside, followed after an interval by her. The curtain was drawn back again, leaving the blank wall of glass, dutifully reflecting the moon. Drawing those curtains and shutting out the sky was sacrilege. The room was an observatory. And he had let it happen; allowed her room to be transformed into a giant grave, in the same callous way he refused to mourn her. What *was* it she had wanted? Comfort? Amy looked at the luminous dial on her watch, a present from him. She was early, like a guest arriving an hour too soon and embarrassing a host still in the throes of preparation. She sat on the bench and fondled the left ear of the dog, remembering not to touch the right. Douglas was like that, too, bits of him where he did not wish to be explored, ticklish bits where the touching was agony even if it was accompanied by the giggles of the tormented which sounded almost like laughter.

'Sit. Stay still.' The dog leaned against the bench, content to be stroked. Amy had invented a history for the animal, based on observation and imagination. A country dog, unused to roads or leads, strong in bone and sinew from a well-nurtured youth and only neglected in later life, it would learn to trust again once it was settled here. It was a curable dog and a good listener. Hidden behind the curtains, the house was still busy. It was not bedtime yet. They would have to wait.

'Do you know, I once thought that woman was my friend,' she told the dog. 'She seemed to be, at first. Probably when she thought I was just a flash in the pan. Better be nice to stepbrother's new woman; she won't last, they never do. But he married me. They took their time, she and her mother. They are the people he loves best in the world. They were his boyhood; they were the ones who nursed him through sickness and forgave him everything; they can do no wrong in his eyes. He wouldn't hear ill of them. He simply couldn't.'

The dog leaned closer, warming her legs. The hair of it would grow thick in winter.

'I can't remember when they started. They hate the dogs, you see. They hated his passion for dirty, hairy, four-legged things. They thought he would stop, see sense and start to live a gracious life. Something like that. They were sick to death of dogs. His father started the sanctuary; his stepmother must have hoped that it would end when he died, but it didn't. She might have thought it would end when he married me, but it didn't. It got worse because of me. I should feel sorry for her. She married a man who cared only for his son, his dogs and his first wife, in that order, and then she finds she's stuck as the dependant of a stepson who still cares more about dogs than anything else and is planning to spend money she thinks should be hers on new stables and a charitable foundation. All that. She's a brilliant actress. Where was I? I know, I was saying, I can't remember when it started.'

The rain began, soft and gentle, pattering against the leaves of the willow tree in a benign, musical drizzle. It was a sound that reminded her of small feet running away, and it was enough to convince anyone of the existence of fairies and elves coming out to play. How could they sit inside that room and hear the rain without wanting to watch it sparkle on the glass? What strange, foreign creatures they were.

'First there was his mother, looking at me with her big, sad eyes. *What a shame,* she would say. You were so pretty when you first came here and now you aren't. Look at you, covered in dog hair. That isn't the way you should look if you want to keep a man.

Can't you cook something better than this, instead of spending all the time in the garden or with the dogs? I laughed and tried to tell him, but he said don't criticise her, darling, she's had enough of that. Standard mother-in-law stuff. But it wasn't. Then, when he was away once, it changed. *He doesn't love you*, she'd say. There's only one person he's ever loved, you're useful, that's all. Because you love dogs and a man has to have a nice, solid wife for the good of his image. Can't have people thinking he fancies little boys. Or his sister.'

The rain stayed soft and the tree shielded them both. The curve of the white house glowed. Upstairs, a light showed. When Douglas was drunk, he took himself to bed, alone. She shuddered, crossed her arms across her chest.

'So I asked Caterina, what does your mother mean? Caterina only came at weekends, not always then, so I was slow to notice the malice in her. I don't know what on earth my mother means, she said at first. I knew about my father by then; I had plenty of secrets to carry around. I had his voice in my ears, telling me how much Douglas would despise him and me for belonging to him and I knew Douglas cannot bear people who hurt others.'

The dog sat closer.

'It was then Caterina told me that she and Douglas were lovers. Told me how he had seduced her when she was little more than a child. Said, in her polite way, not to worry, that was what men did, but she had often wondered since why it was that all the women he fucked, before me, should be her size, her shape, her colouring. She told me this as if she was reciting a recipe for beef stew and it didn't matter at all.'

The rain penetrated the leaves after a while. Amy felt a single, cold drop hit the top of her head and roll down her face like an isolated tear. She caught the drop in her mouth. It felt sweet.

'Oh, I knew they loved him. I just didn't realise what *kind* of love, how strong it was; how essential to him. So what would you have done? These were the risks, dog. If I confronted him with *that* confession, either he would say it was true and he never loved me, which would be the worst. Or he would think that silly little

me had made it up to get attention and Caterina would gasp and
stretch her eyes and say what a wicked liar I was, she never said
any such thing. Or he would believe me and send both of them
packing, which would break his heart. They are his life; I was the
recent addition. The interloper. So I said nothing. Then someone
started sabotaging the dogs. It's no wonder, is it, that when all that
nonsense came up in the newspapers about Douglas buggering
dogs and being cruel to them, I could hardly take it seriously. It
wasn't like the Caterina stuff, because there was absolutely no
prospect of it being true. And I think I know who started it, but I
couldn't say that, either. I behaved as normal, only quieter. Then
I began to think, if I went away, everything would be better.
Everything would go back to normal without me. I think we've sat
here long enough, don't you?'

She got up and stood behind the bench, holding on to the warm
wood, stretching her calves and looking at the watch. Another
light went out upstairs to the far left. Mother-in-law's room; she
slept like a log. Amy attached the dog's rope to the bench and
sidled through the branches of the tree. It was all their fault. If they
had not blackened out the room, she might have been content to
look through the windows, check from that safe distance that
everything was the same. Now she had to get inside. There was a
problem with the raincoat, which rustled louder than the rain
when she moved, so she took it off and left it with the dog. That
way it would know she was coming back.

'*Stayyy* . . .'

The one advantage to those viciously blind windows was the
certainty that no one would see her walk across the lawn of wet
grass. It was springy beneath her feet; she wanted to dawdle and
take off her shoes to feel the damp. The night was hers before the
five a.m. train, all the time in the world. So she held the shoes and
walked the short distance to the steps, disapproving of the short
cut of the lawn. It looked as if it had been taken to the barber's and
she preferred the grass long and shaggy with clover. Near the
steps she trod on something sharp and stifled a scream, sat down
on the step and cradled her foot, brushing away the glass. No

visible damage. She put the shoes back on and winced with pain. It concentrated the mind. This was *her* house; she could enter at will. Passing by the curtains to get round the side, she could see no trace of light from the room.

The back door would be locked. Caterina or her mother would have seen to that; they disliked her preference for an open door and a house where there was nothing to steal. The spare keys Amy never declared and kept entirely for herself were underneath the flowerpot halfway down the side of the house, hidden by an evergreen azalea which did not mind the shade. She felt her way in the pitch dark with cautious ease. The pitter-patter of the rain was louder than her own footfall.

Were they right, Douglas? Did you ever want silly me?

In a way, she did not care in the least if she was heard, and she had the firm conviction that she was invisible. People *were* invisible inside their own houses; latterly she had crept from place to place inside this house and they had ceased to notice her existence. Had he been concerned by her self-effacement? Yes, of course he had. Concerned, inquisitive, and finally impatient. A wounded bear, blundering around, hurt, unable to ask explanations for the inexplicable. Angry at the persistence of her nervous quietness, furious at the accusations of cruelty.

Amy turned on the kitchen light inside the porch. There was none of the usual mess of boots and shoes; instead there was a neat rack of carefully arranged walking sticks, like something out of a magazine. If Caterina had been in residence for any length of time, there would be no dogs, in deference to her allergies, but all the same, the lack of them surprised her. It was as if a large piece of furniture had been removed, leaving a gap. Or as if the walls had been painted a different colour. She gazed round the kitchen. It was the same room and it was no longer hers. There were no flowers dying gracefully in the jug on the sill, no Post-its by the sink with her shopping lists; the table was clear of litter; there were no pots, pans, plates waiting to be put away, but never put away because she would need them again soon. Nothing lingered in the sink; every surface was clear and the dolls' house was relegated to the furthest corner, the roof of it bent as if it had been dropped. She looked inside; all the figures had been removed. A new clock ticked on the wall, replacing the other which had never functioned but stayed because it belonged. Amy's sense of outrage grew; she wanted to cry, bit her lip instead. She turned off the light and went down the corridor to the living room, careless of the sound she made. A single lamp glowed in the furthest corner of the room. Someone had forgotten to turn it off. It was enough to show the differences. The room was smaller with the curtains drawn; it smelled of Douglas's cigars, with an underlying, chemical smell of strong cleansing fluid. The chairs and the sofa were more formally arranged; the carpet was straight. An ornate mirror had been placed over the fireplace instead of the picture which had hung there. A second-rate painting Douglas approved for its sheer size and sentimental depiction of a pack of hounds streaming across a field in pursuit of a long-escaped fox. He had liked these dappled dogs, however amateur and highly coloured their depiction. They had appealed to him. There were other additions – a shawl over a chair, ornaments on the mantelpiece. It was like an elegant museum.

Amy went upstairs. She held the banister and walked carefully at the edge, knowing how some of the stairs would creak like pistol shots if she walked in the centre, but still not much caring if anyone heard. She was dead; they were not expecting her; they were wiping away all traces of her occupation; she hated them. Her foot hurt and felt sticky inside her shoe. It would be nice to find alternative shoes.

The spare room which Caterina habitually used was at the furthest end of a long corridor opposite Mother's room. Facing her was the bathroom she and Douglas used, with the door standing ajar. From the room next to it, she could hear him snoring rhythmically. It was a test of love to sleep with a man who snored. There were the three doors in a row – bathroom, bedroom and his study in this corner of the odd, rectangular extension, all with a view over the garden and the willow tree.

Bathroom first. How he teased her about what he called the

lotions and potions and marvelled how she needed so many. Look at my side of the cabinet, he said. Shaving brush, razor and soap, that's all and there soon won't be room for that. Now there was nothing but the shaving stuff. All her night creams, day creams, eye creams, acquired for the sheer pleasure of their exquisite smells and textures, her grown-up playthings in an otherwise non-indulgent life, all gone. It felt like theft. There was a small airing cupboard in this room, where she kept her underwear; Amy looked: empty. She wanted to shriek *thief, thief,* but that temptation passed and she felt utterly bereft. There was no anger in her wondering how soon after her disappearance it had been before the eradication of her presence, her taste, her methods of doing things, her garments, her toiletries and probably all her clothes. They might have begun the process within hours of the news, probably had. It wouldn't have taken long. The items were not so numerous, however precious they were, and the traces of herself so easily dispelled it was laughable. Useless to think she would find shoes in the hallway cupboard. She backed out of the room into the corridor, quietly, ignoring the opposite door into their bedroom, from where she could still hear the sound of his noisy sleep. He was not always a snorer, only after too much whisky and never when an animal was ill and he was on duty. He had two types of sleep: the solid kind, where he would rest undisturbed by thunder and lightning, and the normal kind where the slightest sound would rouse him, violently. They had never had a night-time prowler foolish enough to ignore the dogs, for which Amy had been grateful. On a night of normal sleep, no intruder who woke Douglas would stand a chance. But on a night of snoring sleep, she could enter that room with impunity, playing a drum. She did not wish to do so, in case she should see herself in that bed, curled away from him in the silence of the worst days. Silence in bed was the worst punishment; she had not meant it as such when she did not know what to say, but that was what it must have felt like. Nor did she want to see her ghost in that bed in the other days when it was she who had made the greatest, unghostlike noise. Also, it was her turn for anger again, of the dull, sad variety. It was he who had let this happen; he who had allowed the women to wipe away her presence with the same ease they might have wiped a basin clean of scum and then run water over it to make sure it was all gone. He was the overseer. She might kill him in his sleep. *Mourn* her? No; he drank and he snored and regarded his empty bathroom cabinet with satisfaction, that was what he did.

She went into his study instead, pausing at the door. This small corner of the house was sacrosanct. Not even his mother would venture here. By some unspoken rule, no one did and no one ever had unless it was her, bringing coffee or tea, or the accountant twice a year. The study required no lock upon the door to preserve its privacy as his domain; custom established it. If he closed the door behind himself, he was not to be disturbed unless he asked; if he closed the same door as he left the room, no one would open it again until he came back. Nor would there be any need for the women to go in there now with their fretful fingers itching to change things, because there were no traces of anyone else to be scrubbed away and nothing that could be altered. There was only a handsome, two-tier desk, a phone fax, hidden beneath a deluge of paper, a filing cabinet and a swivel chair. No curtains to close. The moon swam blearily into view. She had put flowers on top of the filing cabinet, sometimes; he liked that, but the addition of anything permanent and decorative was taboo. The small space was organised chaos; he did not want anyone else to understand it. There was a laptop on the floor, ignored; he preferred pen and paper. Plenty of paper. There were the plans for the new stables and surgery, kept separate on the floor. *Her* plans.

The area of the desk looked as if a bomb had struck. Yellow Post-its were stuck on to letters and bills and on to the edges of the desk, all bearing his scrawl. She switched on the lamp, alarmed for a second at the unfamiliar loudness of the unfamiliar *click* which made her start. The Post-its were the first thing she noticed, but then her eye was caught by the model figure, acting as a light-weight paperweight to a pile of letters in the centre of the desk. It was the little man in his armchair, rescued from the dolls' house downstairs, sitting proud and dust-free with a Post-it attached to the back. Amy sat down in the swivel chair and took the little man in her hands. She peeled away the Post-it and saw his writing on it. He always used a fountain pen and black ink. She bent her head to read it. *The master of the house, ha, ha!* Amy put the figure back, hurriedly. Slowly she looked at the rest of the desk without touching anything, sitting on her hands to keep them safe, her eyes taking in the messages on the Post-its. She had never known him use them before, he found them fiddly; it was she who used the things.

There were messages on the Post-its, senseless scrawls, ready to be scrunched up and replaced with other senseless scrawls.

Where is Amy? Amy is here; Amy will go back to the flat again. Must get back handbag, why, why, why? Amy is not dead, I know she isn't.

Amy, how am I going to find you?

Then, in block capitals on a bigger piece of paper, level with her eyes, dead centre on the top tier of the desk so that she could not miss it: *AMY, MY DARLING, ALL YOUR CREAMS ARE IN THE FRIDGE.* Where did he mean? Fridge downstairs, stables, the flat? She gasped. Felt as if two huge hands were pressing into her shoulders, forcing her down into the seat. The sound of his snoring calmed her. Then she counted these strange notes, as much to stop herself crying as for any other reason. Twenty-five of them, all featuring her name. As if, in the midst of doing something else, he distracted himself by writing it again and again, all of them rehearsing in one way or another the same theme – that she . . . *was not dead,* or rather his own refusal to believe it. *If Amy was dead, I would be dying; I would KNOW . . . Amy is not DEAD she went to the flat, she wiped the messages.* This was his grief, this was the reason for the stoic *lack* of mourning to which the newspaper had alluded. He had never been a reasonable man; he would go on believing black was white until the black consented to change colour. It was the way he achieved things as well as avoided them. Bloody stubborn. She wanted to crawl into the bed beside him; she had always wanted to do that. Get in there with him so they could hug each other silly for hours and hours.

She pushed the chair back from the desk. She must not weep on the paperwork or the black ink would run. And if she were to do any such thing as crawl into the bed next door, what would happen? They would be back to square one, with more to explain and forgive than ever. She would be crawling into bed like a sickly, infectious bitch, pleading forgiveness for her own disease.

She found the last Post-it. *Amy, love you better than life; come home.*

Time was passing; the moon was peering through the window accusingly as she found clean paper and pen and worked out in her mind where she could leave her messages. In the filing cabinet, at the back where he would find it, not tomorrow, but sometime; where he would not be able to guess when she had left them, but know for sure that she had. Five written messages, to be littered through the old paperwork, written with a shaky hand.

AFGHAN LOVES ROTTWEILER. ALWAYS SHALL.

Her foot throbbed painfully, a reminder of reality. She tried to ease it out of the ruined shoe, but it stuck as a punishment for doing as she did now and the pain of it reminded her she was not a ghost. Made her turn off the light with another loud *click*, and close the door behind her before she went back down the stairs. Her foot felt sticky as she crossed the clean kitchen floor and let herself out. Went halfway down the side of the house before she remembered to go back and lock the door.

FACE CREAMS ARE IN THE FRIDGE. The fridge in the stables where medicine and specialist diet food was stored, where she was bound with the dog. She did not care about face creams when she felt like a leper and she began to know she was not invisible and be afraid of her own substance.

She was a leprous blob, crossing the barbered lawn, hobbling slightly under her own weight, spotlit by the moon, jeered by the trees and made heavier by her own tears. Most of all, she wanted to hide beneath the willow tree and cry herself into a stupor. She wanted to cry for not being able to turn back the clock a couple of years in order that she could act and react then with the knowledge she had now; she wanted to remember what it was like to be loved and treasured and respected by a tyke of an awkward, difficult, clumsy, passionate man who would have listened to her if she had believed she had the strength to make him listen; a man who detested lies, told the truth and would recognise it finally, however brutal it was. A man with a short fuse and blinkered faith in those who purported to love him, a terrible vulnerability on that account, an inability to express his emotions, more blind spots than a travelling tortoise and more bloody-minded integrity than anyone should possess, even with shoulders that broad. For God's sake, if he had screwed his stepsister, he would probably be proud of it. Why had she listened? She stopped by the side of the house. One last look at the windows, tears blurring her vision. She had never even been afraid of him, unlike so many others. She shook her head in the darkness. That wasn't quite true. There had been that moment, when he found her in that daft dress, sitting on Blackfriars Bridge with the pigeon in her lap, when she had been absolutely terrified, and that was the only time, the fear tempered by something he said that same first night. *No need to run away. I'm only an ugly old dog.*

The dog sat, tethered to the bench. She sat beside it. It was easier to stay alive as a dog; they had shorter memories and a greater ability to have trust restored, even if they were cursed with a different capacity, on a shorter time-scale, to have it destroyed. And they could equally die of a broken heart and had to be kept, unless they were wolves living in a different landscape. She had an irrelevant memory of another dog they had taken in after it had been living wild for a year and starving and still it bit the hand that fed. Maybe human beings were not so different. That dog had lived in the remoter corner of the stables, refusing succour for a long time. Plenty of pride, and him such an ugly dog too. She had cried when it died and she cried now, but crying upset the animal beside her which was learning trust at a fast rate and had got her on and off the train, and distress was contagious, so she stopped crying. You could not turn clocks back, any more than you were allowed to dwell in British summertime, or command the rain to stop, so she exited the sacred shelter of the tree from the opposite

side without looking back and took the back way towards the stables, carrying the coat. *Going home*, she told the dog softly, *this is
home*.

There was a point on the left wall where she could approach
and not activate the alarm; she would tether the dog there after it
had drunk from the fresh puddle-water. Not so long before dawn,
I promise you, sweetheart, not so long, I promise you and I have
never ever reneged on a promise I have made to a dog. Only to a
man.

How quiet it was; how loud each teeny sound they made, each
footstep sinking with a splishy whisper as if they trod on cymbals.
Closer to the gate of the stables, she could imagine the smell of
herbs and the sweet, sour scent of animals, let her thoughts
wander. Dell of Dell's Animal Sanctuary was a stupid, egotistical
bitch. She never took the ugly ones, not Dell, she never took the
nearly dead, and she wanted what Douglas had, power, authority,
reputation. Dell hated men. She could be behind the sabotage, but
never without an ally. Ahhh; the gate was to Amy's left as she
sidled along the wall. Wait. The lights were all wrong. Jimmy was
drunk again.

Amy stopped. Douglas would have got Jimmy back; it was only
ever a matter of time before he got Jimmy back. And he would not
have drowned his sorrows and gone to bed without someone being
here, not with Dell on the loose; not with *whoever* it was on the
loose, some spirit of malice, dancing in the shadows. There was a
mere hint of damp dawn in the sky, promising warmth. The gate
to the yard stood open. Amy slung her raincoat over it, tied the
dog's rope to the post, patted the grizzled head. Douglas would
find her in the morning. Mission accomplished. Goodbye. But
the gate should not have been open. Something was wrong. She
could smell the herbs, vividly, as she stepped across the threshold.

The stable used as living accommodation was firmly shut;
wrong. The storeroom to the left of it was open, with the light
from within seeping into the yard, along with noises of movement
too slight to disturb the sleeping dogs, *wrong*. Amy stood to the
side of the door and peered round. Someone was busy about the

sacks of dry food which were the staple of the diet for the canine residents, bought in bulk, one sack finished before the next was opened, each sack sufficient for three days. There was an open sack, two-thirds full with which the busy person fiddled industriously, stirring something into the sack, bending over it with her arm inside, elbow-deep, mixing the contents. On top of the adjacent fridge, Amy saw a familiar sight. Three tubs of slug pellets with a familiar logo, unsealed, one lying on its side and ready to roll away, empty.

The bitch, the stinking mad bitch.

Such nice hair, her mother-in-law had, always elegantly coiffed at the expense of a wasted hour every morning. Making duty visits to the stables like a visiting royal often enough to be familiar to the animals, not an intruder, not really. Mixing up a nice mess of poison for the dear little doggies which would make them sick enough to kill the more vulnerable and have these clean stables awash with filthy liquid shit from the rest. That could get them closed down, as it almost had before. *That* would break his heart and make him biddable. That would stop building. Frail mother-in-law, with the elegant, silver-handled stick she scarcely needed propped against the door.

He's never loved you, you know. It's only us he loves. We want all of him. And all of his money.

The moment of shocked objectivity which made her so still melted into incandescent rage. A desire to leap on the woman, scratch her eyes out, claw at her porcelain skin. Hold her by the skinny neck and shove slug pellets down her throat, like stuffing a goose before eating its liver. Amy picked up the stick and lifted it high. Heavier than it looked, the momentum of the downward arc carried her with it into the room and the silver handle thumped into the side of the grey head with a sickening thud. Delicate Mrs Petty screamed and slumped forward into the bag of meal, clutching at it, sliding to the floor, crumbs of dried meal cascading over her clothes in a flurry of dusty movement until everything was still. In the next stable, a dog began to bark, then another, then all of them. Their noise was deafening after the silence. Amy kept hold of the stick and backed out of the door. Kept walking backwards until she collided with the gate, felt for the raincoat as if it would save her. The dog she had left there snarled and joined in the cacophony of barking. The row increased and went on and on, echoing round the walls with the sound of a baying mob, yelling for blood. She ran.

She ran out of earshot of the dogs as fast as she could, so that she could lose the illusion of all of them following her, snapping at her heels, bringing her down to earth in recrimination, making a bloody hole and burying her. She ran through the woods and into the path across the fields, slowed to an unsteady walk and then to a full stop. If she were to run any further she would fall. Somewhere in the initial flight, she lost the stick. Leaning against a fence, she vomited again, stomach heaving painfully to produce a thin stream of bile dribbling into the grass. As the spasms passed, leaving her as weak as a kitten, so did the trembling and breathlessness. Sickness took the last of her energy, leaving nothing but weakness. The sky was growing lighter and the hem of the raincoat was damp with dew. There was mist hanging over the field and she could hear the raucous overture to the dawn chorus. The best time of the day. Too empty for anger or regret, she wet her hands in the dewy grass and wiped them over her face. In the growing light of the day, with the hopeful racket of the birds, she felt the freedom of someone with nothing else to lose. There were no broken bridges behind her; they were burned. She found herself giggling hysterically. *Eat dirt, Mother.* Choking on her laughter until she stopped. The birdsong grew louder, the blackbirds loudest, indifferent to competition. The mist was thinning into parallel strips of floating whiteness. Go back to being dead.

There was a shrouded street with a milk float. The station was conspicuously empty, a noticeboard inviting ticket holders to use the side entrance before seven a.m. Litter drifted the empty platform; with no more than a frisson of disgust, she found some almost unused tissues under a bench and used them to clean her hands with the lubricant of spit. She shook out the coat, checked the pockets. Put it back on.

She hesitated as the train grunted to a halt, on time; it was still a monster, waiting to devour her, and it was only the empty horror of being left behind that cancelled out the fear of getting aboard. The train somehow gulped her in. She glanced at the sprinkling of passengers; none of them looked back. She did not look as murderous as she felt. Strange how one gravitated to the same seat, sat down in the same way with a quick look round before settling, like a dog patting the bed. There was a man sitting in the seat opposite, staring at her. She only noticed him when he got up and moved. A faintly familiar face she forgot as soon as it was gone.

Jimmy trudged over the field, head hurting, mind hurting, hands in pockets, one looking for his cigs, the other scratching his balls. A long time since they'd seen action. What a fool to bring back that wee girl to the stables after a night in the pub, playing tonsil hockey outside up the alley, and then getting into the banger, a good idea at the time, even if it had been winter. Only that was the night that poor pregnant bitch decided to go premature with her pups and her bad hips and he'd been too pissed to notice, lying in a stupor after a wee bit of the other and the postcoital fag burning a hole in the mattress while he contemplated the fact that he was such an irresistible personality, to say nothing of his prodigious cock, that the girl was gone long before he woke in his own stink. Maybe it was the dogs spooked her, or one whimpering bitch, to be precise. Funny he should think of it now, all these months later when he was back with the job from which he knew he had well deserved the fucking sack. Must be on account of thinking of bitches in general and that one in particular. 'Scuse me, Caterina fucking Petty, you can come down the stables like lady bitch of the manor at nine in the evening and order me home, but you can't stop me walking back at five in the morning if I please. Couldn't sleep, you see, as if you fucking cared. It must take fourteen hours of insomnia-free kip a day to keep the lines off that face of hers, so there was fat chance she would notice anything in the middle of her beauty sleep. Who the fuck did she think she was anyway? And why had he been daft enough to obey?

He grumbled his way across the field to disguise the fact that while early rising was second nature, it was not usually quite as early as this and it was a weird premonition that had jolted him awake in his room on the edge of town and got him so far. Something wrong, daft images whirring round in his head, not far away from the dread of waking up and finding Douglas standing over him alive and well and wanting to bludgeon him to death. Daft. Then he saw the stick, sticking out of a bush with the silver handle uppermost, which he would never have noticed if he had not almost collided with it. Old Mother Petty's stick, not that she was so fucking old, still looked at her son as if she wanted to eat him . . . wait a wee minute. Something wrong here. He plucked the stick and broke into a run. Nearer the stables he could hear the barking, one or two of the noisy ones sustaining a chorus which the others had dropped, all punctuated by the howl of the one tied to the gate. Dilly to the life, shockingly similar, apart from the howling, because poor Dilly never said a word, just listened all the time.

Still carrying the stick, he found the storeroom with Mrs Petty on the floor, lying there covered in dog meal, the sack of it dragged down with her and all over the place on her moaning face and her skirt which had ridden up to show knickers, *knickers*, on that one, who'd have thought it? She lay in profile with a purple contusion spreading from her grey hair into her forehead, above the left eyebrow, one hand outflung, the other clawed to her chest and her breathing unhealthily audible. Jimmy was still holding the stick, grasped in the middle, as if he was the leader of the majorettes and about to twirl the thing. He twisted his fist and looked at his watch, 5.45, Jesus help him. First things first. He took the stick to the sink, ran it under the tap, wiped it all over with paper towel and propped it by the door. The rain, which was probably the only thing that had woken him after all with its intermittent, indecisive pattering, began again. Even as he washed the stick and noticed how the imprint of the fresh bruise on her ladyship's fucking forehead bore a surprising resemblance in scale to the handle, and long before he had connected the slug pellets to the meal and the spillage and the bod on the floor, his own motives for cleansing the thing were perfectly clear. He was getting rid of the traces mainly on account of the fact that whoever had clonked the woman deserved a break. They deserved a fucking medal.

And now, at long bloody last, the shit could hit the fan.

Chapter Thirteen

Amy Petty limped across the almost empty station concourse, taking the same route to the left she had taken with all the others after the crash. There were video cameras discreetly placed above the exit. A man followed, keeping his head down and his hands in his pockets; she did not notice him or anyone else.

Everything was clean in the morning. The view from the top deck of the bus was crystal-clear; the river had been lit with gold and even the endless cars of the hinterland gleamed. The bus covered the distance efficiently, filling and emptying with quiet, morning workers. Amy told herself that one day soon, she would get one of those jobs where a person worked at night and came home in the early hours like this, at the only time of the day when it was possible for her to admire this present world without making comparisons to another. She was built for work and made herself think about nothing but work all the way back, until, two stops before the regular stop, she saw a sign for a supermarket, neon-lit. Asda Superstore, so near to home and yet so far, it made her feel ashamed for not noticing it before. The omission pointed to a kind of blind laziness. She would go there, later. Buy a bottle of whisky, keep it as a memento. She wanted the smell of it. There was nothing else she could buy here to remind her of home.

Back in the treeless zone, the traffic was lighter as she walked past the newsagent's and down Bayview Road, her steps growing slower and slower. Not even the cool morning of almost eight o'clock could redeem Ratview from ugliness. There were footsteps behind her own which slowed with hers. She kicked a lump of polystyrene into the road, looked at the closed doors. There was something she had seen in a magazine about the Far East, where houses turned in on themselves, presenting drab, dark walls to the outside world in order to misrepresent the riches within.

Photographs of beautiful, hidden courtyards came to mind, vistas of plants and stone fountains and cool, welcoming rooms. The whole façade of this street might hide scenery like that, where every family kept its aspirations indoors. That was what she would make herself believe. It was one way to live. Her father did it. He had placed his real houses inside his own makeshift house and lived in fantasy. Dwelling among the work of a lifetime, the prince of a kingdom. The dolls' houses were his real passion and without them he would be nothing. Each to his own deficiency. Amy had no judgement to make of herself, yet, and none she could honestly make of him. The sound of the blow in the bright light of the stable echoed in her mind with a strange liberating effect and yet she was heavy with grief. She could not judge anyone.

She unlocked the front door to the smell of white spirit in the hall, and in the middle of the kitchen table there was a pair of shoes in her size, standing on a piece of paper on which her father had written, *My dear daughter, I hope you are home safe. Please don't wake me early, I haven't been well. I thought you needed these. PS From Asda, they also have clothes.*

He was not well, she remembered. He had grown more feeble in the weeks of her residence, a visible decay evident in his growing indifference to food. The shoes on the table were cheap and ugly canvas ones, but their very existence made her tearful. There was nothing she needed more. She stared at them, her mouth forming the words, '*he does care for me, after all*', then sat at the table, picked up a Biro and wrote on the border of a newspaper the word '*DISLIKE*'. There was a boy who had once come to the stables for a job, with the word '*H.A.T.E.*' tattooed on his knuckles; there was a difference between the two and how you lived with them. You could dislike your daughter and still buy shoes for her, she thought earnestly, but surely you could not buy the shoes at the same time as *hating*. You could not do a single kind thing for someone you hated. She missed the dog. She would think more clearly if there was a dog.

In the fridge, alongside a loaf of the kind of everlasting bread her father preferred, there was a surprise cache of sweets, pushed to the back. Three tubes of fruit gums and two bars of nut and raisin chocolate, next to pink and yellow jelly babies, the colourful packets bright against the other, bland contents. He never ate sweets. Amy stuffed the bread back inside and went out into the back yard. The persistent sun was hard on her eyes, a reminder of the exhaustion which made her wired for sound, unable to remain still, weary and yet not able to crawl into the ugly little room upstairs in the hope of sleep because she was afraid of crying and waiting for the ghosts of regret to come haunting. Better to stay awake, even moving like a drunk with all of a drunk's awareness of time and space. The flowers in the plastic pots were wilting; she noticed that the homemade kennel for the dog had been tidily demolished. Raising her face to the sun, she tried to think of the implications of her father keeping sweets in the fridge. The desire to weep was almost overpowering. There was movement from a corner of the yard. The dark head of the child ducked down, almost out of sight, showing only the top of her sleek hair.

Amy shouted at her. 'Go away! Go away or I'll hit you. I'll hit you hard, I can do it.'

There was a scuttling sound, followed by silence and the slamming of a door. Amy went back inside, made tea and sat at the table. *My father is not a bad man*, she repeated to herself, *only a sad one*. There was nothing wrong in buying sweets in the hope of small visitors, provided they came openly, through the front door, not by the back in response to the crudest of temptation. But she knew he was neither innocent nor harmless, even if he had never been guilty as charged so long ago. She had seen him staring at the children when they came home from school with that hopeless look of longing in his eyes, as if he would reel them with hoops of wire if he dared. And how could he change, how did anyone change? How could he, even old as he was, redefine desire, emasculate, lobotomise himself, cut chunks out of his own heart and soul to make himself different? Wanting what you could not, should not have, she knew all about that. She was his daughter. She had none of his tidy dimensions, but she had his nose, his eyes, the same obstinacy. She was angry with him, but along with the anger there was a furious pity. He could not help what he was.

Amy sat for a long time, trying to fathom if there was any good in either of them. She needed to do that for the sake of her sanity. The shoes stood centre stage on top of his note and yesterday's unread newspapers, while the new ones dropped through the front door. Amy was consumed with trembling weariness until she heard him in the bathroom, stirring, her alter ego, her daddy. She could not face him yet, not now. She might shout at him, curse him and, whatever else, he had been kind. He had left her the shoes, he had let her in; he had no life, wanted what he must not have and the act of kindness was more than she could bear. She thought of the anonymous hiding place of the supermarket she had passed, full of space and people. Hurriedly she peeled off her wrecked shoes and put on the new ones. They fitted loosely and again she felt a rush of gratitude. She left a note for her father, *Thank you, back soon*, picked up the keys and hurried from the house.

The morning was still kind, the air still fresh. Mr Oza in the newsagent's smiled as she bought a bar of chocolate. He only smiled when he forgot to stare at her clothes – she had left the coat behind. She smiled back and walked to the bus stop. Going to Asda had a purpose. She was a freak, an ungrateful child, possibly a murderess, and dressed as she was in the hideous skirt, she was not even in disguise. Waiting for the bus, wondering why it was her father had never mentioned the existence of the supermarket before, she thought of Elisabeth in her careless, good-quality clothes, rather like her own used to be and then, reminded by the bus driver, thought fleetingly of Rob the trolley man, and his lighter blue uniform. A uniform would be good. She wondered, with an ache of longing, where they were, and was glad that neither of them could see her now.

There had been footsteps behind her on the way. In canvas shoes, her own footsteps were silent.

The sun shone through the stained-glass windows of the High Court, adding a discordant note of cheerfulness to the gloom.

'Rob? Look, someone has told me that there was a man in your carriage who tried to kill the woman next to him . . . before the crash . . .'

'You've found her, haven't you? No one else saw that.'

'Well . . .'

'Did she ask about me? No, no, no, doesn't matter. She's OK, is she?'

'About the man . . .'

'Yes, he threw her off the train. She didn't die in the crash, none of us did. But if you think I'm ever going to say anything about that, you're off your fucking trolley! Don't want no bogeyman after me. Is she hiding?'

'Yes.'

'Give her my love. She didn't ask about me, did she?'

Repeating to herself this conversation of the night before, Elisabeth sat and watched the passersby. There was the clicking of a stick on the mosaic of the tiles which sounded louder than anything else. It *tap-tapped* from left to right slowly, the man with the stick taking his time, attracting no attention except her own. The sound of the stick reminded Elisabeth of something she could not grasp and she watched the slow movement with scepticism. No one who really required the solid support of a stick used one with a silver tip. It needed a ferrule.

Inside these august halls there was an officer, formally known as the Tipstaff, with a duty to parade on ceremonial occasions in nineteenth-century clothes and also to arrest those malefactors who evaded the jurisdiction of the High Court or were violent within it. Rather than a stick, the Tipstaff carried a short staff, decorated with a crown and hollow in the middle to hold his official warrant. The staff was a fourteenth-century invention, also useful as a weapon and an early model for the police truncheon both in size and weight, all of which Elisabeth remembered from a history lesson personally delivered by John Box inside these very walls, which lesson included the fact that what a modern Tipstaff did more often than not was to take into custody children who had been made wards of court.

Could *one*, she wondered, make a *wife* a ward of court? Have a judge declare on the application of a husband that his lawfully wedded spouse be returned by her abductor, in the way that a father could be ordered to return a kidnapped child? Alas, not. The man with the stick exited stage left up the stairs, where someone held open a door for him, the old fraud. *Tap, tap, tap.*

Today, the High Court was gloomy, gothic and quiet. Sitting where she was, Elisabeth was overwhelmingly conscious of the thousand rooms and three and a half miles of corridor squatting oppressively above, alongside and below where she sat. It was late lunchtime and the place was beginning to buzz, like a railway concourse, with the difference that most of the movers were soberly dressed and heavily laden. There was little enough of the early summer frippery in evidence here. Long sleeves and dark suits.

In evidence . . . If she ceased to be a lawyer, would she stop using this terminology, or was it so ingrained that she would talk like a legal parrot until the day she died, and think like one too, as if the law was branded on her brain. She was stuck with the vernacular and she was distracting herself with *irrelevancies* because she was bursting with speech and, if she had not arranged this meeting, might have found herself burbling at the bus stop or on the train to any stranger who was prepared to listen, like one of the poor nutters who lurked on the Circle Line, looking for someone to abuse. She really needed a friend. A more confidential friend than she was herself, because although she could keep secrets perfectly well, they burned holes in her pockets like money waiting to be spent. A friend. There were few enough of those and all the same, when she saw Helen West standing by the noticeboard, dwarfed by the scale of the place, looking around as if she expected a reception committee, Elisabeth wanted to shrink. A friend she had neglected over the years but one with all the right legal knowledge, a friend she was *using*. When Helen cantered over to where Elisabeth sat by the wall she had all the elegance of a dancer. This was not a woman who had difficulty finding clothes to fit. She dumped her bag and lit a cigarette in one fluid movement. At least there were some bad habits.

'So what's all this about then?'

No accusations, such as why do you only keep in touch when you want something and why should I interrupt my day to walk up Fleet Street and meet you here? None of that. Simply a brief, once-over inspection, followed by a critical nod.

'Elisabeth Manser, you're in a pickle and you haven't brushed your hair this morning. So tell me what you want me to do about it. Smoke?'

Elisabeth shook her head. She could feel dust shaking itself out of her brain, like dandruff. Helen never prevaricated and it was best to respond in the same way, taking a deep breath first.

'I need to find out about a case twenty-five years ago, in which a man called Rollie Fisher was convicted for indecent assaults on little girls. I don't know how to get them, but I need to know the facts.'

'Why?'

'Because it connects to a libel case. Fisher is Amy Petty's father . . .'

'And she's married to that *bugger* Douglas Petty. Got it. That was the reason for the last time you phoned. You wanted to know if he was going to be prosecuted. Likes dogs. Amy's the dead one. Train crash.' There was no sentiment about Helen, whom Elisabeth remembered as reading every page of every newspaper like someone addicted to newsprint. She had a prodigious memory, pursued information like a beggar after coins and would have been the better libel lawyer. A better lawyer full stop, but it didn't prevent her from being a human being. Or from styling her long dark hair into a clever knot at the nape of her neck from which only the minimum escaped.

'Amy Petty might not be dead,' Elisabeth muttered, wishing it did not sound so melodramatic.

'Well you're either dead or you aren't. There's no middle way.' Helen gave a rude chuckle, loud only because it was an unfamiliar sound in here. It had a perversely calming effect.

'What offence do you commit if you fake your own death?'

A spiral of cigarette smoke escaped towards the ceiling. 'Depends if you actually *fake* it. I mean if you actually hatch a deliberate plot to make people think you're dead. Or if you did it to facilitate a theft. Instead of just buggering off and letting every-one assume you're dead. I can't think there's any offence quite covers that. Is that what you wanted to know?'

'Supposing that's what she did – the latter, not the former – but before she disappeared from the train crash, she saw something which would indicate that someone was killed, non-accidentally. Murdered, and the train crash used to cover it. Supposing she has a conscience about that . . .'

'Yes. The woman you mentioned when you phoned. In *The Times*.' At least Helen did not react as if she was off her head. She had always been like that, paying close attention without respond-ing until the end. You could sit down with Helen and announce an ambition to have a sex change and she would not bat an eyelid.

'And she wants someone to know,' Elisabeth ended lamely, watching Helen considering the problem as if contemplating a chess move.

'Well I know what I'd do. I'd write a series of anonymous letters to the police, my MP, the DPP and a couple of newspapers, sug-gesting the death be reinvestigated. If I didn't want anyone to know my identity, that is. It would do the trick, without achieving much. A witness can't be clandestine and effective. And if she did come forward, she might not be believed either. She's hardly showing signs of reliability and credibility at the moment, is she? Why do you want to find out about the father?'

'Because . . .'

'Let me guess. Douglas Petty might abandon his libel case if that particular skeleton crawled out of the cupboard. Wouldn't do much for his *reputation*. And you and your learned leader would lose the chance to make all that lovely money.'

'I'm not like that,' Elisabeth protested. 'Honestly I'm not.'

Helen nodded. A little of the shining hair escaped from the knot on the back of her neck. Interesting earrings, like small, curled flowers.

'I know you aren't. Which is why you're probably in the wrong line of work.' She puffed contemplatively, brushed away the smoke with a wave. 'You know the one thing which always struck me about libel? How easy it would be to orchestrate. You only need a bent journalist – plenty of those – in cahoots with the victim or someone close. The so-called victim and the journo create the libel and the journo gets it published. There's no real defence to it, so the newspaper has to pay out. If they have to pay out at the end of a trial, so much the better, because juries hate newspapers and give ridiculous awards. The journo doesn't suffer, only the newspaper. Then he and the victim can split the proceeds. A bit like an insurance scam.'

Elisabeth thought about this, not for the first time. 'The victim himself wouldn't need to be involved, would he?' she said. 'It could be somebody wanting to ruin him. Or achieve another purpose.'

'You've surely been long enough in this game to know that every law made to protect the weak or the innocent is infinitely exploitable by those who are anything but. The right to silence, the right to privacy, they're all exploitable. What I want to know is who's exploiting you? Are you in the grip of some mad dead-woman or is it still John Box?'

Elisabeth was silent. They both watched as the foyer began to clear, the busy to-ers and fro-ers crossing the floor as in some ritual dance, before disappearing into the corridors and rooms. There was a sprinkling of robes and wigs, looking entirely natural in the setting, as if their wearers had emerged like that from the stonework.

'OK, you don't know,' Helen was saying evenly, gathering up her bag. 'And you want me to go and look at the Crown Prosecution Service archives from before the days of computer records, as if I had nothing better to do, so that I can tell you what this Rollie Fisher was accused of doing. All in such complete breach of the rules about the rehabilitation of offenders, I'll likely get sacked. Fisher won't be on some convenient register for paedophiles, you know. That's only for the recent ones. It's as hard for me to get this information as it would be for you.'

Elisabeth was stricken with remorse. 'Oh, Helen, I'm sorry, I didn't think . . . of course you mustn't . . . it was only . . .'

'You didn't know who else to ask? Story of my life.' She was standing and patting Elisabeth reassuringly on the shoulder. No need for her to say that none of this was ever to be repeated. That was a given. Even when they were students, Helen was famous for gathering gossip without ever repeating it.

'Shame on you, Elisabeth,' she said, grinning. 'I was only teasing. If you remembered any criminal law at all, you'd know that R v Fisher is in all the casebooks, if it's the same Fisher. You can't keep your anonymity if you make a point of law. He was one of the first to establish the principle that the evidence of a child can be accepted without corroboration. And it was in the bad old days when a wife couldn't give evidence against her husband, even if she wanted to, so there was some point made about that. I'll find it and fax you a transcript this afternoon. I've still got your home number, even though you seem to have lost mine. Bless you, all this cloak-and-dagger stuff for something you might have found out easily yourself.'

She was laughing.

Elisabeth felt monumentally ashamed. 'I am in the wrong job, aren't I?'

'Yes, you are,' Helen said. 'Why didn't we do something sensible and marry rich men?'

'You mean like Amy Petty?'

'Perhaps not.'

They had reached the doors of the Court and emerged into the grey daylight of the Strand. Elisabeth watched her go and wanted to call her back. It was suddenly lonely without her.

Lonely, *amen*. Everyone needed friends. A lover was no replacement, especially if he was not also a friend.

She took the mobile phone out of her handbag and stared at it, willing it to ring. Please, Amy, *ring*. Even if there is nothing to say, please ring. POETS day: Push Off Early Tomorrow's Saturday. John was firmly in the bosom of his family for the weekend that stretched ahead without promise. A two-day interlude of keeping company with the cat and trying not to drive herself mad. Feeling guilty all the time, as if she had done nothing and nothing had been learned. But it had. And it was not as if there was nothing to do but wait and wonder. She could write anonymous letters for Amy; she could tend her garden, all three inches of it, and if Helen was true to her word, read about Rollie Fisher. It would not be the same Fisher, life was never as simple as that, and of course, if she were the private detective of fiction, she would have had a grizzled police contact to assist with vital information, unearthed from illegal sources and freely given for the price of a drink in a grubby bar in Soho. Recasting herself as another kind of woman altogether, fleet of foot and as fearless in enterprise as an avenging angel, amused her somewhat on the way home, but not for long. Helen's blithe remarks about how profitable it could be to orchestrate a libel were only an echo of what had already entered her mind and stayed there like indigestion. Who *had* started the Petty libel which seemed so unimportant now? That aspect of the thing had never been touched; nor had John been assiduous in trying to find out. *Like an insurance scam.*

Supposing Douglas was short of dosh, and he had set the whole thing up as a gamble, and hadn't he been a bit of a gambling man? Nobody set up a libel which made them look such a fool. Not a vain man, anyway. Her handbag remained silent on the way home. With the mobile phone inside it, it gave her the impression of being alive, a small animal in its own right, ready to squawk. POETS day afternoon was dull and cloudy. The flowers in the tiny garden did not need her. Amy Petty needed her and Amy did not ring. Amy's tan handbag sat on the kitchen table, squatting there in mute imitation of a cat. There were three bottles of wine in the rack, pushing their necks to her, temptingly.

★

Slowly, without thinking about it in advance, Elisabeth rummaged in the *Petty v Associated Press* folder which stood by her bed and found the video the newspaper had supplied, declining to name the source or the cameraman. The photos came from that. She slotted it into the video.

It could have been any wintry lawn. There was the golden dog, lolloping across the grass in the direction of the woods, the road and freedom. Followed by the ungainly figure of Douglas Petty, with his bare legs and barrel chest half-covered in the striped pyjama jacket, brandishing a piece of wood. Elisabeth froze the frame. The wood looked heavy enough to hurt. She shivered. The man with his naked genitalia and fierce expression launched himself on the animal, bringing it down. They squirmed together on the ground, for all the world like lovers locked in the combat of copulation. She could see the steps leading into the house, the white of the stucco faintly visible as a backdrop to the thrashing couple, before the picture flickered into a blur of branches, then nothing. Elisabeth went back to the beginning. She did not laugh as she and John had done when they first saw it; instead she felt squeamish, felt it was she herself pointing a camera through the bare branches of the willow tree to catch a man being a beast, salivating at the sight of nakedness and an act of bestial madness. Maybe they were both growling. Something was. There was a thunderous knocking at her front door.

It was only a small house; the application of a fist on the door was enough to make it shake, or so it felt, and interrupted in this voyeuristic viewing which was already making her feel ashamed, Elisabeth was annoyed. Why not ring the dinky little bell which gave delicate warning of visitors? The thumping resumed after a pause and she had the unpleasant image of a burly policeman outside, ready with a warrant of arrest, flanked by a posse of curious neighbours. Guilt made her think like that. She ran to the door. There was a peephole she never used and did not use now. The thundering on the door indicated emergency. What the . . . ?

'What the *fuck* do you want?' she shouted. Christ, her language was getting worse.

There was no time for words. Little Jimmy, the Pettys' factotum, stood on the other side, his fist raised to knock again. A large fist, she noticed, for such a small man. The battered estate car was parked in the street, dirtier than any other vehicle. Greetings were not in order.

'What fucking kept you?' he said and pushed her inside.

Pushed, pulled, could have been either. They half stumbled into the living room where she had been watching the video, the freeze-framed picture glowing on the screen, Douglas locked on the bucking dog. Close, like this, Jimmy smelt of dog hair and sweat, a smell she remembered from the front seat of the car with the closed windows.

'Get your *fucking* hands off me!'

'Oh, don't be a silly bitch. I've been sent to fetch you.'

'You *what*?'

'*You what*?' he mimicked. 'Are you deaf? S'pose you must be if you don't hear the fucking door. You're to come over for a drink, he says. Since you won't bring the fucking handbag back. I been sent to fetch it and you alongside. If you'd be so kind. Won't take long. Same fucking county.'

His slightly squint eyes were taking in the details of the room in a way that made her feel peculiarly self-conscious about it, as if he was a prospective buyer for her house and she should be hurling herself over the cracks, the rude bastard. She was not afraid of him, merely angry and desperately wanting to hide the television, with the frozen frame of Douglas Petty. Possibly that frame on the screen said more about her taste than the whole house put together and she moved to stand in front of it. He pushed her aside. She heard the phone in the kitchen which she had turned on to fax bleeping the receipt of a paper message.

'Fuck you, lady . . . is that the kind of thing you watch, is it? Well bugger me. I seen that one, too. It's himself, isn't it? Nice arse, for his age. A wee bit more photogenic than my own.'

'Wouldn't be difficult,' she snapped.

He looked at her and laughed. There was something primeval about him, like a goblin lately arrived from a swamp, dried-off and scaly, pleased with himself, utterly confident in this alternative world of fucking suburbia.

'Nooo. He's plenty of backside, that one. Like yourself. Needs to lose a wee bitty weight, maybe. Here, go back to the start. It's a good one, this. People'd pay good money to see this. Turn it back to the start.'

She picked up the remote and did exactly as she was told, rewinding the tape to the beginning of its two-minute stretch, amazed, at one remove, at her own complicity. It did not seem surprising that Jimmy slumped into a chair as if he had been invited and she had offered to slip out to the kitchen for a cold beer.

'This is good, this is,' he repeated. Somehow the remote was in his hands. She could feel the imprint of his fingers on her arm where he had grabbed her, sat in the seat opposite and listened while he used the same hand to stab towards the screen, explaining his commentary.

'See this dog here? That's Josh. He's a wanderer, he. Came tae us with his sillybitch sister, too big for the old woman who kept them. Only handsome hound we have. The bitch is pregnant, see, with bad hips and all, retrievers, they have that, overbred bitches, wee hips, big pups, no good. Got me sacked, that sillybitch. Didn't realise she'd whelp so soon, had to be watched, pups might kill her. I get drunk, he sacks me. This is later.'

She was lost and he was entirely at home, beginning to chuckle. Bring on the ice creams.

'Well, there's a man over the way who'd shoot Josh if he comes near their bitch. Douglas won't take the bollocks off a dog. Stupid bastard. Plus Dell wanted to kidnap him, to prove some fucking point – she likes the good-looking ones. Fucking pedigree. Dougie would have been down there to look after the bitch and her pups, that time of year, anyways. He'd have made Amy stay in bed. That Josh is a wily bastard. Look at the great daftie! Did you ever see any such thing?' He roared with laughter. Douglas was romping over the screen.

Elisabeth could not work out what Jimmy was laughing at. Maybe he just laughed, the way hyenas did; he had the same pointy face and funny eyes. The golden dog moved. Jimmy was fumbling in his pockets with one hand, fetching out cigarettes and crumbs of tobacco. She wished she could open the window, but she did nothing of the kind. The car stood dirtily in front of her house, darkening the room, and then the cat, the treacherous cat, crept into the room and stole into his lap as if it knew that warm, smelly space was there and she hated it for that.

'See this? He'll have been sleeping down there, gone out for a pee and let the damn dog out. It runs, he chases, that bloody dog loves a game. Retriever? Won't swim, won't *retrieve* a fucking thing, except a stick. See how he throws the stick to one side? Makes him veer a bit. Gives Dougie a chance to bring him down. Yesss! Goal! Fucking dog always stops for a piece of wood to chew. Never fucking brings it back. Look at the daft bastard. That Josh, silly as arseholes.'

'He looks like he's fucking it,' Elisabeth said.

'You *what*?'

'*Fucking* fucking it. Douglas fucking it.'

Jimmy looked gobsmacked. His mouth hung slack and then he giggled. '*Douglas,* fucking it? But it's a fucking *dog*. Fucking impossible. Give us a break.'

'So what's he doing then?'

'Look, sunshine, he's chasing a wandering dog to save it getting shot. Or give Dell a chance. He's been out for a pee in the cold and lost his trousers when he sees him go. He's thrown a stick and got it to go sideways, then he grabs the sodding dog any way he can, right? What do you think a dog would do if a man tried to bugger it, for God's sake? Bite his fucking head off, for God's fucking sake, that's what it would do. Get him in the leg, at least. Dogs might trust you, yeah, but not that much. Fucking hell. Don't you know *anything*? Josh'd take your arm off. Didn't you see him throw the stick?'

The film blurred to the end. Jimmy shook his fist at the screen and drew a deep gasp of his fag before grinding the stub beneath his heel on her carpet. It was an oatmeal carpet, easily scarred. Maybe tomorrow it would matter, or next week, when John would notice. *Shit.*

'They're strong, retrievers,' Jimmy said admiringly, as the video blurred into branches. 'Muscular dogs. Couldn't be buggered, oh no. Never a dog, they know when they're being hurt. A bitch in heat, though, that's another matter. Take anything. Tried it myself, but I was only an ignorant lad then. Only the once. I think she liked it. Come on, we gotta go.'

'I'm not going anywhere.'

'The fuck you are. All that pissing about with trains you do. Same fucking county, what's wrong with a car? Shall I switch this off? Good one, this was. Come on.'

The cat fled off his lap as he rose.

'You can fucking wait, Jummy!' she shouted. 'I'm going to wash my face and comb my hair and—'

'Why? Fancy our Douglas, do you? You've got no fucking chance. He's in love already—'

'SHUT UP! What does he want?'

He grinned, showing brown teeth. It was a slow smile of satisfaction. 'He wants a fucking referee. Stop him doing murder, mebbe. OK, I'll wait.'

What to look like? A fucking lawyer? She went upstairs and put on jeans and a long shirt. Brushed her hair with a trembling hand, thought of shinning down the drainpipe outside the back window, went back to the kitchen instead, collected Amy's handbag, stowed it in her briefcase with a notebook. This way, she could pretend that the expedition was official. Jimmy did not disturb these preparations. He was watching the television, roaring with laughter at some cartoons, not a care in the world, listening out for her all the same. There was a brief temptation to open the back door and attempt to escape over the garden wall, but embarrassment made her hesitate. The thought of hauling herself over the prickly roses onto next door's minute lawn was a deterrent. The TV fell silent.

'I think you've had time enough,' Jimmy said from the doorway. 'Anyway, it's a nice evening for a drive.'

'It's your bloody driving I'm worried about.'

'What d'you mean? What's wrong with it?' He was hurt.

Pretending to be hurt, while being at the same time manically cheerful, steering her out of the house and opening the car door for her like an assiduous cab driver working towards a large tip, grinning at her as if she was his favourite fare. She settled into the seat obediently. Surprised to find that she did not really mind the bullying; it was almost pleasant to relinquish control. Then she was afraid; she knew he would black her eye and break her nose without a second thought; there was a challenge in behaving as if it was almost normal. A rural ride on a late Friday afternoon. Ha ha.

And it was a novelty, almost, to travel by car. Other people lived in them, treated them as an extension of their homes and themselves in a way she could not imagine.

'Clean this car often, do you, Jimmy? Smells nice.'

'Aw, shut your face, woman. What's the point in cleaning a car? It only gets dirty again.'

He drove slower than she remembered, perhaps in deference to her presence, or perhaps to the traffic, it was difficult to tell. She could not visualise the route in her mind; train travel ruined her sense of geography; she followed the logic of train lines rather than roads. He might be taking her to a different destination than the one promised, a deserted quarry, a railway siding, a rubbish tip for a ritual homicidal dispatching, but reason predominated; she had done nothing to deserve that and besides, she no longer cared. The weather was muggily warm; black-fly weather, pleasant with the window open. At a set of traffic lights, Jimmy shrugged off his jacket, revealing a grubby singlet and releasing his underarm smell. Not as bad as she feared. Like his legs, Jimmy's arms had slender, well-defined muscles. He would be a good subject for a life-drawing class. Then, as he indicated left and hauled at the wheel, she noticed how both forearms were purpled with bruises, some old, some new.

'Where'd you get the bruises, Jimmy? Fighting?'

He laughed. 'Naa, I'm too fucking old. Bruises are just something you get if you hang around dogs. Occupational hazard.'

'How's that?'

'Don't you know anything? They knock you over. They play; they nip.'

'Oh.'

The car lurched on to a stretch of motorway. There was an ominous knocking sound as it gained speed. She saw a sign for London and felt slightly reassured.

'What *is* all this about, Jimmy?'

'He said not to tell you, just bring you.'

'Those puppies, Jimmy, the ones that got you fired, what happened to them?'

'They went to good homes. Easy to find good homes for pups with a touch of *pedigree*,' he added scathingly. 'Old, sick dogs, not the same. You keep those until they die.'

The knocking in the engine stopped as if it was tired of making the noise. They left the motorway and turned through a recognisable town. The conversation was between bouts of gazing at the green fields, listening to Jimmy whistling. The briefcase looked incongruous in this car. Only twenty-six hours since she had promised Amy Petty she would keep silent; she must remember that.

It was the most beautiful time of the day when they turned into the valley which held the white house hidden discreetly in a fold. The sun was low in a rosy sky; the colours of the trees so vibrant they hurt the eyes. Look at me, they seemed to say; look how fine I am. The curve of the bright white house disappeared as they went round the back. A house without an entrance; a secret house. *Everyone who deals with dogs has a few bruises.* Now, there was a context to that, and she was struggling with it, even while mesmerised by the light and clutching her briefcase as if it contained state secrets. Amy Petty bruised by contact with dogs rather than a husband. Douglas not a rude *bugger*, but the soul of sweet nature, merely addicted to the protection of animals . . . For reasons he did not explain, Jimmy parked the car by the stables and led her up the rutted track round the side of the house and over the lawn. The willow tree breathed appreciation of the day; there were brilliant green hostas by the steps. The great semi-circle of windows basked in the sun. Surely this house civilised all who lived within it, the master included. There was no need to be afraid. An echo of Amy's voice . . . *Douglas? Beat ME?* She followed Jimmy into the room, via those glorious windows, ready to be cool, calm, collected, forgiving and discreet, whatever Mr Petty, the master of this house, wanted, her eyes adjusting to the indoor light. He was the client. She had the handbag; she was in control. The curtains confused her; the room was different, dark and dramatic with the windows shrouded. She stumbled over the step, saw the interior and screamed, short and sharp, before Jimmy put his hand over her mouth.

Caterina Petty was sitting on a stool, fetched from the kitchen, with her legs twisted round the legs of the stool and her feet bare. Her back was supported by the pillar of the fireplace surround. With her legs parted and her feet shoeless, she looked inelegant and her once pristine white linen shirt was creased and stained with a slick of brown down the front. Her face was pale. Mrs Isabel Petty lolled in the armchair to the left of the fireplace, both of them facing outwards towards the windows. There was a large pressure bandage on the left side of her head, which she held with her left hand. The other hand was taped with Elastoplast to the arm of the chair. Her face was pink, and she moaned softly. Her feet were also bare. The lack of shoes and the dirtiness of their clothes seemed to strip them of dignity. It was as if they were prisoners. To Elisabeth's eyes, the scene was barbaric.

'Don't worry,' Jimmy said in her ear, pointing rudely at Mrs Petty, 'we've had the vet out to her.'

Douglas was standing between the women in front of the fireplace. The mirror above him reflected the light which entered, almost like a spotlight, from the French doors. The room was muffled. Each woman had a small side table to her left with a glass on it. He held a bottle of whisky. Another empty bottle was on the floor. The smell of cigar smoke lingered.

'Took your time, Jimmy, didn't you?' Douglas said mildly, nodding at Elisabeth. She sat in an armchair as bidden, facing the

ghastly tableau of sickly women. Caterina glared at her, then she
tried a conspiratorial smile. Elisabeth churned with sudden pity for
her, mixed with fear.

'So what've you been doing that's so fucking useful?' Jimmy
snapped back at Douglas.

'Language, Jimmy, please, not in front of the ladies. I've been
keeping them comfortable and making sure they have enough to
drink Take another sip, Mother, please do. It's good for you.'

He took the glass from the table and, with one hand round her
shoulder, guided the half-full whisky glass to her lips. She drank
obediently, but weakly and slowly as if beyond protest. He wiped
her chin with a clean handkerchief and patted her arm gently.
'Mustn't have *too* much with the paracetamol, must we? But
enough. And you mustn't keep scratching yourself.' He turned to
Caterina. 'And now you, my dear,' placing the other glass in her
grubby hands. His solicitude was appalling.

'No.'

'Yes. All of it.' She drank.

Elisabeth smelt the liquor and felt sick. 'Mr Petty,' she said
loudly. 'This is bloody monstrous. They're ill, both of them. You
can't do this . . . If you don't—'

'Thank you for coming,' he interrupted her, with the same
dreadful mildness. 'Very kind of you. I wanted you to take notes,
if you wouldn't mind. And they aren't ill. They're intoxicated with
my sole company, perhaps. And all *girls* get a little demoralised, I
suppose, if someone discourages them from washing or changing
their clothes. Or wearing their shoes. They love their shoes. Jimmy,
get the lady a drink. I think she'd prefer wine. White or red?'

'I . . . white.'

'Good. Did you bring the handbag?'

She took it out of the briefcase.

'Thank you so much.' He had a lovely voice.

He cradled the handbag briefly in his arms and then put it
gently on the floor. Jimmy shuffled back with a wineglass so full,
the liquid slopped over the sides as he put it down beside her. She
hunted in the bottom of the briefcase for a notebook and paper.

Douglas beamed approval. His geniality was utterly intimidating, compelling obedience.

'I'd better bring you up to speed, Miss Manser. I'm afraid my dearest relatives – although, of course, we don't share any blood apart from the bad kind – have been a bit naughty. Something I've suspected for a while, although my lovely stepsister, Caterina, has been very good at deflecting suspicion. Do you know, she had the nerve to tell me that she thought Amy might be the one behind the sabotaging of the dogs? Amy, I ask you. Suggesting a touch of mental instability, perhaps, in poor, silly Amy, who was longing for city life and maybe, just maybe, a lover, although to be fair she didn't suggest that until recently. Where was I? Ah, there you are, Dilly, come in.'

The dog slunk into the room from the kitchen. Elisabeth looked at it. A brindled half greyhound of some age and startling familiarity. Amy's sillybitch, the one without road sense, which came and sat at Douglas's feet between the two women, facing her. The shock paralysed her. No, of course it was not the same animal; it was just another old dog.

Douglas addressed his sister. 'This is a new dog, sis. Just to let you know. She's only here to put things in perspective, make us behave, and she needs to feel at home. Now where was I?'

'Bringing the lady up to speed,' Jimmy murmured.

'Ah yes.' Douglas turned to Elisabeth. 'This morning, very early, my frail stepmother was found mixing slug poison into the dogs' food. Would have made some of them sick, and maybe some of them die. This has happened before, but we never knew who. Then I suppose she might have phoned the local newspaper. Luckily, someone stopped her by hitting her on the head. Jimmy found her. Caterina was next on the scene, I wonder why, and came rushing up to tell me Jimmy had done it. He's hit my mother, sack him. He's hit my stepmother and poisoned the animals, she says. Well, once I saw, I knew it wasn't Jimmy. He'd have made a better job of it, he'd have killed her. And he might be a sad bastard, but he does love dogs. There was a bit of a contretemps. Are you taking this down?'

Elisabeth nodded.

'Right. Question time. Now Mother, why did you do that?' His tone was wheedlingly sweet.

Hers, in reply, was embarrassingly childlike, anxious to please and definitely tipsy. 'I hate those dogs, Dougie dear. All my married life I've lived with them. No one ever put me first. I *hate* those *fucking* dogs. You used to love us best when you were a little boy. We were your world then. We had nice furniture and beautiful things. Then it's dogs, dogs, dogs. Just like your father. Then, with Amy, there was going to be more dogs. No money or comfort for me. I wanted you back. *I HATE DOGS*.'

It was a rapid, breathless delivery. Elisabeth almost admired it.

'Is that why you hated Amy?'

Mrs Petty seemed to consider the question and gave a deep sigh. 'I didn't hate Amy,' she slurred. 'How could anyone hate Amy? There's nothing to hate. I sometimes hate you, though. For what you did to Caterina. Funny how I can hate you and love you at the same time.'

There was a pause. Douglas put his hands on his hips. 'What did I do to Caterina? Apart from squire her round and introduce her to suitable males, bail her out, put her up here between jobs, support her so-called, non-existent career, act as a prop to all those insecurities . . . pick her up and dust her down, try and make her *work* for a living and stop exploiting men . . . What did I *do*?'

Isabel Petty sighed dramatically. Her voice descended to a whisper. 'You know very well. You screwed her, Douglas dear, when she was only twelve and made sure she could never have anyone else but you. She *can't*, you see. And why should she work? *You* don't. You screwed her. Then you screwed her again.'

There was a deathly silence. Douglas leant against the mantelpiece, heavily, his head bowed. The silence continued. The sitting dog got to its feet, the only movement in the room.

'My God, how I get people wrong,' Douglas murmured. 'Tell them it isn't true, Cat. Tell them.'

Caterina smiled glassily. 'Of course it's true.'

She threw back her head and laughed. A shrill, drunken laugh which went on and on. The dog did not like the laughter. It moved next to her stool and growled. Then, in a curious change of mood, began to lick her bare feet with a long, wet tongue.

Caterina screamed.

CHAPTER FOURTEEN

Elisabeth stared at Caterina's toes in disgust. So did Caterina, cringing away from her own feet and then kicking out at the dog. There was a dull thump as the heel of one foot struck the dog's head. The dog lay down without protest, as if this was normal and the best thing to do was to stay quiet. It smelt as if it had been rolling in manure. Only Isabel Petty did not seem to notice what had become an overpowering smell, although her delicate nose wrinkled. Somehow, Elisabeth was not perturbed by the behaviour of the dog and yet shocked by the realisation that yes, it was the same animal and no more surprising that it should recline on an Indian carpet within reach of a dirty, vicious foot than that it should try to kill itself on a busy road. It seemed to have no sense of self-preservation. Nobody said anything until she spoke.

'Well,' she said brightly, 'do I record that as a comment?'

Nobody heard. Caterina, closest to the smell of the dog, pursed her mouth and turned her head away, clenching her fists and presenting a fine profile to the audience. The dog began to whine and paw at the carpet, conscious of wrongdoing, raising a muzzle to regard Caterina's sticky feet. Douglas shushed it. All the time he stared at Caterina, willing her to turn her head. Elisabeth gazed at Douglas. His face was as sad as a bloodhound; he looked every day of his fifty years.

'That's some allergy you have, Miss Petty,' Jimmy ventured, finding the silence unbearable. 'You should be out in fucking hives by now. It'll crap in a minute. Does it all the time.'

'Shut up, Jimmy.' Douglas moved to Caterina's side and touched her shoulder. She flinched, her head still averted. 'Come on, Cat. Can you look at me and say it's all true? I'm afraid the animal's attention was quite misguided, not really affection at all, but don't kick her, she might bite.' He was still terrifyingly mild.

'Any confession obtained under duress is not worth the paper used to write it down,' Elisabeth said loudly. 'It means fuck all, Mr Petty, as you know.'

"Thank you, *Miss* Manser, for that reminder of why I needed a lawyer present, and one of such integrity, too. You're quite right. But this isn't a court of law and no one is going to get hanged. *Yet.* Speak to us, Cat, please.' He ruffled her hair. Finally she turned and let her head rest on his chest. She was very drunk.

'Always loved you,' she said.

'Needed me, Cat.'

'Yeah. That's it. And you needed someone like *her.*' She pointed her tied-up hands at Elisabeth, one holding the other with a single finger extended from her two fists, mimicking a gun. 'Silly cunt.' She let out a deep sigh. 'You never even touched me. Nope, I tell a lie. You slapped me on the leg once. Shame, really. Certainly got her attention, though, didn't it? Stupid Amy.' She turned the gun salute on her mother. 'Bloody tough it is, too. When your mother loves her stepson so much, she won't even challenge him for raping you. Worships the ground he walks on. Jus' like I did. So whadya think it's like, brother? After all those years of trying, all those years of *helping* you, you have everything. Me, nothing. A mother with a conscience, at last.'

She let out a dry sob and clutched at the whisky glass he had already refilled.

'I think you're rewriting history, Cat,' Douglas said wearily. 'A rich stepdaddy who didn't like you much, that was your disease. Amy tried to tell me that before she stopped talking and I stopped listening. And I never counted the money I gave you, Cat, you know that. I simply trusted you and I felt guilty. I thought you respected me.'

She giggled. 'Respect? When you fuck up a career by fooling round and taking your clothes off when you might have loved me? Oh, you *ARSE* . . . When you could have had me for the taking. *Adored* you,' she said dreamily.

He let go of her gently, so that her long back remained supported by the fireplace pillar. He seemed uncertain of what to do next. Elisabeth intervened. Cross-examination came naturally, after all, and she could not resist it. Both women looked ghastly. She could not get over her impression that they were somehow stripped and bound, had to remind herself they were not. The dog and the whisky were the only incentives to tell the truth.

'Did you discuss this with Amy, at all? I mean, is there any chance you did that? Told her how much Douglas had loved you for so long?' *Always address the witness in a manner which encourages them to believe you respect them.*

Caterina turned her bleary eyes in the direction of the windows, squinted at the last of the light coming through, nodded and raised the hands to shield her eyes from the single shaft of the sun. 'Course I did. She had to know he was my love and I was his.'

It seemed as if Douglas might punch her, so tightly were his fists clenched; Jimmy moved across and took hold of his arm. There was a muttered exchange while Douglas shrugged him off, during which Elisabeth sat impassively, shivering. It felt cold, suddenly; not full-scale summer yet and the house had cooled. With the curtains covering the windows in their dramatic folds, the room could not store up the fragile heat of May. Then they were all back in their places.

'And she trusted you,' Elisabeth continued. 'Because you were a good friend to her and helped her with everything. After all, she didn't know anything about any of you, did she?'

'Stupid cow.' The last slug of drink made Caterina more sober by the second. She straightened up and looked smug, just at the point when Elisabeth began to feel sorry for her. 'She didn't know what *he* was like. He'll fuck anything. Except me.'

'You're a fine one to talk,' Jimmy said angrily. 'You've even made a fucking pass in my direction. And that lawyer fella.'

'Which lawyer?' Elisabeth asked.

'Don't be silly,' Caterina said with disdain, looking towards Jimmy. 'When you saw me and Mr Box in The Wheatsheaf, we were merely discussing business. And as for you, you don't even count as *anything*. I'd rather be fucked by a pig. A fucking pig!' Her laughter was shrill.

Jimmy got up and took two steps towards her. 'If that dog craps,' he said, 'it would make a lovely wee face mask.'

'Stop it!' Elisabeth yelled. The dog leapt to its feet. Jimmy retreated and sat down. He fumbled in his pocket for fags. 'Mr Petty, I really do think you should untie your mother.'

'Are you all right, Mummy?' he crooned at her, mimicking her childish voice. She inclined her head, weakly. 'She says she's fine as she is. Jimmy, please do not mention crap.'

Elisabeth leant forward, grasped her wineglass and took a long pull, as if it was beer, conscious as it hit the back of her throat that it was too good for gulping. In the pause, Douglas lit a small cigar. The smell of it was sweet relief. He seemed to be abdicating control of the proceedings to her, like a ringmaster at a circus introducing the clowns. Elisabeth sipped the wine this time, took up her pen and scribbled in the notebook. So far, the page was pristine clean.

'Perhaps Miss Petty can cast some light on the libel which got everyone so upset,' she suggested soothingly. Silence from Caterina. Jimmy nudged a roll in the carpet with his foot. It was Mrs Petty who rallied and spoke, trillingly, from the depths of her chair.

'Such fun,' she said. '*Such* fun. Catty thought of it. Get someone to take some pics. Maybe have Jimmy swearing at the bloody dogs, he does it ever so nicely. Or pics of Amy *talking* to the bloody things, she did it all the time. We could have her declared mad. But then *you*, Douglas dear, you turned up trumps, running about with a stick like that . . . In your jim-jams.'

'Who took the video?' Elisabeth asked.

Isabel Petty waved the hand with the dressing in it, impatient with detail. 'Someone Dell knows. We like Dell, don't we, Cat, even though she is such a *vulgar* woman.' Caterina kept her head turned away. 'Dell would have taken all the dogs away. And Dell's got a cousin in the local paper as vulgar as she is. And we thought it would stop people bringing more dogs, but then the big newspaper took it up and you got furious, didn't you, Douglas dear? No sense of humour.' Her girlish giggle was embarrassing. It made her speak faster so that she could get out the words before the uproarious funniness of the situation quite overcame her. Whilst scribbling doodles in the notebook, Elisabeth was trying to imagine her stirring poison into the animal feed and found it all too easy.

'So, whoopsadaisy, all these lawyers. Well, that was all right. Nice to have visitors and Amy so upset too. Cat wanted it to go on, because Douglas might get lots of money at the end and give her some. Or lose Amy somewhere along the line, something like that . . . Give me a drinkipoos, darling.'

Douglas obliged. Her polished nails clinked on the glass as she drank like a hungry bird.

'Where was I? Oh yes. It all went too far. Once Amy was gone and we had Douglas to ourselves, it was all going to be all right, you see. But Douglas was still going to go on with it, that lawyer *insisted* . . .'

'Which lawyer?' Elisabeth asked, sharply this time.

Isabel Petty squinted at her. 'Not *you*, dear, the other one. That thin man who sniffed. Lovely face, like a statue.'

Elisabeth wrote in her notebook, *Box the Fox*, and kept silent.

Isabel fixed her with a radiant smile. 'So I thought,' she said, with amazing clarity, 'it was time for another disaster. Only someone hit me.'

'Who hit you, Mummy?' Caterina crooned.

The smile receded and the question confused her. With the wavering hand, she pointed at Elisabeth. '*She* did. I think.'

'It was Jimmy,' Caterina said through gritted teeth. Jimmy picked a clump of fur from the carpet, moulded it into a neat lump and lobbed it into her lap. She screamed and squirmed until it fell on to the floor. Then she began to cry, slumped against the support of the fireplace pillar, tilting dangerously.

'What exactly did you tell Amy?' Douglas asked quietly.

'I think we can guess the rest,' Elisabeth interrupted. 'I think she would have manipulated Amy's sense of inferiority into believing she was neither valued nor loved. And I think that's enough, Mr Petty. I really do. There are limits and you're going way beyond them.'

He nodded. There was a weariness in the nod which did not correspond with the deftness of his movements. He reached a piece of damp towel from the mantelpiece and, for a split second, Elisabeth thought he would wrap it round his stepsister's throat. Instead he simply wiped her feet, gently, and caught her as she fell sideways. Then he hoiked her over his shoulder and carried her in a fireman's lift towards the door. He patted her on the back like someone burping a baby. 'Bedtime,' he stated. His heavy footsteps sounded in the stone corridor and, more distantly, up the stairs. Jimmy went across to Mrs Petty and removed the Elastoplast which held her wrist to the arm of her chair. He chafed her wrist.

'She would keep scratching,' he said. 'Wee bit of arnica for this bruise on the head, maybe,' he murmured briskly. 'Works a treat.' Mrs P did not respond. Her head settled comfortably against the leather of her seat and she began to snore, softly. Jimmy shook his head in amazement. 'Don't know how you can sleep with a conscience like that,' he said admiringly. 'And that son of yours can take you to bed, cos I'm not going to carry you.'

Douglas came back into the room and repeated the fireman's lift with his mother, disappearing again in the direction of upstairs. The atmosphere was suddenly lighter.

'More wine?' Jimmy asked. Her glass was empty. The image of the women as captives suddenly faded.

'I'd kill for another glass of wine.' She could have drunk the whole cellar, felt mildly hysterical. Jimmy left and came back with the wine. He seemed to be able to traverse the passageway between kitchen and here with remarkable speed and presented a clean glass, again overflowing, with the cool, pale liquid spilling over his grubby brown hand. The same hand which dealt with dirty dogs. She tried not to think of that, slumped back against her own chair, looked round the room and took several deep breaths. The feeling of hysterical relief faded. She tried to focus, took refuge in looking around.

'It's different in here, Jimmy. Why the hell have the curtains gone up? It's so gloomy.'

'Cos it's supposed to be elegant. Fucking art.'

'Wouldn't take long to pull them down.'

'Dead right it wouldn't.'

There was a brief silence, with noises in the distance. 'Did you know about any of this before, Jimmy?'

He shuffled, uncomfortably, not uncomfortable enough to hide a gleeful gaiety. 'Aye, I did, I suppose. Some of it. Sometimes I heard Amy chatting to the dogs. I saw the way those bitches treated her and watched her change. I never knew about the fucking libel, though, I really never. Is there really money in that rubbish?'

She thought of John Box and his need of money. 'Yes, there is.'

'Well I never. One fool born, two to take him. What's keeping the man? Can't take so long to bed down a couple of drunks. Come here, you daft creature, you've not done badly.'

The dog ambled across, put a head on his knee and wagged its tail.

'She's nice enough but she's got no road sense, though,' Elisabeth said, and then corrected herself hastily. 'I *bet* she has no road sense. Not much by way of domestic manners, either. She smells and she goes towards the person who hates her.'

'Manners? In that case, we'll get along fine. There's no point having manners if you live here.'

Mrs Petty's slender stick still rested by her chair. It looked as if the silver had been polished to a shine. A useless stick, except as a weapon. The assailant had not drawn blood. Elisabeth tried not to think of Amy Petty wielding that stick. The woman she had met the day before did not seem capable of getting on a bus, let alone driving a car. How had she done it? Of course she had not done it. But if it had been Amy wielding the stick which struck her mother-in-law, surely that exonerated Elisabeth herself from her promise of silence? Was that the reason Amy had been borrowing time? To cause mayhem? No, it was impossible; the dog was a different dog, and a promise was a promise, regardless. Douglas came back, sat in his mother's place, recharged his glass and raised it to her. He took a sip, reached for his wife's handbag and put it in his lap.

'They'll sleep like babies and no harm done, Miss Manser. Does that reassure you?'

She sipped and considered her reply. 'It might, Mr Petty, if you could give me a guarantee of good behaviour towards them in the morning. Steady on the threats of dogshit and the booze, if you see what I mean. Whatever they've done.'

He sipped his whisky. 'It may be far too old-fashioned to say I give you my word on that, but I do. For what it's worth.' He sipped again. 'Besides, they'll be busy packing their bags. They can both go and live in Cat's cottage. Don't worry, they won't starve. Even though they have a daft notion of how much I'm worth and it'll never be enough.'

'It was love that they wanted,' she said quietly.

He smiled at her, not the ferocious smile she had seen him bestow on John Box, but a real smile. Then he sighed. 'That's as maybe. But mine was spoken for.'

'Dogs,' she said flatly, eyeing the beast with its muzzle in Jimmy's lap. 'Spoken for by dogs.'

'Not entirely. The animals and the two women were a sacred trust given to me by Father. I love the dogs because I can make a difference, and I love them more because Amy does. Amy herself is another matter. I didn't choose Amy because she shared my passions. I chose her because she is the greatest of them. Do you know where she is, Elisabeth?'

The use of the present tense for Amy and the question, delivered like a lethal bullet at the end, shook her newfound composure and she spilled the wine. Scrubbed at the mark of it on her jeans with the sleeve of her shirt, ineffectually, affected by his voice. So smooth, almost without inflection, almost hypnotic. No wonder John Box envied him.

'I beg your pardon? Amy's *dead*, Douglas.' Saying his name out loud sounded odd, as if she had never referred to him as such in private.

'*Afghan loves Rottweiler*,' Douglas said dreamily. His voice had a mesmeric quality when he spoke as softly as this. 'And now at least, I know how my darling wife came by the extraordinary notion that I neither needed nor adored her. Post-its, bloody footprints on the kitchen floor. Clarins creams gone from flat, my own conviction. A dog like Dilly. I was so relieved to be right, I could have wagged my fucking tail.'

'I haven't got the faintest idea what you're talking about,' Elisabeth said with complete conviction.

He sighed again. 'Probably not. Did you find anything in the handbag?'

'Plenty.'

'And?'

'And nothing. I met a man on the train who thought the world of her. He served the tea.'

Douglas shouted with laughter. 'That figures. Probably small, perfectly formed and rude to her. Like Jimmy. She has the knack of liking the unlikable.'

HAS. Jimmy grinned, manifestly unoffended.

'I should like to go home now,' Elisabeth said. She sounded to her own ears like a child wanting to be taken away early from the party, pompous and petulant.

'Of course,' Douglas said quickly. 'Don't you like the wine?'

'I like it far too much. It bears no comparison to what I usually drink. In other circumstances, I would enjoy it hugely; but if you'll excuse my prudishness, I'm in a state of shock. What on earth possessed you to cover the windows?' They were talking in non sequiturs. She could not help it. She wanted neither to go nor to stay. She felt like an alien recently landed on the wrong planet where the air did not allow for quiet breathing.

'Caterina did them,' Douglas said. 'She said it lent style to the room. It probably does. Jimmy, for God's sake have a drink and call the taxi. Luscious Lizzie's had enough alarms without being driven home by you. Besides, I don't want to ruin her reputation and I'm worried about the suspension. Sorry, I do mean the car.'

Jimmy took what looked like a quarter pint of whisky into a glass and exited again, to the kitchen. The dog followed. Elisabeth was relieved about that. The dog puzzled her to death. Jimmy came back in his jaunty, jack-in-the-box style with another glass of wine for her.

'Ten minutes, petal. Time for you to drink it.'

'You'd be a good butler, Jimmy,' she said. They all sipped in unison. It felt ridiculously easy, although the curtains shrouding the room from the dusk outside made it seem as if they were all talking underwater. She had been here four times before and missed the view from here to beyond as if she belonged.

'There is this funny business about *trust*,' Douglas said to her. 'I don't know what it is. Or how it's formed, I really don't. Sometimes it takes an age to acquire, sometimes a second. I haven't the faintest idea why I trust you, but I do. I learned it from my father. Blind trust, sometimes, but always worth repeating. Amy didn't have that chance. She didn't have the chance to learn it and I managed to deny her the chance to acquire it. I don't trust that leader of yours, I'm afraid. It's a strange phenomenon, isn't it, *trust*? Something akin to respect. Acknowledgement, mutual recognition. The bare bones of love, but not the same. Dogs trust Amy. There's a kind of power in her innocence. I hope I never lose the habit of trusting to instinct. It works far more often than not.'

Elisabeth bowed her head, humiliated for no reason she had time to analyse. She knew she had been trusted, even if she had been bullied into it. She did not trust him, any more than she could have thrown him, which was a matter of inches, but she knew the accolade of being trusted and she knew she liked Jimmy. Probably because of his poetic influence on her language and all the *fuckings* he employed in his own. She pulled herself together with a visible effort. Pushing up the sleeves of her shirt, squashing the useless briefcase shut, which was easy with only the notebook inside it. A notebook of the type widely used in the profession, blue on the outside, serrated and lined pages within, slimline and harmless. The sound of a car horn sounded from the back. She finished the wine and stood up, slightly unsteady, put the handbag over her shoulder. Douglas extended his hand. It was warm and dry.

'Goodbye, Elisabeth. Thank you for bringing back the handbag.' He hesitated. 'I do know that trust isn't reciprocal, but if you do happen to know where my wife happens to be and trust me enough to tell me, please do.'

'I think she's dead at the moment, Douglas.'

He shook her hand. The grip was so strong she had the suspicion the forearm would fall off at the elbow.

'Thinking's a far fucking cry from believing.' That was Jimmy, grumbling at her side as they went through to the back door, crossing the alien kitchen, where the new dog skulked, luxuriously, beside a Rayburn oven which looked as if it had been born in the last millennium.

'Know any good jokes, Jimmy?' she said.

'Don't know no fucking jokes.'

'Well there's one about ovens. Do you know the correct way to refer to a middle-class pregnancy? You can't say she's got a bun in the oven. You have to say she's got a fucking ciabatta in the Aga. Oh, forget it.'

He was ushering her into a new-looking Ford with polished interior, a swinging deodoriser over the back window and a woman driver winking at him from behind the wheel.

'What are you going to do now?' she shouted at him from the back seat as he shooed her into it in the same way he had shooed the dog out of the room.

'Pull down those fucking curtains,' he yelled back. 'It's the only way I'll get the bastard to mourn. He can't do it with the windaes shut.'

★

The car slid away, bumping down the track with cautious ease. She looked back towards the house, seeing the white curve of the half-dome with no idea of whether she would ever see it again and, as soon as it was out of view, missing the sight of it like a mild indigestion, all the way home.

A short way home, quicker than arrival, the roads emptier now. Not black night, but dusk night, dark without being entirely dark, fumbling on the brink of night. Rain out there, somewhere, fucking up the view. A nice car, three colossal glasses of wine, the equivalent of a bottle, and fuck this, did she have the fare? Life was an empty briefcase. *Luscious Lizzie*; the bastard, how dare he?

The car cruised neatly between country and town, across motorway and centre and side road and finally into the terrace where she lived. She played cat's cradle with her fingers. Laced them one over another and turned them inside out. It was a nice car, without bumps and crumps, with a silent, efficient driver. The sight of her own door was a shock on account of it being so small, she felt she should stoop to open it. Jimmy's fistprints were in the dust, lit by the useless security light, the imprints of his knuckles lit above the central handle. All paid, the driver said; must've cost a fortune. She fumbled with the key and opened her own little door as if she was a stranger.

Stored heat. A yowling cat, as well it might. Food for it. The winking answerphone, the mobile phone she had left behind. *Shit.* The fax machine, attached to the phone, last heard whirring as she went out, a year ago.

She wanted to bury her head in a piece of nice warm sand somewhere. Or lie in a hot bath and think, but she also wanted something to do. The relative harmlessness of paper was easier to deal with than the accusing sound of voices, so Elisabeth began with the fax, postponing the messages. Coffee in one hand, chocolate in the other as the proper way to read. She would never have thought that the sight of neat handwriting attached to several sheets of legal prose would be soothing. Her friend Helen was always legible, probably thought in legal prose, or at least formal prose, infected with the sometimes sonorous language of judges.

No effing and blinding – neat, unadorned work. Helen would never call her Lizzie. Helen was as sleek as an otter.

Dear Elisabeth,

Here's an extract from the judgement in R v Fisher. He was forty years old at the time, in 1975; would that make the ages correspond to indicate it's the same Fisher?

The judgement deals with points of law, of course, and there's only a short precis of the facts, so I'm allowing myself to read between the lines. Apart from the legal points, the case had some notoriety at the time, because he was an art teacher and it was early days for the 'outing' of 'respectable' sex offenders in positions of authority. What he actually DID was not so bad; if you put activity short of penile penetration or fellation in that category. It must have been more titillation and gratification for him than release. (Put another way, he kept his tackle inside his trousers, but liked copping a feel.) The worst aspects were his isolation of each little girl in turn, his penchant for what he sweetly called 'duskies', and his chosen method of keeping them quiet. Which was to introduce them to glue-sniffing (I suppose you may as well use what comes to hand.) They were all about ten years old. A very persuasive man, but, unfortunately for him, the aberrant behaviour caused by fun and games with glue was what brought the thing to light, although it dented the credibility of the witnesses and confused their memories. (One had also been encouraged to 'taste' lead paint. I think they have less poisonous materials in schools these days.)

Two interesting facts: (Why do I do this for you, the way I used to write your essays? Why don't I let you read it for yourself?)

ONE: Fisher's daughter was to have been his alibi for the occasion of the most serious assault, but denied being with him at the time.

TWO: THE PROSECUTOR WAS ONE DOUGLAS PETTY. An old hand here says he was a real tough one in his

*youth and did a lot of deviancy cases. Perhaps it infected him?
Turned him into an animal?*

*More importantly, my dear, I spoke to Superintendent
Bailey, who is working on the train crash. The victim with the
broken neck you mentioned is down on record as travelling
alone. However, the partner to whom the death was reported at
home later that day is a travelling salesman 'not unknown to
police'. (I can't say more than that.)*

*And FINALLY, I have to tell you that I can't let your cryptic
remarks about Amy Petty rest there. It just isn't on. Why should
conscientious people spend days investigating these terrible
deaths only to have the facts distorted by someone pretending to
be dead or hurt? It isn't right and it isn't fair. I know you meant
it to be confidential but some things just cannot be that. There's
such a thing as public duty, you know. So Bailey will be coming
to see you tomorrow and if there's anything to tell, I advise you
to be frank.*

*Yours, whenever you need me,
Helen*

Oh why oh why did she always get people so wrong?
Underestimate them, overestimate them; inflate them, deflate
them, but consistently misjudge? And what price promises? The
coffee burned her mouth, the chocolate furred her teeth and the
cat twined round her ankles. 'Bugger off,' she told it. Oh Christ,
and now she was talking to animals, too. She threw the coffee
down the sink and resisted the impulse to smash the mug against
the wall. Faced with a police interrogator tomorrow, she would
blab, of course she would; she was not an investigative journalist
insured to protect her sources. Her and her own big mouth and
fuck Helen, what about trust? She put down the fax with shaking
hands. The paper had an unpleasant texture which stuck to her
fingers. Should have done the phone first, maybe it was easier
after all.

★

There were two messages on the mobile phone, the first echoing with desperation.

'Elisabeth, where are you? Oh I wish you were there. It's Amy. Can you come back tomorrow, soon? Now? *PLEASE?* Save me . . . from myself . . .'

Elisabeth phoned back the number shown on the mobile's screen. Heard the lonely, continuous ring and imagined the deserted callbox with the traffic thundering by.

CHAPTER FIFTEEN

The bright lights of the Asda superstore were very bright. It was an alternative world, all by itself. When she entered the place that Friday morning on her flight from Bayview Road, Amy concluded that this was where everyone went. Into the equivalent of the parish church, built on a larger scale. They came here from the deserted pavements as soon as they had discovered where it was. They got into their cars and came here to pay homage. A pedestrian like herself, approaching a side door, felt like a pilgrim, entirely different to the imperfect country housewife she had been before, dumping the car, grabbing the family-sized trolley, safe in the knowledge of the credit card and the large, affordable order. Without people and dogs to feed, she felt strange, limped through the aisles, distracted by the music, unenchanted by the place but busy, concentrating. It was another kind of normality. She wished she had found it sooner; it was a hopeful hive of activity.

She selected one cheap tracksuit, the same dun green of the canvas shoes, carefully chosen for price and lack of pattern. She did not like patterns. The clothes section looked as if it had been picked over by a million hands, feeling for bargains, but the presence of *new* things was thrilling. She put the suit into her basket, turned to tour the other aisles. Two pairs of socks, two of knickers, one tube of E45 moisturising cream, which she clutched like a talisman. She wandered through the two dozen aisles of food, unable to focus, but planning all the time. There was everything here; even on a budget her father did not need to eat in the way he did. She would come back, get food to whet his appetite, make him think of food rather than anything else. A well-nourished body would make for a quieter soul. For the moment, all she selected was a litre bottle of whisky and a packet of cigarillos, because she wanted the smell of both, all of which went into the basket along with a packet of bright hair slides. She paid carefully and found the ladies' lavatory by the exit. In the safety of a cubicle, she changed into the tracksuit. The sleeves of the top and the legs of the bottom were too long; the fabric was harsh and mostly synthetic, but the freshness of it was delicious. She bound back her hair with a purple hairgrip and saw in the mirror a renewed, almost respectable person, less alien than the one who had arrived, and felt an enormous sense of achievement, exaggerated into pride as she stuffed the skirt into a rubbish bin.

At the checkout, she had watched someone slide a packet of sweets into his pocket and wondered if her father might have done that. Perhaps she could be a thief, Amy thought as she waited at the bus stop with the whisky in a bag bumping against her thigh, feeling almost competent. She could be a thief who simply sat in one of those parked cars and drove it away: she could live on stolen food. But a thief required sleight of hand rather than clumsiness, and what would happen when she was arrested? What would they do to her if she simply smiled and smiled, saying nothing, with nothing to identify her? They would have to put her somewhere, if not a safe place, safer than this. Suddenly there seemed to be choices; she would find work, begin again. She felt a surge of optimism; she had new clothes and moisturising cream; her father had bought her shoes. She would get back her money from him and buy good food; she would plan their lives for a week and make a difference. She would protect him.

She should have bought something for him today, as a start, a reminder to him of how they could go on. She remembered that as she opened the front door to see the door of his workroom locked with him busy inside, and despite the determination to somehow begin afresh with him on an honest basis, she was secretly relieved to postpone a conversation again. The fatigue hit her like a brick. She wanted him to see her with all the authority of her new clothes, notice her, ask where she had been, talk to her openly, but she needed above all to close her eyes. She was monstrously tired; she had tricked her grief into submission for a few hours but now her need for sleep was as relentless as toothache.

The new newspapers were on the kitchen table, still folded. Amy placed the whisky by the sink and crept upstairs. When she had slept, she would find the right words to speak to him clearly. He had bought her the shoes. They would sort out a way of living with dignity, protecting each other for a while. In the bathroom, she scrubbed herself in cold water. The habits of cleanliness died hardest. It felt as if a decade had passed since last she slept. She took off the new tracksuit and folded it carefully; it had to last. The sheets on her bed were grey . . . must wash . . . must scrub teeth . . . must sleep . . . must . . . avoid grief. Not cry. A dream-filled sleep. Nonsense dreams, when she was cleaning a house belonging to someone else, rubbing at stains which would not go away on an oatmeal-coloured carpet which was as hairy to touch as the coat of a dog. Elisabeth Manser asking her, why do you bother? The question ballooning out of her fine-featured, expressive face which became as large as the moon. Bother with what? Coarse, chauvinistic, bullying men and old, sick dogs. Her face was nose-down into the pillow. Someone was pressing the back of her head so that it was difficult to breathe; a hand touched her hair. She brushed it away, but still the question had to be answered. *I have always loved dogs ever since I had one and it was taken away. I love them because I am never clumsy with them. I know what to do. I am never afraid of them as I am of almost everything else; they are never afraid of me. I am deft and clever with dogs . . . I make a differ-ence. I have always wanted to make a difference. And Douglas? He was just love.* She could feel Caterina's manicured fingers next, pretending to massage her shoulder, her long nails biting into the flesh, a voice telling her, *Sleep, darling, don't worry about a thing.* Voices drifted from downstairs, entering the room like fog. A door slammed.

Amy woke, breathless. The curtains of the room were stretched shut. Light filtering through the thin fabric showed the contours of the room. The wardrobe stood still, like an empty coffin. There was a sharp smell of whisky in her nostrils and the sound of quiet, cackling laughter. Then a tuneless singing.

Rollie Fisher sat on a chair in the middle of the room, as far away as he could get from the bed, always keeping his distance. '*Rock-a-bye baby, on the tree top, When the wind blows the cradle will rock, When the bough breaks, the cradle will fall, Down will come baby, cradle and all . . .*' He crooned the rhyme in a cracked voice and then laughed some more until she closed her eyes against the sound. Opened them again to see that he was nursing a tumbler of whisky. There was a teacup on the rickety table at the side of the bed, half full of liquid.

'My dear silly daughter, WAKE UP, pet.'

She raised her head.

'Ah, that's better. Isn't it nice to see you? Such a popular woman you are. A man called to see you just now. Said he knew you from the train, you tart, and followed you home. I told him there was no woman here. A *nasty* man.'

'No one's looking for me,' she murmured, groggy with sleep, but still enraged by the lie and the irrational hope it created.

The whisky smell grew stronger. Rollie Fisher reeked of it as he shook with mirth. He was drunk, something she had never seen. He hated drink; said it had almost killed him; she remembered the whisky, left by the sink, her silly, sentimental purchase, made for the smell. Rollie was wicked drunk, uninhibited, talkative, manic. Gleeful.

'I told the man you weren't here so that you would have time to *leave*,' he said with heavy emphasis. 'Soon, sooner, *soonest.* I don't want you here any more, never wanted you at all. You've stayed quite long enough. Tee-hee-hee. I won, didn't I? I won! Don't want you here. I want you to go. I mean go, just bugger off. Those shoes were made for walking.'

'Go?' she said stupidly.

He slurped at the whisky. The pouch of skin beneath his chin trembled; he seemed to be brimming with triumph. He put down the drink, clapped his hands loudly, picked it up again. Part of him was entirely in control.

'You went home, didn't you? I knew you did. And when you went you knew you could never go back. He'd *hate* you if you did. A man like that loathes to be fooled. They dish it out but they can't take it. Too late to go back now, isn't it? You've blown up your own home, ha ha ha.'

She could see that his face was scarlet, his eyes peculiarly bright, like the glass eyes of some of his dolls.

'So you can get out now, Go, go, go. I'm finished with you. Besides, I need the room.'

Amy struggled for words. 'You said I could stay. As long as I wanted.' She knew she was plaintive and frightened, hating it in herself. Panic rose in her throat. She could not imagine how she had ever craved the smell of whisky.

'Listen, dear, I got you the little shoes so that you could walk away. As soon as you can, dearest, before it gets dark, anyway.' Again, the giggle. 'Otherwise I don't know how I shall feed you. Turpentine in the tea, perhaps, please don't tempt me. I can resist anything but.'

Amy sat up, pulling the sheet to cover her shoulders.

'Ugh,' he said, sipping more of the whisky, grimacing at the sight of her.

'Why do I have to go?' she said slowly. 'Where would I go?'

He waved his empty hand. 'Oh, I don't know. Anywhere. I've finished with you really. Even before you frightened away that lovely child next door and invited a strange man to the house. Rock-a-bye baby, great big lump.'

She folded her arms across her knees, watching him.

'Do you know, when I was in prison, I dreamed of this,' Rollie said, tapping the glass. 'All the time. And then when I was out, it made me ill. But it took my mind off his voice, the bastard. Do you know, when you were ten years old, you were as much a conniving little bitch as any of them?'

'I don't know what you mean, Father. Which voice?'

'*His* voice, of course,' he scoffed. 'As if you didn't know it. You probably think of it all the time, too. That lovely, *manly* voice. Making me squirm and cry with his questions. In court, in front of everyone. For years I could hear his voice . . . He made me out to be a leper, made me admit . . . Bastard DOUGLAS PETTY. Handsome Petty once, with a fucking fortune . . .' He transferred the glass from right hand to left and wagged his finger at her. "Such a *gifted* teacher you were, Mr Fisher," he mimicked. "An *artist*. A trustworthy man. They adored you, those children, did they not? And all you could do was *lust*." He made me admit . . . he made me cry. He made me say . . . He damns with faint praise, assents with civil leer, and without sneering, taught the rest to sneer . . . He *diminished* me into *nothing* . . .' His voice was rising to a scream.

Amy hugged herself tighter. Rollie Fisher went into a paroxysm of coughing, still holding the glass steady.

'That hypocrite, with his *voice*,' he choked. 'Your *spouse*. Was him I wanted, not you. I followed what he did. How could he talk about *lust* when he had all those women? How could he brand ME a *pervert* for loving innocence? And then I saw you,' he went on dreamily, his voice subsiding into a chant. 'In a newspaper. You in that frock, looking ridiculous. He must have loved you to be so blind. He'd forgive you anything if he could forgive that frock. It must have been real *lurve*. Must have loved you to *death*. He had what he wanted, poor fool. He *trusted* you with his happiness. So I thought I would take you away. Leave him with dreams, like me. Mr *Petty* wrecks my life; I wreck his. Simple.'

The outburst exhausted him. His voice became a triumphant whine. 'And then you came to see me and *pitied* me, Mrs *Petty*. *My* daughter who marries my *persecutor*. And you let yourself believe you were my precious, important little thing, even after that treachery! I could never have planned it as good as this. You helped . . . you believed, you *pitied* . . . You *let* yourself be taken away. You came willing. You preferred me to him. How he'd *detest* you if he knew what a credulous fool you are. You can't go back. You can only go to the gutter. And he won't die wondering, because one day I'll tell him and make him squirm. I'll tell him what you became because you believed me, not him. I won, I won, I won. Do you understand, you big lump?'

She did understand, perfectly. She had never mattered at all. *Hatred; dislike; indifference; contempt.* She had never even merited any of these. Amy got out of bed, naked. There was a small ration of space in the room. Her clothes were over the chair in which he sat and she needed the armour of clothes. Kicking her way out of the blanket, she knocked over the teacup he had left; the sharp stench of white spirit was sickening. He leapt from the chair and backed towards the window; stood there gazing at her. The laughter died. His face was contorted with disgust.

'Look what Douglas can never have. Christ. And you thought I cared about *you*? You were only a means to an end. You aren't even an *enemy*. You're *nothing*.'

'What about my money?'

'*Your* money? I deserve that for keeping you.'

She loomed above him, trembling, feeling for the clothes and staring him in the eyes. Rollie put his hand over his mouth and stumbled from the room. She heard his clumsy thumping down the stairs, the chanting voice drifting back, '*I won, I won, I won . . .*'

She yanked back the curtains with such force they tore in her hands. Later afternoon daylight, diffused with clouds. The sounds of a street full of hidden eyes. Music through the wall from next door. She did not want daylight; she wanted darkness.

The shoes were on the floor where he had left them. Her left foot slipped inside easily; the other was swollen. She could not wear his shoes. She dressed slowly in the new clothes, waited a while and followed him downstairs, barefoot. The door to his workroom stood open, presenting his theatre, ready for admirers, clean and swept and spotlit, the heavier curtains left partially open, so that the interior could be glimpsed from the outside. Houses and dolls built as honey traps a modern child could resist. He would be better to have lined his lair with computer games. On his workbench there was the almost finished shell of a new building, $\frac{1}{12}$ scale, balsawood, bigger than the others, the paint of its red roof still gleaming wet. Amy laced the fingers of both hands together into a single fist and brought the fist down like a hammer. The red roof crumpled. Such large, strong, capable hands she had. Her face burnt in the warmth of the spotlights; her mind registered the fantastical shapes of the houses and the years it had taken to make them.

She left the room.

In the kitchen, Rollie was slumped back in his habitual place, sleeping an unhealthy, noisy sleep with long, ragged breaths. Drink was a dangerous, unpredictable novelty. The whisky bottle stood where she had left it, empty. His arms were crossed over his slight tummy, his neck bent back and his throat exposed. He was like the one of his dolls she knew best, the defenceless master of the house, lolling in his chair. She could pull him apart in a minute. Her hands hovered above his thin throat, touched his paper skin. Not a real man; it would be a painless death; she could do it, it would be easy. She leant forward and whispered into his ear.

'What kind of man strangles love out of people, Daddy? Douglas didn't deserve you. He didn't make you guilty; you were guilty. You aren't fit to lick his shoes. All he does is tell the truth. He always does that. You can do what you like to me, but I'll kill you for hating him.' Her fingers tightened on his throat, her thumbs pressing into the flaccid flesh of the neck, harder, tightening around bone. She could shake him until he was dead, dead, dead. Douglas deserved enemies he could see and fight, not these cunning shadows. The touch of her father's skin repelled her; her paint-sticky hands smeared crimson against his chin; there was the reek of whisky-sour breath, bringing sanity. Then his eyes opened wide and looked straight into her own. Clouded eyes, widening in terror, closing again as she backed away, retreating until her hip collided with the sink. The empty bottle fell to the floor with a thud.

Amy washed her hands, repeatedly and compulsively. The red paint stuck. Real blood would be a different colour, almost brown. It was dark outside, the day gone. Nothing changed nature. She breathed deeply. Nothing changed what she was. If she killed him, she would murder herself. Then he would have won; that might be what he wanted. Part of the game, the bequest to Douglas of a murderous wife, even better revenge than a deserting, deceitful wife. Revenge was not hers, not now; violence was unnatural to her, but she hated him, hated him, hated him. She made herself breathe steadily and look down at his smeared throat for a long time. Until, through long concentration and an effort of will, all she could see lying in the chair was an old, sick dog with incurable diseases, a pathetic piece of existence. He was also still a man she desperately wanted to hurt. He stirred, opened his eyes again. 'Don't leave me,' he murmured.

'No,' she said.

His eyes closed; the ragged breathing resumed.

Amy went back to the room of the dolls' houses. She closed the curtains tight and shut the door behind her.

Now she was at the phone box. The phone stood by the edge of the road, near the bus stop, defying anyone to enter the bubble surrounding it to make themselves heard over the traffic. A midnight phone for using when all the lorries had gone to bed. She had lost all notion of time. Amy dialled the number she knew by heart and heard the neutral voice of a recording, speaking in clipped, electronic English, *please speak after the tone.* She heard herself shouting back, 'Elisabeth, is that you?' Yelling into the foul-smelling phone. *'Are you there, Elisabeth? Speak to me, please. Can you come?'* Then a male voice, cutting across her own. Jimmy's voice, shouting back, *'Amy! Amy! Hallo, hallo, hallooooo!'* Slammed back the phone as she realised what she had done. Dialled home. Silly, silly, silly.

She paused for a deep breath and dialled the other number she had learned by heart and meant to dial the first time. Slightly calmer, she heard the same, neutral voice and left a message.

'*Elisabeth, please come. Come and save me from myself. Please.*'

There was a man outside the bubble, waiting. He seemed to be waiting for her. He stared at her bright red hands, tear-streaked face, wild eyes and bare feet and backed away.

The traffic was lighter and faster. Cars whined into sight and whined away, speeding into the night. They moved faster, this time of night. Amy paused at the edge of the kerb, listening to the murderous hum of engines. It would be so easy, so simple to run amongst them. Better than going *home*. If she went home and her father taunted her with his triumph over Douglas, she might still stab him. She was feverish with rage; she could do anything.

Amy walked barefoot, parallel with the traffic. Red paint smeared the front of the new tracksuit. The trousers were covered with multicoloured dust and fragments, and she did not know from where they came. The Asda sign she had never noticed winked in the distance and she suddenly remembered her father's phrase. '*. . . must have loved you to death . . . he'd forgive you any-thing.*'

She opened the palm of her hand and saw that she was clutching a single pound coin, nothing else.

The lights of the cars tantalised her.

The light at the end of the tunnel is the train coming in the other direction.

CHAPTER SIXTEEN

Elisabeth hated the watery light of early morning 'C'mon, c'mon . . .' she fretted. *Come and save me.* That was what Amy said. What could she have done at midnight but wait for morning? Nothing.

There was a *tick, tick, ticky* sound. *Tick, tick, tick.* This was a sick train, sulking while a few of them stood on the platform, waiting for permission to board. *Tick, tick, SHIT.* There was something wrong with it. The ticking mimicked the racing of her heart.

Elisabeth sat on a bench with her hands pressed between the backs of her legs and the metal, all the better to resist chewing her fingernails. The metal was early-morning moist and scaldingly cold. It was the wrong time for a train to break down, although there was a kind of relief in the delay. Better to travel hopefully. *Tick, tick . . . sigh*; a human, scolding sound, mocking anxiety.

Six-thirty a.m., in time for the first train in the doubtful light. Elisabeth removed her hands to the pockets of her jacket. There was a Saturday-morning sprinkling of people, nothing like the weekday commuter crowd, all of these hell-bent on innocent pleasures. She should have set off the night before, only she had not. *Should have, should have . . . shoodav, shoodav,* a pointless recrimination sounding like the train, but the darkness had taken away courage. *Should* have been at home when Amy rang. Should *not* have phoned John at home and heard the icy voice of his wife saying, 'Do you know what time this is, Miss Manser? Of course you can't speak to him' Exercising the inalienable rights of a protective spouse.

The train fell silent, then stuttered into life with a show of vigour, became a lazy animal recovering from a dawn chill, responding to the weak heat of the sun on the carriage roofs, deciding that movement was preferable. Orders were shouted; everyone got on and settled down, none of them, except a mother and daughter, sitting together. The carriage gathered speed in the interludes of countryside between stations, too fast for her uncertain digestion, although the movement was better than staying still. It meant progress, a sense of purpose, as if she was driving the thing herself, a lulling of the gnawing anxiety, and it meant having to do nothing for a little while. Which presented the fact that she did not know what she was doing anyway. Running in the direction of Amy's danger, like a headless chicken; running away from a severe policeman, responding without planning. Typical. She chewed her nails. Why the hell hadn't she just called them first? The one thing she could do was use a phone. But there was that bloody promise of two days' silence, which seemed insane in daylight, even though it made sense the night before. Fear, that was all it was, fear and cowardice that made her wait. What the hell she was going to do when she got to Bayview Road she had no idea. Drag Amy away by the scruff of her neck, as if she was a fighting cat? Take her home? Find a way to deliver this piece of property back into the hands of its rightful owner, like a lost dog which might well be beaten by its master for the crime of its defection? She would be sick with relief if she found Amy feeding some old dog. That would be fine, but she would be too late and it would be her own fault. Rollie Fisher might have killed her. Elisabeth yearned for coffee while knowing it would only make her shake; it always had that effect the morning after the night before, even if the hangover was purely emotional. *Do you know what time this is, Miss Manser? Can't it wait until morning?* This journey was unbearably lonely.

She thought of other journeys on this train, to and from, always on her own, and knew this was the loneliest of all. She had not asked Helen for help; she was disgusted with Helen. She had wanted John's help, forgotten it was never really there. So she had tried sleep instead and regretted it now.

The Lloyds tower was visible in a blue sky, giving the illusion of closeness to a city signposted by similar obelisks. More passengers had joined at the intermediate stops, a tribe of men going north for a football match, girls with sportsbags, team players all. With her gaze fixed outside the window, Elisabeth nursed the handbag on her knee, half waiting for a crash, until someone occupied the seat beside her. She angled both body and handbag further towards the window. A hand poked her arm; she turned her head, ready to glare.

'Oh *fuck.*'

There was Jimmy, with his crumpled brown face like a paper bag, his finger on his lips, saying, 'Shhhhh.' The evening before was a distant dream, far further away than a matter of hours. His face was remote enough to surprise her; it was out of context. It did not belong on a train; it belonged on a planet where trains and cities did not belong. She felt shocked at the sight of him. Jimmy belonged somewhere else, and all the same, she was numb with relief.

'I've seen you looking better, Liz. Not used to getting up early in the morning, are we?'

She clenched her hands around the handbag and turned her head back to the window. A blush was spreading over her face and she was furious, the pulse pounding again. The fury sank into a flutter of irritation, followed by resignation. No one could keep secrets; they were infectious, with the hidden life of a virus, spread by the sheer act of breathing, and she was glad not to be alone. So pleased, she could have screamed and hugged him. There was *someone.* Even a rude, aggressive bundle of skinny muscle and bone like Jimmy was someone.

'You look like a piece of shit yourself,' she said.

'Ah, but that's normal.'

She frowned and stayed silent, lost for words. The train stopped at London Bridge at a side platform flanked by dark and sinister brickwork, a platform to avoid at night. There was an exodus of the football party, the train moved off again, moaning and groaning in a slow crawl over complicated tracks. Jimmy clutched her arm fiercely, so that his fingers dug through the fabric of her sleeve.

'I never go on trains,' he said. 'Fucking things scare me to death.'

'Shame.'

'She phoned last night,' Jimmy said tremulously, still clutching her arm. 'By mistake. Asking for you. Always was dysfuckinglexic with numbers, Amy. Know that voice anywhere. I didn't tell him, I just came over to follow you.'

She suppressed the joyous relief that he had. There seemed no point in explanation or denial. 'Why didn't you tell him?'

'He might fucking murder you for not saying you knew where she was. Though God knows why, he guessed you did. I fucking didn't, not until she called by mistake. I knew then he was right. Oh, Jesus Christ, look at that,' he said, still holding her arm with one hand and pointing out of the window with the other. 'Will you just look at that?'

The Millennium Wheel rose above the river as if it owned the landscape, including the gleaming, moving expanse of the river below. The train slid into the darkness of the station. Jimmy dragged at the strap of her handbag like a dog on a lead.

'You're going to see her, aren't you, I know you are. I've been waiting outside your house. We need to bring her back, he'll have those two out by this afternoon.' Jimmy spoke like a spluttering firework.

'Because of Amy?'

'Aye, because of Amy.'

'That might not be the problem, Jimmy. She's got this father who's an ex-con . . . paedophile. That's where she is.'

'So what fucking difference will that make to Douglas?' Jimmy shouted, missing the point entirely. 'It'll be the same bastard been writing him hate-mail for years. Besides, his own father was a fucking crook.' He tugged at the window, slamming it down, ready to jump, poised on the step, ready to run.

'Her father hates her, Jimmy. He's filled her with lies. She's coming apart . . . he might be dangerous.' To her horror, she could feel tears welling in her eyes.

Jimmy stood on the platform, hands on hips, a bantamweight man with the physique of a terrier. 'Don't even think of fucking *crying*. Why didn't you say so, for God's sake? Just take us.'

She was fumbling in her handbag for her purse, unconsciously mimicking the way he was feeling in his pockets for tobacco. 'I need cash for the taxi.'

His brown hand produced a wad of notes, bunched in his fist.

Taxis did not want to go to SE23. Jimmy kept the notes visible until one of them did. The morning was fine, clear, calm, the population harmless. Cruising through the City, she was struck by the irrelevant wish that Jimmy had brought one of the dogs. The cityscape rolled by; the details went unnoticed. He was entirely unmoved by the Westminster spires and the density of buildings.

'Her father might try to poison her,' Elisabeth said wildly. 'He might have tried to kill her.'

Jimmy turned his head from the window. 'You don't know Amy, do you?' he said.

Elisabeth shook her head. 'No, I don't know her at all.'

It was a quiet street when they reached it. Not as ugly as she remembered. Just another street where people lived and breathed and nothing much happened.

There was a figure in the doorway of number seventeen. A crumpled heap of dirty clothes, sleeping. Emerging on touch into a woman. The overlong trouser bottoms covered her feet. She uncurled and stood upright, unsteadily, revealing cold, bare feet. Squinting at them. Smiling that deceptively vacuous smile, which embraced them both and gave no indication that she had expected to see them, only hoped.

'Hallo,' Amy said. 'I forgot my keys. Aren't you glad I forgot my keys? It means I haven't killed him.'

'. . . *The house was so dark,*' Elisabeth wrote to John at the very end of the day. '*Darker than I remembered. It faced east, I think; a dark, cold house. It would have killed your spirit to live in it the way it was. There was so much newspaper in it. Thank God for Jimmy. It was him who broke down the door and went upstairs and found Rollie Fisher in his bed. Not dead, the bastard. Not even dying. He kept saying SHE'S DONE FOR ME, SHE'S DONE FOR ME. He was sleeping with his bedroom door barricaded and a range of broken miniature dolls by his bed. He was gibbering. Jimmy cleaned him up and got an ambulance on his mobile. They said, who'll be here when we bring him back? I said no one, none of us were relatives, only passing strangers. I can be heartless, sometimes.*

The dolls' house room (see above, if you haven't been following) was a pile of rubble. Everything smashed to smithereens. Who did this, I asked Amy. She was frozen, not monosyllabic, but oddly composed, as if something was settled. "It will take him a long time to put them together," she told me. Looking at the carnage was the only time I felt regret for him. I told her they were beautiful creations as I remembered them, and she said that all depended on why they were made. I didn't understand. She kept on saying how glad she was she had forgotten to take the keys when she went to phone. There was red paint on his neck. He screamed when he saw her, I don't know why. She said thank you to him. Thank you for what you said about some people loving each other to death.

I said we would take her home. When I said that, she trembled so much, I thought she would shake to pieces, but there was not much choice. And I knew I had to go with her. Protect her, and I can't tell you how much I dreaded that. She wanted to wash and borrow makeup, fretted about her shoes . . . Ah, I can hear you say, the priorities of women.

I wondered why her father was suddenly so afraid of her. Gentleness, thy name is Amy. I thought the danger came from him, but it was him who was afraid . . .

★

Cash talks and cash hires cars. There was piercing, dappled sun-shine through the trees, the beginning of a brilliant June before the rain as they emerged from the town and into the valley. All three of them were in the back of another car with Elisabeth in the middle. They were going home. Amy was dozing, with her head leaning against the window, eyes closed, like a person dreaming for courage. Jimmy was calm and whistling.

'Is this really the right thing to do?' Elisabeth whispered.

'What else to do?'

'She could come and stay with me.'

He stopped whistling. 'Nope. My job is to bring her home. She wants to go.'

'Does she? What are you Jimmy, a bounty hunter?'

He looked at her scornfully. 'You know what, Miss fucking Manser, I reckon that somewhere in between yesterday and today, Amy got to understand something, which is more than you ever seem to do.'

'Understand what?'

'The nature of the beast,' he said. 'The one who goes by scent and instinct, just like she does. You don't know anything.'

Elisabeth subsided into her seat. 'He could have come and fetched her,' she said.

'I told him, no. He would have crashed the car.'

The whistling resumed.

The car stopped by the side of the house. All three of them crossed the lawn, their figures casting shadows. Elisabeth stayed close to Amy, looking up at the white façade of the house, noticing that the windows of the big room were bare. Douglas shambled out of the French doors like a bear, moving at a run. Elisabeth put her hand on Amy's arm, pulling her back. Amy pushed her aside, gently, and went towards him, unconscious of anyone else. Not Jimmy or the dogs keeping a distance. The two of them collided, slowly, as if conscious of their fragility. Then they were hugging, Douglas crying like a helpless child and murmuring over and over, *Oh, you silly bitch, you sillybitch, my dearest sillybitch, my darling* . . . They could have been surrounded by fire and never noticed. With the peculiar, intoxicated walk of addicted lovers, arms entwined, they disappeared inside the house, leaving the swishing salutation of the willow tree.

Jimmy had turned away, shuffling in his pockets for the fags.

Elisabeth tried to stay cool, like a fucking lawyer. 'The nature of the beast?' she asked, voice quavering.

'Yeah, tha's it,' he sniffed. 'It's not what you fucking say that counts. It's what you do. Who needs fucking discussions? Animals don't need them.'

She could hear the sound of barking in the distance.

Jimmy adjusted the cigarette. 'I'll have to feed the dogs. C'mon with me. Nobody needs us here.'

She felt peculiarly light-headed, followed down the path to the stables, turning back to look at the house.

Much later, going home on the train, she cried and cried and cried and tried to compose the words she should use to tell all this to John Box, while knowing she could never explain to him the nature of the beast.

CHAPTER SEVENTEEN

Rain, relentless rain, persisting through Saturday night and all of Sunday. Appropriate rain; rain was her background for writing and reading and confessing, sitting in her tiny kitchen with Helen West's policeman, an uncritical confessor, better than a priest and far more sympathetic. A discursive man with a surreptitious note-book; a person who forced her to analyse. To the tune of the rain, Elisabeth Manser found it all too easy to cry. Sundays, he told her, were always sad days.

There were phone calls. Many.

It still rained on the Tuesday morning, when John Box and Elisabeth Manser met inside the portico of the High Court entrance.

'You're late,' he said.

'The train was late. Weather.'

He looked at the grey clouds and felt for his handkerchief. Today's was a paper napkin from Starbucks. He looked as he felt, uncertain and exposed.

'I got your letter,' he said. 'One from Douglas, too.' His face was haggard; for a moment, Elisabeth pitied him. They walked inside, beyond the phalanx of security desks and sat beneath the vaulted ceilings on the cold stone bench which ran along the side. The rain dulled the light from the stained-glass windows.

'You mustn't send letters to home,' he said, putting the handkerchief back into his pocket. 'And you should have told me sooner.'

She could feel the hardening of her heart, looked at him and wondered what it was she had so found to admire. It was his cleverness most of all, the presence of a fine brain behind a noble forehead, an articulate mind and a seductive voice. She always remembered voices. She had expected to be nervous, but she was nerveless.

'I suppose I should have done. But you were never there to be told. And I couldn't communicate on a Sunday, could I? So I wrote you the letter. I've got into the habit of writing. The news will break tomorrow. Newspapers will have a field day. You needed to know.'

He nodded. 'There'll be an uproar, I suppose. No doubt the Pettys will retain you to help with the fallout.'

There was a trace of bitterness in his voice; a touch of jealousy. She had stolen the client.

'So they say, but I doubt if I'm diplomatic enough. Besides, they don't need help. They have each other. They won't care about being libelled or scorned. They just don't care. They know what they are . . .' Her voice broke. She coughed and recovered, kept her voice light and her hands stuffed in her pockets, still wanting to touch him. 'Listen, my dearest dear, am I wrong or am I right? Nod once, or twice for the latter. You set up the whole libel, didn't you? No, *you* didn't. Caterina came to you with it all tied up neatly in a package. Video and photos ready to roll, friends in the trade ready to grab. Outraged victim, encouraged by his sister, everything ready primed and big damages a safe enough gamble. An anonymous journalist gets it all past the night lawyer for a share. You knew none of it was true before we started.'

'That wasn't quite how she put it . . .'

'*Fuck* the way she put it. You followed a lie for the money.'

He winced. He was a handsome man, in his slender, aesthetic

way, generous sometimes, a skilful, patient lover. She would miss him. 'It could have been a lot of money, Elisabeth. It could have been freedom.'

She looked at him as she might a stranger on a train, with dispassionate curiosity.

'Freedom to be with you,' he said. 'We make a good team.'

Elisabeth shook her head, hoisted her handbag and walked away. Her footsteps were loud on the mosaic floor, moving smartly towards the rain. Endings were best kept brief.

ENDPIECE

September

Dear Helen,

I still can't write this report. Not even with numbered paragraphs. Rescue me.

I hope you preferred the way I told it to you, in chapters, with scenes. How many bottles of wine went into the telling? I've lost count. And you still think I should write an official report, for the sake of my legal intellect, to say nothing of my reputation.

But I keep getting sidetracked by REPUTATION. What a flimsy construction it is. A cardboard edifice, built on only the most obvious impressions. Such as being blonde and shy, short-tempered and loud, well-dressed and calm, rough or smooth, old and harmless. All made of paper. Take Douglas. I always assumed he was capable of beastliness, without a scintilla of evidence that he had ever done anyone harm. Rather the opposite; he always did what he said he would do, a strange sort of weakness. I can understand him better than Amy.

Because she did kill her father in the end. Effectively. She smashed the dolls' houses. I know in my bones that she did that; it was woman's work. She could not have killed a living thing; she did worse. She took his lures and his real reason for living, left him with the wreckage. She emasculated him and rendered him harmless. I can see her in that room, destroying everything bit by bit. I don't know if she locked herself out before or after, but she did it and left him with nothing. There's more violence in that, to my mind, than a straightforward throttling. She had her revenge; she may be the strongest of them all, and if I were her enemy, I would watch my step.

I don't think she did it for herself. She did it out of anger for Douglas. And it was her father's perception of how much Douglas loved her which made her know she could go home. So he did something for her after all. I'm guessing that part. Maybe she simply came to understand that he could love her as much as she loved him, and if she found there was nothing to forgive, then so would he.

I can't write this fucking cathartic report for other reasons. I've got better things to do. I'm aware that you and your peers, you wise ones whose voices form the choir of authority, have made your decisions about the murder on the train. NO CASE, you say, on account of a dearth of reliable witnesses, the chief of whom is an attention-seeking blonde with big tits and a fevered imagination, who might well have been in the throes of a nervous breakdown at the time, corroborated only by a bolshie trolley man who hates uniforms and won't say nothing. Not to the likes of you, anyway. You also take the view that the victim of the murder was no better than she should be because she was obviously having an affair. I may be a lousy lawyer, but this officious, defeatist, hypocritical attitude completely enrages me. I'm going to find the truth, if it kills me. Nobody should get away with wanton murder. Not even a lover. Not even on a train. Watch this space.

I don't know much about love, any more than I did when I started, only to have the vain imagination that I might now recognise it when I see it. What about you?

Anyway, must rush. This fellow, Jimmy, is driving round with a bottle. The cat adores him. I find I rather like politically incorrect endearments, and I've always had a thing about skinny men. Besides, I no longer give a shit where a man keeps his brains.

Love,
Elisabeth.